REG
Reputation

Diane Gaston

MILLS & BOON

First Published in Great Britain 2017
By Mills & Boon, an imprint of HarperCollins*Publishers*
1 London Bridge Street, London, SE1 9GF

REGENCY REPUTATION © 2017 Harlequin Books S.A.

A Reputation for Notoriety © 2013 Diane Perkins
A Marriage of Notoriety © 2014 Diane Perkins

ISBN: 978-0-263-92380-3

52-0517

Our policy is to use papers that are natural, renewable and recyclable products and made from wood grown in sustainable forests. The logging and manufacturing processes conform to the legal environmental regulations of the country of origin.

Printed and bound by
CPI Group (UK) Ltd, Croydon, CR0 4YY

A REGENCY

Collection

A Reputation
for Notoriety

In fond memory of my Aunt Loraine,
who taught me to enjoy life, no matter what.

Diane Gaston always said that if she were not a mental health social worker she'd want to be a romance novelist, writing the historical romances she loved to read. When this dream came true she discovered a whole new world of friends and happy endings. Diane lives in Virginia, near Washington DC, with her husband and three very ordinary house cats. She loves to hear from readers! Contact her at www.dianegaston.com or on Facebook or Twitter.

Prologue

London—June 1819

Rhys noticed the woman as soon as she appeared in the game room doorway. Taller than fashionable, she held her head high as she perused the room. Her face was half covered by a black mask reminiscent of those he'd seen in Venice, crowned with feathers and painted with gilt filigree. A large garnet was set between the eyes. Visible still were her full lips, tinted and enticing.

In her deep red gown, matching the reds, greens and golds of the game room, she might have been an item he'd personally selected. He watched as she moved gracefully through the room, stepping carefully as if uncertain the space worthy of her. Did she intend to play hazard? Or one of the other games? He was keen that this woman should admire what he'd done to the gaming hell and enjoy herself.

He wanted her to return.

Rhys intensely wished for this gaming house to be a success. He would settle for nothing less than it becoming London's most desirable place to gamble, a place both gentlemen and ladies would be eager to attend. Not for the profit it would earn, but to show he could be the best at whatever he tackled.

The challenge exhilarated him, in a way he'd not experienced since the stimulation of battle. Only this time there was no carnage in its wake.

This time there was a beautiful woman here to enjoy herself and it was his job to see that she did.

She paused in the middle of the room and he quickly made his way to her.

'Good evening, madam.' He bowed. 'I am Mr Rhysdale, the proprietor of this establishment. It will be my pleasure to assist you. What game do you wish to play?'

She lifted her eyes to him. Through the black mask he saw they were an intriguing green. Her hair, a walnut-brown laced with gold, was loosely piled on her head.

Who was she?

'Mr Rhysdale.' She nodded and her voice was surprisingly soft and reticent. 'I would like to play whist, but I do not have a partner.'

How he would relish partnering her himself, but he did not play in his own gaming house. He would have to find a gentleman willing to be her partner, but he'd find no enjoyment in the task. His friend Xavier would play cards with her if Rhys asked, but women much too easily succumbed to Xavier's handsome features. No, Rhys would not pass her on to Xavier.

Rhys wanted her for himself.

Chapter One

London—May 1819, one month earlier

Rhys and his friend Xavier sat at a table in the dining room of Stephen's Hotel. They had just been served their food when Rhys glanced towards the doorway.

Two men stood there, scanning the dining room.

Rhys knew them. Had known them since childhood. Viscount Neddington, né William Westleigh, and his brother Hugh, the legitimate sons of Earl Westleigh.

His brothers.

Rhys turned back to his food.

Xavier put down his fork with a clatter. 'What the devil?' He inclined his head towards the doorway. 'Look who is here.'

Rhys glanced up. 'They are looking for someone.'

Stephen's Hotel catered to military men, or former military men like Rhys and Xavier. Not the usual stamping ground of the Westleighs.

Rhys waited for the inevitable moment one of the Westleighs would notice him and slip his gaze away as if Rhys had never existed. Over the years when their paths had crossed, Neddington and Hugh always tried to act as if he'd never existed. Certainly that was their wish.

Ned, the elder, taller brother, turned his head in Rhys's direction. Their eyes locked, but this time Ned did not look away. This time he nudged his brother and the two walked straight for Rhys's table.

'They are headed here,' Rhys told Xavier.

His friend blew out a breath. 'I'll be damned…'

Rhys continued to hold Ned's gaze. Rhys always stood his ground with the Westleighs.

They stopped at the table.

'Rhys.' Ned inclined his head in an effort, Rhys supposed, to appear cordial.

'Gentlemen.' Rhys would be damned if he'd greet them by name and pretend an intimacy that had never existed. He gestured towards Xavier. 'My friend, Mr Campion.'

'We are acquainted.' Ned bowed in acknowledgement.

'We are indeed.' Xavier's tone was sarcastic.

Rhys cut another piece of meat. 'Are you merely paying your respects, or do you seek me out?'

'We seek you out,' Hugh replied, his voice taut and anxious.

Xavier glanced from one man to the other, obviously curious as to the purpose of this unusual visit.

Rhys made his expression neutral. Years of card-playing taught him to conceal his thoughts and emotions. He certainly had no intention of revealing anything to a Westleigh. He lifted a piece of beef into his mouth.

'Forgive us for interrupting your dinner.' Ned's tone was conciliatory, if somewhat stiff. 'We need a word with you.'

They *needed* a word with him? Now this was unique.

Rhys deliberately kept his attention to his plate, but he gestured to the empty chairs at the table. 'Have a seat.'

Hugh, shorter and always more hot-headed, emitted an indignant sound.

'We would prefer to speak in private.' Ned seemed anxious to avoid offending Rhys in any way.

Xavier straightened. If his friend were carrying a sword, Rhys suspected he'd have drawn it.

Rhys gazed at the two men, seeing only the boys they once were. The bitter memory of their first encounter, when Rhys was nine, flashed through his mind. He'd confronted them with what he'd just learned—that they shared a father.

That moment, like countless others from their childhoods, had resulted in flying fists and bloody noses.

Rhys stared into eyes identical to his. Dark brown, framed by thick eyebrows. Like his, Ned's and Hugh's hair was close-cut and near-black. Rhys might be taller and thicker-muscled, but if he stood side by side with these two men, who could ever deny they were brothers?

He exchanged a glance with Xavier, whose lips thinned in suspicion.

Rhys shrugged. 'Wait for me in the parlour off the hall. I'll come to you as soon as I've finished eating.'

Ned bowed curtly and Hugh glowered, but both turned and walked away.

Xavier watched their retreat. 'I do not trust them. Do you wish me to come with you?'

Rhys shook his head. 'There never was a time I could not take on both Westleighs.'

'Just the same, I dislike the sound of this,' Xavier countered. 'They are up to something.'

Rhys took another bite of his food. 'Oh, they are up to something. On that we agree. But I will see them alone.'

Xavier shot him a sceptical look.

Rhys took his time finishing his meal, although he possessed no more appetite for it. In all likelihood this would be an unpleasant interview. All encounters with Ned and Hugh were unpleasant.

Xavier clapped him on his shoulder before parting from him in the hall. 'Take care, Rhys.'

Rhys stepped into the parlour and Ned and Hugh turned to him. They'd remained standing.

He gestured. 'Follow me to my rooms.'

He led them up the two flights of stairs to his set of rooms. The door opened to a sitting room and as soon as Rhys led the men in, his manservant appeared.

'Some brandy for us, MacEvoy.'

MacEvoy's brows rose. MacEvoy, a man with an even rougher history than Rhys, had been his batman during the war. Obviously he recognised Hugh Westleigh from the battlefield.

'Please sit.' Rhys extended his arm to a set of chairs. It gave him a perverse pleasure that his furnishings were of fine quality, even if the items had been payment for various gambling debts. Rhys was doing well, which had not always been true.

MacEvoy served the brandy and left the room.

Rhys took a sip. 'What is this about, that you must speak with me now? You've made such a point of avoiding me all these years.'

Ned glanced away as if ashamed. 'We may not have… spoken to you, but we have kept ourselves informed of your whereabouts and actions.'

Ned was speaking false. Rhys would wager his whole fortune that these two had never bothered to discover what had happened to him after his mother had died and their father had refused any further support. The earl had left him penniless and alone, at a mere fourteen years of age.

No use to contest the lie, however. 'I'm flattered,' he said instead.

'You've had a sterling military record,' Ned added.

Hugh turned away this time.

'I lived,' Rhys said.

Hugh had also been in the war. The two former officers had come across each other from time to time in Spain, France and finally at Waterloo, although Hugh had been in a prestigious cavalry regiment, the Royal Dragoons. Rhys ultimately rose to major in the 44th Regiment of Foot. After the disastrous cavalry charge at Waterloo, Rhys had pulled Hugh from the mud and saved him from a French sabre. They said not a word to each other then, and Rhys would not speak of it now. The moment had been fleeting and only one of many that horrendous day.

Ned leaned forwards. 'You make your living by playing cards now, is that not correct?'

'Essentially,' Rhys admitted.

He'd learned to play cards at school, like every proper schoolboy, but he'd become a gambler on the streets of London. Gambling had been how he'd survived. It was still how he survived. He had become skilled at it out of necessity, earning enough to purchase his commission. Now that the war was over his winnings fed the foundation of a respectable fortune. Never again would his pockets be empty and his belly aching with hunger. He would be a success at…something. He did not know yet precisely what. Manufacturing, perhaps. Creating something useful, something more important than a winning hand of cards.

Hugh huffed in annoyance. 'Get on with it, Ned. Enough of this dancing around.' Hugh had always been the one to throw the first fist.

Ned looked directly into Rhys's eyes. 'We need your help, Rhys. We need your skill.'

'At playing cards?' That seemed unlikely.

'In a manner of speaking.' Ned rubbed his face. 'We have a proposition for you. A business proposition. One we believe will be to your advantage, as well.'

Did they think him a fool? Eons would pass before he'd engage in business with any Westleigh.

Rhys's skin heated with anger. 'I have no need of a business proposition. I've done quite well…' he paused '…since I was left on my own.'

'Enough, Ned.' Hugh's face grew red with emotion. He turned to Rhys. 'Our family is on the brink of disaster—'

Ned broke in, his voice calmer, more measured. 'Our father has been…reckless…in his wagering, his spending—'

'He's been reckless in everything!' Hugh threw up his hands. 'We are punting on the River Tick because of him.'

Earl Westleigh in grave debt? Now that was a turn of affairs.

Although aristocrats in severe debt tended to have abundantly more than the poor in the street. Ned and Hugh would never experience what Rhys knew of hunger and loneliness and despair.

He forced away the memory of those days lest he reveal how they nearly killed him.

'What can this have to do with me?' he asked in a mild tone.

'We need money—a great deal of it—and as quickly as possible,' Hugh said.

Rhys laughed at the irony. 'Earl Westleigh wishes to borrow money from me?'

'Not borrow money,' Ned clarified. 'Help us make money.'

Hugh made an impatient gesture. 'We want you to set up a gaming house for us. Run the place. Help us make big profits quickly.'

Ned's reasonable tone was grating on Rhys's nerves. On Hugh's, too, Rhys guessed.

Ned continued. 'Our reasoning is thus—if our father can lose a fortune in gaming hells, we should be able to recover a fortune by running one.' He opened his palms. 'Only *we* cannot be seen to be running one, even if we knew how. Which we do not. It would throw too much suspicion on our situation, you see, and that would cause our creditors to become impatient.' He smiled at Rhys. 'But *you* could do it. You have the expertise and...and there would not be any negative consequences for you.'

Except risking arrest, Rhys thought.

Although he could charge for membership. Call it a club, then it would be legal—

Rhys stopped himself. He was not going to run a gaming hell for the Westleighs.

'We need you,' Hugh insisted.

Were they mad? They'd scorned him his whole life. Now they expected him to help them?

Rhys drained the contents of his glass and looked from one to the other. 'You need me, but I do not need you.'

Hugh half rose from his chair. 'Our father supported you and your mother. You owe him. He sent you to school. Think of what would have happened if he had not!'

Rhys glared at him, only a year younger than his own thirty years. 'Think of what my mother's life might have been like if the earl had not seduced her.'

She might have married. She might have found respectability and happiness instead of bearing the burden of a child out of wedlock.

She might have lived.

Rhys turned away and pushed down the grief for his mother. It never entirely left him.

Ned persisted. 'Rhys, I do not blame you for despising

our father or us, but our welfare is not the main issue. Count-less people, some known to you, depend upon our fam-ily for their livelihood. The servants. The tenant farmers. The stable workers. The village and all its people in some fashion depend upon the Westleigh estate to be profitable. Too soon we will not be able to meet the expenses of plant-ing. Like a house of cards, everything is in danger of col-lapsing and it is the people of Westleigh who will suffer the most dire of consequences.'

Rhys curled his fingers into fists. 'Do not place upon my shoulders the damage done by the earl. It has nothing to do with me.'

'You are our last resort,' Hugh implored. 'We've tried leasing the estate, but in these hard times, no one is forth-coming.'

Farming was going through difficult times, that was true. The war left much financial hardship in its wake. There was plenty of unrest and protest around the coun-try about the Corn Laws keeping grain prices high, but, without the laws, more farms would fold.

All the more reason the earl should have exercised pru-dence instead of profligacy.

'Leave me out of it.'

'We cannot leave you out of it!' Hugh jumped to his feet and paced the room. 'We need you. Do you not hear me? You must do this for us!'

'Hugh, you are not helping.' Ned also rose.

Rhys stood and faced them both. 'Words *our* father once spoke to me, I will repeat to you. *I am under no obligation to do anything for you.*' He turned away and walked over to the decanter of brandy, pouring himself another glass. 'Our conversation is at an end.'

There was no sound of them moving towards the door. Rhys turned and faced them once again. 'You need to leave me, gentlemen. Go now, or, believe me, I am quite capable of tossing you both out.'

Hugh took a step towards him. 'I should like to see you try!'

Ned pulled him away. 'We are leaving. We are leaving. But I do beg you to reconsider. This could bring you a fortune. We have enough to finance the start of it. All we need is—'

Rhys lowered his voice. 'Go.'

Ned dragged his brother to the door. They gathered their hats and gloves and left the rooms.

Rhys stared at the door long after their footsteps faded in the hallway.

MacEvoy appeared. 'Do you need anything, sir?'

Rhys shook his head. 'Nothing, MacEvoy. You do not need to attend me.'

MacEvoy left again and Rhys downed his brandy. He poured himself another glass, breathing as heavy as if he'd run a league.

He almost wished Hugh had swung at him. He'd have relished planting a fist in the man's face, a face too disturbingly similar to his own.

A knock sounded at the door and Rhys strode over and swung it open. 'I told you to be gone!'

'Whoa!' Xavier raised his hands. 'They are gone.'

Rhys stepped aside. 'What were you doing? Lurking in the hallway?'

'Precisely.' Xavier entered the room. 'I could not wait a moment longer to hear what they wanted.'

Rhys poured another glass of brandy and handed it to his friend. 'Have a seat. You will not believe this, I assure you…'

Sending away the Westleighs ought to have been the end of it. Rhys ought to have concentrated on his cards that night rather than observe the workings of the gaming hell on St James's Street. He ought to have slept well without his thoughts racing.

Over the next few days, though, he visited as many gambling establishments as he could, still playing cards, but taking in everything from the arrangements of the tables, the quality of the meals, the apparent profitability of the various games.

'Why this tour of gaming hells?' Xavier asked him as they walked to yet another establishment off of St James's. 'A different one each night? That is not your habit, Rhys. You usually stick to one place long enough for the high-stakes players to ask you to play.'

Rhys lifted his shoulders. 'No special reason. Call it a whim.'

His friend looked doubtful.

Rhys did not wish to admit to himself that he was considering his half-brothers' offer, although all the people who had been kind to his mother in the village kept rising to his memory. He could almost envision their suffering eyes if Westleigh Hall was left in ruins. He could almost feel their hunger.

If he pushed the faces away, thoughts of how much money he could make came to the fore. The Westleighs would be taking the risk, not Rhys. For Rhys it was almost a safe bet.

If only it had been anyone but the Westleighs.

Rhys sounded the knocker on the door of an innocuous-appearing town house. A huge bear of a man in colourful livery opened the door. Rhys had not been to this house in perhaps a year, but it appeared unchanged.

'How do you do, Cummings?' he said to the liveried servant. 'I have been gone too long from here.'

'G'd evening, Mr Rhysdale,' Cummings responded in his deep monotone. He nodded to Xavier. 'Mr Campion.'

Cummings might act the doorman, but he'd be better described as the gatekeeper, allowing only certain people in, chucking out any patron who became rowdy or combative.

Cummings took their hats and gloves. 'Nothing has changed here. Except some of the girls. They come and go. The game room is up the stairs. Same as always.'

Rhys was not interested in the girls, who often sold their favours on the side.

He glanced around the hall. Nothing appeared changed.

Three years ago he'd been a frequent patron of this place. He, like so many gentlemen at that time, had been intrigued by a masked woman who came to play cards and often did quite well. She'd been a mystery and that intensified her appeal. Soon the men were wagering on which of them would bed her first, all properly written down in the betting book. Rhys had not been interested in seducing a woman just to win a bet.

He shook his head. He had not thought of that masked woman in years. Who had won her? he wondered.

He turned back to Cummings. 'And Madame Bisou. Is she here tonight?' Madame Bisou owned this establishment.

'Aye. She should be in the game room.' Cummings turned away to store their hats.

Rhys and Xavier climbed the stairs and entered the game room, all a-bustle with activity as the time approached midnight. The hazard table was in the centre of the room, encircled by eager players. The familiar sound of dice shaken in a cup and shouts of 'Seven!' reached Rhys's ears, followed by the roll of the dice on the green baize and more shouting. Now and again a patron might win big, but the odds always favoured the bank, as they did in faro and *rouge et noir*. The two faro tables stood against one wall, nearly obscured by players; the other side held the games of *rouge et noir*. Rhys avoided all these games, where winning was almost completely dependent on luck. He confined himself to games of skill.

'I thought you came to play cards.' Xavier nudged him.

'I have,' he responded. 'But I have not been here in a year. I am taking stock of the room.'

At that moment, a buxom woman with flaming red hair hurried towards them. 'Monsieur Rhysdale. Monsieur Campion. How good it is to see you. It has been *trop longtemps,* no?'

Rhys smiled both at the pleasure of seeing her again and at her atrocious French accent. 'Madame Bisou!' He leaned over to give her a kiss on the cheek and whispered in her ear, 'How are you, Penny?'

'*Très bien, cher,*' she responded, but her smile looked stressed. She turned to greet Xavier before Rhys could ask more.

In those difficult London days of his youth Madame Bisou had been Penny Jones, a decade older than he and just as determined to free herself from the shackles of poverty. They'd both used what God had provided them: Rhys, his skill at cards—Penny, her body. But she did not spend all the money she earned on gin like so many of the other girls. She'd saved and invested and finally bought this place. She'd been running it for almost ten years.

'Why has it been so long since you have been here?' She took Rhys's hand and squeezed it.

'I am asking myself that same question.' Rhys smiled at her, genuinely glad to see an old friend.

Her tone changed to one of business. 'What is your

pleasure today, gentlemen? Do you wish a woman? Or a game of chance?'

Xavier answered her. 'A game of whist, if we can manage it.'

Rhys would have preferred merely to watch the room for a little while, but Penny found them two willing high-stakes partners.

When the play was over, Rhys and Xavier collected their winnings, more modest than most nights, but Rhys had to admit to being distracted. They moved on to the supper room. One of the girls began a flirtation with Xavier. Rhys spied Penny sitting in a far corner.

He walked over to her. 'It is not like you to sit alone, Penny. Is something amiss? Might I help?'

She sighed wearily and appeared, for the moment, much older than her forty years. 'I have lost the heart for this, Rhys. I wish I could just walk away from it all….'

Rhys's heart beat faster. 'Are you thinking of selling the business?'

'How can it be done? I cannot advertise.' Her gaming hell was illegal. 'I am too weary to even think how to accomplish it.'

This was unlike her. Penny always found a way to do precisely as she wished.

Rhys's nostrils filled with the scent of opportunity.

Fate was shoving him in the direction he must go. He was the solution to Penny's problems. He could save his old village. He could enrich his coffers.

All he must do was sell his soul to the devil.

His father.

The next day Rhys presented himself at the Westleigh town house. He'd not told Xavier his intention. He'd not wanted to be talked out of it.

It was well before the fashionable hour for making calls. Probably well before Ned and Hugh rose. It was half-past nine, a time working men and women were well into their day while the wealthy still slept. But Rhys needed to do this first thing or risk the chance of changing his mind.

The footman who answered the door led him to a drawing room off the hall. Unfortunately, the room was dominated by a huge portrait of the earl. Painted with arms crossed, the image of Earl Westleigh stared down, his expression stern and, Rhys fancied, disapproving.

Let his image disapprove. Rhys knew his own worth. He was determined the world should know it soon enough.

Still the earl's presence in this house set his nerves on edge. Would he join Ned and Hugh for this interview? Rhys half hoped so. He would relish standing in a superior position to this man who once held power over his life.

But it was far more likely the earl would do anything possible to avoid his bastard son.

Rhys's brothers, to their credit, did not keep him waiting long. He heard their hurried footsteps and their hushed voices before they entered the room.

Ned walked towards him as if he would offer his hand to shake, but he halted and gestured to a chair instead. 'Shall we sit?'

Hugh held back and looked solemn.

Rhys calmly looked from one to the other. 'I believe I'll stand.'

His response had the desired effect. Both men shifted uncomfortably.

'Are we to assume your presence here to mean you have reconsidered our offer?' Ned asked.

Rhys inwardly grimaced. Ned called it an offer? 'I came to further the discussion of whether I am willing to rescue you and our father from penury.'

'Why?' Hugh demanded in a hot voice. 'What changed your mind?'

Rhys levelled a gaze at him. 'Call it an attack of family loyalty, if you like. I did not say I've changed my mind.'

Ned placed a stilling hand on Hugh's arm, but spoke to Rhys. 'What do you wish to discuss?'

Rhys shrugged. 'Well, for one, it takes a great deal of money to start a gaming establishment. Will I be expected to invest my own money? Because I would not stake my fortune against something so risky.'

'How is it risky?' Hugh cried. 'The house always has the advantage. You know that.'

'The house can be broken,' Rhys countered. 'It is all chance.' Rhys succeeded at cards by reducing chance.

'But it is not likely, is it?' Hugh shot back.

Ned's eyes flashed a warning to Hugh, before he turned to Rhys again. 'The monetary investment will be ours.' He lowered his voice. 'It is now or never for us, Rhys. We've scraped the last of our fortune to bank this enterprise. All we want from you—all we need from you—is to run it.'

They must truly be desperate to devise a plan like this, especially as it involved him. Desperate or mad.

'A gaming house will not make much money right away unless it can quickly build a reputation. It must distinguish itself from other places. Give gamblers a reason to attend.' Rhys paused. 'You want to attract the high-stakes gamblers who have money to throw away.'

'It must be an honest house,' Hugh snapped. 'No rigged dice. No marked cards.'

Rhys gave him a scathing look. 'Are you attempting to insult me, Hugh? If you do not think me an honest man, why ask me to run it?'

Hugh averted his gaze.

'No cheating of any kind,' Rhys reiterated. 'And no

prostitution. I will tolerate neither.' He'd keep the girls at Madame Bisou's employed, but he'd have nothing to do with them selling their bodies.

'We are certainly in agreement with all you say,' Ned responded.

Rhys went on. 'Within the parameters of honesty, I must be given free rein in how the house is run.'

'Of course,' Ned agreed.

'Wait a moment.' Hugh glared. 'What precisely do you mean by free rein?'

'I mean I decide how to run it,' Rhys responded. 'There will be no countering of what I choose to do.'

'What do you choose to do?' Hugh shot back.

Rhys kept his tone even. 'I will make this house the one every wealthy aristocrat or merchant wants to attend. I want to attract not only wealthy men, but ladies, as well.'

'Ladies!' Hugh looked appalled.

'We all know ladies like to gamble as well as gentlemen, but ladies risk censure for it, so I propose we run the house like a masquerade. Anyone may come in costume or masked. That way they can play without risk to their reputation.' This had worked for the masked woman who'd come to Madame Bisou's and caused such a stir those years ago. No one had ever learned who she was.

Rhys had thought this all through. It had been spinning in his mind ever since Ned and Hugh first proposed he run a gambling house. He would call it the Masquerade Club. Members could join for a nominal fee. They could dress in masquerade as long as they purchased their counters with the coin in their pockets. If they sought credit or were forced to sign a promissory note, they must reveal their identity.

He continued explaining to Ned and Hugh. 'This is my plan thus far. It is not up to negotiation. If I come up with a better idea, I will implement it and I will not confer with you beforehand.'

'See here—' Hugh began.

Ned waved a hand. 'Leave it, Hugh. As long as it is honest and profitable, what do we care how the place is run?' He turned to Rhys. 'Anything else?'

'I want half the profit.'

'Half?' Hugh shouted.

Rhys faced him again. 'You risk money, but it is my reputation that will be at risk. We can charge a nominal subscription and call it a gaming club, but there is still the risk that it will be declared illegal. I must be compensated for that risk.' Besides, he intended to give Penny a portion of his profits, as part of the sale, and Xavier, too, if he was willing to help.

'I think your terms are agreeable,' Ned responded. 'Shall we discuss how much money you need to get started?'

Rhys nodded, but tapped a finger against his lips. 'I do have a question.'

Ned looked up suspiciously. 'What is it?'

'Does the earl know you wish me to do this?'

The brothers exchanged glances.

'He knows,' Ned answered.

And was not happy about it, Rhys guessed. Something Rhys counted upon. Besides earning a profit, Rhys wanted the gaming house to provide him another pay-off. He wanted to rub the earl's nose in the fact that it was his bastard son who pulled him from the brink of ruin. Rhys wanted revenge against the man who sired him and never, ever, acknowledged that fact, who had instead turned him away without a penny, not caring if he lived or died.

He tapped on the back of a chair with his fingertips.

'Very well, my *brothers*—' he spoke sarcastically '—I agree to run your gaming house.'

The two men who so resembled him visibly relaxed.

'On one more condition,' Rhys added.

Hugh rolled his eyes. Ned looked nervous.

'Our *father*—' Rhys spoke this word with even greater sarcasm '—Earl Westleigh, that is—must publicly acknowledge me as his son. It must seem as if I am accepted into the family as one of you, an equal member. I must be included in family functions and social occasions. I must be treated as one of the family.' What better revenge than this?

Ned and Hugh gaped back at him with horrified expressions. Apparently the idea of accepting him as a brother was as anathema to them as it would be to the earl.

'That is my condition,' Rhys reiterated.

Ned glanced away and silence stretched between them.

Finally he raised his eyes to Rhys. 'Welcome to the family, brother.'

Chapter Two

Rhys accomplished the sale and reopening of the gaming hell within three weeks of calling upon his half-brothers. He changed the décor and the menu and retrained all the workers. Madame Bisou's became the Masquerade Club and news of its opening travelled swiftly by word of mouth.

The first days had been stressful, but each night the numbers of patrons had grown, as had the profit, which made the Westleighs less fraught with worry. Rhys could count on one of them—Hugh mostly—to come in the guise of an ordinary patron. Rhys knew they were keeping tabs on what he had created.

He'd been watching for one of them when he spied the beautiful masked woman who had just told him she wished to play whist.

Rhys had experienced his share of affairs with women. He and Xavier had enjoyed some raucous nights in Paris with willing *elegantes,* but rarely, if ever, had he been so intrigued as with this woman.

Her posture was both proud and wary, and she had come to the gaming house alone, in itself a courageous act for a woman. What's more, her lips were moist and pink and her voice like music to his ears.

'How might a lady find a willing partner?' she asked.

What man could refuse her?

For the first time since opening the gaming house, Rhys regretted that he could not play cards. He would have relished being her partner and showing her his skill.

As it was, he must find her another man—to partner her in whist.

He bowed. 'Give me a moment to fulfil your desire.' A serving girl walked by with a tray of port. He took one glass and handed it to her. 'Refresh yourself in the meantime and take a look at all the house has to offer.'

He quickly scanned the room and spied Sir Reginald, a harmless man who frequented gaming hells and flirted with the ladies, but rarely followed through. His card playing was competent, if not inspired. Sir Reginald would be forgiving if she turned out to be a poor player, but would not disappoint if she was skilled.

Rhys could not imagine her not being skilled at whatever she tried. He wanted her to enjoy herself. He wanted her to like the Masquerade well enough to return.

He brought the unmasked Sir Reginald to her. 'Madam, may I present Sir Reginald.'

Sir Reginald bowed gallantly. 'It will be my privilege to partner you.'

She smiled at Sir Reginald, her pink lips parting to reveal pretty white teeth. Handing Rhys her empty glass as if he were a servant, she accepted Sir Reginald's arm and walked with him to a card table with two other men. After speaking with the men, the lady and Sir Reginald sat. One of the other men dealt the cards.

Rhys had no intention of being so easily dismissed by this mysterious masked woman. He had other duties to occupy him at the moment, but, before she left, he intended to speak with her again.

* * *

Celia Gale breathed a sigh of relief to finally be seated at a card table, staring at diamonds, hearts, clubs and spades.

Entering the game room had been like crossing through the gates of hell. It had taken all her courage to do something so potentially damaging to her reputation. A lady, even a baron's widow, did not go gambling alone in the dead of night.

Even worse, it meant entering a world where other, even greater, risks existed—the lure of cards and dice, the heady thrill of winning, the certainty that losing could be reversed with one more hand, one more roll of the dice.

Cards and gambling once took away everything she held dear. The road to ruin was only one bad hand of cards away.

But what choice did she have? How else was she to procure the money she needed?

She'd heard of this gaming hell at a recent musicale she'd attended and immediately thought it was a godsend. Two men had spoken of it within her earshot.

'Thing is, the ladies can attend. It is called the Masquerade Club and anyone may come in disguise,' one had said.

'They do not have to reveal themselves?' the other asked.

'Not at all. Any lady may gamble without fear of ruining her reputation.'

She could gamble for high stakes and no one would know! At last a way to earn the funds she so desperately needed.

'Your deal, my dear,' Sir Reginald said, bringing her back to the present.

She'd spied Sir Reginald at a few of the entertainments she'd attended, but they had never been introduced. There was little reason to suppose he would recognise her. The other two gentlemen, also unmasked, were unknown to her before this night.

She dealt the deck slowly and with deliberation.

'Nicely dealt.' The man on her left smiled condescendingly.

She inclined her head in acknowledgement.

Her father taught that gambling was part skill at cards and part skill with people. Let these gentlemen condescend. It was to her advantage if they underestimated her. They might become careless in their choice of cards to lay down.

When the serving girl came around offering spirits, the gentlemen accepted, but Celia nursed one glass of port. She needed all her wits about her.

She purposely played as if this were her first time at a green baize table, and, by so doing, the counters grew into a pretty little pile at her right elbow. These gentlemen were betting quite modestly and, she suspected, were sometimes letting her win.

She indulged their mistaken impression. Soon enough this room would know her skill and then the competition—and the risk—would intensify.

She glanced up. The establishment's proprietor, Mr Rhysdale, was watching her. Too often when she looked up he was watching her. It set her nerves on edge.

Her blood had raced with fear when he'd approached her after she'd entered the room. She'd thought she'd done something wrong, transgressed some secret code of behaviour that was known only to those who frequented gaming hells.

He was a magnificent man, tall and muscled and intense. His eyes assessed everything, but his expression remained inscrutable. What was he thinking as he me-

andered through the tables, when he turned his gaze towards her?

He raised a glass to her and she quickly looked away.

What earthly reason made him watch her so closely?
There were other masked ladies playing cards in the room.

She took the last three tricks of the hand, winning the
game.

'That is it for me,' one of the gentlemen said.

'And for me,' his partner added.

Sir Reginald straightened. 'Would you like to try your
luck at *rouge et noir,* my dear?'

She shook her head. 'No, thank you, sir.'

She wanted to play more cards. Games of skill, not
merely of chance. She was at a loss as to how to manage
it. Certainly she would not seek out Mr Rhysdale to find
her a new partner.

All three gentlemen bowed and excused themselves,
leaving her alone. Celia rose. She busied herself with slip-
ping her counters in her reticule. The night had been profitable. Not overwhelmingly so, but it was a good start.

'Was luck with you, madam?'

She startled and turned, knowing who she would find.
'Luck?' She smiled. 'Yes, luck was with me, Mr Rhysdale.'

'Do you cash in, then?' He stood so close it seemed he
stole the air she needed to breathe.

She clutched her reticule, but tilted her head so as to
look in his face. 'Frankly, sir, I would like to continue to
play. Dare I presume on you to arrange another game for
me?'

'My pleasure, madam.' His voice turned low.

Within a few minutes he had rounded up two gentlemen and a lady needing a fourth and Celia played several
more games. The gentleman who became her partner was
more skilled than Sir Reginald and her counters multiplied.

When the players left the table, Mr Rhysdale appeared again. 'More partners?'

Her heart fluttered. Why was that? 'I am done for the night.'

He took her arm and leaned close. 'Then share some refreshment with me.'

She did not know what to say. 'What time is it?'

He reached into a pocket and pulled out a fine gold watch. 'A quarter to three.'

Her carriage came at three-thirty.

She glanced around the room. There was not enough time to join another whist game, or even find someone willing to play piquet. 'Very well.' She was certain her tone sounded resigned. 'Some refreshment would be welcome.'

He escorted her out of the game room to the door of the supper room behind. His hand remained firmly on her elbow. Her heart raced. Was he about to tell her why he watched her so intently as she played?

If he discovered she was a card sharp, her plans could be ruined. If he presumed she was cheating, it would be even worse. Was not her father's fate proof of that?

She wished Mr Rhysdale would simply leave her alone.

When they crossed the threshold of the supper room, Celia gasped.

The room was lovely! It was decorated in the earlier style of Robert Adam. The pale-green ceiling with its white plasterwork mirrored the pattern and colour of the carpet and walls. The white furniture was adorned with delicate gilt. Servants attending the buffet or carrying trays were dressed in livery that belonged to that earlier time, bright brocades and white wigs.

Rather than appear old-fashioned, the room seemed a fantasy of the elegance of bygone days. With all its lightness, Celia felt conspicuous in her dark red gown and black mask. There were four or five tables occupied, some with men entertaining ladies, some with men in deep conversation. Several of them glanced up as she and Rhysdale passed by.

'Are you hungry?' Rhysdale asked as he led her to a table away from the other diners. 'We can select from the buffet or, if you prefer, order a meal.'

Her nerves still jangled alarmingly. 'The buffet will do nicely.'

'And some wine?' His dark brows rose with his question.

She nodded. 'Thank you.'

At least he displayed some expression. She otherwise could not read his face at all, even though it was the sort of face that set a woman's heart aflutter. His eyes were dark and unfathomable and his nose, strong. But his lips—oh, his lips! The top lip formed a perfect bow. The bottom was full and resolute, like the firm set of his jaw. In this early pre-dawn hour, the dark shadow of his beard tinged his face, lending him the appearance of a dangerous rogue.

It was his position as the proprietor of the Masquerade Club that posed the most peril to her, though. She did not want the attention of the proprietor. She wanted only to play cards and win as much money as she could.

He pulled out a chair and she lowered herself into it, smoothing her skirt. Her chair faced the curtained window, but she wanted to face the room, so she could see what he was doing behind her back.

When he walked to the buffet, she changed seats.

Even as he made his selections at the buffet, he looked completely in charge. There was no hesitation on his part to pick this or that tidbit. His choices were swiftly accomplished. When a servant came near, Rhysdale signalled the man and spoke briefly to him. A moment later, the servant brought two wine glasses and a bottle to the table. He poured wine in both glasses.

Celia sipped hers gratefully. The night's play had given her a thirst and the mellowing effect of the wine was a balm to her nerves.

When Rhysdale turned from the buffet, he paused slightly, noticing, she supposed, that she had moved from the seat in which he had placed her.

He walked towards the table and her nerves fired anew.

Setting a plate in front of her, he lowered himself into the chair directly across from her. She would be unable to avoid those dark eyes while they conversed.

'I hope my selections are to your liking.' His voice rumbled.

She glanced at her plate. 'Indeed.'

He'd provided some slices of cold ham and an assortment of cheeses, fruits and confections, all items she enjoyed, but she would have given her approval no matter what he had selected.

She pushed the food around with her fork.

'I am curious.' His tone was casual. 'Why did you come to the Masquerade Club tonight?'

She glanced up, her heart pounding. 'Why do you ask?'

The corner of his mouth twitched, ever so slightly. 'I am eager to make this place a success. I want to know what entices a woman to attend.' He paused. 'And what would entice you to return.'

Her brows rose. Was this all he wanted from her? She could not believe it.

She chose her words carefully. 'I heard that a woman might play cards here without revealing her identity.'

He nodded. 'I had hoped anonymity would be an appeal.' He took a sip of his wine. 'And where did you hear this of the place?'

Now it was she who must avoid the truth. To answer truthfully would reveal that she moved in society's finest circles and that she could not do.

What could she say that would avoid tipping her hand? 'At the theatre.'

Yes. That ought to suffice. Anyone might attend the theatre.

He stared at her for a moment too long for comfort.

Finally he tasted the food on his plate. 'And what do you think of my establishment now you have seen it?'

She relaxed a little. Perhaps he was being honest with her. It made sense that a proprietor would want to know if his place appealed or not.

'It meets my needs very well.'

He glanced up. 'And your needs are?'

She swallowed a piece of cheese. 'A place to play cards where a woman might feel secure.'

'Secure.' He held her gaze.

She struggled to explain. 'To feel safe from...the stories one hears about gaming establishments.'

He pinned her with his gaze again. 'You have felt safe here?'

'I have,' she admitted.

What she witnessed from behind her mask was not the worst of what she'd heard of gaming hells, where drinking and debauchery might share the night with charges of cheating and, worst of all, challenges to duels. It almost seemed as civilised as a Mayfair drawing room, except for the wild excitement in the eyes of those on a winning streak and the blanch of despair on the faces of losing players. Those highs and lows were part of gambling. Something she must guard against at all costs.

As well as guarding against this special notice from the proprietor. His watchful dark eyes made her tremble inside.

He turned again to his plate. 'And what about the gaming here appeals to you? You played whist. Would you also be interested in the hazard table? Faro?'

She shook her head. 'I do not trust so much in luck.'

Too often in her life luck had totally abandoned her.

His eyes bore into her again. 'You prefer to rely on skill?'

Her gaze faltered. 'One must have some control over one's fate.'

'I quite agree.' To her surprise he smiled and his handsome face turned into something wondrous.

She found it momentarily hard to breathe.

His smile turned wry. 'Although you might say opening a gaming hell cedes too much of one's fate to luck.'

She forced her voice to work. 'Chance favours you at the hazard and faro tables, which is why I do not play them. Nor *rouge et noir.*'

She finished her wine, aware that he continued to stare at her. She fingered her reticule, heavy with counters. 'May—may I ask the time, please?'

He pulled his watch out again. 'Three-twenty.'

She stood. 'I must go. My carriage arrives at three-thirty and I need time to cash out.'

He also rose and walked with her to the ground floor where the cashier sat in a room behind the hall. She felt a thrill watching the coins she'd won stack up in front of her. After scooping them into a leather pouch and placing it in her reticule, she collected her shawl from the dour-faced servant attending the hall.

And Rhysdale remained with her.

He walked her to the door and opened it. 'I trust you will return to us?'

She suddenly was very eager to return. So eager a part

of her wanted to re-enter the game room and deal another hand of whist.

She curbed her excitement. 'Perhaps.' Curtsying, she said, 'Thank you for your assistance, Mr Rhysdale. And for the refreshment.'

'You are very welcome.' His voice turned low and seemed to resonate inside her.

She crossed the threshold, relieved to take her leave of him, but he walked out into the dark night with her.

The rush lamp at the door must have revealed her surprise.

'I will see you into your carriage,' he explained.

Her coachman drove up immediately and she was grateful her carriage no longer had a crest on its side.

Rhysdale opened the coach door and pulled down the steps. He held out his hand to assist her. His touch was firm and set her nerves trembling anew.

He closed the door and leaned into the window. 'Goodnight, madam. It has been my pleasure to assist you.'

His pleasure? She took a breath.

'Goodnight,' she managed.

The coach pulled away, and she swivelled around to look out the back window.

He stood in the road, illuminated by the rush light.

Still watching her.

Rhys did not leave the road until her carriage disappeared into the darkness.

Who the devil was she?

He did not need to be captivated by a woman. A woman could become an inconvenient distraction and he needed to keep his wits about him. The gaming house must be his priority.

Rhys had known too many women who made their living by acting pleasing at first, then cutting the man's purse and dashing away. He expected that sort of woman to show up at the gaming hell—women who played at gambling, but who really merely wished to attach themselves to the evening's big winners.

This woman was not a cutpurse, however. Neither did she come to the gaming hell on a lark.

She came to win money.

He'd watched her play, had seen the concentration in her posture, the calculation in her selection of cards. She was here for the card play.

She was a kindred spirit, a gambler like himself.

Would she return? She must. He wanted her in every way a man wanted a woman.

He walked back into the house, nodding to Cummings as he passed him. When he reached the door to the game room, Xavier appeared, leaning against the wall in the hallway, his arms crossed over his chest.

'What was that all about?' his friend asked.

Rhys did not know how much he wished to say about the woman, even to Xavier. 'She intrigues me.' He gave his friend a warning look. 'If she returns, do not aspire to make her one of your conquests.'

Xavier, who attracted female company so easily he never needed to make a conquest, replied, 'I comprehend.'

They walked into the game room together.

'Do you know who she is?' Xavier asked.

Rhys grinned. 'Not yet.'

Chapter Three

Celia sat at the desk in her library in the rooms she'd taken for the Season, rooms she now had more hope she could afford. Her winnings were stacked in piles on the desk, one half set aside to stake her next venture to the Masquerade Club.

What would she have done had she not discovered the new gaming house? Her widow's portion had been stretched to the breaking point and the bills continued to pour in.

Now she could transfer some of the bills from one stack to another—ones to pay now, ones to pay later.

She rolled some of the coins in her hand, almost giddy at their cool texture and the clink of them rubbing against each other.

She stacked them again and leaned back, appalled at herself. To be giddy at winning was to travel a perilous path. She must never succumb to the mania that was gambling. Not like her father—and, by association, her mother. They both died of it.

If she played with her head and not her emotions, she should be able to resist. She planned to visit the place often enough to learn who the high-stakes players were. Think of the money she could win in games with such gamblers!

Stop! she warned herself. No emotions. Playing cards must merely be what she did to earn money, like any tradesman or skilled workman.

Celia turned her face to the window and gazed out into the small garden at the back of the house. At the moment she must depend on Rhysdale to find her partners, but soon she would become known to the regulars. Then she hoped to be sought after as a partner.

At least Rhysdale had set her up with partners skilled enough to bring her a tidy profit.

She riffled the stack of coins. She needed more. Her stepdaughter's Season cost money and her mother-in-law refused to stop spending recklessly.

Her late husband had been another whose gambling and debauchery ruled his life. Her husband had been excessive in everything. Gambling. Spending. Drinking. Mistresses.

He'd even been excessive in his disdain for his young wife.

Not that it mattered now. His death had freed her from a marriage she'd never wanted and from a husband she'd abhorred. It had left her with a stepdaughter nearly her own age and a mother-in-law who despised her.

'Celia!' Adele, her stepdaughter, called.

Celia's singular joy, the closest Celia would ever come to a daughter of her own. Adele. Bright and starry-eyed, and full of hope that her first Season in London would bring her the love match she pined for. Celia was determined Adele should achieve her dreams, dreams that might have been Celia's own.

If gambling had not robbed her of them.

'I'm in here, Adele,' she responded.

Dreams aside, it was pragmatic for Adele to make a good match. The girl deserved to be settled and happy with a husband wealthy and generous enough to support

Adele's grandmother, as well. Celia's modest widow's portion might be enough for her to live in some measure of comfort if she economised very carefully, but it definitely did not stretch so far as to support her stepdaughter and mother-in-law.

Besides, Celia had no wish to be shackled to her mother-in-law forever.

Adele bounced into the room and gave Celia a buss on the cheek. 'Grandmama and I went shopping. We went to the new Burlington Arcade. It was a positive delight!'

'Was it?' Celia would miss Adele. The girl was the delight of her life.

Adele danced in front of her. 'There must have been a hundred shops. We did not see half of them.' She sobered. 'But, I assure you, I did not purchase a thing.'

Celia smiled. 'I hope you enjoyed yourself, none the less.'

'I did. I cannot tell you of all the items I saw for sale.' Adele lowered herself onto a nearby chair. 'Do not tell me those are bills.'

'They are bills, but do not fret. I have funds to pay some of them.' Celia moved the stacks of bills to pay farther away from those that would have to wait. 'Including the modiste. So you may order a new gown or two.'

Adele shook her head. 'I do not need them. I can make do with my old ones.'

Celia rose from her chair and went over to the girl. 'Indeed you may not!' She took Adele's hands. 'It is very important for you to put in a good appearance! Your grandmother and I agree on that score. Besides I've—I've found some funds I did not know we had. We are not so poverty-stricken after all.'

Adele looked sceptical. 'I hope you are telling me the truth and not shielding me as if I were a child.'

Celia squeezed her hands and avoided the issue. 'Of course you are not a child. A child does not have a Season.' Adele was nineteen years old. Celia herself was only twenty-three, but she felt ancient in comparison.

'I am sending Tucker out with the payments today.' Tucker had been one of the footmen who had served the Gales for years. Without overstepping the boundaries between servant and master, he'd been loyal to Celia through her marriage and widowhood. He was now her faithful butler.

'Where did you find the money?' Adele asked.

Celia pointed to the coins. 'The silliest thing. I was looking for something else and I discovered a purse full of coin. Your father must have packed it away and forgotten about it.'

Adele's expression saddened. 'That was a fortunate thing. Had he found it he would have lost it gambling.'

What would Adele think if she knew where the money had really come from?

Only three people knew of Celia's trip to the Masquerade Club—Tucker, her housekeeper, Mrs Bell, and Younie, Celia's lady's maid. Younie was lady's maid to all three women since Lord Gale's death.

What would Adele think if she knew Celia planned to return to the gaming hell tonight?

An image of Rhysdale flew into her mind. Would he watch her again? Her heartbeat accelerated.

The Dowager Lady Gale, Celia's mother-in-law, entered the room. 'There you are, Adele.' She did not greet Celia. 'We must decide what you are to wear to the musicale tonight. It cannot be the blue gown again. Everyone has seen that gown twice already. It will be remembered.' She finally turned to Celia. 'She absolutely needs new dresses. You are excessively cruel to deny them to her.'

Celia pasted a smile on her face. 'Good afternoon, Lady Gale.'

Like Celia, Lady Gale wanted Adele to have a successful Season, ending in a betrothal. The difference was, Celia wanted Adele to find someone who could make her happy; Lady Gale cared only that Adele marry a man with a good title and good fortune.

Celia adopted a mollifying tone. 'You will be pleased to know Adele and I have been talking of dresses. I have payment for the modiste, so Adele may order two new gowns.'

Her mother-in-law, silver-haired and as slim-figured as she'd been in her own Season, narrowed her eyes. 'Only two? I cannot abide how tight-fisted you are!'

Celia forced herself to hold her tongue. Engaging in a shouting match with the dowager would serve no purpose. 'Only two for now, but I am confident our finances will soon improve and Adele may order more.'

Her conscience niggled. How many times had her father purchased something, saying he'd win enough to pay for it?

Lady Gale pursed her thin lips. 'And I am to wear my old rags, I suppose.'

Celia's smile froze. 'You may order two gowns for yourself, if you like.'

'Will you come with us tonight, Celia?' Adele looked hopeful. She was too kind to say she did not find her grandmother's company altogether pleasant at such gatherings.

Celia calculated what time the musicale would end. It would still give her time to attend the gaming house for a few hours of play. 'If you wish.'

'I do!' Adele's countenance brightened.

Her grandmother rolled her eyes. 'You will dress properly, I hope.'

'I will, indeed.' Celia always dressed properly. Her most daring gown was the one she'd worn to the Masquerade

Club the night before. Its neckline had always seemed too low. She'd only worn it because she thought no one would recognise her in it, as if anyone at these society events noticed what she wore. None the less, she would change into it to wear to the gaming house tonight, as well.

She turned to Adele. 'Why don't you see if Younie has any ideas of how to alter one of your old gowns for tonight? She is very clever at that sort of thing.'

Adele jumped to her feet. 'An excellent idea! I will do that right away.' She started for the door. 'I beg your leave, Grandmama.'

Lady Gale waved her away. 'Go.' She called after Adele. 'Younie is in my room, Adele. She is mending.'

Adele skipped away and Lady Gale turned to Celia. 'I do not see why my granddaughter and I must share your lady's maid.'

Celia kept her voice even. 'Because we do not have the funds to hire more servants.'

'Money!' the older woman huffed. 'That is all you ever talk of.'

Money had consumed her thoughts, Celia would be the first to admit. Except this day thoughts of money were mixed with combinations of hearts, spades, clubs and diamonds.

Would Rhysdale be pleased at her return? Celia wondered.

She gave herself a good shake. Why was she even thinking of the man? It was not a good thing that she had come to his notice, no matter how attractively masculine he was. She planned to win and win often.

What if he accused her of cheating?

Lady Devine's musicale was a sought-after event and Celia's mother-in-law said more than once how lucky they were to have received an invitation. Celia, Adele and Lady Gale were announced amidst Lady Gale's grumbling that they ought to have had a gentleman escorting them.

They strolled through the rooms where the pink of the *ton* were assembled. Celia recognised some of the men as having been at the gaming house the previous night and she wondered how many more of these people—ladies especially—had been there, as well, but wearing masks as she had done.

Some of the gentlemen's faces at this entertainment had been quite animated at the gaming house, impassioned by the cards or the dice. Here in this Mayfair town house their expressions were bland. It seemed as if the risks of winning or losing made them come alive.

She did not know their names. The *ton* were known to her only from newspaper articles or books on the peerage. When her parents had been alive she'd been too young for London society. By the time she was married, her husband chose to keep her in the country so as not to interfere with his other 'interests.' The arrangement had suited her well enough. She preferred him to be away.

If she had been with him in London, though, she might have had some warning of his profligacy and the condition of his finances. She would have seen in him the telltale signs of gambling lust. Her childhood had honed her for it.

Her mother-in-law ought to have known how debauched her son had become. Lady Gale had spent most of her time in London as part of the social scene. In fact, it was because of Celia's mother-in-law that they received as many invitations as they did. But her mother-in-law would never countenance anything negative being said about her only son.

Except his choice of a second wife.

One of the men who had been at the gaming hell passed

close by. Celia had an impulse to ask her mother-in-law who the gentleman was, but Lady Gale gestured to her dismissively before she could speak.

'Get me a glass of wine,' the older woman ordered. 'It is so tedious not to have a man about to perform such niceties.'

'I will get it for you, Grandmama,' Adele said. 'Do not trouble Celia.'

Before either lady could protest, Adele disappeared through the crowd.

Lady Gale pursed her lips at Celia, but something quickly caught her eye. 'Look. There is our cousin Luther.'

Luther was second cousin to Celia's husband. And he was the new Baron Gale.

Needless to say, Luther was none too pleased at the state of his inheritance, mortgaged to the hilt, all reserves depleted. He had not the least inclination to offer any financial assistance to the former baron's mother, daughter or wife, as a result.

'Yoo-hoo! Luther!' Lady Gale waved.

The man tried to ignore her but, with a resigned look upon his face, walked over to where they stood. 'Good evening, ladies.' He bowed. 'I trust you are well.'

'We are exceeding well,' Lady Gale chirped, suddenly as bright and cheerful as she'd previously been sullen. 'And you, sir?'

'Tolerable,' he muttered, his eyes straying to elsewhere in the room.

'My granddaughter is here, Luther, dear,' she went on. 'You will want to greet her, I am sure.'

Luther looked as if he'd desire anything but.

'It is her Season, do you recall?' Lady Gale fluttered her lashes as if she were the girl having her Season. 'We expect many suitors.'

'Do you?' Luther appeared to search for a means of escape.

'Her dowry is respectable, you know.' That was because her father, Celia's husband, had been unable to get his hands on it.

Luther's brows rose in interest. 'Is that so?'

Celia felt a sudden dread. Surely Lady Gale would not try to make a match between Adele and Luther? Luther had already proved to be excessively unkind. After all, he'd taken over Gale House as soon as Celia's year of mourning was completed, removing Celia, Adele and Lady Gale without an offer of another residence. Even now he was rattling around in the London town house by himself when he could very easily have hosted the three women for the Season. That simple act would have saved Celia plenty of money and would have given Adele more prestige.

'Gale!' some gentleman called. 'Are you coming?'

Luther did not hesitate. 'If you will pardon me.' He bowed again.

'But,' Lady Gale spoke to his retreating back, 'you have not yet greeted Adele!'

'He can see Adele another time,' Celia assured her. 'In fact, he could call upon us, which would be the civil thing for him to do.'

Lady Gale flicked her away as if she were an annoying fly. 'He is much too busy. He is a peer now, you know.'

A peer who cared nothing for his relations.

Adele returned, carrying two glasses of wine. 'I brought one for you, too, Celia.' She handed a glass to her grandmother and one to Celia.

Adele was always so considerate. Sometimes Celia wondered how the girl could share the same blood as her father and grandmother.

Lady Gale snapped, 'Adele, you missed our cousin,

Luther. He was here but a moment ago.' She made it sound
as if Adele should have known to come back earlier.

'Oh?' Adele responded brightly. Did Adele simply ignore her grandmother's chiding or did she not hear it? 'I
have wanted to meet him and ask how all the people are
at Gale House. I do miss them!'

One of Lady Gale's friends found her and the two
women were quickly engaged in a lively conversation.

Adele leaned close to Celia. 'The kindest gentleman
assisted me. I—I do not know if I properly thanked him.
I must do so if I see him again.'

Celia smiled at her. 'You will be meeting many gentlemen this Season.' She so wanted Adele to pick a steady,
responsible, generous man.

Luther was certainly not generous.

'You grandmother will wish to select your suitors, you
know,' Celia added.

Adele frowned. 'I do want her to be pleased with me.'

Celia sipped her wine. 'You must please yourself first
of all.'

Adele would not be pushed into a marriage she did not
want and should not have to endure—as Celia had been.
Celia would make certain of it.

The start of the programme was announced and Lady
Gale gestured impatiently for Celia and Adele to follow
her while she continued in deep conversation with her
friend. They took their chairs and soon the music began.

Lady Devine had hired musicians and singers to perform the one-act French opera, *Le Calife de Bagdad* by
Boieldieu. The comic opera was ideal for an audience who
were intent on marriage matches. In the opera, the mother
of the ingenue Zétulbé, refuses to allow the girl to marry
the Caliph of Baghdad, who meets her disguised as an or-

dinary man. When he tries to impress the family with extravagant gifts, the mother merely thinks he is a brigand.

It should be every family's fear—that the man marrying their daughter is not what he seems. It certainly was Celia's fear for Adele. If only Celia's experience had been more like Zétulbé's, discovering the generous and loving prince disguised as something less. Celia's husband had been the opposite. Presented by her guardians as a fine, upstanding man, but truly a cruel and thoughtless one in disguise.

As the music enveloped Celia she wondered if all men hid their true colours.

Of course, she disguised herself, too. She pretended to be a respectable lady, but she visited a gaming hell at night. Once there, she disguised herself again by wearing a mask and pretending to be a gambler, when gambling and gamblers were what she detested most in the world.

The tenor playing the Caliph's part stepped forwards to sing of his love for Zétulbé. Celia closed her eyes and tried to merely enjoy the music. An image of Rhysdale flashed through her mind. Like the tenor's, Rhysdale's voice had teemed with seduction.

Rhys watched the door from the moment he opened the gambling house. He watched for her—the woman in the black-and-gold mask.

'Who are you expecting?' Xavier asked him. 'Someone to make our fortunes or to take it all away?'

He shrugged. 'The woman I told you about last night.'

Xavier's brow furrowed. 'This is not the time for a conquest, Rhys. Your future depends upon making this place a success.'

Xavier was not saying anything Rhys had not said multiple times to himself. Still, he flushed with anger. 'I will not neglect my responsibilities.'

Xavier did not back down. 'Women are trouble.'

Rhys laughed. 'That is the pot calling the kettle black, is it not? You are rarely without a female on your arm.'

'Women attach themselves to me, that is true.' Xavier's blue eyes and poetic good looks drew women like magnets. 'But I've yet to meet one who could distract me from what I've set myself to do.'

'I did not say she was a distraction. Or a conquest.' Rhys tried to convince himself as well as his friend. 'I am curious about her. She is a gamester like me and that is what intrigues me.'

Xavier scoffed. 'Is that why you warned me away last night?'

Rhys frowned. 'That prohibition still stands. I do not wish to have *you* distract *her.*' He paused, knowing he was not being entirely truthful. 'I want to see what transpires with this woman gamester.'

Xavier gave him a sceptical look.

Truth was, Rhys did not know what to make of his attraction to the masked lady gamester. Xavier was correct. The woman did tempt him in ways that were more carnal than curious.

But not enough to ignore his commitment to the gaming hell, not when his main objective was to show the Westleighs he could succeed in precisely the same world in which his father failed.

The buzzing of voices hushed momentarily. Rhys glanced to the doorway as she walked in, dressed in the same gown and mask as the night before. Sound muffled and the lamps grew brighter.

His body indeed thought of her in a carnal way. 'There she is.'

He left Xavier and crossed the room to her. 'Madam, you have returned. I am flattered.'

She put a hand on her chest. 'I have indeed returned, Mr Rhysdale. Would you be so kind as to find a whist partner for me once again?'

Xavier appeared at his side. 'It would be my pleasure to partner you, madam.'

Rhys glared at him before turning back to the masked woman. 'May I present Mr Campion, madam. He is a friend and an excellent card player.'

She extended her gloved hand. 'Mr Campion.'

Xavier accepted with a bow. 'I am charmed.' He smiled his most seductive smile at her. 'Do me the honour of calling me Xavier. No one need stand on ceremony in a gaming hell.'

Rhys groaned inwardly.

'Xavier, then,' she responded.

He threaded her hand through his arm. 'Do you wish to play deep, madam?'

She did not answer right away. 'Not too deep, for the moment. But neither do I wish a tame game.'

Xavier nodded in approval. 'Excellent. Let us go in search of players.'

He looked back at Rhys and winked.

Rhys knew Xavier well enough to understand his intent was merely to annoy. Xavier would always honour his wishes in matters such as this. Rhys was less certain about the lady. Most women preferred Xavier to Rhys. Most women preferred Xavier to any man.

Rhys went back to patrolling the room, watching the play, speaking to the croupiers running the tables. He kept a keen eye out for cheating in those winning too conveniently and desperation in those losing. Gamblers could easily burst out in sudden violence when the cards or the dice did not go their way. Rhys's plan was to intervene before tempers grew hot.

His eyes always pulled back to the masked woman. She sat across from Xavier, posture alert, but not tense. Tonight her handling of the cards was smoother than the night before. She arranged her hand swiftly and never belaboured a decision of what card to play. She'd said she preferred games of skill and she was quite skilled at whist.

She was a gamester, for certain. Rhys could wager on that. He'd also bet that she remembered every card played and that she quickly perceived the unique patterns of play in her partners and her opponents.

He strolled over to the table to watch more closely.

'How is the game?' He stood behind the masked woman.

Xavier looked at him with amusement. 'We make good partners.'

Judging from the counters on the table, Xavier and the masked woman made very good partners indeed. Card partners, that was.

Rhys stood where he could see the woman's cards. If it bothered her, she gave no sign. He watched the play for several hands. She was clever. Deal her four trump and she was certain to win with three of them at least. Give her a hand with no trump and she took tricks with other cards when trump was not played.

She was a gamester all right.

He instantly looked on her with respect.

But, as fascinated as he was watching her play, he needed to move on. No gambler wanted such acute attention to his or her play, especially by the house's proprietor.

Rhys sauntered away.

An unmasked Ned Westleigh approached him. 'How are things faring?' Ned asked in a conspiratorial tone.

Rhys lifted his brows and raised his voice. 'Why, good evening, Lord Neddington. Good to see you back here.'

'Well?' Ned persisted.

'We are near to recouping the original investment,' Rhys replied. 'So all is as it should be.'

'Excellent.' Ned rubbed his hands together.

'There is more to our bargain, do not forget,' Rhys added.

He expected these Westleighs to try to renege on the earl's obligation to claim Rhys as a son. More than once Rhys wondered why he'd made that part of the bargain. Another man might wish for the connection to the aristocracy such an acknowledgement might bring, but Rhys cared nothing for that. Neither was the money he'd reap from this enterprise a motivation. He could always make money.

No, all Rhys really wanted was to force his father to do what he ought to have done when Rhys was a child—take responsibility for Rhys's existence. Once that was accomplished, Rhys was content to spurn him and his sons as they had once spurned him.

'Hugh and I do not forget,' Ned said in a low voice. 'Our father…requires some time.'

Rhys lifted a shoulder. 'I will not release the money until that part of the promise is assured.' The Westleighs, in their desperation, had ceded all the power in this matter to him.

Rhys glanced over to the masked woman and caught her looking back. She quickly attended to her cards.

Rhysdale was talking to the gentleman Celia had seen earlier at the musicale, she noticed. It was fortunate she had changed her gown, even though she doubted the gentleman would have noticed her. The widow of a dissolute baron who never brought his wife to town did not capture anyone's attention.

Rhysdale caught her watching and she quickly turned back to the cards and played her last trump. She guessed Xavier still had two trumps remaining. That should ensure they won this hand.

They'd won most of the games and each time Celia felt a surge of triumph. Their opponents, however, grew ever-deepening frowns. Xavier took the next trick and the next and the game was theirs.

Their opponents grumbled.

Celia shuffled the deck and the man on her right cut the cards. She dealt the hand and the play began, but this time Xavier did not play in the manner to which she'd accustomed herself. The opponents took tricks they ought to have lost. Xavier suddenly was playing very sloppily indeed. He was losing *her* money. She gave him a stern glance, but he seemed oblivious.

When the hand was done, the opponents won most of the tricks and won the game, to their great delight. Luckily that game's wagers had been modest, but Celia's blood boiled at losing so senselessly.

'That was capital!' the man on her right said. 'I'm done for now, however. Excellent play.' He stood, collected his small pile of counters and bowed to Celia. 'Well done, madam.' He turned to Xavier. 'You chose a capital partner, sir. We must play again.'

'I'm done, as well,' the other man said.

Both begged their leave and wandered over to the hazard table.

'They must wish to lose more,' Xavier remarked.

Celia gathered her counters. 'You let them win that last game.'

'You noticed?' Xavier laughed. 'Better they leave happy. Otherwise they might choose other opponents next time.'

Her eyes widened. 'You made certain they would be willing to play us again.'

He nodded. 'Precisely.'

He smiled and his incredibly handsome face grew even more handsome. He'd been an excellent partner, she had to admit. She now possessed even more money than she'd won the night before. Still, she sensed he'd had motives of his own for partnering her, something that had nothing to do with trying to win at cards.

Another man hiding something.

She stood and extended her hand to him. 'It was a pleasure, sir.'

His smile flashed again. 'The pleasure was mine.' He held her hand a moment too long for her liking. 'What's next for you? The hazard table?'

She shrugged. '*Vingt-et-un*, perhaps.'

'Ah, there is a *vingt-et-un* table. Let me take you to it and see if we can get you in that game.'

Vingt-et-un was another game where she could exercise her skill. All she need do was remember the cards played and bet accordingly.

Xavier led her to the large round table with a dealer at one end and players all around. Xavier facilitated her entry into the game and it soon occupied all her concentration.

When the croupier reshuffled the cards, she glanced up.

Mr Rhysdale was again watching her. He nodded, acknowledging that she'd again caught him watching. She nodded in return and refocused on the cards.

Time passed swiftly and Celia's excitement grew. She was winning even more than the night before. Her reticule was heavy with counters. She fished into it and pulled out her watch.

Quarter after three.

In only a few minutes her coach would arrive and she still must cash out.

Mr Rhysdale appeared at her elbow. 'Almost time for your coach, madam?'

Her senses flared with his nearness. 'Yes.'

He touched her elbow. 'I will escort you.'

'That is not necessary, sir.' His attention made it hard for her to think. And to breathe.

He touched her reticule. 'I cannot allow you to walk into the night alone. Especially with a full purse.'

As he had done the night before, he escorted her to the cashier and waited for her while the hall servant collected her wrap. He again walked her out the door and onto the pavement.

It had apparently rained. The street shone from the wet and reflected the rush lights as if in a mirror. From a distance, the rhythmic clopping of horses' hooves and the creaking of coach wheels echoed in the damp air. Celia's coach was not in sight.

Rhysdale stood next to her. 'How did you find the cards tonight, madam?'

She closed her hand around her reticule. 'Quite satisfying.' She glanced down the street again. 'Although I may not spend much time at *vingt-et-un* after this.' She feared he would catch on that she had been counting the cards.

'You did not lose.' He spoke this as a fact, not a question.

She smiled. 'I try not to lose.'

His voice turned low. 'I noticed.'

Her face warmed.

'You have an excellent memory for cards, do you not?' he went on.

Her stomach knotted. He knew. 'Is that a problem?'

'Not for me,' he responded. 'Not as yet.'

Her hands trembled. 'Are you warning me away?'

'Not at all.' His tone remained matter of fact. 'If I saw you make wagers that would jeopardise my establishment, I would certainly warn you away from my tables, but, as long as you play fair, it matters not to me how much you win off of any gentleman brave enough to challenge you.'

'Do you suspect me of cheating?' The very idea filled her with dread.

And reminded her of her father.

He shook his head. 'You are a skilled player.' He paused. 'I admire that.'

She relaxed for a moment, then glanced down the street, looking for Jonah, her coachman.

'Who taught you to play?' Rhysdale continued conversationally.

She averted her gaze, not willing to reveal the pain she knew would show in her face. 'My father.' Her throat grew dry. 'He once was also a skilled player.'

Before he died.

She faced Rhys again, wanting to take the focus off of her. 'And who taught you to play, sir?'

He made a disparaging sound. 'Certainly not *my* father.' He looked reluctant to tell her more. 'I learned in school, but I honed my craft later when it became necessary.'

'Why necessary?' she asked.

It was his turn to glance away, but he soon faced her again. 'I was living on the streets.'

She was shocked. 'On the streets?'

He shrugged. 'When I was fourteen, I had no one and nothing. I came to London and learned to support myself by playing cards.'

No one and nothing?

How well she remembered the desolation of no one and nothing.

She opened her mouth to ask why he'd been alone, what had happened to his parents, but her coach turned the corner and entered the street. She was silent as it pulled up to where they stood. As he had done the night before, he put down the steps for her and opened the door.

He took her hand and helped her inside, but did not immediately release it. 'Will you come play cards again, madam?' His voice seemed to fill the night.

She wanted to return. She wanted to win more.

And she wanted to see him again.

All seemed equally dangerous.

'I will return, sir.'

He squeezed her hand.

After he released her and closed the coach door, Celia could still feel the pressure of his fingers.

Chapter Four

Ned waited until almost noon for his father to rise and make his appearance in the breakfast room. He'd tried to confront his father on this issue before and knew he must catch him before he went out or he'd lose another day.

Hugh had waited with Ned most of the morning, but stormed out a few minutes ago, swearing about their father's decadent habits.

Not more than a minute later Ned heard his father's distinct footsteps approaching.

Wasn't it always the way? When Ned needed Hugh, his brother disappeared.

The earl entered the room, but paused for a moment, spying his oldest son there.

He gave Ned an annoyed look. 'I thought to have breakfast in peace.'

Ned stood. 'Good morning to you as well, Father.'

His father walked straight to the sideboard and filled his plate with food that had already been replaced three times. The earl detested cold eggs. 'Do you not have something of use to do? Itemising my bills? Recording my debt in a ledger?'

Ned bristled at his father's sarcastic tone. 'You ought to be grateful to me and to Hugh.'

His father sat down at the head of the table. A footman appeared to pour his tea. Ned signalled for the footman to leave.

His father waited until the door closed behind the man. 'I am anything but grateful that you treat me as a doddering fool. Makes me look bad in front of the servants.'

Ned sat adjacent to his father. 'You were the one to speak of bills and debts in front of Higgley.'

His father glared at him and stuffed his mouth full of ham.

Ned went on. 'But I do need to speak to you.'

His father rolled his eyes.

Ned did not waver. 'It has been a month since Rhysdale opened the gaming house and you have yet to fulfil your part of the bargain.'

'You truly do not expect me to speak to that fellow, do you?' He popped a cooked egg into his mouth.

'Speak to him?' Ned felt his face grow hot. 'You gave your word as a gentleman to do more than that. We need to include him socially. You need to acknowledge he is your son.'

His father waved a hand. 'I already did my part. I sent him to school. What more can he want?'

Ned gritted his teeth. 'You agreed to this, Father. Rhysdale has already amassed the amount we invested to get the place started. But he will not release the money until you do what you are honour-bound to do.'

'Honour?' His father's voice rose. 'Do you call it honourable that *he* is holding *my* money? It is more like extortion, I'd say.'

'I'd say it is more like sound business,' Ned countered.

'Rhysdale is no fool. The money is his leverage. You must do as he says.'

'I do not have to do anything I do not wish to do.'

Good God. The man sounded like a petulant schoolboy.

Ned would not put up with it. 'Father. You must do this. We are running out of time. No one will advance you more credit. The fields need tending. The livestock need feed. Our tenants need to eat—'

At that moment Hugh entered the room. 'Your voice is carrying, Ned.'

So much for keeping this private from the servants—not that one could keep anything secret from servants for long.

'Where were you?' he asked Hugh.

Hugh looked apologetic. 'I was going mad waiting for Father. I just took a quick walk outside.'

He sat across from Ned and poured a cup of tea.

'Father is reneging on his word.' Ned inclined his head towards their father.

Hugh took a sip. 'I presumed.' He slid his father a scathing look. 'Your bastard son has more honour than you, you know. He's kept his part of the bargain.'

Their father straightened in his seat. 'I'll brook no disrespect from you, you ungrateful cub.'

Hugh faced the earl directly, his face red with anger. 'Then be a man I can respect, sir! Do what you agreed to do. Introduce Rhys to society as your son. You gave your word.'

'Only to the two of you,' their father prevaricated. 'I never gave my word to him.'

Ned lowered his voice. 'Your word given to your sons means nothing, then?'

Hugh rose from his chair. 'Let him go, Ned! He is not thinking of us. Nor of the Westleigh estates. Nor the Westleigh people. Let him watch his creditors come ransack the house, carrying away our heritage and that of our own sons. He cares nothing for nobody. Only for himself.'

'See here, you cur!' the earl cried, jumping to his feet.

Ned stood and extended his arms, gesturing for them both to sit down. He had one more card to play. 'Let us bring Mother into this conversation.'

'You'll do no such thing!' his father cried.

'Ned's right.' Hugh seized on this idea immediately. 'Mother needs to know what a sorry excuse for a gentleman you've become.'

Ned suspected their mother already knew what a sorry creature her husband was. But she probably did not know the extent of his debt and the dire consequences that were imminent unless they could begin paying the creditors. This information would certainly shock her.

She, of course, knew of Rhys's existence and Ned did feel sorry that she must endure the humiliation of having him welcomed into the family.

'Very well,' the earl snapped. 'I'll go the gaming hell and make nice to Rhysdale. I'll do that much.'

'You'll have to do more,' Ned warned him.

The earl nodded. 'Yes. Yes.' His tone turned resigned. 'But first I want to see this place and ascertain for myself whether he is swindling us or not.'

'He is not swindling us!' Hugh said hotly.

Their father ignored him. 'If all is as it should be, then we may plan how to divulge the rest to your mother.'

Rhys wandered through the tables of the gaming house, watching the gamblers, perusing the croupiers at their work. He wished he had more eyes, more people he could trust to check on the tables. To make certain the croupiers stayed honest and the gamblers refrained from cheating. With so much money changing hands every night, it was a rare man or woman who would not at some time or another become tempted.

Cheating was the great danger of a gaming house. Gentlemen could accept losing huge amounts in honest games, but the whiff of a dishonest house might swiftly destroy everything.

He also had to admit to watching for the masked woman to arrive. She'd been attending almost every night. Whenever she came, Rhys contrived to spend a few minutes alone with her.

The mystery of her sometimes filled his thoughts.

Where had she come from? Who was she? Why had she chosen gambling to make money?

She had a life outside the gaming hell, a life she wished to protect, that much he understood. Was she married and hiding her gambling from her husband? He hoped not. Married women held no appeal for him.

He'd had some opportunity to attend the Royal Opera House and Drury Lane Theatre. He and Xavier had joined Xavier's parents in their theatre box. But Rhys had seen no one who resembled her. He knew he would recognise her without her mask. He'd memorised her eyes, her mouth, the way she moved.

He glanced up at the doorway, for the hundredth time. But it was not she who appeared.

He stiffened. 'Well, well,' he said to himself, looking around to see if Xavier noticed, but his friend was deep in play.

Earl Westleigh sauntered in with one of his cronies.

Rhys had spied the earl from time to time in the two years he'd been back from the war. He and the earl had sometimes gambled at the same establishments. At those times, though, Rhys doubted the earl noticed him. Even if he had, how would he recognise Rhys now from the scrawny fourteen-year-old he'd been when he'd begged the earl for help?

Rhys watched the earl survey the room in his self-important way. He leaned over to say something to his friend and both men laughed.

Rhys flexed his fingers into a fist, feeling as though the men were laughing at his youthful self, near-helpless and so desperately alone. He was not alone here. Not helpless. This was *his* place. Under his control. His to build into a success beyond any of the earl's expectations.

He straightened his spine.

'Where is the owner of this establishment?' Lord Westleigh asked in a booming voice. 'I should like to see him.'

Rhys turned to one of the croupiers and asked the man about the play at his faro table. It was the sort of surveillance he might do, but this time, of course, his motive was to avoid responding to the earl's beck and call.

Out of the corner of his eye he saw someone point him out to Lord Westleigh. He also saw Xavier looking up from his play, his gaze going from the earl to Rhys. Xavier appeared ready to vault out of his chair, daggers drawn.

Rhys did not need his friend's aid. He could handle the earl. He knew he was the better man.

He deliberately busied himself with checking the faro deck, but the hairs on the back of his neck rose when Westleigh came near.

'Rhysdale!' The earl made his name sound like an order.

Rhys did not respond right away, but finished replacing the faro deck in its apparatus.

Slowly he raised his eyes to the earl. 'Lord Westleigh,' he said in a flat voice.

'I've come to see what people are talking about. A gaming hell and a masquerade.' He made a somewhat disparaging laugh.

'What do you wish to play?' Rhys asked, treating him like any other gentleman—but with a bit more coldness.

'I fancy some faro,' the earl's companion said. 'Haven't tried my hand at faro in an age.'

It was a game going out of fashion, but still making enough here to satisfy Rhys.

'I do not know you, sir.' Rhys extended his hand to the man. 'I am Mr Rhysdale and, as the earl so loudly announced, I am the owner.'

The man clasped his hand. 'Sir Godfrey's the name.'

Rhys made room for Sir Godfrey at the faro table. 'I hope you enjoy yourself, sir.'

He turned to Lord Westleigh. 'And you, sir, what is your fancy?'

Lord Westleigh's attention had turned to the doorway where the masked woman for whom Rhys had been waiting all night entered.

'I'd fancy that,' the earl said under his breath.

Rhys's fingers curled into a fist again.

He stepped in front of the earl, blocking his view of the woman. 'This is an establishment for gambling and nothing more. Do you comprehend?' His voice was low and firm. 'The ladies who play here will be left in peace. Am I speaking clearly enough?'

Lord Westleigh pursed his lips. 'Meant no harm.'

Rhys narrowed his eyes.

Westleigh glanced away. 'My sons tell me this establishment is making money. Is that true?'

'It is true.' Rhys guessed the earl wanted his share. Not a damned chance until he met his part of the bargain.

'But you have not paid my sons a farthing.' Westleigh had the gall to look affronted.

Rhys levelled his gaze at the man. 'It is you who have held up payment, sir. I await you.'

'Yes. Well.' Westleigh looked everywhere but at Rhys. 'It is complicated.'

Rhys laughed dryly. 'And distasteful to you, I might imagine.' He shook his head. 'Matters not to me whether you do this or not. This place is making me rich.' He walked away.

Rhys had begged once from his father, but never again. Let his father beg from him this time.

As soon as she walked in the room, Celia's gaze went directly to Rhysdale. He stood with an older man, a gentleman, to judge by the fit and fabric of his coat. This man had not visited the gaming house before, at least not when she'd been here, and she had not seen him at the few society functions she attended with Adele and Lady Gale.

Whoever this man was, Rhysdale did not seem pleased at his presence. That piqued her curiosity even more.

She detested herself for looking for Rhysdale as soon as she walked through the door, for wondering about who he was with and how he felt about it.

As the days had gone on, she'd come to enjoy his attentions.

It felt almost like having a friend.

She turned away and made her way through the room, returning greetings from players to whom she was now a familiar figure. She no longer needed Rhysdale to find her a game of whist; plenty of men and some ladies were glad to play.

She passed by Xavier Campion. That man's eyes usually followed her, not with the interest of other gentlemen. She swore he watched her with suspicion. Tonight, however, Xavier watched Rhysdale and his brow was furrowed.

Who was that man?

Rhysdale turned away from the gentleman and walked away, his expression one of distaste and suppressed rage.

She lowered her gaze and set about finding a whist partner.

Not too long after, she was seated at a table and arranging a hand of cards into suits. Still, she was acutely aware of whenever Rhysdale passed near.

She no longer feared he was trying to catch her cheating. She liked his attention. It seemed as if the air crackled with energy when he was near, like it might before a summer storm. She liked him.

Even though he made his living from gambling.

To her distress, the cards did not favour her this night. Even when she had partnered with Xavier, she lost hand after hand. Counting in her head, she knew it was not a trifling amount. She kept playing, thinking the next hand would turn her luck around. When that did not happen, she counted on the hand after that.

As the night advanced, her pile of counters grew lower and lower. She'd lost over half the money she staked. Still, the urge was strong to keep playing, to bet more, to keep going so she could change it all back to the way it had been before.

But still she lost.

Celia stared at her counters and came to her senses. *Stop!* she told herself. *Before you return home with nothing.*

She stood up abruptly. 'I am done.'

Before the others at her table could protest, she hurried away and made her way to the cashier. She wanted the counters changed back to coin so she would not be tempted to return to the games.

It was only two in the morning, too early to wait outside

for her coachman. Instead, after cashing in her counters, she walked to the supper room, not hungry, but greatly desiring a glass of wine or two to quiet her nerves.

Several of the tables were occupied, but her gaze went instantly to the table where she'd sat before with Rhysdale.

He was there, staring into nothing, a glass in hand.

She approached him, needing at least the illusion of a friend. 'Hello, Rhysdale.'

He glanced at her with a look of surprise that turned into a smile. 'The lady with the mask.' He stood and pulled out a chair. 'Would you care to sit with me?'

She sat.

'What is your pleasure?' he asked. 'Shall I fix a plate for you?'

'Wine.' She sighed. 'Just wine.'

He signalled a servant to bring her wine.

Now that she'd so brazenly approached him, she did not know what to say.

'How was your night?' he asked finally.

'Not good,' she replied.

What more was there to say? Losing called into serious question her whole plan to finance Adele's come-out with winnings. Worse than that, it showed how easily she could slip into a gambling fever where nothing mattered but trying to win back her money.

The wine arrived and she quickly downed half of it.

His brows rose. 'Bring the bottle,' he told the servant and turned back to her. 'I take it you lost.'

Her fingers drummed the tabletop. 'I did.'

He reached across the table and quieted her busy hand. 'Do you need assistance? Are you in distress?'

She glanced into his eyes, which conveyed only concern and earnestness. His hand was warm against hers, even through the thin fabric of her glove.

She slipped her hand away, shaken at how comforting his touch felt and how much she needed comfort.

'I'll come to rights,' she said, although her voice lacked any semblance of confidence.

'I can lend you money,' he went on.

She shook her head. 'I know better than to borrow from moneylenders.'

His eyes flashed. 'I am not a moneylender. I offer as a friend.'

She took in a breath. 'But…you do not even know who I am.'

He traced the edge of her mask with a finger. 'Tell me, then. Who are you?'

She sat very still at his gentle touch while her heart fluttered in her chest.

'I am nobody,' she said, speaking with a truth that had been proved over and over. She had not mattered enough for anyone to care what the impact of their actions would be to her.

She raised her eyes to his.

His promise seemed so genuine, as if he was a man she could believe. Would he truly lend her money if she needed it? And then what? Without gambling she could not repay him. What would she do then? Turn to moneylenders?

She shivered as the memory of her father returned. He had to sell her pony, he'd told her. He had to pay the moneylenders. Life after that had been filled with more times of want than times of plenty.

Until the day her mother told her news even more horrible than losing a pony. Her father was dead. He'd been accused of cheating at cards and a man—an earl—had shot him dead in a duel.

'I do not need a loan,' she said absently, still caught in the memory of her father's senseless death.

At every society entertainment she feared she would encounter her father's killer. What would she do then?

Rhys spoke. 'But you need money.'

'I'll find another way.' Although she knew there was no other way.

She, Adele and Lady Gale would have to find a set of rooms that Celia's widow's pension could afford. She'd have to let the servants go and Adele's chances of making a good marriage would become extremely slim. At least Celia would not have to encounter the earl who killed her father.

She finished her glass of wine as the servant placed the bottle on the table. Rhysdale poured her another.

'Thank you.' She lifted the glass and decided to push the attention off herself. 'What of you, Rhysdale? When I came in you looked as if you were the one who had lost money.'

A corner of his mouth rose. 'The house never loses, you know. We are doing well.'

She smiled. 'I am glad of it. You seem to have more players each time I've come.'

'More women, as well.' Again he touched her mask. 'The Masquerade seems to be working.'

She put her fingers where his had touched. 'It has worked for me.'

He sat back. 'Until now.'

She shrugged. 'I shall have to consider whether to come again and try to recoup.'

He leaned forwards again. 'Do you mean to say you might not return?'

'I might not.' She paused. 'I should not.'

'Do not say so!'

Her heart started pounding faster again. She took another sip of wine. 'Does one gambler matter so much?'

His gaze seemed to pierce into her. He did not answer right away. Finally he said, 'I believe there are men who come merely in hopes of playing with you.'

She scoffed. 'Surely you are not serious.' She supposed the men who'd partnered with her and those who played against her recognised her skill. 'In any event, I doubt any man will want to partner with me after my losing streak tonight.'

She'd not only lost her own money, but her partners' money, as well.

'You place so little value on yourself?' He continued to pin her with his eyes.

No one else had valued her.

She glanced down. 'Who wants to partner with someone who is losing?'

He drummed on the table like she had done earlier, while his steady gaze began to unnerve her.

'I have a proposition,' he said finally. 'Come work for me.'

Rhys did not know why he had not thought of this before.

Hire her.

'What do you mean, work for you?' She looked shocked. 'Doing what?'

'Gambling,' he rushed to assure her. 'Nothing more.' The idea grew in his head as he spoke. 'I would pay you to gamble. And to encourage others to gamble, as well.'

Her eyes through her mask grew wary. 'Am I to cheat?'

He waved a hand. 'Never! It is not cheating to pay you to gamble. You will receive no advantage.'

She glanced away, as if deliberating.

It gave him time to think, as well. Would he compromise the gambling house by paying her to gamble? He only knew he wanted her to come back. He needed her to come back.

She turned back to him. 'How much would you pay?'

He threw out the first number that occurred to him. 'Two pounds a night?'

'Two pounds?' She looked astonished.

Was that not enough? He paid his man only fifty pounds a year. 'That is more than generous, madam.'

She sat very still, but he fancied her mind was calculating.

Finally she spoke. 'I need money, sir, but if my task is to gamble, then, as generous as two pounds a night might be, it does not allow me to play for bigger stakes. What is more, I still stand a chance that I will lose as I have lost tonight. That I cannot risk.'

She had a point. In gambling there was always the possibility of losing it all.

He wanted her to agree, though. He wanted to see her again. If he did not offer enough to entice her, she might never return.

He tapped on the table again. 'Very well. I will stake you.' He thought for a minute. 'Say, for one hundred pounds. At the end of the night, you return my stake to me but keep your winnings. If you lose, you make an accounting to me of the loss.' If she lost too often, he'd reassess this plan, but his gamble was that she would bring in more money than she would lose.

Her eyes showed interest. 'Do I still receive the two pounds a night?'

He was not that big a fool. 'One pound. Plus your winnings.'

She calculated again, her eyes on his. What did she look like under her mask? He imagined lifting it off her face, discovering the treasure underneath.

In the back of his mind he could hear Xavier's voice, questioning his motives, accusing him of succumbing to the first pretty lightskirt who'd caught his eye in a long time.

She was not a lightskirt, but Rhys would wager she belonged on the fringes of society as did he. His money was still on her being an actress.

She opened her lovely mouth and, God help him, all he could think of was tasting her lips. She was about to agree—he could feel it.

Celia was so tempted. He'd handed her a way to gamble without losing her money. What could be better than that? What did it matter, then, if she succumbed to the excitement of the game? Losing would not imperil her.

It was as if he was handing her the future she so desired. To see Adele well settled. To retire to the country and live quietly within her means with no one directing her life but herself.

Rhysdale did not press her. He poured her another glass of wine and waited.

She accepted the glass gratefully and took a long sip, but even the wine did not loosen the knots of panic inside her.

He'd offered her this help as a friend. When had she last had a friend? For that matter, when had she last been able to trust a man? Even her beloved father broke promise after promise.

What if she refused Rhysdale's offer? Her mind spun with what she would have to do to economise. She'd have to try to pay back most of the creditors. She'd have to give up her coachman, her carriage, her servants. She'd have little left for rooms to let and food to eat. Adele did not deserve such a life. Even her mother-in-law did not deserve such a life.

Rhysdale's gaze was patient and, she fancied, sympathetic. 'You are not required to decide this minute. Come to me tomorrow, in the afternoon.' He glanced about the room. 'We can discuss it without anyone around.' His voice deepened. 'If you refuse employment, my offer of a loan still stands.'

She felt tears prick her eyes. 'You are kind, Rhysdale.'

A smile grew slowly across his face. 'Do not say so too loudly or you will ruin my reputation.'

She almost laughed.

Some gentlemen entered the room and she came to her senses. 'What time is it?' She fished into her reticule to check her timepiece. 'I must take my leave.'

He stood and offered his hand to assist her.

As they walked towards the door, they passed the older man she'd seen with Rhysdale when she'd arrived that night.

'Charming supper room!' the man remarked to his companion.

When he spied Rhysdale, his eyes hardened to ice. He walked past them without a word.

Even the air seemed chilled as he passed.

Celia inclined her head to Rhysdale. 'Who is that gentleman?'

Rhysdale's entire manner changed into something dark and bitter.

'No one you need know,' he answered.

It pained her to see him so disturbed. 'Does he come here often?'

'Never before.' Rhysdale's voice rumbled with suppressed emotion. 'But I suspect he will come again.'

He led her out into the hallway and down the stairs to collect her cloak. As had become his custom, he escorted her into the street to wait for her coachman.

Clouds hid the stars and made the night even darker than usual. Celia's own woes receded as she stood waiting with him for her carriage, an overwhelming desire to comfort him taking over.

She touched his arm. 'Rhysdale, it will not do for the both of us to be glum.'

He covered her hand with his and his typically unreadable face momentarily turned pained and vulnerable. 'Come this afternoon. Let us talk more about my offer.' His grip on her hand tightened. 'Do not leave me entirely.'

She blinked and her throat constricted. 'Very well. I'll come.'

He smiled and his gratitude was palpable. He leaned down, his eyes half closing.

Celia's heart thundered in her chest as the night itself wrapped around them and his head dipped lower and lower. She wrestled with an impulse to push him away and a desire to feel his arms around her.

The *clop-clop* of a horse team sounded in her ears and he stepped away. Her carriage approached from the end of the street. When the coach pulled up to where they stood, he put the steps down and reached for her hand to help her into the couch.

When she placed her hand in his, she suddenly turned to face him, her words bursting from her mouth. 'I will do it, Rhysdale. I will come work for you.'

His face broke out in pleasure. 'Indeed?'

She smiled, as well. 'Yes.'

For a moment he looked as if he would pull her into his arms and kiss her. Instead, he gently cupped her cheek. 'We will talk more this afternoon.'

'Until then,' she whispered.

She climbed into the coach and he closed the door.

As the carriage pulled away, her heart raced. Had she been afraid he would kiss her or had she yearned to feel his lips on hers?

Chapter Five

A gnarl of nerves amidst a flutter of excitement, Celia donned her hat and gloves. It was half-past twelve, barely afternoon, but she wished to be finished with her interview with Rhysdale before two, when no respectable woman dared walk near St James's Street.

She supposed she was not truly a respectable woman. Not when she spent her nights gambling in a gaming hell. But that did not mean she wished to suffer the taunts and catcalls of dandies who loitered on corners for that very purpose.

Her mother-in-law descended the staircase. 'And where are you going?'

Celia had hoped to slip out before her mother-in-law knew she was gone. 'I have an errand. I shall be back shortly.'

'Do you take Younie with you?' the older woman snapped. 'Because I have need of her.'

Celia kept her tone mild. 'She is at your disposal. My errand is not far. I have no need of company.'

'Hmmph!' her mother-in-law sniffed. 'I expect you will not tell me the nature of this errand of yours.'

'That is correct.' Celia smiled.

Lady Gale continued to talk as she descended the stairs. 'Most likely it is to pay a bill or beg for more credit from shopkeepers who ought to be glad to have our business. Needless to say you are not off to meet a man. My son always said you were frigid as well as barren.'

The barb stung.

The cruelty of this woman was rivalled only by that of her son. Ironic that Lady Gale was blind to her son's faults, but took great enjoyment in cataloguing Celia's.

Primary among Celia's shortcomings, of course, was her inability to conceive a child. Neither Gale nor his mother had forgiven her for not producing sons, but neither had they ever considered how crushing this was for Celia. A baby might have made her marriage bearable.

Knowing she could never have a child hurt more than her mother-in-law would ever know, but today her mother-in-law's abuse merely made her angry.

After all she'd sacrificed for the woman's comfort…

Celia faced her. 'You speak only to wound me, ma'am. It is badly done of you.'

Her mother-in-law stopped on the second stair. She flushed and avoided Celia's eye.

Celia maintained her composure. 'Recall, if you please, that your son left you in more precarious financial circumstances than he did me, but I have not abandoned you.' Much as she would like to. 'Nor have I abandoned Adele. I am doing the best I can for all of us.'

Lady Gale pursed her lips. 'You keep us both under your thumb with your tight-fisted ways. You control us with the purse strings.'

Celia tied the ribbons on her hat. 'Think the worst of me, if you wish, but at least have the good manners to refrain from speaking your thoughts aloud.' She opened the door. 'I should return in an hour or so.'

Younie had sewn a swirl of netting to the crown of Celia's hat. When she stepped onto the pavement, Celia pulled the netting over her face so no one would recognise her if they happened to spy her entering the Masquerade Club.

The afternoon was grey and chilly and Celia walked briskly, needing to work off her anger at the woman.

Lady Gale had well known of her son's debauchery, but still she preferred to blame all Gale's ills on Celia. In truth, the man had countless vices, many more than mere gambling. He'd treated Celia like a brood mare and then thrust her out to pasture when she didn't produce, all the while taunting her with his flagrant infidelities and profligate ways. As if that were not enough, he neglected his daughter.

And his mother.

Celia had known nothing of men when her aunt and uncle arranged her marriage to Gale. She'd still been reeling from her parents' deaths and barely old enough for a come-out. Her aunt and uncle simply wished to rid themselves of her. She'd never felt comfortable with Gale, but thought she had no choice but to marry him. She never imagined how bad marriage to him would be.

The only thing he'd wanted from Celia was a son and when she could not comply, he disdained her for it. Over and over and over. Life was only tolerable for her when he went off to London or anywhere else. Celia cared nothing about what he did in those places as long as he was gone.

Little did she know he'd squandered his fortune, leaving only what he could not touch: Celia's widow's portion and Adele's dowry.

She'd worn widow's black after Gale died, but she had never mourned him. His death had set her free.

And she would free herself of his mother, as well, when Adele was settled. As long as her husband would be generous enough to take on the responsibility of the Dowager Lady Gale.

It was not until Celia turned off St James's on to Park Place that she remembered her destination. She was indeed meeting a man. Would not Lady Gale suffer palpitations if she knew? She was meeting a man who offered her the best chance of escaping life with her mother-in-law. A man who had almost kissed her.

The gaming hell was only a few short streets away from her rooms. In daylight it looked like any other residence.

But it was an entirely different world.

As she reached for the knocker, her hand shook.

For the first time he would see her face. Was she ready for that?

She sounded the knocker and the door opened almost immediately. The burly man who attended the door at night stood in the doorway.

Celia made herself smile. 'Good afternoon. I have an appointment with Mr Rhysdale.'

The taciturn man nodded and stepped aside for her to enter. He lifted a finger. A signal for her to wait, she supposed. He trudged up the stairs.

Celia took a breath and glanced around to try to calm her nerves.

At night this hall looked somewhat exotic with its deep green walls and chairs and gilded tables. At night the light from a branch of candles made the gold gilt glitter and a scent of brandy and men filled the air. To her right was a drawing room, its door ajar. To anyone peeking in a window this house would appear as respectable as any Mayfair town house.

The doorman descended the dark mahogany stairs and nodded again. Celia assumed that meant he'd announced her to Mr Rhysdale. He then disappeared into the recesses of rooms behind the hall.

A moment later Rhysdale appeared on the stairs. 'Madam?'

She turned towards him and lifted the netting from her face, suddenly fearful he would not approve of her true appearance.

He paused, ever so slightly, but his expression gave away nothing of his thoughts.

He descended to the hall. 'Come. We will talk upstairs.'

Dismayed by his unreadable reaction, Celia followed him to the second floor where sounds of men hammering nails and sawing wood reached her ears.

'Forgive the noise,' he said. 'I'm having this floor re-modelled into rooms for my use.' He lifted the latch of a door to her right. 'We can talk in here.'

They entered a small drawing room. Its furnishings appeared fashionable, as well as comfortable. They were stylishly arranged.

He gestured for her to sit on a deep red sofa. He sat on an adjacent chair. 'I've ordered tea.'

She might have been calling upon one of her mother-in-law's society friends. Escorted into a pleasant drawing room. Served tea. The conventions might be identical, but this was no typical morning call.

In daylight Rhysdale was even more imposing. His dress and grooming were as impeccable as the most well-attired lord, even though he managed to wear the pieces as casually as if he'd just walked in from a morning ride. His eyes, dark as midnight in the game room, were a spell-binding mix of umber and amber when illuminated by the sun from the windows.

His gaze seemed to take in her total appearance, but his expression remained impassive. Did she disappoint? She was too tall to be fashionable. Her figure was unremark-able. Her neck was too long; her face too thin; her lips too full; her hair too plain a brown—she could almost hear her husband's voice listing her faults.

But what did Rhysdale think?

And why was it she cared so much for his approval?

He blinked, then averted his compelling eyes. 'I assume you have not changed your mind about my proposition?' His smooth voice made her quiver inside.

She swallowed. 'I would not have kept the appoint-ment otherwise.'

A smile grew across his face. 'Then, perhaps an intro-duction is in order?'

She was prepared for this, at least. He would be a fool to hire her without knowing her name.

And he was no fool.

She'd already decided to give him her true name. Her maiden name.

She extended her gloved hand. 'I am Celia Allen, sir.'

It pleased her to be Celia Allen again. The surname was common enough and her father minor enough that no one would connect the name to Lord Gale's widow.

He took her hand, but held it rather than shake it. 'Miss Allen or Mrs Allen?'

She pulled her hand away. 'Miss Allen.'

Rhys felt the loss of her hand as if something valuable had slipped through his fingers. With this first glimpse of her face, he wanted her more than ever.

She reminded him of a deer with her long regal neck and alert-but-wary eyes that were the colour of moss at twilight. She seemed wrong for the city. She was meant for the country, for brisk walks in fresh country air. The bloom in her cheeks, the hue of wild raspberry of her lips looked out of place in London.

But he was becoming distracted.

And much too poetic.

He could almost hear Xavier's voice in his head, admonishing him to keep his focus on the gaming house. He would tell his friend later about employing her—not of almost kissing her—both had been too impulsive to meet the approval of his friend.

Not that Rhys cared if his zealously protective friend approved of his employing Miss Allen. Or of wanting her in his bed.

He fixed his gaze on her again. To call her Miss Allen seemed wrong to him. He had no wish to be so formal with her.

'Will you object if I address you as Celia?' he asked. 'You may call me Rhys.'

She coloured.

Her discomfort made him wonder. A woman of the theatre would expect the presumption of intimacy of using given names.

She paused before answering. 'If you wish it.' She met his eyes. 'Not in the gaming house, though.'

Clever of her. 'Of course not. You are exactly right. No one must know you are in my employ. They will suspect us of manipulation.'

'Manipulation?' Her lovely brows knit in anxiety.

'I hire you because your presence in the gaming house encourages patrons—men—to gamble. You are not expected to do anything different from what you were doing before.'

She nodded.

He leaned closer and put his hand on her wrist. 'That is not my only reason for hiring you, however—'

A knock at the door interrupted. She slipped her hand away and Rhys straightened in his chair.

MacEvoy entered with the tea tray, managing to give her an un-servant-like look-over. Undoubtedly Rhys would hear Mac's assessment of the lady later.

'Shall I pour?' She looked rattled. 'How do you take your tea?'

'No milk, no sugar.' He'd accustomed himself to drinking tea that way from times when he could not afford milk and sugar. It pleased him that he did not need those inconsequential trappings of wealth.

He gestured to MacEvoy to leave.

MacEvoy closed the door behind him and Celia handed Rhys his cup of tea.

He lifted the cup and took a sip.

Perhaps it was for the best that Mac had interrupted him. His desire for her was making him move too quickly. When he got close, he sensed her alarm, another clue that his theory about her identity might be wrong.

He changed the subject. 'I should explain something else about your employment here.'

She gave him her attention.

'Some time ago, before I owned this gaming house, a woman came here in disguise to play cards. It is where I got the idea to set up the place as a masquerade.' He waved that tangent away. 'But no matter. About this woman. She created a stir. Men were taking wagers on who would be the first to unmask her.' He paused. 'And who would be first to seduce her. Men came and gambled merely for the chance to win the wager.'

She paled. 'You wish me to offer myself as some sort of prize?'

He shook his head. 'No. No, indeed. I am merely warning you. Some men who come to gamble may ask more of you than merely to partner them in a game of whist.'

Her eyes narrowed in calculation. 'Like that man who so distressed you last night?'

Westleigh, she meant.

His voice hardened. 'Yes. Men like him.' He looked directly into her eyes. 'I will be near if any men ill treat you. Do not hesitate to alert me or Xavier. We will protect you.'

She put her hand on her heart and glanced away.

He took another sip of tea. 'You are a good card player. And that is all that is required of you. None the less, your feminine allure will attract admirers.'

'Feminine allure?' She looked surprised.

How puzzling. Did she not know she was alluring?

'You are a beguiling mystery. A lovely young woman who knows how to play cards. You will—you *do*—attract men. Men will want to partner you, play against you, sit next to you.' He gave her another direct look. 'But they must not cross the line of proper behaviour. If they do, you must let me know.'

She became absorbed in stirring her tea. Finally she answered. 'If such a thing should happen, I will let you know.'

He became even more convinced he'd been wrong about her being an actress. If not someone connected to the theatre, who was she?

'May I know more of you, Celia Allen?'

She turned wary again, like a deer about to bound away. 'There is nothing else I can tell you.'

He must not push her further. He would learn about her in due time, he resolved. Even though he knew solving the mystery of her would not diminish his desire.

She placed her teacup on the table. 'The terms of payment are what we agreed upon last night?'

He nodded, regretting the conversation turning businesslike. The desire to taste her lovely lips grew more difficult to resist. 'One pound per night, plus all your winnings. I stake you one hundred pounds, which you will return if you win. I will forfeit if you lose.'

She stood. 'I will try not to lose.'

'I know you will try not to lose. You are a true gamester.' He rose with her. 'Chance sometimes does not favour us, though, Celia. You will lose. At hazard or faro, at least, but those losses will come directly to me, so I do not credit them. Play all the hazard and faro you like. At whist or *vingt-et-un* I suspect you are skilled enough to win most of the time.'

'I hope I do not disappoint.' Her lips formed a tremulous smile. 'For both our sakes.'

That was another thing. Why did she need money so urgently?

She pulled on her gloves. 'I will try to come to the gaming house as many nights as I am able.'

What might keep her away? She was one mystery after another, even without her mask.

'Good.' He adopted her businesslike tone. 'When you arrive, stop at the cashier. He will be instructed to provide you your stake.'

'Is there anything else?' she asked. 'I must leave now.'

'One thing more.' He extended his hand. 'We must shake on our agreement.'

Slowly she placed her hand in his. He liked the feel of her long graceful fingers and strong grasp.

He drew her closer to him, just short of an embrace. 'I am glad of our partnership, Celia Allen,' he murmured, his lips inches from hers.

Her eyes widened. The deer wished to bolt, he feared.

He released her and she started towards the door.

'Will I see you tonight?' he asked.

She reached the door and turned. 'If I can manage it.'

He let her walk out on her own, but when he heard the front door close, he stepped to the window and held the curtain aside to watch her.

She paused for a moment on the pavement, as if getting her bearings. Seeming to collect herself suddenly, she walked down the street with purpose.

He watched until he could see her no more.

'I'll solve the mystery of you, Miss Celia Allen,' he said aloud. 'And I will see you in my bed.' He dropped the curtain. 'Soon.'

Celia gulped in air and tried to quiet her jangling nerves. Taking one more quick breath, she hurried away.

God help her, being with Rhysdale excited her even more than the prospect of gambling without losing her own money. What was wrong with her?

She'd had no experience with men—other than Gale, that is. Rhysdale looked as if he wanted to try to kiss her again, but she could not be sure. He'd called her *alluring,* but had he meant it?

Gale had poured on pretty compliments at first, when he'd been courting her. He'd obviously not meant them. How was she to know if Rhysdale spoke the truth?

She paused.

Why was she even *thinking* this way?

Her task was not to become enthralled with the handsome owner of the gaming house. He was blowing her off course, robbing her of the power to think straight. She must never allow another man any power over her. Not emotionally. Certainly not legally. Never would she marry again and become the property of a man, legally bound to his every whim.

Once had been enough.

Rhys represented a different sort of bondage, one that captured her thoughts and senses. She had no idea how to cope with the temptation to allow his kiss, to allow what was simmering below the surface to burst forth and consume her.

All Celia needed to do was return to the gaming house and play cards, but that presented another temptation. Rhys's offer encouraged precisely what she should battle. She should eschew the cards and games, not throw herself into playing them. How did she know she would be able to escape when Rhys's employment ended? Would she be able to stop gambling then, or would she become like her father, compelled to return to the tables against all good sense? Gambling might not be content to have merely killed her father and mother and ruined her young life; it could destroy her future, as well.

She started walking again, though her vision was blurred by the storm of thoughts inside her.

There would be no future at all for Adele unless Celia accepted this risk.

Adele was everything to her. The daughter she could never have, even though only a few years younger.

Rhysdale had given Celia this chance to secure Adele's future and Celia must embrace it.

She quickened her pace.

All she needed to do was remain resolute. Resist temptation. Play cards and nothing else. What did she care what Rhys or any man thought?

He'd suggested that men might become attracted to her while she played cards with them. What utter nonsense. If anything, it was the mask and nothing more. The novelty of a disguised woman who liked to play cards.

Rhysdale, though, had seen her face. He'd still thought her alluring.

A frisson of pleasure raced through her. She closed her eyes and again stopped walking.

She was back to Rhysdale. He could so easily invade her thoughts.

How pitiful she was. The first time a man showed her any kindness she turned as giddy as a girl fancying herself in love with Lord Byron after reading *Childe Harold's Pilgrimage.*

Had Rhysdale been the reason she agreed to his proposition? Was he, not money, the reason she agreed to face the gambling demons again?

Chapter Six

That evening William Westleigh, Viscount Neddington, searched Lady Cowdlin's ballroom as he had done every other entertainment he'd attended this Season.

He'd thought she was a vision when he first gazed upon her. Pale skin flushed with youth. Hair a shimmer of gold, its curls looking as artless as if she'd just stepped in from a breezy day. Lips moist and pink as a summer blossom.

She'd turned him into a romantic in an instant. He'd felt both exhilarated and weak when she'd allowed him to assist her in selecting wine at the musicale, but he'd lost her in the crowd afterwards.

He needed an introduction to her. If she appeared tonight—if he found her again—he'd beg someone to do the honours. He'd try his damnedest to dance with her and share supper with her.

Thinking of her was a welcome respite from worry over the finances, the estates, the welfare of his sister and mother. Those matters were largely out of his hands and under the control of his father at the moment.

Unless his father fulfilled the bargain they'd made with Rhysdale, they were about two weeks from disaster.

He walked the rooms of this ball three times without

finding her, but it was early yet and guests continued to arrive.

'The Lord Westleigh and Lady Westleigh,' the butler announced.

Ned twisted away. He was too angry at his father to witness his joviality, as if he had not caused his family the extreme stress that currently plagued them. How his mother could walk at his father's side foxed Ned.

Of course, she did not yet know how severely her husband had squandered their fortune.

If only the beauty he encountered at the musicale would walk in, Ned could momentarily free himself from thoughts of their troubles. He glanced around the room once again, looking everywhere but in the direction of his father.

The butler's voice rang out again. 'Lady Gale, Dowager Lady Gale and Miss Gale.'

Ned turned to the door.

It was she!

She stood a little behind two other ladies, one tall and as young as herself and the other certainly the dowager. This family was unknown to him, but the name *Miss Gale* now pressed into his mind like a hot iron brand.

She was as lovely as he remembered, this night donned in a pale pink gown that had some sort of sheer skirt over it that floated about her as she moved. Her lovely blonde hair was a mass of curls on top of her head and was crowned with pink roses.

As she and the other two ladies made their way to greet the host and hostess, she paused to scan the ballroom and caught him staring at her. He bowed to her and she smiled, ever so slightly, but enough for his hopes to soar.

Hope that he could find someone to present him to her. Hope that she was unattached. Hope that her smile meant

she felt the same strong attraction to him that he felt towards her.

Ned kept her in view and occasionally he caught her
eye again. But he'd seen no one of his acquaintance talking or dancing with her. The time neared for the supper
dance and he was determined to partner her.

He marched over to the hostess. 'Lady Cowdlin, may
I beg a favour?'

'A favour?' She patted his hand. 'Tell me what I might
do for you.'

'There is a young lady here…' He paused. 'I need an
introduction.'

'Who is it, my dear?' She smiled.

'I believe she is Miss Gale.' He inclined his head in
her direction.

'Ah, I knew her mother. A lovely lady.' Lady Cowdlin
gave him a knowing look. 'I understand, Neddington, that
Miss Gale is worth five thousand at least—'

As if he cared a fig about that.

'But she is not very grand. Her father was only a baron,
you know. This is her first time in town and Edna—her
grandmother—wants her to marry her cousin who inherited the title.'

That was not welcome news. 'Who is her cousin? Do
I know him?'

'Luther Parminter. He is the son of her father's cousin. I
am certain you have seen him around London. Of course,
now he is the new Baron Gale. He inherited, you see.'

Ned knew who the man was, but could not even count
him an acquaintance. Now must he think of him as a rival?

Lady Cowdlin took his arm. 'Come with me. Let us
make this introduction forthwith.'

She brought him directly to where Miss Gale stood
next to her grandmother's chair. Lady Gale stood nearby.

Lady Cowdlin spoke to the dowager. 'Ma'am, may I present this young man to you and the other ladies.'

The dowager looked up.

'This is Lord Neddington.' She turned to the younger Lady Gale, who looked upon him with a quizzical expression. 'Lady Gale and Miss Gale.' She nodded towards Ned. 'Lord Neddington.'

Ned bowed. 'Madams.' He looked into the eyes he'd longed to see up close again. 'Miss Gale.'

She lowered her long thick lashes and curtsied. 'Lord Neddington.'

'May I perform any service for you ladies?' He glanced at Miss Gale. 'Bring you some wine, perhaps?'

She coloured and looked even more lovely.

'That is kind of you, young man.' The Dowager Lady Gale smiled.

'None for me, thank you,' the younger Lady Gale said.

'I will return directly.' He hated to leave Miss Gale's presence.

Ned quickly found a servant toting a tray of wine glasses. He took two and returned to the ladies.

When he handed a glass to Miss Gale, their fingers touched and his senses heightened.

'Thank you, sir,' she murmured.

He took a breath. 'Are you engaged for the supper dance, Miss Gale?'

She lowered her lashes. 'I am not.'

'Adele,' the Dowager Lady Gale broke in. 'I have asked your cousin to claim you for that dance.'

'But, Grandmama…' she murmured.

The younger Lady Gale spoke up. 'He did not ask Adele, though, Lady Gale. Let her decide.' She turned to Miss Gale. 'You do not want to sit out at a ball when you could dance, do you?'

Miss Gale smiled. 'Indeed not.'

Lady Gale faced him. 'Then it is settled.'

Ned peered at this woman who had just helped him engage the dance. He had the oddest notion that he'd seen her before.

Ned bowed. 'I will return for the pleasure of dancing with you, Miss Gale.' He walked away, hoping the supper dance would be announced very soon.

Celia noticed the change in Adele as she danced with Lord Neddington. The girl gave evidence of enjoying every dance and every partner, but never had such a dreamy look crossed her face as when she glanced at this man.

'He is likely a fortune hunter,' Celia's mother-in-law commented.

'Her dowry is respectable, nothing more,' Celia responded. 'Perhaps he just fancies her.' That he visited gaming hells was Celia's prime worry. She'd recognised him immediately.

'Hmmph.' The dowager frowned. 'You ought not to have encouraged that young man, in any event. You know I am determined she should marry her cousin.'

Celia probably should not have encouraged Neddington. She'd done so only to oppose her mother-in-law. And because she'd seen the look in Adele's eye, how much she wanted to dance with the man.

'Luther shows very little interest in Adele, Lady Gale,' Celia said.

Luther was the more likely fortune hunter.

Celia would not see Adele forced into a marriage, but could she allow Adele to marry a gambler? She had seen Lord Neddington at the gaming hell more than once. She could never recall seeing him play more than once or twice at hazard. He spoke to Rhysdale on occasion.

Rhysdale.

Rhys, he'd asked her to call him, although could she really think of him in such intimate terms? Her heart skipped at the mere thought of speaking his name aloud. Her name on his lips came back to her, as well as his smile and the way those lips touched the edge of his teacup.

And had almost touched hers.

She placed her hand over her heart.

She would see him tonight after the ball. And once again yield to the temptations of the gambling den, with no need to wager her own money. She felt a dangerous excitement at the prospect of playing cards with a hundred pounds to wager. Think how much she could win!

The Dowager Lady Gale's voice broke through Celia's thoughts. 'You should have refused Neddington the supper dance. Now he will spend supper with her. That is entirely too much time.'

Her mother-in-law had a point.

Celia gazed in Adele's direction. Adele was glowing with pleasure each time the figures joined her with Neddington. His face was filled with admiration.

Was this how young love appeared?

Celia had been given no chance to experience a youthful romance. She could not bear to take such joy away from Adele.

She turned to her mother-in-law. 'Do not interfere, Lady Gale. Allow your granddaughter the pleasure of supper with an admirer.'

Lady Gale's nostrils flared. 'I've half a mind to fetch her to me for supper.'

Celia seized her arm with just enough pressure to make her point. 'You will do no such thing. Do you hear me clearly?'

Lady Gale shrugged. 'You are indeed a wretch, are you not?'

'Interfere with Adele's life and you will see what a wretch I can be.'

Celia's conflicting wishes for Adele waged inside her. Let the girl choose her suitors. Let her fall in love with whom she wished. But not a man who would be cruel or thoughtless or more enamoured of gaming than of a wife and children. Celia had endured all of those.

Later that night Celia's lady's maid helped her get out of her ballgown and prepare to dress for the Masquerade Club. Celia sat at her dressing table, pulling pins from her hair so that they could fix it to fit under the new turban Younie had fashioned, to go with a new mask of white silk adorned with tiny seed pearls taken from one of her mother-in-law's discarded gowns.

There was a knock on the door and Adele entered. 'Celia, I saw the light under your door.'

Celia grabbed the new mask and hid it under her table. 'I am still awake.'

Younie, new gown in hand, quickly retreated to the dressing room.

Adele flopped onto Celia's bed. 'I cannot sleep!'

Celia brushed out her hair. 'What is the matter?'

Adele stretched and sighed. 'Nothing is the matter! Everything is wonderful!'

'What is so wonderful that you cannot sleep?' Celia asked, although she was certain she knew.

'I had such a lovely time at the ball. The best ever!' Adele sat cross-legged. In her nightdress with her hair in a plait, she looked as young as when Celia first met her six years ago.

Celia smiled. 'And to what do you attribute this pleasure?'

Adele wrapped her arms around herself. 'I—I think I met someone I really like.'

Celia turned back to the mirror. 'Lord Neddington?'

Adele's reflection showed surprise. 'How did you know?'

Celia kept brushing her hair. 'A lucky guess, I suppose.'

'He is so wonderful!' She flopped back onto the bed. 'And so handsome.' She sat up again. 'Do you not think he is handsome?'

'I do,' Celia agreed. 'Very handsome.'

'And very gentlemanly,' Adele continued. 'It was he who helped me procure the wine for you and Grandmama at the musicale. And tonight he fixed me the nicest plate at supper and gave me the choice of sitting with my friends. He was so agreeable, do you not think?'

'Indeed.' Celia had watched Neddington carefully and had seen nothing to object to in his manner towards Adele. It was his activity after the society events that concerned her.

Adele bounded off the bed and paced. 'I do not know how I can sleep. Do you think he will call? I hope he will call. But I'm afraid Grandmama does not like him. Do you think she will send him away if he calls?'

Celia rose and hugged the girl. 'She would not be so impolite.' Celia would see to it.

Adele clung to her. 'But she wants me to marry Cousin Luther and I do not even know him!'

'Leave your grandmother to me. She will not interfere in your wishes.' She loosened her hold on Adele and made the girl look into her eyes. 'But know that neither your grandmother nor I would let you marry a man who was unsuitable.'

'Lord Neddington is very suitable!' Adele cried.

Celia hugged her again. 'Indeed he seems to be, but you must not put your hopes beyond tomorrow. Merely hope he calls and, if he does, see if you still like him so well.'

'I will like him tomorrow and the next day and the next,' Adele cried. 'But will he like me?'

Celia kissed her on the cheek. 'Any man would be a fool not to fall heels over ears in love with you. But you should go to sleep now so you will not have dark shadows under your eyes tomorrow.'

Adele's hands went to her cheeks. 'Oh, my goodness, yes! I must look my very best.' She kissed Celia and hugged her tightly. 'Goodnight, Celia. I hope you sleep well.'

'Sweet dreams,' Celia murmured as Adele rushed out of the room.

Celia breathed a relieved sigh and looked towards her dressing room door. 'It is safe to come out, Younie.'

Her maid appeared in the doorway. 'That was a near go, wasn't it?'

'Indeed.' Celia retrieved the mask from beneath her dressing table. 'We'd best wait until we are certain she is sleeping.'

Celia arrived at the Masquerade Club later than she'd ever done before. Would Rhysdale—Rhys—be angry at her for being late?

She rushed inside, undeterred by the doorman, who seemed to recognise her even with the new gown and mask.

Rhys stood in the hall, as if waiting for her. Her breath caught. He wore an impeccably tailored but conservative black coat and trousers. With his dark hair and glowering expression he looked as dangerous as a highwayman.

'You are late,' he said.

'I had difficulty getting away.' She handed her shawl to the footman and tried not to sound defensive.

Rhys walked her out of the hall and she prepared to hear him ring a peal over her head as soon as they were out of earshot.

But he said nothing. When they stepped up to the cashier's desk, Rhys withdrew. The cashier was the same man who had served the tea in Rhys's drawing room and the only other person connected to the gaming house who had seen her face. He obviously knew precisely who she was, even masked, because he counted out the exact number of counters Rhys had promised her.

As she turned to make her way to the game room, she caught Rhys still standing in the doorway. She forced herself to lift her chin and meet his gaze head-on.

His eyes shone with admiration, much like Neddington's had done when looking upon Adele. 'The new gown is effective.'

Celia felt an unfamiliar rush of feminine pleasure and immediately forced herself to sober. She would not melt at mere compliments.

Her smile was stiff as she clutched her reticule, the counters safe inside. He stepped back for her to pass, but he followed her into the game room.

The room was crowded and she recognised many gentlemen who a couple of hours before had been dancing in Lady Cowdlin's ballroom.

Xavier Campion approached her with his disarming smile. She sensed something unpleasant beneath it.

'Madam.' He bowed. 'Do you fancy a game of whist?'

She glanced at Rhys, who frowned.

'I came to play,' she answered, unsure if she should accept Xavier's invitation or not.

'I will partner you if you wish,' he said.

She glanced back to Rhys, but his back was to her and he was conversing with a group of gentlemen.

'Yes, Mr Campion. Do you have some opponents in mind?'

He smiled again as he took her arm. 'It is Xavier, remember. Let us go in search of some worthy opponents.' His grip was firmer than was necessary. He leaned towards her and murmured in a tone that seemed falsely convivial. 'I understand you are in Rhys's employ. How did you manage that, I wonder?'

She did not miss a beat. 'He made me the offer and I accepted. How else might it have been accomplished?'

'He is my friend,' Xavier said through gritted teeth. 'I will not have him trifled with.'

Celia lifted her chin. 'Rhysdale seems capable of selecting his own employees. Ought I to tell him you think otherwise?' His concern was ridiculous. 'Or perhaps he has asked you to protect him from me?'

Xavier's eyes flashed. 'He does not need to ask. I protect all my friends. Do you tell tales on all of yours?'

'I do not.' Celia paused. 'But, then, you are not my friend, are you?' She shrugged from his grip. 'I have changed my mind, *Mr Campion*. I believe I will try my luck at hazard.'

She left him and did not look back.

It made her feel wonderfully strong. A man had tried to intimidate her and she'd held her own against him.

The hazard table was crowded with mostly men. Celia faltered a bit, then remembered Rhys said she was equally as alluring as his mysterious masked woman who had played here before.

She'd just stood up to a man; perhaps she could also be a little bit alluring.

'Pardon me.' She made herself smile in what she hoped was a flirtatious manner. 'Might a lady play?'

The gentlemen parted. One was the man who had so disturbed Rhys the previous night. Her skin turned to gooseflesh. He, too, had been at Lady Cowdlin's ball.

What did such a gentlemen say to his wife to explain going out again after a ball? Did the wife pace with worry as Celia's mother had done?

'You are welcome to play, my dear.' The gentleman flicked his eyes quickly over her person. 'Have you played before?'

Disgust roiled through her. She remembered Rhys's warning.

She dropped any flirtatious affectations. 'I am accustomed to card games like whist and piquet and *vingt-et-un.* I've not tried a game of dice before.' But tonight she had money she could afford to lose.

The croupier at the hazard table was a pretty young woman with curly red hair. 'Do you play, miss?'

The gentleman rose on his heels in self-importance. 'I will assist the lady, if she so desires.' He scooped up the dice. 'I will stake you for this first round.' He put a pound counter on the table and placed the dice in her hand. 'Call a number between five and nine.'

'Nine,' she called, the date her father died.

'Nine,' he repeated.

Around the table there was a flurry of side-betting accompanying her call.

'They are betting on your chances to win,' he explained. 'If you roll a nine, you will win. If you throw a two or a three, or an eleven or a twelve, you will lose. Now shake the dice in your hand and roll them on the table.'

She shook the dice and threw them down. They landed

in the middle of the green baize, one landing on three, the other, on five.'

'Eight!' the croupier called.

'That is a called a *chance,*' the gentleman explained. 'You did not win, but neither did you lose.' The croupier handed him the dice. 'Roll again.'

He dropped the dice into her palm.

'I want a nine, correct?' She shook the dice in her hand.

'No, this time you want a two or a three to win. Or anything but the *main*—your nine—to continue to roll.'

She dropped the dice onto the table, this time rolling one pip on one die and two on the other.

'Three!' called the croupier. 'A winner.'

Westleigh handed the winnings to her.

A man next to her pushed the dice back to Celia. 'Let the lady keep playing. She has the luck.'

Celia continued to play and to win. The rules of winning and losing changed depending upon what number she chose as chance and she quickly calculated that choosing the numbers five or nine reduced the odds of winning. The crowd around the hazard table grew, most betting with her.

Each time she won she jumped for joy and could not wait to throw the dice again. Her heart was beating fast and her breath as rapid as if she'd run all the way to Oxford Street. Even knowing this gentleman was having a grand time as her host did not dampen her excitement. The impact of his presence faded with each roll of the dice, each possibility that her pile of counters would increase.

As the gentlemen betting with her gathered their winnings, she caught sight of Rhys. He stood at the edge of the crowd, his face a dark cloud.

No wonder he was upset. Every time she—and those who bet with her—won, Rhysdale lost. It woke her from her reverie.

When the dice were again handed to her, she held up her hands. 'I am done, gentlemen.' She made herself smile. 'I wish to keep all these lovely counters.' She'd won at least forty-five pounds.

She gathered her counters and backed away from the table, shocked at herself. She'd lost all sense of time, all reason.

Rationally she should continue to play until losing again and lead her followers to do the same.

She blinked.

Like a swarm of bees around a hive, the other players filled her space at the table and resumed the play.

To her dismay the gentleman who had assisted her was not among them. Instead he remained at her side.

'Allow me to introduce myself.' He bowed. 'I am Lord Westleigh.'

She felt the blood drain from her face. 'Lord Westleigh.'

Lord Westleigh was the man who'd accused her father of cheating at cards, who'd accepted her father's challenge of a duel, who'd fired the pistol ball that pierced her father's heart.

Because he was an earl with friends and influence, he'd walked away from killing her father with impunity, broke her mother's heart, destroyed her health and, in effect, killed her, as well.

Celia tried to remain upright, even though her legs trembled. She tried to keep her face expressionless.

Westleigh waited, as if expecting she would reveal her name.

He finally smiled. 'You will not tell me who you are?'

She took a breath. 'I have chosen to wear a mask. That means I do not wish to reveal myself.'

He laughed. 'I thought you might make me an exception.'

Never for him.

Undaunted by her obvious reserve, he glanced around the room. 'Shall we find some partners for whist?'

'No!' she snapped.

She scanned the crowd for Rhys, needing him. He'd said she should find him if this man bothered her. He was bothering her greatly. He was making her ill.

She caught herself and moderated her tone of alarm. 'I—I am looking for someone.'

Rhys stood some distance away and he did not glance her way.

She found another familiar face. Sir Reginald. 'There he is. I must speak with him.' She inclined her head. 'Thank you for teaching me hazard.'

Before he could protest, she started to cross the room to where Sir Reginald stood, but someone stepped in her way.

Rhys.

Tears of relief pricked her eyes.

He touched her arm. 'I saw you with Westleigh. Was he uncivil to you?'

'Yes,' she blurted out. 'No. Not really. He wanted me to play cards with him.' She took a deep breath. 'I did not know that man was Westleigh. It—it surprised me.'

His brows lowered. 'What do you know of Westleigh?'

'I cannot tell you here.' Her knees weakened.

He must have noticed because he offered her his arm. 'Come with me.'

He walked them to a back staircase, one used by the servants, perhaps. They climbed to the second floor. They passed dark rooms that smelled of sawed wood and linseed and entered the drawing room where he had received her earlier.

He led her directly to the sofa. 'Sit here.'

She removed her mask and rubbed her eyes, trying to

calm herself from the shock of learning she'd spent the greater part of her night in the company of her father's killer.

Rhys handed her a glass. 'Have some brandy.'

She took the glass gratefully and drank, the liquid warming her chest. She sipped more. And finished it.

Rhys sat in an adjacent chair and poured her some more. He asked nothing. Just sat with her.

She finally calmed enough to look up at him. 'Thank you, Rhys.' The brandy was helping. 'I am afraid it was a shock to learn that gentleman was Westleigh.'

He did not press her to tell him more.

Since her mother's death she had spoken to no one about Westleigh, but suddenly it seem too great a burden to carry alone. 'You must wonder why I became so upset.'

He shrugged. 'With Westleigh, nothing would surprise me.'

She stared into his eyes. 'Would it surprise you to learn he killed my father?'

His brows rose, but his gaze did not waver.

She glanced away. 'My father enjoyed gambling...too much. He sometimes played unwisely. He played cards with Lord Westleigh and apparently was winning when Westleigh accused him of cheating.' She looked back to see his reaction to that information. Would he think her father a cheat? 'My father would never cheat. He was outraged and challenged Westleigh to a duel.' She blinked away tears. 'The duel was fought and Westleigh killed my father.' She choked on her words and quickly took another sip of brandy. 'He walked away with impunity.'

The sound of her mother's voice telling her of her father's death returned to her and the horror and grief struck her anew. Dear God, she was about to lose control of her emotions.

He moved from the chair to the sofa and took her into his arms.

Celia collapsed against his chest, heaving with sobs, and he held her and murmured to her. She could not even tell what he said, she just felt his voice, low and rumbling.

It had been so long since she'd been held, so long since anyone had comforted her. The years of loneliness and loss overwhelmed her and his arms were so warm and strong.

She had to pull herself together, though. She could not do this.

Rhys held her close, relishing the feel of her in his arms, but, even more, feeling her pain and wanting to do anything he could to ease it.

Damned Westleigh! The man had killed her father? It was more than even Rhys would have suspected. Fighting a duel over a game of cards was foolish beyond belief. Killing a man over cards was a million times worse.

'There, there,' he murmured, realising he sounded like his mother. His own throat tightened with the memory of her loss. Another deed he could throw at Westleigh's feet. His mother might have lived a long happy life if not for that cursed man.

She pulled away, wiping her eyes with her fingers. 'I am so sorry.'

He handed her his handkerchief. 'Do not say so.'

'It is the surprise of seeing him.' She blew her nose. 'I wondered how it would be. I did not know I would turn into a watering pot.'

He suspected that weeping was not something she often allowed of herself. 'What would you like me to do about Westleigh?'

She gaped at him in surprise. '*Do* about him?'

'It cannot be comfortable for you that he comes here.

I can prevent him, if you like.' Rhys disliked seeing the man here anyway.

She finished her second glass of brandy. 'I do not know what to say. I do not know what to think. I do not want him to know who I am.'

Rhys did not know who she was.

Her face hardened. 'I would like to make him pay in some way.'

'Revenge?' He well knew the need for revenge.

'Yes!' She covered her mouth with her hand. 'I suppose that is wrong of me.'

A corner of his mouth turned up. 'Quite natural, I would say. You are probably one of many who would like revenge on Lord Westleigh.'

She peered into his eyes. 'You detest him, as well.'

He could explain to her that Westleigh was his father, but, at the moment, the idea that the blood of such a man flowed in his veins filled him with disgust. He did not wish to take the chance she would feel the same.

They could each keep their secrets from the other, could they not?

He held her gaze. 'I detest him. It will give me pleasure to throw him out for you.'

She stared for a moment, as if thinking, then shook her head. 'It would not do to ban an earl from your gaming house, would it? Especially one who likes to gamble. I would never ask this of you.'

'Nonetheless,' he responded. 'It would be my pleasure to do so, if it will ease your mind.'

She reached over and touched his hand. 'It is enough to know I have an ally.' She withdrew her hand almost as quickly and turned away. When she turned back, she smiled the ghost of a smile. 'Perhaps there is some restitution I can force on him. Engage him in a card game and win all his money...'

As if he had any sum of money to lose, Rhys thought.

She straightened. 'At least that would be something, would it not?'

He would have preferred an excuse to toss Westleigh out on his ear, although her course was undoubtedly the wiser for both of them. He preferred a more subtle revenge, one that would cause Westleigh even greater pain.

'It will be as you wish.'

She dabbed at her face again and folded his handkerchief. 'I will launder and return this.'

He waved that away. 'It is of no consequence.'

She picked up her mask. 'I have taken up enough of your time. We should return to the game room, do you not think?'

Leaving her was the last thing on his mind, but she was correct. He should get back. 'You may stay here, if you wish. Stay until it is time for your coachman.'

She shook her head. 'I think it is like falling from one's pony. One must remount immediately.'

She'd ridden a pony? Riding a pony seemed unlikely for an actress.

He'd pursue that thought another time. 'Then I will go down first. You may follow a moment later. It will not seem as if we have been together.'

She gave him a grateful smile.

They both rose. She lifted the mask to her face and fussed with its ribbons. He stepped behind her and tied the mask in place.

She stood very still as he did so.

When he finished, his hands hovered over her shoulders, wanting to explore more of her.

Instead, he stepped away and walked out of the room.

* * *

Down in the game room, he found Westleigh almost immediately, laughing at something his companion had said. Westleigh caught his gaze and froze for a moment, an icy expression on his face. Rhys returned the unfriendly glare and resumed his patrol of the room.

In a few moments Celia appeared, searching the room, her reaction to finding Rhys as warm as Westleigh's had been cold. She appeared perfectly composed, strolling to where Sir Reginald stood.

Sir Reginald greeted her like a long-lost friend. This man was a member of the aristocracy who Rhys could like. Sir Reginald was kind and friendly to everyone.

Westleigh also noticed Celia's entrance. Rhys watched him leave his friend and make a beeline to where Celia stood.

Xavier appeared beside Rhys. 'Would you mind telling me what all this is about?'

'All what?' Rhys countered.

Xavier inclined his head towards Celia and Westleigh.

Rhys waved a dismissive hand. 'Nothing of consequence, I am certain.'

Xavier frowned. 'Between Westleigh and the woman who captivates you? Do not take me for a fool.'

Celia watched Westleigh make his way across the room and knew he was coming after her. She cast a glance towards Rhys. He stood close by.

She turned to Sir Reginald. 'Do you need a whist partner tonight, sir?'

Sir Reginald smiled in a jolly way. 'Is that an invitation, madam? If so, I would be honoured.'

Westleigh came up to her side. 'There you are, my dear. I feared I had lost you forever.'

She inclined her head slightly and spoke without expression. 'Lord Westleigh.'

He bowed. 'Are you ready for our game of whist?'

He presumed she would play cards with him? 'I fear you are too late.' She managed to sound civil. 'Sir Reginald and I will be playing.'

That did not daunt him. 'Whist? You will need partners, certainly. Allow me and my companion to challenge you to a game.'

Whist had been the game that Westleigh had played with her father that fateful night.

Her eyes narrowed.

Sir Reginald broke in. 'Madam, I am completely at your disposal. We do need partners, but I leave it to you to say who that should be.'

She glanced over to Rhys, who had stepped away from his friend, but looked her way.

He was still near.

It emboldened her. 'Very well. Sir Reginald and I will play whist with you.'

Westleigh fetched his companion. Celia wondered if his companion had been his partner when Westleigh engaged her father in play. If so, why had the man not intervened? Someone should have stopped such folly.

They took their places at a card table and the cards were dealt.

Soon Celia focused on the play instead of the detested player who sat at her right, too often brushing his arm against hers or fussing over her counters as if it were his job to tend to her.

The play was tame. Westleigh and his partner were particularly predictable in which cards they put down and when. Even Sir Reginald's limited skills more than outmatched them. Westleigh could not have been a challenge to her father, who was very good at whist. Her father would have had no reason to cheat.

That knowledge was like a burden lifted from her shoulders. She now had no doubts that the charge of cheating against her father had been unfounded.

It also made Westleigh's actions that night all the more reprehensible.

Perhaps the revenge she could enact against him was to play cards with him as often as she could. To take as much of his money as she could. It would probably not put a dent in an earl's fortune, but it would be some restitution—the sort of restitution her father might admire.

While Sir Reginald shuffled the cards for the next hand, Celia glanced around the room, as she often did, looking for Rhys. Instead, her gaze caught upon Lord Neddington.

It did not please her that this young man was so frequent a visitor to this place. She had no wish for Adele to be enamoured of a gambler.

Celia watched Neddington walk through the room aimlessly. He turned towards her table and she quickly averted her eyes, but Neddington was not concerned with her. He was scowling at Lord Westleigh.

At least that was in the young man's favour.

Between hands Celia kept tabs on Neddington who walked around, but never seemed to gamble. How odd. It did make her a bit less concerned about his character, though.

After several games Westleigh's partner threw up his hands. 'No more!' He turned to Celia. 'You have emptied my pockets, madam.'

He was even worse a player than Westleigh.

She smiled good-naturedly. 'Perhaps you would like a rematch another night, sir.'

He laughed. 'A night when luck is with me.' He winked. 'At least I won when you played hazard. We must coax you back to the hazard table, must we not, Westleigh?' He turned to the earl.

'It would be my pleasure to play whatever game the lady wishes.' Westleigh eyed her in the same manner her husband had done before they were married.

It made her cheeks burn.

Sir Reginald, so harmless and friendly, said, 'Well, madam, you may count on me to partner you any time.'

'You are an excellent partner, Sir Reginald.' She dropped her counters into her reticule and stole a glance at her watch. It was nearly time for her coach to arrive.

She stood.

Westleigh took her elbow. 'Shall we play more hazard, my dear?'

'Thank you, no.' She drew her arm away. 'I bid you gentlemen goodnight.'

She looked for Rhys, but he was not in the game room, so she made her way to the cashier and repaid the hundred pounds she'd not touched in her play. At the end, she carried away over seventy pounds. The huge sum filled her with guilt. Winning at hazard would cost Rhys directly. It was a poor way to repay his generosity.

Celia wanted to see Rhys before she left. After cashing out, she glanced in the supper room, but he was not there. She asked the hall servant where Rhys was.

'Drawing room,' the man told her.

Celia climbed the stairs. As she neared the doorway to the drawing room, she heard Rhys's voice and held back.

'Your concern is unfounded, Xavier,' Rhys said. 'And insulting, as well.'

'Insulting?' His friend's voice rose.

'I am well able to make my own decisions about business and about women.' Rhys spoke with heat. 'I do not caution you against dallying with any of the several women who vie for your attention, you know.'

'There would be no need.' Xavier's tone was just as angry. 'I know how to handle women.'

'And I do not?' Rhys countered.

'Come now.' Xavier turned placating. 'This infatuation with the masked woman is something else. You do not know who she is. Or what she wants.'

'She wants what I want. Money,' Rhys answered. 'And she has given me her name. That is enough for me.'

'Rhys—' Xavier began.

'Enough,' Rhysdale broke in. 'I need you as a friend, not a nursemaid. Do not press me further on this matter.'

Celia stepped away from the doorway as Xavier strode out of the room. Seeing her, he hesitated only briefly, long enough to look half-apologetic, half-provoked. He continued on his way down the stairs.

She knocked on the door.

Chapter Seven

'May I speak to you, Rhys?'

Rhys turned in surprise at the sound of her voice. 'Celia! Come in. Close the door.'

She looked wounded, as well she might. He'd been about to pour himself some brandy. Now he needed it even more.

He lifted the decanter. 'Would you like a glass?'

She nodded.

'How much of that did you hear?' he asked as he poured.

She took the glass from his hand. 'Enough to know that Mr Campion does not like that you hired me.'

He'd been afraid of that.

'It is none of his affair,' he assured her. 'He thinks he is acting out of friendship.'

'If my employment causes you a problem—' she began.

'You cause me no problem.' He reached over and gently removed her mask. 'That is better.' He brushed a lock of hair off her face and gestured to the sofa. 'Please sit, Celia.'

By God, she looked lovely this night. The white of her gown was embroidered with a cascade of flowers created from shimmering silver thread. In the game room amongst the sea of black-coated men, she'd glowed like moonlight.

She lowered herself onto the sofa where she'd sat before. Where he'd held her before.

'I did not mean to overhear,' she said. 'I only came upstairs to thank you again. And to let you know that I managed being in Westleigh's company without too much distress.'

'I was watching.' He sat in the nearby chair. 'I also noticed that you won.'

'I did.' She shook her head. 'He is a terrible player.'

Their conversation was stilted and devoid of the intimacy they had so recently shared in this room. That she'd overheard Xavier did not help.

'Terrible?' That knowledge pleased him. Rhys was a master of cards. He took a sip of brandy. 'A competent card player would have no need to cheat against him, then.'

Her face shone with pleasure. 'You have guessed my thoughts.'

She looked even more lovely.

He took another sip. 'How much did you win?'

'From Westleigh and his partner? About twenty-five pounds.'

His brows rose. 'So much?'

She waved a hand. 'They were reckless in their betting, as well. I decided to play him as much as I can. Take as much of his money as I can.' Her voice cracked. 'For my father.'

He understood her need for revenge, but it puzzled him. How did Westleigh have that much to lose? He was supposed to be on a tight leash regarding his spending.

She lowered her gaze. 'I must confess that I won much more than the twenty-five pounds from Westleigh. I won even more from hazard.'

He'd noticed. 'You had a winning streak. How much did you win finally?'

She looked apologetic. 'Fifty pounds.' She quickly added. 'I know it was not well done of me. It is a great deal of money out of your pocket.' She opened her reticule. 'I wanted to see you so I could pay it back. I only regret I cannot repay all that the patrons betting with me must have won.'

He pushed the reticule away. 'I'll not take your winnings. And do not concern yourself about the gentlemen betting with you. Those who stayed at the hazard table will have lost it all again. Or will another night.' He gazed at her. 'Not everyone is so wise as to stop when ahead.'

'I was not wise....' She made a nervous gesture with her hand. 'To own the truth, I was terrified. The excitement made me lose all sense.'

'Not all sense, or you would have played until your reticule was empty.' He finished his brandy. 'That excitement is all part of the game. I have been a gambler too long not to have felt that same exhilaration.'

'It makes a person foolish,' she rasped. 'I cannot afford to be foolish. It will hurt me, but tonight my foolishness hurt you.'

'Gambling is always a risk, but remember that this was a risk I agreed to take. This night you won and I lost. Tomorrow it may be different. We will keep an eye on it.' He reached over again and touched her cheek. 'Do not fear. I will not let you be harmed by it.'

Her eyes grew wider and her fair skin glowed like an angel's.

Xavier was right when accusing him of wanting to make her a conquest. He wanted her as intensely as a man could desire a woman. But Rhys also genuinely liked her. He felt a kinship with her.

It was rare for him to feel kinship with anyone. He'd long ago accepted that he was alone in the world. He even expected to lose Xavier's friendship eventually, when the man finally found a woman he wished to marry. Xavier's allegiance would shift, as it should, to a wife and family of his own making.

Or perhaps his friendship with Xavier was ending over Celia.

Rhys dared not hope for anything more than temporary with Celia. No doubt her secrets would eventually separate them.

As his secrets might from her.

But for the moment he relished her company. When had a woman ever made him feel such sympathy as he felt towards her? He wished he could make Westleigh pay for killing her father, for bringing her such pain.

He wanted to enfold her in his arms and take all her pain away.

He looked into her eyes. 'I like you, Celia Allen.'

Her eyes darted around the room. He'd frightened her.

She smiled nervously at him. 'You have been…like a friend. I cannot tell you how grateful I am to you for paying me to gamble. For enduring my fit of tears over Westleigh.'

He held up a hand.

She twisted the laces of her reticule. 'I should go. My coachman will be here soon.'

He stood and offered her his hand. She hesitated a moment before placing her hand in his. He pulled her to her feet, but did not stop there. He pulled her into an embrace.

He could not tell if she was alarmed or pleased.

'I suspect we are two of a kind, Celia,' he said. 'I am glad you are in my employ. I am glad I will see you night after night.'

Her eyes grew huge and her voice trembled. 'You are holding me. Are—are you going to kiss me?'

'Is it what you wish?' He could feel the rise and fall of her breast against his chest.

It fired his senses, but he waited. She must want this, too.

She rose, no more than an inch, but it was all the invitation he needed.

He lowered his mouth to hers.

Her lips were warm, soft and tasting of brandy and he wanted more, much more. She melted into him and her lips pressed upon his, as if she, too, could not get enough. He lost himself in the pleasure of her, his hands eager to explore her, undress her, pleasure her—

She broke away. 'This is not wise, Rhys,' she cried.

His body was still humming with need, but he forced himself to give her the space she needed.

'You are sounding like Xavier.' He smiled. 'It probably was not wise to hire you in the afternoon and kiss you in the night, but I do not feel like being wise with you, Celia. I want more from you.'

Her eyes grew big. 'More from me?'

Did she not understand?

He would be clear. 'I want you in my bed.'

She stepped away. 'I—I do not know.'

He honoured her distance. 'It is your choice, Celia. No matter what you decide, our employment agreement still stands.'

Her expression turned puzzled. 'My choice,' she said to herself.

The clock on his mantel chimed four bells, causing them both to jump.

She rubbed her forehead. 'I must go. I am already late. My driver will be concerned.'

He reached out and took her hand. 'Tomorrow, give your driver a later time.'

She looked like a frightened deer.

He did not wish her to bolt. 'Do not distress yourself,' he spoke in a soothing voice. 'You know what I want, but do not let that keep you from coming back and gambling. You need not answer me now. I am a patient man.'

She stared at him, but finally said, 'I will think about it.'

It was not the answer he had hoped for, but he contented himself that it was not a definite no.

'Do not think.' He touched her cheek. 'Feel.'

She made a sound deep in her throat, before turning away from him and hurrying towards the door.

'Celia,' he called to her.

She stopped and looked over her shoulder at him.

'You forgot your mask.' He picked up the piece of white silk and crossed the room to her. 'Stay still. I will put it on you,' he said.

Her breath accelerated as he affixed the mask to her face and tied the ribbons that held it in place.

'There you go,' he murmured.

She stepped away, but turned and gave him a long glance.

He opened the door. 'I will walk you to your coach.'

As they left the room he kept his distance, but walked at her side down the stairs to the hall where Cummings quickly retrieved her shawl. She put it on herself carelessly, but as soon as they were out the door, he wrapped her in it to protect her from the misty night's chill. Almost immediately the sound of her coach reached their ears even before it became visible.

She stepped forwards so her coachman could see her. He stopped the horses and Rhys lowered the steps. He squeezed her hand as he helped her into the coach.

He watched her face in the window as the coach started off, disappearing into the mist as if only a dream.

* * *

The next day Rhys sounded the knocker at the Westleigh town house. It was time to confront Westleigh.
He'd had enough of the man, especially after what he'd
learned from Celia.

He was ready to drop the whole bargain with the Westleighs, but Celia wished her revenge and Rhys would not
deny her it. He would, however, push along his own dealings with the Westleighs and be done with them.

A footman opened the door.

'Mr Rhysdale to see Lord Westleigh.' Rhys handed the
footman his card.

The footman stepped aside and gestured for him to enter
the hall. 'Wait here a moment.'

The last time Rhys called at this house, he'd been escorted into the drawing room. Why not now?

Likely Westleigh had left instructions to treat him like
a tradesman.

The footman disappeared towards the back of the house.

Rhys gazed at the marble-tiled floors and swirling staircase. Such grandeur in contrast to the set of rooms in
which he and his mother had lived. Or how he had lived
after her death.

Gazing at it all, Rhys realised this was not what he
wanted in life. Yes, he wanted comfort, but comfort would
be enough. More than anything, he wanted to build something. A business. A factory. Something useful. He wanted
not to be like his father, who had wasted his life and squandered his fortune.

He did not give a fig about being acknowledged as
Westleigh's bastard son. In fact, he'd just as soon not be
known to have the connection. He'd go through with it,
though, only because it was *his* revenge against Westleigh.
He would make the man do what he would detest the most,

what he ought to have done when Rhys was born—to declare openly that Rhys was his son.

This bargain with the Westleighs had become like a game of cards. Westleigh behaved as if he held all the trumps, but he was bluffing. It was time to up the ante and win the hand.

It was a gamble. Everything in life was a gamble. Westleigh could choose poverty over admitting Rhys was his son, but how likely was that? Rhys knew a good bet when he saw one.

A servant who could only have been the butler entered the hall. He lifted his nose at Rhys. 'Do you have an appointment with his lordship?'

Rhys glared at the man and used the voice he'd once used to command men in his regiment. 'I do not need an appointment. Announce me to Lord Westleigh.'

The butler shrank back and quickly ascended the stairs. Rhys's eyes followed him. Westleigh would show himself promptly or Rhys would go in search of him.

A huge allegorical painting hung in the hall. Rhys turned to examine it. The painting depicted Minerva, representing wisdom, pushing Mars, the god of war, away from the goddess of peace. He chuckled to himself. Would Minerva prevail with Westleigh? Or would he and Westleigh engage in battle?

A woman's voice said, 'Ned! I thought you had gone.'

He turned to see a finely dressed woman descending the stairs.

She looked startled. 'I beg your pardon. I thought you were my son.'

He recognised her from the times he'd glimpsed her in his old village, an older but still beautiful Lady Westleigh.

He bowed. 'Allow me to present myself, my lady. I am Mr Rhysdale, here to speak with your husband.'

Her eyes flickered at the mention of his name. Did she know of him? Did she remember that poor woman who'd once been in her service so many years ago?

'Mr Rhysdale.' Her voice tightened. 'Perhaps you can tell me why you call upon my husband.'

'I have no objection to doing so, ma'am, although perhaps Lord Westleigh ought to be present.' He inclined his head. 'As a courtesy.'

She swept across the hall. 'Come into the drawing room. I will ring for tea.'

It was the same room where he had spoken to Ned and Hugh. She pulled a bell cord and the butler appeared.

'Some tea, Mason,' Lady Westleigh ordered. 'Do sit, Mr Rhysdale.'

He waited for her to lower herself into a chair and chose one a distance from her that she might consider comfortable.

She could not look at him.

Rhys took pity on her. She was merely one more person who had been ill-used by Lord Westleigh. 'I surmise you know who I am, my lady.'

She glanced at him and gathered some pluck. 'Why would you show your face here, after all this time?'

He spoke gently. 'Your sons involved me...' he paused, trying to think how to say it '...in a business matter.'

Her mouth opened in surprise. 'Ned and Hugh?'

'Yes.'

Lord Westleigh thundered in. 'See here, Rhysdale. You were told to wait in the hall.' He came to a sudden halt. 'Honoria!'

'Charles.' Her lips thinned.

Rhys rose. 'Lady Westleigh happened upon me and was gracious enough to invite me into the drawing room.'

'Yes, well.' Westleigh wiped his brow. 'Thank you, Honoria. You may leave. This does not concern you.'

She remained in her seat. 'Mr Rhysdale has no objection to my presence.'

Westleigh tossed him a scathing look. 'It is a matter of business, Honoria. You would find it tedious.'

She smiled at him. 'Oh, since it also involves Ned and Hugh, as I understand, I doubt I should find it tedious. You know that nothing about my sons is trivial to me.'

'Did you think you could conceal the whole from Lady Westleigh?' Rhys asked him. 'I do not see how, unless you decided to go back on your word. Which is why I am here. To determine once and for all if you intend to keep to the bargain your sons made on your behalf.'

The butler brought in the tea tray, halting the conversation at that point. He placed the tray on the table in front of Lady Westleigh. 'Thank you, Mason,' she said.

The butler bowed and turned to leave, but she called him back. 'Mason? If Hugh is about, tell him to join us, please.'

The man bowed again. 'As you wish, my lady.'

When he left the room and closed the door behind him, Lord Westleigh spoke again. 'We do not need Hugh here.'

'I would not talk behind his back,' his wife countered. 'I would invite Ned, as well, but he went out a little while ago.'

Rhys realised his revenge upon his father was certainly going to hurt his wife, which suddenly gave Rhys no pleasure. Still, it was better than the complete financial ruin of the family.

'Shall we wait for Hugh?' Rhys asked the lady.

'I would prefer it,' she said. 'Do sit, Mr Rhysdale. How do you take your tea?'

'No cream. No sugar.'

* * *

Ned was surprised at the modest accommodations Miss Gale had on Half Moon Street. He'd expected something grander—not that it mattered to him. She just looked as if she belonged in luxury, protected from any discomfort or stress.

Not that he could provide her such a setting at the moment. He really had no business courting her, except that he could not bear it if her heart went to another.

He sounded the knocker and was admitted by the butler who announced him.

He entered the drawing room where Miss Gale sat with her stepmother and grandmother.

Also present was Luther Parminter, the new Baron Gale.

He bowed to the ladies.

The grandmother frowned in an unwelcoming manner, but Lady Gale extended her hand. 'How nice of you to call, Neddington.'

He glanced to where Miss Gale was seated with the baron. 'Am I interrupting a family visit? Do forgive me.'

'Nonsense,' the young Lady Gale said. 'You are welcome here. Join us.' She gestured to a chair near Miss Gale. 'Shall I pour you some tea?'

'I'll not trouble you.' He bowed to Miss Gale.

She sat in a pool of sunlight from the window, her hair shining like spun gold. Her skin was flawless and her eyes sparkling and clear as a cloudless sky.

She robbed him of speech.

He glanced from her to Luther, whom he'd known in school. 'Gale.'

'Neddington,' Luther said without expression.

Ned was distressed to see him here. Was he courting Miss Gale? Most people liked to keep their wealth and property in the family. Lady Cowdlin said Miss Gale's dowry was a generous one. Was that why Luther was here?

Still, if she had a large dowry, why did she live in such economy?

'I hope you are well today, sir,' she murmured to him.

'Very well, miss,' he responded.

'Hmmph,' the Dowager Lady Gale broke in. 'Our cousin Luther was telling us about Gale House and its people. And the news from the village. We have always made it a point to concern ourselves with the needs of the people, you know.'

Ned turned to Gale. 'I hope you found the people at Gale House in a good situation.'

'Of course,' Luther snapped.

The man was as happy to see Ned here as Ned was to see him. It depressed Ned that he might have a rival. Ned had so little to offer, how could he compete?

His family's partnership with Rhysdale must reap its hoped-for benefits. It all depended upon his father.

Ned could hardly abide the presence of his father these days; he was so angry with the man. His father was being stubborn about Rhysdale and could ruin everything. They'd be worse off than before.

Then there would be no use in pursuing Miss Gale at all.

They chatted about the ball the night before. At one point Luther pulled out his timepiece and examined it.

A few minutes later, Luther stood. 'I must take my leave.' He bowed to Miss Gale, her stepmother and grandmother. 'Ladies, it has been a pleasure.' He tossed an unhappy glare at Ned.

After he left, Miss Gale asked Ned about the weather.

It gave him courage. 'I wonder if you would like to take a turn in the park this afternoon, Miss Gale. I would con-

sider it an honour to drive you in my curricle.' He turned
to her stepmother. 'With your permission, ma'am.'

Lady Gale smiled. 'If Adele wishes.'

'Oh, I do!' she cried. 'I mean, I would like that very
much, my lord.'

Miss Gale's grandmother frowned.

He rose. 'Then I shall return at four.' A good three
hours. How would he be able to pass that much time knowing he would have her company all to himself?

And with everyone else crowding Hyde Park during
the fashionable hour.

Ned took his leave, his heart soaring.

'What is this?' Hugh entered the Westleigh town house
drawing room. 'Rhysdale, what are you doing here?'

Rhys was accustomed to Hugh's brashness. He had always been so.

Rhys straightened and glanced at each of them. 'I will
not prevaricate. I came to get what is due me. I fulfilled
my part of our bargain and—' he turned to Lord Westleigh '—you, sir, have not fulfilled yours. I am done being
trifled with.'

'See here, Rhysdale—' Lord Westleigh snapped.

'What bargain?' Lady Westleigh asked.

Rhys gestured to Westleigh and Hugh to explain.

Hugh glared at his father. 'You explain it to her, Father.'

Lord Westleigh, still standing, wrung his hands.

'Well.' He looked at his wife. 'Your sons made the plan.
Just because finances have become a little strained these
days—'

'A little strained!' Hugh broke in. 'It is more serious
than that.' He turned to his mother. 'We are a hair's breadth
from complete ruin. We owe everybody and Father has not

kept up with payments to the bank, for money he borrowed to cover his gambling debts.'

Her gaze flew to her husband, who did not deny this. 'What has this to do with Mr Rhysdale?'

Hugh answered her. 'Ned and I went to him with a proposition.' He explained the scheme to run a gaming house. 'But Father will not do what he gave his word he would do.'

'What is that?' Lady Westleigh asked.

Her husband made a sound of disgust.

Rhys spoke up. 'My lady, I fear what I've asked may cause you some distress. For that, I am sorry.' He riveted his gaze on his father and spoke only to him. 'I once came to you with one request—to support me after my mother died until I had a means of supporting myself. You refused. Now I have no need of your money, so I ask more.' He turned back to Lady Westleigh. 'Your husband must acknowledge me publicly as his natural son. It must seem to society that I am welcomed into the family. I do not ask for a true welcome,' he assured her. 'This is more a matter of recompense. But I insist upon a plan for this to be done and done soon. If it is not accomplished in a reasonable length of time, I will not release any of the money from the gaming hell to your sons.'

Hugh swung around to his mother. 'We need the money, Mother. We need it *now*. Matters are desperate.' His eyes shot daggers at his father. 'If you had behaved with any decency, with any thought to our mother and sister, you would have done the right thing in the first place and you certainly would not have gambled and caroused until money for their food and clothing would be in jeopardy!'

Lady Westleigh's eyes grew huge. 'Is it as bad as that?'

'It is desperate, Mother. Desperate.' Hugh dropped into a chair.

The lady closed her eyes and pressed her fingers to her

temples as she took in all this information. Finally she spoke. 'We shall give a ball and introduce you, Mr Rhysdale. I'll arrange the date with you, but it might take a few weeks. The social calendar is full. You will, I presume, wish to have good attendance.' She lifted her chin. 'I will give you my word that it will happen. Will that be enough to release some of the money?'

Rhys stood. '*Your* word will be enough, my lady. I will release the money to Ned today. Have him call upon me this afternoon.' He turned to Lord Westleigh. 'If you prevent this ball in any way, no further profits will be forthcoming.'

'I have no other choice, do I?' Westleigh said.

'As my mother had no choice when you forced her into your bed. As I had no choice but to survive on my own when I was fourteen.' He bowed to Lady Westleigh. 'I will act in a manner that will not embarrass you, my lady. It will suffice that the truth become known.'

She nodded.

'Hugh.' He nodded to his half-brother. 'I'll bid you all good day.'

As he left the house and walked out to the street, he lacked the feeling of triumph that he'd expected. Instead he thought of Lady Westleigh. Her pained expression. Her evident distress.

He'd succeeded in putting his father in a helpless position, but in so doing he'd hurt someone even more helpless. Lady Westleigh.

Another casualty of his father's selfish behaviour.

But it was done.

Rhys would make arrangements with his bank and get the money to Ned this day.

Sun peeked through the buildings and Rhys was reminded of his youth in the village. It had not all been unhappy. He remembered running over hills, fishing in the river, climbing the highest tree he could find to look down on a world where he ordinarily felt quite small. The seeds of his ambition were sowed in that childhood—to succeed. To build something lasting.

The world was changing. The gaming hell belonged to a past where a few had so much money they could throw it away on dice and cards. The future belonged to men with brains and courage, no matter who parented them. Rhys had brains and courage and, with the help of the gaming hell, he'd soon have enough capital to build anything he liked.

His thoughts turned to Celia Allen as the sun warmed the air and lit the buildings in a golden light. Which world did she belong to? He no longer knew. He only knew that in the gaming hell, they were one of a kind.

Would she share his bed this night?

Would she approve of his actions this day?

Not that he would ever tell her, but, somehow his visit to the Westleighs, the family to which he would never truly belong, had left him feeling abandoned.

He wanted the comfort of her arms, her kiss.

He looked up to cross the street and saw Ned approaching from the other side. He stopped and waited. He might as well inform Ned about the afternoon's events.

Ned walked right past him, not pointedly cutting him, as was typical of him, but apparently utterly oblivious.

Rhys called after him, 'Ned!'

Ned stopped then and shook his head as if in a daze. He finally turned around. 'Oh, Rhys. I did not see you there.'

He must be dazed. He called him Rhys, not Rhysdale.

He peered at Ned. 'Are you unwell?'

Ned laughed. 'Not at all. Merely thinking.'

The man looked like a sapskull. 'What is so engrossing?'

Ned grinned. 'Nothing.'

Oh. A woman.

A man only acted in such a manner when he was a besotted fool. 'May I pull your head from the clouds?'

Ned sobered. 'What is it?'

'I've come from your father.' Their father, he meant. 'I have forced the issue with him and I am satisfied that my introduction to society will happen soon. I am prepared to transfer the money back to you. Your original investment and some modest profits.'

Ned brightened. 'My father came through? I feared he would not.' He grasped Rhys's arm. 'This means... This means... We may retrench. We may actually pull out of this!'

Rhys recoiled from this unexpected camaraderie. 'Do not be so hasty. It is not all song and celebration. I am afraid this matter has caused your mother some distress. For that, I am regretful.'

'My mother?' Ned's demeanour blackened. 'Did Father tell her?'

'I did,' Rhys said. 'Although not by design. She encountered me in the hall.'

Ned lowered his head, his euphoria gone.

Rhys felt badly for him. 'Think, Ned. She would have to know of this.'

'I realise that,' Ned responded. 'I just hate what this does to her.'

Rhys actually felt sympathetic to Ned. 'If it is any consolation, she knew who I was as soon as I told her my name.'

Ned nodded. 'That does not surprise me. I am certain, though, that she did not know the state of our finances.'

'Yes, I do think that shocked her,' Rhys admitted. 'I admired her. She handled the whole situation with exceptional grace.'

Ned glanced up at him. 'She is an exceptional woman.'

Rhys clapped Ned on the soldier, surprising himself that their conversation was devoid of hostility. 'Come with me to Coutts Bank. I'll transfer the money to you right now.'

'Excellent!' Ned's mood improved. 'But I must be done by four o'clock.'

'We'll be done,' Rhys assured him.

Celia excused herself after two of her mother-in-law's friends came to call. Adele had already begged to be excused so that she might ready herself for her ride in Hyde Park.

It was endearing to see Adele so excited and happy. This past year of mourning had been so difficult. First the shock of their financial situation, then what amounted to an eviction from the only home Adele had ever known.

And now Luther thought he could court Adele?

Not if Celia could help it.

Although Celia was unsure about Neddington, as well.

But she was getting ahead of herself. Adele was engaged only for a ride in Hyde Park, not marriage.

Celia retreated to her bedchamber.

Her lady's maid emerged from her dressing room. 'Good afternoon, ma'am.' She lifted a gown she carried in her arms. 'I came in for this. Needs some mending.'

'Thank you, Younie.' Celia smiled. 'I am surprised to see you here, though. I thought Adele would be running you in circles to get ready for Hyde Park.'

'Oh, I am to go to her in one half hour,' Younie said. 'After she has rested so the dark circles under her eyes disappear.'

'What dark circles?' Adele looked as fresh-faced as ever.

Younie chuckled. 'The ones in her imagination, I expect. It is best to go along with these notions, though. You cannot convince a girl that age of anything.'

'I am certain you are right.' Celia had never had an opportunity to be so young and infatuated. She'd been married two years by the time she was Adele's age. Love seemed impossible.

An image of Rhys flew into her mind.

'And what of you, ma'am?' Younie asked. 'Do you go out tonight?'

Celia knew what she meant. 'After the theatre? Yes.' Her insides fluttered.

She could hardly think of anything else but going to the Masquerade Club tonight. Or that Rhys wanted to bed her.

Her body roused as if he'd again been near. Could Younie tell? she wondered.

'Which gown do you wear tonight?' Younie asked, appearing not to notice anything amiss.

Celia wished she had something new and even more fashionable to wear tonight. She wanted him to look on her with admiration.

Which made her not much unlike Adele, she supposed.

Celia sat at the dressing table and peered at her reflection. 'Do you think I have dark circles?'

Her maid clucked. 'You ought to have, with the amount of sleep you are getting.'

She looked closer, pulling the skin under her eye taut to examine it better. 'Oh, dear, is it taking a toll?'

Younie put her fists on her waist. 'Does it look like you only sleep four or five hours? No. No one would know.'

'That is good,' Celia murmured.

Younie picked up the dress again and walked over to her. 'You ought to rest, ma'am. You need it more than the young miss.'

'Excellent advice.' Celia touched the woman's hand.

'Perhaps I will lie down a little. Will you make certain I am up before Adele leaves?'

'That I can do! Shall I untie your laces?' Younie asked.

'Yes. I'll take off the dress only, though. I can lie down in my shift and corset.'

After Younie helped her from her gown, the maid left. Celia climbed into the bed.

And thought about Rhys.

His invitation was scandalous.

And exciting.

He *liked* her, he'd said. And he had been kind to her. And protective, all of which was extremely novel to her. Besides, he was young and vital and strong. What would it be like to lie with such a man?

She was inexperienced, but not naive. One could not be naive having been married to a wastrel like Gale. She well knew that men and women engaged in affairs without being married.

What would she discover if she allowed herself to accept Rhys's proposition? Would she feel pleasure?

His kiss had promised pleasure. It made her yearn for more.

That was what shocked her.

She hugged herself and imagined his arms around her again.

Would there be any harm in having an affair with him? Plenty of widows had affairs and society turned their eyes away from it. She would never marry again, so this might be her only chance to see what the sexual act would feel like with a man other than her husband.

It might even erase the memory of what it had been like with her husband.

That was something she very much desired.

Her time with Rhys was limited. As soon as Adele was

settled, Celia would move away and live the quiet, independent life she craved.

She was in no danger of losing her heart to Rhys. He was a gambler. Her mother had shown her that loving a gambler was a very bad risk. The only person she intended to place her bets on was herself. She could trust herself to pay the bills, to live within her means, to do whatever she chose to do.

She sat up and climbed off the bed.

There was the one thing she wished most to do that she could not choose. She could not choose to have a baby.

She paced the room, finally coming to the window. She gazed into the street below, but saw nothing of the carriages passing by or people walking to and fro. Her arms still ached to hold a child of her own, and nothing would replace that void in her life—not even the babies Adele would have.

Those babies would never be hers.

She swung away from the window and sat at her dressing table, staring at her reflection.

Rhys had said she was alluring.

She could not see it, but his words did thrill her.

He admired her, liked her, comforted her, protected her. Why not let him make love to her, as well?

Why not accept what Rhys offered her?

Chapter Eight

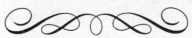

Rhys strolled through the game room, keeping his eye on what he'd laboured to create. The hazard and faro tables were the most crowded, but several patrons also played *vingt-et-un* and *rouge et noir*. The occasional gentleman wore a mask, but all of the women came disguised. More and more of them came each night.

Xavier glanced up at him from a game of whist and gave him a look that showed Xavier was still at outs with him. Rhys could forgive it. Xavier's concerns came from friendship, a friendship Rhys valued. Xavier, and perhaps MacEvoy, were the only people in the world who cared a fig about whether Rhys lived or died.

Rhys nodded to Xavier and continued his rounds.

He turned towards the doorway and saw Celia enter.

She wore the same gown and mask as the night before, but her hair was simply dressed with only a ribbon threaded through it. She paused just inside the room and turned in his direction.

Their gazes caught and held.

He smiled. Her mouth moved ever so slightly.

Was that a yes?

It surprised him how much his spirits were heightened.

He'd not quite allowed himself to think about whether she would come this night. And whether she would agree to his invitation.

Some gentlemen approached her and, amidst her protests, led her to the hazard table. She finally nodded her head and took the dice in her hand.

'Rhys?' A voice at his elbow caused him to turn away from the sight of her.

Both Hugh and Ned stood there. They rarely came to the Masquerade Club on the same night.

'Gentlemen.' He nodded to them. 'Did you make your appointment in time?' he asked Ned.

'My appointment?' Ned looked puzzled.

'At four?'

Ned coloured. 'Ah, that appointment. I did indeed.'

Hugh's brows rose.

Rhys asked, 'How is your mother?'

Hugh glowered. 'Quite upset.'

Rhys said, 'I regret that.'

Hugh turned away.

Ned broke in, 'We came to say again how grateful we are that you paid the money today.'

'Your mother gave her word,' he responded. 'It was enough for me.'

Hugh glanced back at him, his expression quizzical.

Ned surveyed the room. 'It looks like a good crowd.'

Rhys agreed. 'The numbers grow every day.'

Ned paused, but finally said, 'We will not stay long. We came only to thank you again.'

If their situation were different, Rhys might find Ned a comfortable acquaintance. He was sober and earnest, a decent sort. Rhys had known boys like him at school. They'd always treated him fairly. Hugh, though, was a different story. Rhys suspected they were too much alike to ever co-exist without battling each other.

The same blood flowed in their veins, so it should be no surprise that their personalities were similar. Of course, Rhys had learned to hide his emotions. Hugh's emotions were always on display.

'I bid you goodnight, then,' Rhys said, extending his hand.

Ned shook hands with him. Hugh did not.

Rhys turned back to the hazard table. Westleigh had joined the crowd and handed Celia the dice.

'Pass them on, sir,' Rhys heard her say. 'I've lost enough.'

'One more roll,' Westleigh urged. 'Your luck could change.'

She hesitated, but finally accepted the dice and threw them on the table. 'Six!' she called out.

She nicked the roll with a twelve.

A cheer went up from the men crowding around the table. At their urging the young woman croupier scooped up the dice and handed them back to Celia.

She called out a seven this time, but rolled a four and a two. The croupier handed her the dice again and she won this toss with another roll of six.

Another cheer rose from the table.

It looked like she was on another winning streak tonight. Last night's tally showed they had indeed lost at the hazard table, but nothing alarming. The profits at faro and *rouge et noir* more than made up for it. Rhys liked that her winning drew a bigger crowd to the hazard table. In the long run hazard would turn a profit.

Rhys moved through the room again, still keeping an eye on the hazard table. Celia won a third time, and, egged on by the patrons betting with her, she more eagerly accepted the dice from the croupier to try again.

He'd seen winning streaks like this before. He did not mind if she had some big wins, since money was important to her. Better she win than lose.

He wanted her to be happy.

He also wanted her to come to him this night. He felt the twinges of arousal merely thinking of it.

When Celia had entered the game room, she'd immediately caught of glimpse of Rhys. She'd also seen Neddington and another young man approach him, so she avoided speaking to him right away. Before his conversation ended, two gentlemen whisked her over to the hazard table.

'Come give us the luck, madam,' they'd said to her.

'As you wish,' she responded.

She played hazard again because she expected to lose. If she could encourage men to bet with her like the night before, they would also lose and maybe she could return to Rhys some of the money she'd cost him.

It worked, too. An occasional roll was successful, but most were not. She'd set her limit at fifty pounds, which she would then try to recoup by playing card games that gave her better odds.

As she tossed the dice on to the green baize table, a man's hand touched her back.

Westleigh.

Her skin shuddered where he touched.

'Greetings, my dear. Allow me to assist you.' He scooped up the dice, put his closed hand up to his lips and blew. 'For luck.' He smiled.

It made her sick.

She tossed the dice and won. And won again. And again.

Soon she'd lost all sense of time. All she knew was the feel of the dice in her hand, the sound of dice hitting the table, the cheers when the right numbers turned up. Her heart pumped wildly and she became dizzy with excitement. The fever had returned.

This night she woke from her reverie at the sight of Xavier Campion scowling at her.

She came to her senses and threw up her hands. 'I am done!'

She hurried away from the table. Pausing to check the timepiece in her reticule, she realised she'd not even thought about Rhys while in the fever. The dice had been too important.

It was two-fifteen! She'd spent all her time at the hazard table.

Someone touched her back again.

'Would you care for some supper, my dear?' Westleigh had followed her.

She'd even forgotten he'd stood next to her all that time. 'No. Not at all. Forgive me. I must speak with Mr Rhysdale.'

'Rhysdale?' Westleigh sniffed with contempt.

'Yes.' She could not be bothered with this man.

She searched instead for Rhys and found him leaning against the door jamb, his arms folded across his chest.

He saw her, nodded and walked out of the room.

Surely he knew of her new winning streak.

'I must go,' she said to Westleigh.

As she made her way to the door, she suddenly felt unable to breathe. She'd not decided about his proposition, but now she feared he would withdraw it. She walked briskly through the room.

A gentleman stopped her. 'Some whist, Madame Fortune?'

'Madame Fortune?' She did not comprehend.

The man smiled. 'That is what we call you now.'

She groaned inwardly. Her good fortune was Rhys's loss. 'I see.'

'It would honour me if you would partner me in whist,' he persisted.

She glanced toward the door. 'I—I cannot tonight, but perhaps next time?'

He bowed. 'I shall count on it.'

She hurried to the door and made her way to the room where the cashier sat.

'Cashing in early, ma'am?' he asked.

She nodded.

When her accounts were settled she thanked him and made as if she were leaving, but instead of entering the hall, she turned towards the servants' stairway and climbed those stairs to Rhys's private rooms, not knowing what reception she would find.

The drawing-room door was ajar and she could see him in the centre of the room. He'd removed his coat and waistcoat and stood only in his shirtsleeves, his back towards her. Her hands flew to her suddenly flaming cheeks.

She took a breath. 'Rhys?'

He turned, but his expression was impassive. 'I was uncertain you would come.'

'Of course I would come.' She spoke the words without thought. 'I needed to.'

His brows rose.

She entered the room and closed the door behind her, her heart pounding. 'I—I mean I must speak with you.'

He did not move, but she felt him withdraw as she came closer.

'I must explain.' A wave of guilt washed through her. 'I won tonight, Rhys.' Had this been how her father had felt when he lost? Ironic she should feel it for winning. 'I must have cost you over a hundred pounds between my winning and those who bet with me.'

The experience was now a blur of dice hitting the table, people cheering and the intoxication of win after win.

She took a breath. 'Surely you noticed.'

'Is that why you are here?' His posture was stiff and his shirt so white it seemed to light the room.

She gripped her reticule to keep her hands from shaking. 'I expected you to be angry.' Her husband had become angry at so much less.

He stared at her. 'I told you it is of no consequence. You and the others will lose eventually.'

His tone was still so stiff she feared he'd meant the opposite of what he said.

He gestured to her. 'At least take off your mask, Celia.'

Her hand flew to her face. She'd even forgotten her mask. She wearily lowered herself onto the sofa, setting her reticule down beside her. She untied her mask and dropped it next to the reticule.

He crossed his arms over his chest. 'You have not answered my question.'

She searched back, but could not remember what it was. 'I've forgotten it.'

He remained standing, but sipped his drink. 'Did you come here merely to tell me you won tonight?'

She gazed at him, so tall, so taut in his stance that it felt he was coiled like a spring. A flutter of nerves—or excitement—made her press her hand against her stomach. It did not help that his shirtsleeves accentuated his broad shoulders and narrow waist. She was robbed of breath.

'Not only for that,' she answered. No matter her fear or her nerves, her decision was made.

He met her gaze, but remained grim. 'For what, then?'

She blinked. 'Are you going to make me say it?'

One corner of his mouth turned up. 'Indeed.'

Courage was failing her. 'What you asked of me—I might say yes.'

He tilted his head. '*Might* say yes?'

She gathered her resolve and stood. 'Will say yes.'

He took her hand and raised it to his lips, which were warm and firm and sent a thrill deep within her.

'When does your driver return?' he asked.

'Five-thirty,' she said. Three hours away.

Her coachman had raised his brows at the request for a later hour. She herself was surprised she'd asked for it.

Perhaps she'd always known what she would decide.

He raised a hand and touched her cheek. 'You are certain?'

No. She was not certain at all. But she could not make herself refuse.

She did not *want* to refuse.

'Come.' He took her by the hand. 'I will show you my bedchamber.'

He led her to another room on that floor. Candle flames fluttered when they entered, illuminating a chest of drawers, a table, side chairs...and a bed. He'd prepared for her.

She had not thought beyond her impulsive yes. Once inside the bedchamber, she was as unsure as a new bride.

He led her to a table where two glasses of wine stood. 'A toast to you.' He handed her one of the glasses and lifted the other. 'And to pleasure.'

'To pleasure,' she whispered in return, her heart racing in her chest.

The wine was a strong and sweet sack. She drank it quickly and he poured her another. When she finished that glass she felt as if she were floating.

'Come to the bed,' he said.

Acting precisely like an experienced lady's maid, he unbuttoned the row of buttons decorating the back of her gown. She let it fall to the floor. Next he untied the laces of her corset. Each motion of his fingers made her tremble, more and more unsure of herself. Still, she slipped off her corset, leaving only her shift.

His eyes raked over her, dark as the night and full of desire.

He made quick work of removing his shirt, tossing it aside in a flash of white that tumbled to the floor. Dark hair peppered his chest and his muscles were as defined as those of a Greek statue. He moved slightly and the lamp-light caught a webwork of scars on his side.

Her hand reached out to touch them, but he picked her up by her waist and sat her upon the bed. 'Next your shoes and stockings.'

She could not move. Never had a man touched her feet, nor slipped his hands up her legs to remove her stockings. An ache grew inside her, an ache of want.

Her legs still tingled when he stepped back, removed his trousers and stood before her naked.

She stared transfixed. No mere Greek statue could appear as magnificent.

He climbed on the bed, cupped her face and kissed her.

At first his kiss was gentle, a mere touch, but he pressed harder, moving his lips as if needing to devour her. Such a kiss was not one to be endured, but one that made her want to return such ardour. She kissed him back, daring even to touch her tongue to his. His lips parted and the kiss became something wondrous.

Sensation shot through her and his hands moved to explore her body through the thin fabric of her shift. She could do no more than rest her hands on his shoulders, but even that contact gave a thrill. His skin was warm and slightly damp to the touch.

Not cold. Not clammy.

He bunched the fabric of her shift in his hands, pulled it over her head and tossed it aside. Leaning back, he gazed at her, his eyes darkening, his breathing deepening.

Her husband's gaze always made her wish to cover herself. Rhys's felt like a caress.

'You please me,' he said.

Filled with a delight she'd never known before, she lay back on the pillows.

And he rose over her.

All at once it seemed as if the room grew dark.

Her heart raced so hard that it hurt. Her limbs trembled.

He covered her with his body and she gasped for air.

His male member pressed against her skin—

Panic engulfed her. She cried out and flailed at him, struggling to free herself.

He lifted himself off her immediately, shock on his face. 'What?'

She was still trapped by his body. She pushed at his chest, but he seized her arms and held her down.

'What is it?' he demanded. 'Have I hurt you?'

'Get off!' she begged. 'Please get off!'

He released her and moved off her. She scooted away from him, curling up into a ball, trying to hide from her panic and her shame.

'Celia!' He sounded as if he'd run a great distance. 'Tell me. What. Happened.'

She sat up, hugging her knees to her chest. 'I—I remembered.'

'Remembered what?'

For the second time that night she expected anger from

him. Not anger. Rage. Her husband always raged at her if she'd dared push him away.

Rhysdale merely sat up. She braced herself for a blow.

But he did not strike her. He tucked her in front of him, wrapped his arms around her and held her close like her mother used to do when she woke from a nightmare.

'What did you remember, Celia, that frightened you so?' His voice was low. Soothing. Comforting.

It calmed her. 'I—I remembered. The only other man I was with...' She paused, searching for the right words. 'He was not gentle.'

The muscles of his arms bunched. 'He hurt you?'

She nodded. 'It came back. I thought it was happening again.'

'Who is this man?' His voice turned hard. 'I will pay him a call.'

She did not even think of inventing a story. 'My husband,' she answered.

He tensed. 'You have a husband, *Miss* Allen?'

She'd misled him on purpose. Now she regretted it. 'I once had a husband. Not any more. He is dead.'

'How fortunate for him. And me.' He laughed as if in relief. 'Tell me of this husband of yours.'

She owed him an explanation. 'I was very young when I married him. Younger than—' She stopped herself. She'd almost said she was younger than Adele, but giving him a clue to who her husband was—who she was—still felt too exposing. She took a breath. 'It all came back. I am sorry.'

He nuzzled her and rocked her. 'Do not be distressed, Celia. Lovemaking is not supposed to bring pain. It is supposed to bring pleasure. I will not hurt you, I promise.' He paused. 'I will stop now, if you wish it.'

She twisted around to face him. 'No. I—I want to know what it is like without me being so—so afraid.'

She rose to her knees, as did he. He pulled the pins from her hair and released the ribbon threaded through. When her hair fell about her shoulders, he combed it with his fingers.

'I will be gentle, Celia.'

Slowly her panic dissolved. He stroked her, like one might pet a cat. Like a cat, she relaxed under his fingers. She lay down again and urged him down beside her. 'Your touch is gentle.'

He kissed her neck and murmured, 'Say my name, Celia.'

'Rhys.' It was a name to be whispered beneath sheets.

'See? I am not the man who hurt you,' he soothed. 'I will never hurt you.'

He remained beside her, keeping his promise so well her limbs turned to warm butter under his touch. His fingers traced around her nipples and she writhed at the pleasure of it. His hand slipped down her body and rested on her belly.

Aching with need, she pushed it further and still his touch was excruciatingly gentle as he explored her most private of places. Her hips rose to meet his hand, urging him to take greater access.

'You must tell me when you want me,' he whispered.

She wanted him at that very moment, but she held back. The fear hovered near, ready to flood her again. He waited and eventually his touch pushed away the fear and replaced it with more need.

'Now,' she rasped.

He rose over her again and she opened her legs to him even as she braced herself for the event that inevitably brought her pain.

To her surprise his entry was as tender as his touch. He eased inside her and new, unimaginable sensations flooded her. He moved softly as if she might break beneath him.

The rhythm lulled her and slowly a sensation akin to bliss arose inside her, growing more urgent with each thrust.

Suddenly his restraint became torture, albeit an exquisite one. Her hands grasped his backside and a frustrated sound escaped her lips.

He moved faster and she gladly kept up with him. This wonderful new sensation grew. The stronger it became, the more she wanted to rush towards it.

Suddenly pleasure exploded within her. She cried out and, at the same time, he convulsed inside her, spilling his seed, slaking his desire a moment after fulfilling hers.

He did not collapse atop her, as her husband had done, crushing her with his weight. He eased himself off her, settling at her side again. She could feel the rise and fall of his chest against her bare skin.

'Rhys,' she managed to whisper as tears formed in her eyes. She blinked them away.

'We have made love, Celia,' he murmured, his voice rumbling. 'Whatever your husband did to you, it was not making love.'

She curled up against him. 'I did not know of that—that pleasure. It was a surprise. I thought the pleasure was going to be only in how you touched me.'

'You are built for such pleasure, Celia. Settle for nothing less.' He cradled her under his arm.

She placed her hand on his chest, relishing the feel of him.

'Tell me about why you married this husband of yours.' He placed his hand over hers.

At this moment she wanted to pretend Gale had never existed, but she acquiesced. 'I was only seventeen.'

'Seventeen?' He rose on an elbow to look down on her.

'My guardians demanded I marry him,' she explained. 'I had no other choice. To be fair to them, they thought it a good thing for me. He was quite a bit older and—and of good reputation, at least of what they knew. He wanted a young wife.'

He frowned. 'How old are you now?'

'Three and twenty.'

'And he is dead?' His voice turned gruff.

'Over a year,' she said. 'He left me little money. That is why I must gamble. So that I have enough to support... myself.' She'd almost said *us*. 'I want to take care of myself, so that I do not have to do what any one else wants me to do. I do not require much. Not a large fortune. Just enough for comfort and security.' It was not the whole truth, but enough of it.

He kissed her temple. 'I am glad you came here.'

She looked into his eyes. 'I am glad of it, too.' And for more than just the chance to win at cards.

He grinned. 'It seems to me that you may need many lessons in lovemaking, though. To catch up.'

She smiled in return. 'I expect I do.' She feigned innocence. 'I do not suppose you know of a man who might be willing to teach me?'

'Only one.' He lowered his lips to hers for a long, lingering, arousing kiss. 'It would be my pleasure to teach you.'

He made love to her again, every bit as tenderly. The pleasure of her climax was equally as intense and she was left wanting more.

When they were finished he asked, 'Do you need to take care of yourself?'

'Take care of myself?' Her brows knitted.

'Do what women do after. To prevent a baby,' he explained.

Her eyes widened. Women could *prevent* a baby? She'd had no idea.

'I do not need to do anything.' That familiar empty feeling returned. 'I am barren.'

He peered at her, saying nothing, but gathered her in his arms again and kissed her. 'We should check the time.'

He climbed off the bed and searched the clothing on the floor. 'Drat. I left my coat in the drawing room.' He pulled on his trousers.

She wrapped herself in the bed linens. 'There is a time-piece in my reticule.' She scrambled from the bed. 'Oh, my goodness! I left my reticule in the drawing room. It has all my money.'

He lifted a hand. 'I will bring it to you.'

He put on his shirt and walked from the room in his bare feet.

By the time he returned she'd donned her shift.

He lifted the reticule before placing it on a table. 'It feels like you did win a great deal tonight.'

She picked up her corset. 'What time is it?'

'Ten minutes after five.'

'I must hurry.' She turned her back to him. 'Would you help me with my corset?'

She held it in place while he tightened the laces.

In a reverse of the more sensual undressing, they quickly put on all their clothes.

She felt the floor for her hairpins and quickly twisted her hair into some sort of order. She stuffed the ribbon in her reticule.

As they rushed down the stairs, she covered her face with her hand. 'My mask.'

'I'll get it.' He bounded back up the stairs.

She waited on the stairs, covering her face.

Xavier Compier entered the hall. He did not speak to her, merely leaned against the wall and watched her. When

Rhys's footfall sounded on the steps, Xavier retreated into the shadows.

'Here it is.'

She turned away and held the mask in place while he tied its ribbons.

They made it outside and he blew out a breath. 'I think we made it.'

There was the faintest glimmer of dawn peeking through the darkness. She smiled at him. 'Thank you for a lovely time, Rhys.'

He put an arm around her. 'Come to me again tonight.'

She looked up at him. 'For more lessons?'

His eyes darkened. 'Yes indeed.'

After Celia's coach turned the corner, Rhys re-entered the house and saw Xavier standing in the hall.

'You are still here?' He was not particularly pleased. No doubt his friend had known he'd been with Celia.

'I waited for you,' Xavier said.

Rhys gestured for Xavier to come up the stairs with him. 'Well, come upstairs. You might as well have a brandy with me.'

They sat together in the drawing room, a bottle of brandy between them on the table.

'Do you want to stay?' Rhys asked. 'You can use one of the beds upstairs.'

Some of the rooms remained unchanged from when the house's girls once entertained gentlemen in them.

Xavier shook his head. 'I'll go back to the hotel.' He'd kept his rooms at Stephen's.

'Any problems in the game room after I left?' Rhys asked.

Xavier frowned. 'We lost at hazard again.'

Here it comes, Rhys thought. Xavier would have noticed Celia's winning streak. 'I heard about it. We didn't recoup later?'

'Not enough.' Xavier inclined his head towards the cashier's room. 'I asked MacEvoy to count the money right away.'

Rhys tapped his fingers on his brandy glass. 'It happens sometimes. Luck occasionally turns bad, even for the house. You know that.'

Xavier gave him a direct look. 'The only time we lost at hazard was when she was winning.'

Rhys met his eye. 'I know. I watched her, too.'

'I have a bad feeling about this,' Xavier persisted. 'You do not know who she is. What she is about. You don't know what she wants from coming here.'

'We've been through this already, Xavier,' Rhys shot back. 'She wants to win money, like everyone else.'

Xavier's voice rose. 'I know you've taken her to your bed. Your judgement is clouded.'

Rhys levelled a gaze at him. 'Stay out of it, Xavier. I mean this.'

But Xavier went on. 'All I'm saying is, do not close your mind too tightly. Watch her.'

Rhys glared at him. 'Enough. Say no more.'

Xavier opened his mouth, but wisely closed it again.

He stood. 'I ought to be going.' He glanced towards the windows where slivers of light appeared through the gaps in the curtains. 'It's morning already.'

Rhys stood, too, and clapped him on the shoulder. 'Do not worry over me, Xavier. You are like a mother hen sometimes.'

Xavier merely nodded. 'I'll see you tonight.'

Xavier would not let this go, Rhys feared. He'd consider it his duty to look out for Rhys, even if Rhys demanded he stop. It was ingrained in Xavier's character.

Rhys knew precisely what he was doing and had no need of Xavier's caution. Rhys intended to enjoy this affair with Celia for as long as it lasted, and if Xavier did not like it, it would stand like a wall between them.

Chapter Nine

Celia hugged herself during her short ride back to her rooms. Her body felt languorous, at peace with itself for the first time in her memory.

How could she have ever guessed lovemaking could be like this?

The carriage turned a corner.

She'd turned a corner, too. She felt free of her husband at last. There was no reason ever again to think of what it had been like being married to him. That part of her life was over and nothing like it would ever again happen to her.

A new door had opened. A door to new experiences and new delights. Celia planned to enjoy every minute of them.

Her heart was as light as gossamer when the carriage stopped. She gathered her mask and her reticule, opened the door and climbed out.

'Thank you, Jonah,' she called to her coachman. 'Get some rest.'

He touched his hat in acknowledgement and flicked the reins. The coach pulled away.

Celia walked to the door and turned the latch. Tucker

knew what time to unlock the door for her. He would have risen from his bed and be waiting to attend her in the hall.

How good her servants were to her.

She opened the door and stepped inside. Her butler indeed stood before her, but with an anxious expression and wringing hands.

She tensed. 'What is it, Tucker?'

He inclined his head towards the staircase. 'The dowager.'

Was Lady Gale ill? 'What about her?'

His face turned grim. 'She awaits you in your bedchamber.'

Celia froze. She was discovered.

She lifted her chin, though. This would change nothing. Her mother-in-law had no control over her life. The woman was dependent upon Celia, not the other way around.

She gave Tucker a rueful, but reassuring smile. 'Well, this will be unpleasant, will it not?'

'Quite, ma'am.' He relaxed a bit at her calm manner.

Celia climbed the stairs, feeling weary and in a great need of sleep.

Her maid stood outside her bedchamber door. 'She's in there,' Younie whispered. 'Fit to be tied.'

'So I would expect.' Celia opened the door.

Lady Gale had positioned one of Celia's chairs to face the door. She sat on the chair as if it were a throne and wore an outraged expression.

Celia did not give her mother-in-law time to speak. 'You have not been invited into my private room, Lady Gale. Nor were you given permission to rearrange my chairs.' When holding a weak hand, it was always best to make a bold move. Celia's father had taught her that. 'Leave now and never trespass here again.'

The dowager's mouth dropped open and it took time for

her to find her voice. She rose out of the chair. 'How dare you speak to me like that, you little wretch! Especially when you have been out all night. Where have you been?'

'I do not owe you an explanation, Lady Gale.' Celia stood at the open door.

The dowager grabbed her cane and pounded it across the floor. She stopped inches from Celia. 'You have been with a man. I'd wager a fortune on it. Who did you find willing to bed you? Surely someone you had to pay.'

Celia recoiled from the insult and fought the impulse to strike her mother-in-law across the cheek.

Instead she leaned down into her face. 'Remember your place, ma'am.' Her voice trembled. 'It is only because of my affection for Adele that you are here.'

The older woman shook a finger at Celia. 'You need me, girl! You are known to nobody. Without my connections, you would be invited nowhere.'

'I care nothing for your connections, ma'am.' Celia wanted nothing to do with society. 'The invitations are for Adele's sake, not mine.'

'You have obviously found some opportunity through my connections or you would not be out all night.' Lady Gale sneered. 'Unless you merely walk the streets like a common strumpet.'

Adele appeared in the doorway, rubbing her eyes. 'I heard shouting. You said my name. Are you arguing about me? Because I do not want you to argue about me.'

Lady Gale jabbed her finger at Celia. 'This woman is trying to ruin your reputation. She is gallivanting on the streets of London all night. If anyone discovers this, we'll all be ruined. Even your cousin will not wish to court you.'

She was still pushing Luther on poor Adele.

'That would be a good thing,' Celia snapped.

Adele clapped her hands over her ears. 'Stop! Stop!'

Celia caught herself and lowered her voice. 'Lady Gale, please leave now. Say no more.'

Younie stepped forwards. 'Come along, ma'am.' The maid spoke soothingly. 'Let me have Cook fix you a nice posset, so you can have a rest. All this fuss does you no good.'

Lady Gale allowed Younie to put her arm around her and coax her out of the room. 'She has given me palpitations!' she wailed.

'There, there, my lady,' Younie murmured. 'Let me fix you up.'

The maid got her into the hall and halfway to her own bedchamber before Lady Gale turned around. 'Ask her whose bed she's been warming, Adele. She's trying to ruin us all!'

When Lady Gale disappeared into her bedchamber with Younie, Adele turned to Celia, with her lip trembling. 'Is it true?'

'Come in my room.' Celia took the girl's hand and led her to the chair her grandmother had so recently vacated.

She moved another chair closer and sat. 'I will tell you the truth.' Or rather part of the truth, Celia thought. Enough of it, she hoped. 'It is true that I have been out all night, but I have not been walking the streets as your grandmother suggests.'

'Have you been with a man, though?' Adele asked, her voice wobbling.

Celia sidestepped that question. 'I have been at a place called the Masquerade Club.' That was truth enough. She lifted her arm where her mask dangled. 'It is a place where ladies may dress in disguise and gamble.'

Adele's eyes widened. 'Gamble?'

Celia nodded. 'Play cards. Hazard. Faro. It is where I go almost every night.'

'You go to a gambling house?' Adele's voice rose in alarm.

'That is how I have funded your new gowns and paid our bills.' Celia opened her reticule and removed the leather purse, heavy with coin. 'See? These are my winnings. They will pay the servants' wages. And pay for another ballgown for you. And more.'

'You pay for my gowns with money from *gambling?*' Adele looked horrified.

'Adele.' It was time to acquaint her stepdaughter with the realities of their situation. 'I have never had enough money to fund this Season for you. I had to do something.'

'But to *gamble?*' She said the words with disgust. 'Is not gambling what ruined my father?'

Not merely gambling. Debauchery, gluttony and carousing greatly contributed.

'Your father gambled rashly.' As did Celia's own father when he was on a losing streak. 'I am not rash.' At least she would not be rash again. She lifted the purse. 'This is proof.'

Adele jumped to her feet. 'Oh, Celia! What if you are found out? What if Lord Neddington learns you *gamble?*'

Celia did not have the heart to tell the girl that her dear Neddington was a frequent visitor at the same gambling house. 'No one will find out. That is the beauty of this establishment. Because ladies may come in disguise, no one knows who they are.'

'You do not understand, Celia,' Adele cried. 'He comes from an *important* family. He will never look at me again if it is discovered you gamble every night.'

Before Celia could respond, Adele ran out of the room. Her sobs could be heard in the hallway.

Celia rubbed her eyes. Wearily she rose and sat down

at her dressing table, taking her hair down and putting it in a plait.

Younie entered. 'Her ladyship has settled a bit.'

'Thank goodness.' She stood and Younie undid her buttons. 'I fear I handled that badly.'

Younie did not disagree. 'No sense in weeping over shed milk.'

'I am so tired I feel like weeping. I need to sleep. Perhaps I can think better when I am rested.'

She slipped out of her dress and Younie helped her off with her corset. She climbed into her bed in just her shift.

Once under the bed linens she closed her eyes.

She pushed her mother-in-law and Adele out of her thoughts and let her mind wander. It went immediately to Rhys. How it felt lying next to him. How his arms had comforted her and his touch had thrilled her.

Did she not deserve some happiness after all she'd been through? All she needed was to avoid the intoxication of the hazard game and confine herself to whist. She wanted to gamble at the Masquerade Club and share Rhys's bed for as long as she wished, for as long as she needed to stay in London.

When the Season was over, when Adele was settled, it would be over.

That afternoon Ned again called upon Adele for a drive in the park. While he waited for her in the drawing room, he could not even sit, he was so filled with excitement. Rhys had opened the door to restoring his future. Ned could dare to anticipate better fortune from now on.

She walked in and he knew immediately that something was amiss.

'Miss Gale.' He moved towards her.

'I am so sorry to keep you waiting, sir.' She glanced at him and her eyes looked red as if she'd been weeping.

What had upset her? Ned vowed to fix whatever it was, if it was at all in his power.

He did not press her to speak until he turned his curricle in to the park. It was early for the heaviest traffic and he was able to keep some distance from other carriages.

'What is distressing you, Miss Gale?' he began. 'I dislike seeing you so unhappy.'

'Oh.' She sighed. 'Nothing.' She tried to paste on a smile, but he could see it was false.

'Do not say it is nothing,' he pressed. 'I am your friend. Whatever troubles you, I will help.'

She looked away and wiped her eyes with her fingers. 'I ought not to be such a watering pot.'

He wanted to gather her in his arms, but he settled with covering her hand with his. 'Let me share your burden.'

She glanced up into his eyes and it took his breath away. 'It will seem nonsensical to you.'

He squeezed her hand, trying his hardest not to kiss her. 'Nothing you do or say will ever seem nonsensical to me.'

She blinked and one tear slid down her flawless cheek. 'It is just…just that my grandmother and my stepmother are quarrelling and there is nothing I can do about it.'

'What are they quarrelling about?' he asked.

She glanced away. 'I cannot tell you!'

He felt his face grow hot. 'Forgive me. I do not want to pry into your family's business. I only wish to help if I can.'

She sighed. 'Oh, you did not pry. I—I just cannot tell you.'

'I know what it means to keep family matters private.' His whole family situation was a carefully guarded secret. No one—except Rhys, that is—knew how near they were

to financial ruin. 'But I want to help you in any way possible. All you need do is ask.'

She gazed at him again, her blue eyes glittering like
sapphires through her tears. 'You are the kindest of men.'

He took a deep breath. 'There is…perhaps…something
I wish to ask of you. If you feel able to listen to it.'

Her expression softened. 'You may ask anything of me.
I am your friend as you are mine.'

He made himself attend to the horses and the path. 'It
is an impertinence, I know, but I cannot resist.' He dared
glance back to her. 'May I have permission to court you? I
desire it above all things.'

She gasped and covered her mouth with her hand. 'Oh,
my! Oh, yes. Yes!' She laughed, but quickly sobered. 'You
should speak with my stepmother. She will tell you about
my dowry and about—about my family. You should know
our situation before committing yourself so.'

'If you wish it, I shall do so,' he said. 'This afternoon, if
possible. But you must know that your dowry, your family,
will make no difference to me. I want you to be my wife.'

'Oh, Neddington,' she whispered.

He glanced around quickly. They did not seem to be
in view of any other carriage. Holding the reins in one
hand, he cupped her cheek with the other and touched his
lips to hers.

Celia did not wish to receive callers. All she wanted
was to remain in her bedchamber and sleep.

And avoid her mother-in-law.

And wait for night and time to return to Rhys.

But Adele knocked on her door. 'Lord Neddington is in
the drawing room. Will you see him, Celia?'

At least she was dressed. 'Of course I will.'

Adele walked with her down the stairs, whispering in-

structions the whole way. 'Please listen to him, Celia. Do
not tell him about Grandmama's plan for me to marry
Cousin Luther. Tell him the truth about my dowry and
about Father. I do not wish to hold anything back from
him.' She paused for a moment. 'But, do, please, refrain
from telling him about your gambling. I fear he will disapprove greatly and I so want him to like me. And you.
And Grandmama, too.'

Adele walked with her all the way to the drawing-room
door. 'I cannot go in with you, but do treat him well, Celia.
My entire life and happiness depends upon it!'

'I will treat him well, I promise.' Celia reached for the
latch.

Adele seized her arm and pulled her back. 'Come find
me as soon as you are finished. Will you?'

Celia suppressed a smile. 'I will. The moment I am
finished.'

She opened the door and walked in the room.

Lord Neddington stood at the window. He turned
quickly and bowed. 'Lady Gale.'

She hated being called that. In her mind her mother-in-
law was Lady Gale and she was Celia Allen.

'Good afternoon.' He gestured to the window. 'I was
just checking my curricle. Your man was good enough to
hold the horses for me.'

She walked over and peeked out. 'A lovely pair of
horses.'

'Thank you, ma'am.'

She gestured to the sofa. 'Do sit, sir, and tell me why
you wished to speak to me.' She might be standing in the
role of Adele's father, but, ironically, Neddington was probably older than she. She guessed him to be at least thirty.

He waited for her to sit first. 'I will speak plainly. I
wish to court your daughter—your stepdaughter, I mean.

She wished me to seek your permission. I know you are not her guardian, but she said you were the one I should speak to first.'

Adele's guardian was an old friend of her husband's, a man who was in ill health and had retired to Bath. He did not care enough about Adele to oppose anything Celia decided.

'I am very inclined to comply with Adele's wishes.' Celia wanted Adele to be free to make her own choices. 'Whatever makes her happy.'

He frowned. 'I, too, desire her happiness.'

'You have only just met each other.' Adele should not make too hasty a decision. More importantly, she should not marry a gambler.

'I realise this,' Neddington said. 'That is why I request a courtship. Adele must be sure of me. To be frank, there is one matter that may cause you to decide against me.'

Celia's brows rose. 'Oh?'

He rubbed his face. 'I have tried to behave as a gentleman ought, but, at the moment my family finances are strained. I have taken steps to resolve the problem and in a matter of a year, I expect to be on solid ground again.' He paused. 'But it is not a given. It is…a sort of gamble.'

'A gamble?' She tapped on the arm of her chair with a finger. 'Are you fond of gambling, sir?'

He looked surprised. 'Me? Not at all.' Comprehension dawned. 'I do not gamble at cards and such, if that is what you mean.'

As she had noticed at the gaming house. She longed to ask him why he showed up there.

He went on. 'In any event, my family's finances are not yet quite what they ought to be, so I need time before I can in good conscience commit to marriage. I wanted you both to know that.'

She narrowed her eyes. 'Do you know of Adele's dowry?'

He waved a hand. 'I care nothing for her dowry. Whatever the amount, it will satisfy me.'

He certainly sounded genuinely like he was not in pursuit of her fortune. 'It is ten thousand pounds,' she told him.

His brows rose, but he turned thoughtful. 'It will be designated for any children we might have, of course. I'll not touch a penny.'

'Adele also wishes you to know that her father was a gambler and carouser, which was why I asked about your gambling habits. Besides her dowry, she inherits nothing. Her grandmother has only a pittance, as well.'

'And you?' he asked.

'I have enough.' She bit her lip, but decided to speak further. 'It would be desirable for Adele's husband to support her grandmother. It would be, shall we say, a great deal for her grandmother to bear to live with me.'

He bowed. 'It shall be my honour to do whatever is required of me.' His expression turned imploring. 'I would not have presumed to ask permission to court Miss Gale but for my fear of another suitor.'

Cousin Luther, he meant.

'I see,' Celia responded. 'I can assure you that no other man has secured Adele's affections.'

Neddington expelled a relieved breath, but he turned earnest again. 'Miss Gale does, of course, have every right to cry off.' His expression turned miserable. 'If she should ever prefer another gentleman to me.'

She reached over to touch his hand. 'As I said, Adele's happiness is of great importance to me. I think you prudent to request a courtship. Take your time to become acquainted, to see if marriage is truly what you desire.

Perhaps by the time your finances are in order, you will know for certain if you are suited.'

And Celia would have time to find out why Neddington regularly attended the Masquerade Club.

He clasped her hand. 'I am grateful, my lady. Truly grateful.'

She stood. 'Shall I send Adele in so you might apprise her of our conversation?'

He rose, looking as if the sun had come out after a month of rain. 'Yes. Yes. I would greatly desire to tell her.'

Celia walked to the door and called for Adele, who, she suspected, was waiting in the hall. Adele came running. Celia gestured for Adele to enter and the girl rushed in. Instead of joining them, Celia retreated to allow the besotted young couple some privacy.

Celia had already decided not to attend the evening's social event with Adele and her grandmother. It was to be another musicale, and this time the attendees would be providing the entertainment. She did not think she had the patience to sit through such an event.

She'd been able to remain in the background at the few other parties she'd attended. That suited her very well. The less she was noticed, the less chance anyone would guess who she was when she wore her masks.

She rather hoped Neddington's finances would be quickly restored; that is, assuming he told the truth about not gambling. If that were the case, though, she would have no reason to continue her double life and she was suddenly in no hurry to leave London, to leave Rhys.

She would see him tonight.

Avoiding the musicale also meant she could go to the Masquerade Club early...and avoid her mother-in-law's company a little longer.

* * *

Celia had pleaded a headache and confined herself to her room, asking that her dinner be brought to her. It would be assumed she was asleep when Adele and her grandmother returned from the musicale.

There was a knock on her door—Adele, probably, needing her opinion on her gown. 'Come in.'

Her mother-in-law appeared in the doorway. 'Did I behave properly this time?'

It was not worth keeping up the feud, not if it upset Adele so much.

Celia returned a civil smile. 'I do appreciate your knocking. It is very courteous.'

Lady Gale did not look in a conciliatory mood. 'I have something to discuss with you.'

Celia kept her tone mild. 'Certainly.'

The older woman took a deep breath before glaring at Celia. 'Did you allow Adele to make an arrangement with that Lord Neddington?'

Celia stiffened. 'I gave her permission to decide for herself.'

Lady Gale stood with elbows akimbo. 'How dare you! You knew I meant her for Cousin Luther. You must undo this hasty decision.'

Celia met the woman's eye. 'If you can present me with some reason to object to Adele's choice, I will discuss the matter with her. But it is her decision.'

'What can she know of it?' Lady Gale snapped. 'She is but nineteen.'

'She has time to decide,' Celia assured her. 'Neddington is not pressuring her.'

'What do you know of his family? I have heard gossip about his father—'

Celia put up a hand. 'I am certain there was plenty of

gossip about Adele's father, as well. If there is anything to cause undue concern, we will discuss it with Adele. She is a sensible young woman.'

'She is too young—' Lady Gale began again.

Celia levelled a gaze at her mother-in-law. 'Lady Gale, I was younger than Adele and I assure you I knew my own mind.'

The woman's eyes flashed. 'Hmmph! My son should never have married you.'

'Indeed.' Celia did not miss a beat. 'He was a great deal older than Adele's nineteen years and look what an unwise choice he made.'

'That was your fault,' Lady Gale countered. 'You bewitched him.'

Celia stared at her. 'Do not be absurd. I was seventeen. I did not choose him. I was not even given a choice. Adele will have a choice. Do not interfere or you will have to answer to me.'

Lady Gale spun around and made her way to the door. Before she crossed the threshold she turned back in a dramatic flourish. 'You have not heard the last of this from me.'

After she stormed out and closed the door behind her, Celia whispered, 'I agree. I have not heard the last, because you will never leave it alone.'

Chapter Ten

The next three weeks settled into a predictable routine for Celia, encompassing her greatest happiness, but also her greatest risk. Each night she entered the gaming house she risked losing control over her gambling, but when her night was finished she found unspeakable pleasure in Rhys's arms.

She stayed away from the hazard table as often as she could, but sometimes the gentlemen gambling there, Lord Westleigh especially, insisted she play.

'Madame Fortune,' they implored. 'We need you at hazard. We need your magic touch.'

She continued to win more than she lost, but she thought this was because she forced herself to stop as soon as the euphoria of the game bubbled inside her. It was always a struggle, but the other gamblers began to respect her skill at card playing as well as her luck at the dice, and their pressure to play hazard eased somewhat.

They also quickly learned that Madame Fortune had become Rhysdale's lover, preventing any attempts at flirtation. None wanted to offend the gaming-house owner. It suited Celia very well that she did not become an object of seduction like the woman Rhys had told her about, the one who inspired his idea for the Masquerade Club.

Neddington often came to the Masquerade Club, but Celia never saw him play. He talked to other patrons and watched others gamble, but never did so himself. She was relieved for Adele's sake, especially because the two were becoming more and more attached.

Life was splendid at the moment, even if the Season demanded ever more expenditures and the coach required an expensive repair. Other bills were paid. Adele was in raptures over Neddington and even Lady Gale's taunting could not spoil Celia's optimism.

Celia indulged Lady Gale in as many new gowns as she wished, as she did Adele and even herself, although at times she reminded herself too much of her father on a spending binge. She rationalised that looking prosperous for society was still an investment in Adele's future. Celia herself wanted to look presentable to society, but even more she wanted the gowns designed specifically for the night to look alluring. For Rhys. She delighted in nighttime costumes in fabrics of vibrant red, blue or green, with matching masks that grew more elaborate as Younie came up with new ideas for how to make them.

It pleased her when her appearance caused Rhys's eyes to darken with desire as it had this night, when she'd walked in wearing a midnight-blue silk dress embroidered at the hem and bodice with pink roses. Her mask matched the pink and was bordered with tiny green embroidered leaves. It thrilled Celia when Rhys later removed her dress and gazed upon her with reverence.

He constantly surprised her in his ability to delight her and be delighted by her. Celia's old fears about lovemaking had vanished completely. Rhys would never hurt her. Never.

This night brought on yet another new experience.

He was not gentle.

And she did not care.

Their lovemaking took on an urgency, a frenzy that had been entirely new to her. It was she who pushed him, almost violent in her need. She rushed them towards their release as if time was running out, even though the night was young. The pleasure that burst forth from her came with a new intensity. No sooner had they finished than she wanted more.

It felt to Celia that her body had changed into one that always wanted more, more, more.

This night her lovemaking with Rhys was wild with sensuality. The violence of it all was evident in the tangled bed linens and the aching of her womanly parts. She did not feel pain, precisely—nothing like it had been with Gale. But it seemed as if Rhys could not make love to her fast enough or hard enough or often enough.

She'd just propelled them towards another frenzied release when he collapsed atop her and slid to her side. 'I never thought I would say it, but I am worn out.'

She lay back, still throbbing, still needing. 'I do not know what has happened. It feels different. More—more intense. I cannot explain it.' It reminded her disturbingly of when she lost control of her gambling.

He rolled towards her and caressed her face. 'I do not complain of it. You are magnificent.'

She smiled. 'You have heard me say this before. I never imagined lovemaking could feel like this.'

He kissed her lips. 'You have mentioned it. Almost every night.'

She pushed on his chest. 'But this is different.'

He kissed her again. 'It certainly is different.'

If he continued she would start all over again.

The clock struck four. She sat up and the room swam. 'I must go.'

He pulled on his trousers. 'Will you come this night?' he asked.

She nodded.

Unexpectedly her stomach roiled.

Oh, no, please! She did not wish to be ill. She pressed her hand on her abdomen, hoping he did not notice.

'Although I may be later than usual,' she answered aloud.

She never explained why and he never asked.

He kissed her. 'I will wait for you.'

She dressed with his help, always an intimate experience. He tied her mask on last. It came off only when she was in his private rooms.

When he walked her down the stairs, she gripped the rail to keep herself steady.

He noticed. 'Are you feeling unwell?'

'Just tired, I expect.' She smiled. 'Worn out.'

He grinned. 'I know precisely how you feel.'

When they reached the hall Xavier was just leaving with Belinda, the croupier at the hazard table. Celia still felt tension from Xavier, but at least he'd stopped watching her so closely.

When Rhys walked her out into the night air, Celia felt much better. Her carriage came quickly and her kiss goodbye was hurried.

The carriage ride did nothing to help her stomach feel any better, though. She could not be ill! Tonight was a ball Neddington's family was giving and Adele would simply perish if Celia were unable to attend.

That evening Ned invited himself to dine with Adele and her family. He'd hinted very strongly to Adele that it would be a good idea for him to dine with her and her family before the ball.

He wanted plenty of time to talk with them.

At the dinner table, the subject of the ball that night inevitably came up.

He took it as his opening. 'I need to warn you about something.'

Adele's grandmother rolled her eyes. 'I knew all was not well,' she said not quietly enough to prevent his hearing.

He swallowed. 'I—I told you my father was not the best of men—'

'Indeed,' commented Adele's grandmother.

It pained Ned that the Dowager Lady Gale still did not like him, although Ned had tried every way he knew to get in her good graces. What he was about to tell them was not going to help.

He took a breath. Might as well come out and say it straight off. 'I must inform you that my father had a natural child.'

The dowager shrugged. 'He is a reprobate. Everyone knows this.'

'Grandmama!' Adele cried. 'Do not speak so!'

'Neddington is our guest,' warned Adele's stepmother.

Ned turned to Adele's grandmother. 'I must agree with you, ma'am. My father is a reprobate. I do not blame you for holding it against me. I can only say that I am not like him.'

'I am sure great numbers of gentlemen have natural children,' Adele said.

He faced Adele. 'You may meet my father's natural son tonight.' There. He had said it. 'He is to be introduced. At the ball.'

Adele's grandmother pursed her lips in disapproval. 'Hmmph!'

He turned back to her. 'I will not present him to you if you do not wish it, ma'am.'

'I certainly do not wish it!'

'I do not mind,' Adele piped up. 'If you wish to present him to me, I do not object. And neither does Celia. Is that not correct, Celia?'

'Whatever you wish, Adele,' Adele's stepmother responded.

She looked ill to Ned, although she denied it. She merely picked at her food.

'I, for one, am eager to meet your family at last.' Adele gazed at him with eyes full of affection.

How was he to wait to wed her? Perhaps he could ask Rhys if the profits of the gaming house would increase soon. Perhaps it would be enough.

'I am particularly eager to meet your sister,' Adele added.

'You have a sister?' her stepmother asked.

'Phillipa,' Ned responded. 'She is not much in society, but my mother wishes her to attend the ball.'

'I suppose something is wrong with her,' Adele's grandmother said sarcastically.

Ned was determined to tell them all. 'She suffered a terrible…accident when she was a child.' It had been an attack, a mysterious one. His family never spoke of it. 'She has a scar that disfigures her face.'

'Oh, how terribly sad!' exclaimed Adele. 'I am sure I will love her all the same.'

When she said things like this, Ned could only adore Adele more.

He disliked that this shameful family event—introducing Rhys—had to take place the same night he was to present Adele to his parents. He was sorry he had to tell her grandmother all about Rhys and his sister, not that Phillipa

'You are known to each other?' Rhys gave Xavier a glance. 'How interesting.'

'Since we were children,' Xavier explained. 'Our families often summered at Brighton at the same time.'

'And most recently in 1814,' Phillipa added. 'Perhaps you do not recall, though.'

Xavier met her gaze. 'I recall. I was briefly in London.'

Rhys looked from one to the other. This was fascinating. Would Xavier tell him what happened between these two? It was obvious something had. To Rhys's surprise he felt a protective brotherly impulse. Had Xavier ill-used her? He'd certainly done something to cause this chilly treatment.

At that moment, Hugh entered the room and after him the Westleigh butler and several musicians.

Hugh walked directly to his sister. 'I did not know you were here, Phillipa.'

'I thought I was late, but no one was here...except...'

Hugh turned to Rhys and inclined his head. 'Rhys.'

Rhys returned the gesture.

Hugh looked discomfited. Once Rhys would have relished putting Hugh out of ease, in repayment for all the fights Hugh had picked with him when they were boys. But Hugh had restrained himself lately.

Hugh shook hands with Xavier. 'Campion. Good of you to come.' He looked back at his sister. 'Papa is stalling and Mama is dealing with him.'

'Ned?' she asked.

'He rushed in a little while ago. I expect he is getting dressed.'

The musicians set up their instruments and began tuning them. Other servants came in, carrying trays of wine glasses.

Hugh stopped one of them. 'We might as well have a glass while we wait.'

Xavier handed a glass to Phillipa, but she waved it away. Rhys welcomed the refreshment. He was not plagued by nerves, but seemed to be catching the discomfort of all three of his companions. Frankly, Xavier had been more correct than Rhys wanted to admit. This had been a foolish idea.

Lady Westleigh swept in, followed by a dour-looking Lord Westleigh.

He bowed to his hostess. 'Ma'am.'

She extended her hand to him. 'Rhys. Your night has come. I hope it is to your satisfaction.'

He clasped her hand. 'Thank you, my lady.'

Xavier stepped forwards to greet her.

'I expect your parents to attend tonight,' Lady Westleigh told Xavier.

'As they told me, ma'am,' Xavier responded.

Rhys and Xavier had dined with them only a week ago.

She turned to her daughter. 'Phillipa, you forgot your headpiece. After the milliner worked so carefully on it.'

'The feather irritated my face,' Phillipa retorted, her hand touching her scar. 'Besides, everyone knows of my scar. Why should I hide it?'

Rhys looked at his half-sister with new admiration. The young woman had pluck.

Lord Westleigh, Rhys noticed, did not greet him, but instead contented himself with glowering.

Lady Westleigh turned away from her daughter. 'Rhys, I thought we would have you stand in the receiving line with the rest of us. We will greet our guests as a family and Charles will introduce you to each guest in turn. Will that do?'

He preferred that to a general announcement. For one thing, it forced his father to do the right thing over and over and over. 'It seems an excellent idea, ma'am.'

Of all the Westleighs, it was Lady Westleigh who seemed the least affected by this uncomfortable situation. Rhys liked her, he realised. She faced the occasion like a soldier.

'Where is Ned?' She glanced around impatiently. 'I can hear the carriages pulling up to the door.'

'I am here, Mama.' Ned rushed in, still pulling at his sleeves and straightening his coat.

Xavier gave Rhys one more sceptical glance before wandering away from the family.

Lady Westleigh positioned them all in order. She stood first, then her husband. She placed Rhys next to Lord Westleigh, then Ned, even though etiquette would have put Rhys lowest. After Ned came Hugh and Phillipa.

As the guests arrived, Lady Westleigh made certain her husband did not skip a single introduction, although he tried. Some of the gentlemen and a few of the ladies reacted with recognition. A few even said, 'Ah, the proprietor of the Masquerade Club!'

The entire process became tedious as it went on. Ned, for one, fidgeted and spent a great deal of the time leaning over to see who next approached the door.

'Lord and Lady Piermont,' the butler announced.

Xavier's parents.

When they were introduced to Rhys, they reacted with pleasure.

'But we know Rhys!' Lady Piermont exclaimed. 'He is like one of our own.'

Lord Piermont pumped Rhys's hand. 'Good to see you here, my boy.' He looked around to anyone who was in earshot. 'This man saved our son's life on the battlefield.'

'Good to see you both.' He bowed to Lady Piermont. 'Ma'am. Your son is here. He is about somewhere.'

'Is he?' She immediately began scouring the room. 'Oh, do let us find him straight away.'

They quickly moved through the rest of the receiving line and hurried off in search of their son. Xavier was fortunate in his parents, Rhys had always thought.

More names began to blur as other guests arrived. Suddenly Ned seized Rhys's arm. 'She is here!'

'Who?' he asked.

But Ned leaned across him to speak to his parents. 'She is here. The young lady I told you about.'

Lady Westleigh looked interested. Lord Westleigh looked as bored as Rhys felt.

'Lady Gale. The Dowager Lady Gale. Miss Gale,' the butler announced.

'She looks like an angel,' Ned murmured.

Rhys glanced over and froze.

The first woman approaching the reception line stopped suddenly. She was not looking at Rhys, but at Lord Westleigh. Shock and dismay filled her expression.

He glanced at Westleigh, who showed not the slightest sign of recognition.

Lady Gale greeted Lady Westleigh cordially. She moved on to Westleigh, who appeared as uninterested as she was cold.

Westleigh gave his desultory introduction. 'May I present my natural son, Mr Rhysdale.'

She turned to him.

'Rhys,' she mouthed.

Rhys took her hand and applied more pressure than would have been polite. 'Lady Gale.'

She fixed her gaze somewhere in the vicinity of his neckcloth. 'Mr Rhysdale.'

'Hurry up, Celia,' the older woman with her snapped. 'You are blocking everyone.'

The older woman passed by Rhys without a word, as she did Ned and his brother and sister. Ned had already left the line to go directly to the young woman announced as Miss Gale. She was already speaking to Lady Westleigh.

'Mama. Papa,' Ned said. 'May I present Miss Gale to you. You have heard me speak of her, I am sure—'

While they spoke with Miss Gale, Rhys turned back to Celia. She met his glance, but there was no pleasure on her face. She, instead, looked horrified.

His attention was called back to Miss Gale, as Ned presented him to the young lady. Her attention to the family, including to Rhys, was more pointed than any other person going through the line.

Once the young woman had finished exuding her pleasure at meeting Phillipa and moved away from the line, Ned said to none of them in particular, 'There is the lady I wish to marry.'

Who was she to Celia? A stepdaughter? A sister-in-law?

A few minutes later a Lord Gale went through the line. Celia's husband? Had she lied to him?

As the man offered Rhys a limp hand, Rhys said, 'Your family precedes you. They went through the line a few minutes ago.'

Lord Gale did not look him in the eye. 'My cousins?' he said. 'Yes, they would be here, would they not?' He shot a scathing glance towards Ned, who was too happy to notice.

Rhys was relieved.

One thing was for certain. As soon as this receiving line was finished, he would speak to *Lady Gale*.

Celia pressed her hand against her stomach. It felt as if someone had knocked the wind out of her. Twice. She could not even think about Rhys at the moment.

She stopped her mother-in-law. 'Lady Gale, did you know that Neddington was Lord Westleigh's son?'

'Certainly.' Lady Gale sniffed. 'Everyone knows that.'

Everyone except Celia, of course. She'd merely accepted the young man's title without thinking what title his father carried.

She was never meant for London. In that her husband had been entirely correct.

Adele caught up with them. 'I hope they liked me. Do you think they liked me, Celia?'

'I think they liked you,' Celia answered by rote.

'The natural brother seemed respectable enough, did he not?' Adele went on.

Rhys had looked incredibly handsome in his formal clothes. Pristine white breeches and linen. Impeccably tailored coat. How she'd missed seeing him as soon as she was in the doorway was a mystery. Except she'd caught sight of Westleigh and could see no one else.

They were all connected. Adele. Westleigh. Rhys.

'And I adored Phillipa.' Adele was oblivious to Celia's distress. 'I thought her scar was not very evident at all.'

Goodness. Celia had not even noticed.

Lady Gale ignored Celia completely and latched on to one of her cronies. Adele begged to join her friends, obviously eager to pour over each minute detail of her introduction to Ned's family. Celia retreated to the wall. At least her malaise had left her, but now her stomach ached with a different sort of pain.

She glanced back to Rhys at the same moment his eyes found her. Her skin heated and she could feel the tension that fairly raced across the room between them. Matters had changed between them.

Xavier Campion crossed in front of her. She held her

breath. He paused for a moment and his eyes widened ever so slightly.

He bowed and walked on.

Her heart pounded. Had he recognised her? He had never seen her without her mask, but she would wager his had been a look of recognition.

Finally the reception line broke up. Ned made immediately for Adele.

And Rhys came directly to her.

'Lady Gale.' His eyes seemed to bore into her.

'Rhys.'

The music started and Lady Westleigh announced the first dance, taking Lord Westleigh as her partner.

Celia could not even look at Westleigh. It was difficult enough to disguise her abhorrence of him beneath her mask at the gaming house—how was she to do so as a possible family connection? How could she bear being around any of them, knowing he was behind them in the shadows?

How could she again be with Rhys, knowing Westleigh was his father?

'You never told me Westleigh was your father,' she said in a low voice. 'You knew what he did to my father.'

'You never told me you were Lady Gale.' He gazed out to the dance floor as if engrossed in the couples forming for the dance. 'I did warn you about Westleigh.'

She smiled as if they were merely passing pleasantries. 'You acted as if you disdained Westleigh. That does not fit with this family camaraderie.'

He turned to her. In spite of herself her breath caught at how handsome he looked. 'You make an excellent point and I agree with you. I do disdain Westleigh, but I cannot explain here and now why his bastard is suddenly introduced as a son.' He extended his hand. 'Would you do me the honour of this dance? I suspect these people think me deficient in all the social graces.'

'I usually do not dance,' she said.

He held his hand in place. 'Help me, Celia.'

She glanced into his eyes and put her hand in his.

They joined the line and faced each other.

The music began—'Miss Moore's Rant,' a country dance.

Rhys and the other gentlemen bowed to the ladies, who curtsied in return. Then they joined right hands, forming a star with the couple next to them and turning. They completed the figures, changing sides and moving one place down the line.

When she'd been a mere spectator to this dance, Celia appreciated the symmetry. The dancing couples moved like petals falling from a flower.

Inside the dance was an entirely different experience. She was aware only of Rhys. How he turned. How effortlessly he moved. How he gazed at her when the figures brought them together again. He did not look as if he gave any of the steps a single thought, but performed them as if it were as natural as walking down a country path.

His lovemaking was like that, she realised. Confident, natural and so very excellently done. Her senses came alive at the memory of it. When their hands touched, even gloved, she could feel his bare fingers on her flesh. When his gaze caught hers, she remembered how his eyes darkened at the height of their passion.

They reached the bottom of the set and had to stand out one sequence. Celia's body still felt alive to him. She fanned herself with her hand. It was too bizarre to feel so aroused by him after learning who he was, whose blood flowed through his veins.

She glanced away from him.

To her surprise she glimpsed Xavier dancing with Lady Phillipa. Adele, of course, was Neddington's partner and looked the very picture of delight. How could Celia spoil that for the girl even though it now connected Adele to Westleigh?

Lord Westleigh also danced, but she turned cold at the sight of him.

Rhys leaned towards her. 'Do not allow him to dampen your enjoyment.'

It was time for them to move up the line.

Any further pleasure she might feel from dancing with Rhys was spoiled by glimpsing Westleigh, who was like mould spreading through a bowl of fruit, spoiling everything she loved.

The dance moved her apart from Rhys.

When they came together again, he said, 'Is Miss Gale your sister-in-law?'

It was the sort of question a dance partner might ask to further an acquaintance, but everything they said to each other was now replete with hidden meaning and more questions. 'She is my stepdaughter.'

The dance ended and the couples scattered off the floor.

Rhys escorted her back to where they had been standing. He bowed to her. 'There is much more to say, is there not? You will come to the gaming house later?'

Before she could answer, Hugh Westleigh, whom she had so briefly met in the receiving line, approached them.

'Lady Gale.' He bowed perfunctorily to Celia before turning to Rhys. 'Father wants you in the card room. Apparently several gentlemen are eager to have you play.'

Celia recognised Hugh as another frequent visitor to Rhys's gaming house. The family certainly supported Rhys's enterprise, did they not? At least the family connection explained why Neddington attended the gaming house even though he did not gamble.

Rhys nodded and turned to Celia. 'Thank you again, Lady Gale.'

Rhys followed Hugh through the dancers gathering for the next set. They walked out of the ballroom.

Hugh turned to him. 'Smart of you to dance.'

'Was it?'

Hugh was probably surprised he knew the steps.

'And to ask Lady Gale,' Hugh added as they walked back to the hallway.

'Oh?' Rhys had been certain asking Celia had been unwise. 'And why is that?'

'Surely you noticed Ned is besotted with her stepdaughter.' Hugh spoke with sarcasm. 'Lady Gale would certainly not want to offend the family by refusing you.'

Rhys took hold of Hugh's arm and pulled Hugh back to face him. 'I am accustomed to your insults, Hugh, but Lady Gale does not deserve them.'

He expected Hugh to flare up in anger. Hugh's face turned red, but he averted his gaze. 'By God. I did not realise...' He looked back to Rhys. 'Accept my apology, Rhys. You behaved decently.'

Rhys could not help but smile. 'Almost like a gentleman, I suppose?'

Hugh's mouth twitched as if he'd contemplated smiling. 'Precisely like a gentleman.'

'Did you think I meant to embarrass all of you?' Rhys asked.

Hugh faced him. 'That is exactly what I thought.'

'Then you do not know me.' Rhys released him.

'None of us know you, do we?' Hugh responded in a low voice.

* * *

Rhys did not see Celia again until the night grew late. Half the gentlemen at the ball were frequent patrons of the Masquerade Club and were eager to engage its proprietor in play.

The aristocracy foxed him. Ned and Hugh were certain they would be ruined if the *ton* knew they owned a gaming hell, but he, their bastard brother, somehow earned cachet for the role.

Although he'd bet none of these gentlemen would want him to marry their daughters.

As if a gambler should marry at all.

He returned to the ballroom and immediately found Celia. She stood against the wall near her mother-in-law who was chatting to another lady. He watched her.

He'd never guessed that she belonged to the world he scorned, the world he wanted to join merely so he could turn away from it.

Xavier came to stand beside him. 'Did you win?'

'Enough to impress.' He had learned long ago the benefits of not winning every hand. 'I want them to come back to the gaming house.'

'Wise man.'

'How have you been occupying yourself while I was in the card room?' Rhys asked.

Xavier shrugged. 'Dancing, of course.'

'Careful,' Rhys warned. 'These young ladies will think you are looking for a wife.'

Xavier looked completely serious. 'Perhaps I am.'

Rhys was taken aback. 'Are you serious?'

He shrugged. 'I am merely humouring my parents, who would so like to see me settled.'

Rhys said, 'They were more than gracious to me, as they always are.'

Xavier nodded. 'They are excellent parents, I would say.' Which made it all the more mysterious to Rhys why Xavier rarely saw them and rarely attended events that would include him in their circle. Xavier had come to this ball at Rhys's request, not his parents'.

Xavier glanced around the room. 'It has been a much more interesting ball than I had imagined, has it not?'

Rhys's eyes narrowed. 'What is your meaning?'

Xavier gave him an intent look. 'I recognise her, Rhys.'

Xavier knew? Had any others recognised her?

A waltz was announced.

Xavier cocked his head. 'I am engaged for this dance.'

He walked quickly away to where Lady Phillipa stood alone.

Rhys hesitated only a moment more before striding directly to Celia.

He bowed to her. 'Another set, Lady Gale?'

She hesitated and her mother-in-law's face flushed with disapproval.

She suddenly said, 'I'd be delighted, sir.'

He took her by the hand and together they joined the circle of couples forming for the dance. The music began and, facing each other, Rhys bowed and Celia curtsied.

Rhys put his hands on her waist and Celia rested hers on his shoulders. He remembered their first lovemaking when she'd rested her hands in just this way. Their gazes caught and he swirled her into the dance.

No wonder many thought this dance scandalous. The intimacy of moving as one, touching with hands and eyes, left the illusion of being alone on the dance floor, even as the circle of dancers rotated like a wheel.

He was reminded of their lovemaking, of watching her face as pleasure built inside her, her skin flushing, her lips parting. He wished they were this moment in his bed rather than in this ballroom. He did not know how a respectable widow justified an affair with the proprietor of a gaming hell. The secrecy enabled it, he suspected.

They did not speak during the dance; nor did they change position, even though there were several different holds that could be used in the waltz. Rhys saw only Celia. At the same time he fancied he was losing her, that this was their goodbye.

He wanted to hold her tighter, closer, and never release her.

But the music concluded and he blinked as if waking from sleep.

He reluctantly released her. 'Come to me tonight.'

She stepped back. 'I—I do not know.'

He stiffened. Perhaps he'd been correct about the goodbye. 'We need to talk…about who you are, who I am. Will you come?'

She averted her gaze. 'Yes.'

He walked her back to where her mother-in-law stood. 'I bid you goodnight, then.' He leaned to her ear and whispered. 'Until later.'

Chapter Eleven

When Celia walked in to the game room that night, Rhys caught Xavier. 'Watch the room, will you?'

Xavier, for once, did not lecture. He merely nodded.

Celia had transformed herself from the very proper aristocratic widow to the slightly scandalous, mysterious and masked Madame Fortune. Not only by her costume, its deep red more theatrical than the pale green gown she wore to the ball, but by the way she carried herself with a seductive confidence. At the ball she made herself fade into the background, unnoticed apparently, although to him, there had been no other women present.

It was like that in the gaming house, as well. Other women attended, some masked, some not, and he was not blind to the fact that some left with gentlemen patrons. For Rhys, though, Celia was the only one worth a second glance.

He moved through the game room to where she was chatting with other gamblers. Her gaze flicked to him and back to the others.

He touched her arm. 'Madame? May I have a moment of your time?'

She stiffened. 'Certainly.'

He escorted her out of the game room and together they climbed the servants' stairs to his private drawing room.

He closed the door behind them.

She pulled off mask, no longer looking like Madame Fortune or the Lady Gale of the ballroom, but a woman ready to fend off an attack. 'It is good you approached me. Better we discuss this right away. Do we start with who you are or who I am?'

'I think it more to the purpose to talk of who you are.' He lifted a decanter. 'Some port?'

'Please,' she responded.

He poured them each a glass.

She took the glass of port and he noticed her hand trembled. 'Why is it more to the purpose to discuss who I am? Why is that more important than discovering that my lover is Westleigh's natural son and my stepdaughter is being courted by his heir?'

He took a gulp of his drink and set down his glass. 'Because it makes your being here more of a risk.' He moved closer to her and grasped her arms. 'Xavier recognised you. What if others do, too? Your reputation—'

Her eyes widened, but she quickly recovered. 'If your friend wishes to expose me, there is little I can do now, is there?'

He tightened his grip on her. 'He will not expose you, Celia. But if anyone else guesses who you are…it is already known we are lovers. A lady cannot take the owner of a gaming hell as a lover without tarnishing her reputation.'

Her eyes gleamed like the coldest emeralds, but behind them he could see her pain. 'My reputation? I assure you, no one cares enough about Lady Gale to even think she has a reputation.' Beneath her bravado he could see her pain. 'Except you, perhaps. You clearly would prefer not to be a lady's lover.'

'Of course I would not.' Could she not see? 'I would not put a respectable woman in such a position. And I certainly would never have offered you employment, had I known you were Lady Gale.'

She lifted her chin. 'You regret bedding me.'

'Never.' He released her. 'You regret bedding me.'

She turned away and walked towards the window. 'Because of Westleigh. I cannot bear your connection to him and this change of heart towards him—'

'There has been no change of heart,' he broke in. 'I detest Westleigh.'

Now more than ever. Once again Westleigh stood in the way of something Rhys wanted. Needed. He could lose Celia.

In this moment Rhys knew, as strongly as he had ever known anything, that he did not want his affair with Celia to end.

She gave him a sceptical glance. 'Do not take me for a fool, Rhys. You just attended a ball which, for all I could see, had the purpose of welcoming you into Westleigh's family.'

'It was not how it appeared.' Rhys could almost hear Xavier's voice: *I warned you...*

'Then why did you do it?' she asked.

He averted his gaze. 'For restitution.'

'Restitution?' She shook her head. 'Your restitution was to *join* his family? I wish to escape him.' She walked towards the door. 'I need to return to the game room.' She turned. 'That is, if I am still in your employ.'

He frowned. 'Celia, it is not worth the risk.'

She straightened her spine. 'My situation is unchanged. I need the money. Does our bargain still hold?'

* * *

Celia kept her posture stiff as she waited for his answer. Inside she felt as bleak as she'd ever felt.

Rhys looked ashen. 'If you wish it, our bargain remains.'

'Thank you.' She donned her mask and walked out, deliberately not looking back at him.

Nothing was settled between them. They'd said nothing to any purpose at all. And nothing made sense.

Her emotions were raw, as raw as if she'd just heard that Westleigh had killed her father. As if she'd just witnessed her mother's last laboured breath. As if she once again heard her own voice speak the marriage vows shackling her to Gale.

She wanted to forget it all, to escape this new pain.

Instead she adjusted her mask and descended the stairs to the game room.

'There she is!' cried one gentleman when she entered.

'Come play hazard, Madame Fortune,' said another. 'We need your luck.'

She straightened and made herself smile. If ever there was a night to lose herself in a game, this was it. 'I hope to be lucky tonight.'

She played hazard, losing more than she won, but still recklessly playing on. The men still cheered her on and bet with her, but one by one they left the table. When she realised they had stopped betting, she woke from the reverie and rid herself of the game quickly.

'Enough,' she said to the croupier.

'Surely one more game will not hurt.'

She looked to see who had spoken. It was Lord Westleigh. She felt a wave of nausea, but forced herself to greet him congenially. 'You are later than usual, are you not?'

He bowed. 'I am flattered you noticed, madam.' His

words were slurred as if he'd imbibed too much wine. He picked up the dice. 'One more roll?'

She waved him away. 'No more hazard.'

He placed the dice back on the table. 'How about *vingt-et-un?*'

She glanced around the room, but did not see any likely partners for whist. At least at *vingt-et-un* she would not have to face him across a table. 'Very well. *Vingt-et-un.*'

She allowed him to escort her to the *vingt-et-un* table. He walked unsteadily. Another gentleman and a masked lady were playing against the dealer. Celia and Lord Westleigh joined them.

Celia ignored Westleigh as best she could and concentrated on each turn of the cards, remembering which had been played and calculating the odds of her being dealt what she needed. It worked. She recouped some of her losses and almost forgot her pain.

Then she would glance up and her eyes would inevitably turn to wherever Rhys stood. Her pain would return.

At least she won as often as Westleigh lost. She suspected his vanity was wounded that a mere woman was more skilled than he.

The dealer dealt them each one card down, one up. Westleigh peeked at his hidden card and tapped the table. The dealer placed another card on his pile and his face fell. Celia requested another card and won.

Westleigh glanced around the room as if looking for someone. 'I fear I must leave you, my dear. Unless you desire more of my company?'

She did not look at him. 'I'm winning. I want to play.'

He grunted and staggered off, unsteady on his feet. She had no time to feel relief at his absence.

Xavier joined the table.

'It seems your luck holds here, as well, Madame Fortune,' he remarked.

'Indeed!' she said with false cheer.

He distrusted her, she knew. And now he was a threat.

He was also as skilled as she at the game, and, ironically, she suspected it was her skill that made Xavier distrust her.

Could he not accept that she was good at cards? And now, after nearly a month of playing several nights a week, she was even better than before. She made money nearly every night, and, so far, she'd been able to stay mostly in control.

She suspected Xavier had noticed every single time the gaming fever overtook her. He watched her that closely.

The dealer reshuffled for a new game and Xavier leaned towards her, speaking low. 'So we meet twice in one night, do we not, my lady?'

She nodded. 'You recognised me.'

'Yes.'

She glanced around. 'Please say no more.'

He merely smiled his charming smile at her.

The dealer asked Celia to cut the cards and she tried to turn her attention to the game, but her concentration failed her.

After losing three hands in a row, she gathered her smaller pile of counters and told the dealer, 'That is all for me.'

Xavier left the table at the same time. Without being too obvious she followed him to a corner of the room where a servant served wine and other spirits.

When she was certain no one else could hear, she said to him, 'I beg you, sir. Tell no one who I am.'

He did not smile this time. 'I will not.'

She nodded. 'Thank you.'

The scent of the wine made her stomach feel queasy and she was so exhausted she could not stand on her feet. She excused herself to Xavier and made her way to the supper room. Westleigh was there, sitting with a group of gentlemen. She stayed clear of him and made her way to the sideboard where she chose the blandest food she could find.

She chose a table alone and one far from Westleigh, but, to her dismay, he left his table and joined her. 'Would you like some company, madam?'

She did not feel friendly. 'No. I will not stay long. I just needed something in my stomach.'

He lifted his wine glass. 'As did I.'

She glanced down at her plate, thinking he would leave, but he lowered himself into the chair adjacent to hers.

He took a big gulp from the wine glass in his hand. 'Perhaps you wonder why I mostly play only the table games.'

She bit into her biscuit and swallowed lest she retch in front of him. 'I had not.'

She had noticed that he played whist infrequently; thus she'd had few opportunities to revenge her father by winning Westleigh's money.

He leaned towards her. 'It is a secret.' His breath smelled of the wine.

She waved her hand in front of her nose. 'I see.'

He wagged a finger at her. 'You must tell no one.'

She broke off another piece of biscuit. 'Do not tell me.' She did not want to share confidences with this man.

'I am certain I can trust you,' he slurred.

He steadied himself by gripping the back of her chair. It was nearly an embrace. Or a trap within his arms.

He again leaned towards her ear. 'I mostly play games where the losses go directly to the house, not to the other players. Do you wonder why?'

She shrank back, but could not escape him. 'No, I do not.'

He leaned away and gestured expansively. 'I own this place. It is mine.'

Ridiculous. 'Rhysdale owns this place.'

He lifted a finger. 'Rhysdale is my natural son, you see. Everything is in his name, but only to protect my reputation. It was my money that bought this place.'

She did not want to believe him. She did not want to believe that Rhys kept this information from her. She did not want to believe that Rhys was merely Westleigh's figurehead.

She swallowed her piece of biscuit.

Westleigh went on. 'So, you see, if I lose at the tables, the money goes right back into my pockets.'

She pressed her fingers to her now-aching head. 'How very clever of you, my lord.'

He seized her hand. 'I can be clever at other things, if you will allow me to show you. There are rooms upstairs, you know.'

She gaped at him, horrified, and pulled her hand away. 'How dare you speak to me in that manner! Surely you know, as well as everyone else here, my attachment is to your son.'

He did not even have the grace to look contrite. 'My dear, the son is nothing to the father.'

A wave of nausea washed through her. She clamped her hand against her mouth.

One of the gentlemen from the table where Westleigh had previously sat called to him. 'Wes, we are leaving. Are you coming with us?'

He looked at Celia with regret. 'I might as well.' He seized her hand again and kissed it. 'I will say goodnight, madam. You must let me know if you change your mind. I can make it quite worth your while.'

Worth her while? He would pay her as if she were a common prostitute?

'Leave me, sir,' she said in a clipped tone.

As soon as the men left the supper room, Celia rose and went up another flight to Rhys's private rooms. She glanced to the floor above. Were those rooms for Lord Westleigh's use? The idea sickened her.

Rhys noticed when Celia left the game room, but could not follow her at that moment. It was late before he could get away, so late, in fact, the patrons were leaving. Even Xavier bid him goodnight.

Cummings manned the door and would know if she had left.

Rhys made his way to the hall. 'Did Madame Fortune leave yet?' Rhys asked.

'I didn't see her,' Cummings said.

She must be waiting upstairs. Rhys had not expected her to stay. His tension eased and he took the stairs two at a time. He checked the drawing room, but she was not there. He hurried to his bedchamber and opened the door.

She was seated on a chair, resting her head against her hand, her eyes closed.

He crossed the room to her. 'What is it, Celia? Are you ill?'

She raised her head and it seemed that all colour had left her face. 'I waited for you.'

'I am glad.'

Her eyes narrowed. 'Do not mistake this. I waited to tell you what Lord Westleigh said.'

His spirits fell. 'What did he say?'

She stiffened. 'He said you are working for him. That this gaming house is his, not yours.'

Rhys clenched his fist.

Her voice turned raw. 'I will not be back, Rhys. I will not work for Westleigh. I cannot. I detest him!'

Rhys walked over to the side table and poured himself a brandy. 'He lies, Celia. I own this place. It is mine.' He gripped the brandy glass so hard he thought it might shatter. 'And I detest him, as well. Even more for lying to you. For speaking to you!'

'How do I know what is true, Rhys? I do not know who to believe.' Her hand trembled.

He sat across from her.

'This is the truth, Celia.' He ought to have told her this long ago. 'Westleigh brought the family to near ruin with his gambling and excessive spending. Ned and Hugh came to me, needing a great deal of money quickly. They asked me to run a gaming hell for them. They scraped together the initial investment. In exchange, they receive half of the profits. The property is in my name. I paid back the original investment, but I paid it to Ned. None of it goes to Westleigh. I own the gaming house. I am fully in charge of it. Those were my conditions in agreeing to do this for them.' He paused. 'My other requirement was that Westleigh publicly acknowledge me as his son, something he should have done when I was a child.' He glanced away. 'Or when my mother died.' He faced her again. 'That was why I was introduced at the ball.'

She shook her head. 'It mattered that much to you? To be known as *his* son?' She spat out the words.

He did not answer right away. 'There was more to it. There were many people who were kind to my mother when I was a boy. If the Westleigh estate failed, they would suffer. That was why I agreed to run the gaming house. No other reason.' Except his own desire to make his father beholden to him for something.

'But you wanted him to acknowledge you. You wanted to be known as his son.' Her voice was scathing.

He glanced away. 'I thought it the one thing he would most object to.'

She made a disparaging sound. 'That was your restitution?'

It was time he faced the truth. 'The restitution was for my mother. My birth was the ruin of her life. She might have lived a respectable life if it had not been for me. She might have married, borne legitimate children. She might not have died so young.' His throat tightened.

She leaned towards him and placed her hand on his. 'Oh, Rhys. I am so sorry.'

He'd not told her how Westleigh had left him penniless and alone. He was not trying to win her sympathy. He merely wanted her to understand the truth.

She stood and began to pace. 'I cannot be *connected* to him. I cannot. If I am with you, I will be connected to him. And if Adele marries Ned, I will be connected to him.' She turned back to him. 'I will lose her like I lost... everyone else. Because of him.'

He rose and walked over to her, putting his arms around her. 'He can't make you lose your stepdaughter.'

She took a deep, shuddering breath. 'She will become a part of that family. I would not blame her for it—it is the natural course of things. But I want no part of that family. Or of him.'

'Celia.'

Eventually she melted against him. He wanted to kiss away her pain. He wanted to make love to her and show her that now she was not alone. He would not leave her.

But he had connected himself to the one man she could not abide.

Rhys wished he could open a vein and rid himself of

any Westleigh blood flowing through him. 'Do not let him come between us, Celia.'

She held her head between her hands. 'I cannot think any more. I am so weary. I just want to go home. This night has brought too much back.'

'It is almost time for your carriage,' he said, releasing her. 'I'll walk you out.'

Like so many nights before this, Rhys escorted her outside and waited with her until she was safely in her coach, although this time it felt as if everything had changed between them.

Because of Westleigh.

Chapter Twelve

The next day Adele insisted upon calling on Lady Westleigh, to pay her respects to the hostess of the ball and Ned's mother. Celia's mother-in-law refused to go with her to *that house,* so the task fell to Celia.

She wanted to refuse. She did not want to be in surroundings that reminded her of Westleigh, where there was a chance she might see him and have to pretend to be cordial.

She and Adele were announced to Lady Westleigh and entered the drawing room, which had been transformed into a ballroom only the night before.

Immediately Celia noticed the portrait of Lord Westleigh that dominated the room. She had to see him after all.

'How good of you to call.' Lady Westleigh extended her hand to them and the ladies exchanged greetings.

There were no other callers at the moment, although Lady Westleigh was with her daughter. Lady Phillipa wore her hair pulled back into a simple knot. It made her scar even more prominent.

'Come sit with me, Miss Gale.' Lady Westleigh patted the space next to her on the sofa for Adele. 'Let me become better acquainted with you. Last night I did not have a chance to really converse with the young miss who has so captivated my son.'

'Oh, my lady, I would be delighted.' Adele was in raptures.

'I will pour tea,' Phillipa said. 'How do you take it?'

At first the conversation was general enough to include all of them. Compliments from Adele and Celia about the ball. Comments about the weather and the next society event, an opera that night.

Lady Westleigh was a puzzle to Celia. Such a gracious lady to be married to a man who did not care about taking a life and leaving a family in tatters.

The lady took Adele's hand. 'I should tell you, my dear Miss Gale, that I knew your mother.'

'You knew my mother?' Adele's eyes grew wide with excitement. 'Oh, please tell me something about her. I miss her so terribly!'

Celia turned to Phillipa, allowing Adele to have her private conversation with Lady Westleigh. 'Did you enjoy the ball, Lady Phillipa?'

The young woman picked up a piece of needlework. 'It went well, I suppose. I do not attend many balls, but my mother seemed satisfied.'

She did not answer the question.

Phillipa pushed her needle through the fabric. 'You danced with our—our natural brother, I noticed. It was kind of you.'

'Kind?' He'd been a wonderful dancer.

'No one else danced with him.'

Celia had not seen him ask anyone else to dance. She felt compelled to defend him. 'I found nothing to object to in him.' Except his connection to this family.

Phillipa frowned. 'I did not know of him until lately.'

Celia did not want to make Rhys the topic of conversation. She took a sip of tea and felt the eyes of Lord Westleigh's portrait upon her. 'You danced with Mr Campion, I noticed.'

Phillipa shrugged. 'I suspect his mother or mine put him up to it. Our families have known each other a long time.'

Celia did not know what to say in response to that.

'To own the truth,' Phillipa went on, 'I do not like to attend balls or any of the London events.'

'Will you not come to the opera tonight?' It was the event everyone was attending.

'I think not,' Phillipa said.

At that moment Neddington entered the room. 'Forgive me for intruding, Mother,' he said. 'I merely wished to say hello to Miss Gale and Lady Gale.' He bowed to Celia. 'How do you do, my lady?'

'Very well, Ned. Thank you,' she responded, thinking now that he looked like a younger version of his father. Why had she not seen it before?

He turned to Adele and his voice softened. 'And you, Miss Gale?'

She glowed. 'I am very well, sir.'

Celia felt like weeping. She would surely lose Adele when she married this man.

She would lose Rhys, as well.

She glanced at the clock on the mantel. 'We ought to be on our way, Adele.' They'd been there longer than the typical fifteen minutes.

'Will you allow me to see you to your carriage?' Ned asked.

'Oh, we walked. It is such a fine day,' Adele said.

Ned smiled. 'Then might I escort you both back home?'

Adele gave Celia a pleading look.

'That would be kind of you,' Celia said.

* * *

Rhys prowled around the gaming house like a bear in a cage. He'd felt like a caged beast since the night before, the night of the ball, the event that had changed everything with Celia. How could he have guessed that Celia would be present at that ball? At any ball?

She was nothing like the aristocracy.

He should have told her his connection with Westleigh right from the beginning—especially after she confessed that Westleigh had killed her father.

He'd used that fact as an excuse not to tell her.

Would she come tonight?

He wanted another chance to make her understand.

To ask her to forgive him.

He wandered to the cashier's office and stood in the doorway. MacEvoy was busy with a patron, but Rhys did not need to speak aloud. He merely raised his brows.

MacEvoy shook his head.

She had not arrived.

Rhys spun around, his frustration growing.

Xavier stood there, leaning against the wall, arms folded over his chest. 'Let me guess. Mac told you matters were unchanged since the last time you checked with him. Twenty minutes ago.'

Rhys scowled at him. 'Were you counting the time on your pocket watch?'

'I probably could have set my watch by you.' Xavier straightened. 'Care to tell me why you are pacing the rooms?'

He was in no mood to go into this with his friend and hear again Xavier's cautions. 'I'm merely making certain all is well.'

He pushed past Xavier and re-entered the game room.

A few minutes later, Rhys spied Xavier at the hazard table watching the play.

Rhys wandered over to him. 'It seems slow tonight.'

'Everyone is at the opera,' Xavier answered in a good-natured tone, somewhat easing Rhys's guilt for having snapped at him.

A patron threw the dice on the table.

'Nine!' Belinda called.

'I'm out,' the man cried.

'How do you know everyone is at the opera?' Rhys asked Xavier.

'I called upon my parents today,' his friend replied. 'They were bound for the opera and said that was the entertainment for the evening.'

Rhys nodded. 'Your parents looked in good health last night.'

'As always.'

Xavier's parents were, in Rhys's eyes, a rarity—members of the *ton* who were selfless and generous, and not at all concerned with the status of one's birth. Xavier's brothers and sisters had each found their places in society. Xavier had not.

Rhys noticed Xavier's attention shift and his brows rise.

Lord Westleigh had entered the game room. Celia was at his side, but looked as if she were trying to remove a leech.

'Now what?' Xavier commented.

'Now what indeed,' growled Rhys who crossed the room to get his father away from her.

'Westleigh,' he said in a sharp voice.

His father gave him a contemptuous look. 'Well, well. If it isn't my *son*.'

Through her mask, Rhys saw Celia's eyes reflecting distress. She took advantage of the situation and turned to greet other gamblers who walked in behind them.

'Some whist, Madame Fortune?' Rhys heard one of them ask.

He faced his father. 'What are you about, Westleigh?'

Westleigh made a helpless gesture. 'Whatever do you mean, my *son?*' He smirked. 'Are you fearing I will steal your paramour from you?'

Rhys leaned threateningly into his face. 'Do not plague her. Do you hear me?'

They were attracting some attention, so Rhys walked away from him. He searched for Celia, but she was seated at a whist table with Sir Reginald and another masked couple he strongly suspected were Lord and Lady Ashstone. Ashstone's pockets were deep and Rhys hoped Celia would win a good sum from him.

She raised her eyes and caught Rhys's gaze, but her opponents gestured to the cards and she looked away.

Rhys wandered back towards the hazard table where Xavier was now in conversation with Belinda, the table's croupier, whose complexion had brightened at his attention.

Rhys approached Xavier from behind and heard him say, 'Let me know if anything seems amiss. Especially if Madame Fortune plays.'

Rhys stepped back quickly, but caught sight of Westleigh intently watching the exchange.

Had Westleigh heard Xavier, as well?

Celia should have skipped the gaming house this night. She was so weary. She supposed the constant late hours were taking a toll. She'd come, she told herself, to win more money, but truly, she had come to see Rhys. Except she doubted she could last long enough to see him. All she could think about was sleep.

She struggled to make it through the whist game. Her

play was so badly off that quitting was the only decent thing to do.

'Another game?' Sir Reginald asked eagerly. 'We need a chance to recoup.'

The masked couple playing them were eager to continue.

'By all means,' the lady said with a smile.

Celia scooped up the few counters she had left. 'I must beg off. I fear I am so fatigued that I cannot think straight.'

Her gentleman opponent chuckled. 'All the more reason we wish to play you another game.'

She smiled at him. 'I am no challenge tonight. You both would be bored by me.'

'I suppose you are correct, madam,' the man responded.

She dropped her counters in her reticule and stood. 'Another time, perhaps.'

Her feet felt leaden as she walked to the cashier's room.

She poured out her counters. 'I am done for the night, Mr MacEvoy.'

He looked surprised. 'Early for you, is it not, madam?'

She tried to smile. 'It is, indeed. If—if you think Mr Rhysdale would not wish to pay me, just cash in what is left.'

'You may pay her, MacEvoy,' came a voice from behind her.

Celia turned. Rhys stood there, filling the doorway, his expression indiscernible.

'Forgive me, Rhys. I am so very tired. I cannot stay.' She took four crowns from MacEvoy's hand and placed them in the leather purse inside her reticule.

When she stepped towards the door again, he did not move. She raised her eyes to his and he gave way for her.

But he walked with her to the hall.

'You are fatigued?' He made it sound as if she were making an excuse.

'I am, Rhys. Truly. There is no other reason.'

He touched her arm, an expression of concern on his face. 'How do you plan to summon your carriage?'

She placed the back of her hand against her forehead. 'I had not thought that far ahead.'

He took her arm. 'Come. I'll sort it out for you.'

She was too tired to protest.

They reached the hall.

Rhys said, 'Tell me where your coachman waits for you and I'll send for him.'

She shook her head. 'I do not know where he waits. I think he goes back to the stable.'

'Then I will send for a hackney coach and alert your coachman when he calls for you.'

He'd have to send someone to Piccadilly to a coach stand. It seemed a foolish fuss. 'Rhys, I do not live far from here. Would you have someone walk me home?'

'I will walk you home.' He turned to Cummings and asked for Celia's shawl and his hat and gloves.

When they stepped outside, he asked, 'You do not mind me knowing your address?'

She shrugged. 'You know who I am. It would be a simple matter for you to discover where I live.'

He offered his arm. 'Which way?'

She held on to him, grateful for his strength. 'To Half Moon Street.'

As they walked to St James's Street and turned towards Piccadilly, Celia removed her mask and carried it by its ribbons.

The night air felt cool on her face, reviving her. 'I feel better in the fresh air.'

'Are you ill?' he asked.

'Not ill, I do not think. Tired.' Her limbs felt heavy. 'All I wish is to go to bed.'

Her gaze flashed to him. She realised what she'd said. He simply kept walking.

Finally he spoke. 'The late nights are too taxing for you.'

They hadn't been. She'd been energised by the success of her gambling—and the pleasures of her affair with him. The fatigue came on all of a sudden.

'I just need a little rest, I expect,' she told him.

In spite of herself she relished the feel of his strong arm under her fingers. It reminded her of how it felt to be held by him.

Her body flared merely at the memory and the intensity of her desire momentarily drove away fatigue. She wanted him so desperately she thought of asking him to take her back to the Masquerade and put her to bed in his room.

And remain there with her.

But an image of Rhys standing next to Westleigh, greeting guests in the ballroom, also flashed through her mind. She tried to shake it away.

She broke the silence between them. 'One could almost like London if it always felt like this.'

'Like what?' His voice matched the night.

'Quiet and still.' A carriage sounded in a nearby street, the horses' hooves and the wheels loud even at a distance. She smiled. 'At least, mostly quiet and still.'

He reached over and touched her hand, but released it and kept walking.

They reached Piccadilly and he gestured down the length of the street. 'It is an impressive sight.'

Gas lamps bathed the street in gold and the busy traffic of the day was reduced to a carriage or two. All the dirt of the day was obscured by the night.

'It is lovely,' she admitted.

They crossed Piccadilly.

'But you plan to leave.' He said this as a statement.

'I am not meant for London,' she said.

They fell silent again.

This time he spoke first. 'I want you to stay.'

She stopped and turned to him, but she could not speak. Instead she reached up and touched his cheek.

He clasped her hand and pressed it to his lips. 'I do not want what we've had to end.'

Neither did she. 'Oh, Rhys.'

He pulled her into an embrace and she could not help but melt against him. Encircled in his arms she did not feel alone.

She rested her head against his heart and was comforted by its steady beat. 'I am not leaving yet, Rhys.'

She felt his voice rumble in his chest. 'Then come to me as often as you can, Celia.'

She pulled away, only to nod her head.

She'd endure the contact with Westleigh and risk the intoxication of gambling to be with him a little longer.

They walked arm in arm along Piccadilly, the night wrapping them in an illusion that there was no one else in the world except the two of them. For the first time since the ball, Celia felt at peace.

They approached Half Moon Street. 'My street,' she said.

They turned on to the street and she wished her rooms were at the far end instead of so close to Piccadilly.

'Here.' She stopped, already bereft at parting from him.

He gathered her in his arms again and lowered his head, touching his lips to hers. 'Come to me tomorrow,' he whispered. 'If you feel well enough.'

He kissed her again and desire flamed through her, its

intensity taking more of a toll on her body than her fatigue. All she wanted was to share a bed with him and re-experience the delight of joining her body with his.

She threw her arms around him and hugged him close. 'I will if I can, Rhys,' she cried.

It would be impossible for her to stay away.

Celia knocked lightly on the door to her rooms and listened through it until she heard footsteps approach. 'Tucker?' she called through the door. 'It is Lady Gale.'

The lock turned and the door opened.

Her butler looked surprised.

'Do not be concerned, Tucker.' She walked inside. 'I merely decided to leave early.'

He leaned outside. 'The carriage, ma'am?'

She turned around and glimpsed Rhys walking away, a mere shadow in the darkness. 'No carriage, but I was escorted home. Someone must tell Jonah.'

'I will see to it, ma'am.' He closed the door and turned the lock again.

'You can go to bed early.' She gave a wan smile. 'I am indebted to you for the long hours I force you to keep. Please know how grateful I am.'

He bowed his head. 'I can only admire you, my lady.'

She started up the stairs. Her flesh ached from missing Rhys and her fatigue returned. Suddenly it was like scaling the Alps to reach the first floor.

She opened her bedchamber door and startled her maid.

'Oh!' The woman popped up from a chair. 'I must have dozed. What time is it? Forgive me, ma'am.'

'I do not mind if you doze, Younie.' Celia yawned. 'I am home early. It must only be half-past two. I became so fatigued.'

Younie hurried over to her. 'Are you ill, ma'am? Let me

feel your forehead.' She put the back of her hand against Celia's forehead.

'I do not feel feverish,' Celia responded. 'Merely tired.'

Her maid took her shawl from her shoulders and Celia dropped her reticule and mask on a table.

As soon as she was all dressed and ready to crawl into bed, the door opened. 'Another night of gallivanting, I see.' Her mother-in-law strode in.

Celia turned to her maid. 'You may go, Younie. Goodnight and thank you.'

Younie ducked her head down and walked out of the room.

Celia turned away from her mother-in-law. 'I did not hear you knock, Lady Gale.'

'Well, I didn't knock,' the woman answered without apology. 'Was that the man whose bed you are warming? I saw you with him outside.'

Celia rubbed her temples. 'What were you doing at the window at this hour?'

The older woman pursed her lips. 'Why, waiting to see you, of course. Otherwise I'd be asleep.'

Celia swung around. 'Why? Is something amiss? With Adele?'

Lady Gale put her fists on her hips. 'Nothing is amiss with Adele except having a stepmother who is a strumpet.'

Celia's fingers pressed into her temples. 'So you have merely come to lash me with your tongue. I have no patience for it. Leave me, Lady Gale. I will not discuss my private affairs with you. I cannot tolerate you any longer.'

Lady Gale lifted her chin. 'What will you do? Toss me out?'

Celia speared her with her gaze. 'Do not tempt me, ma'am.'

Her tone must have penetrated, because her mother-in-law turned around and left the room. Celia climbed into bed, but now was so agitated by her mother-in-law that sleep evaded her.

By morning Celia was convinced she was ill. When she woke she felt so nauseated she feared she could not reach the chamberpot in time to vomit. She remained in bed the whole day and begged off from attending the social event of the evening.

She also had Tucker deliver a message to Rhys to tell him she could not come to the gaming house that night.

When she felt equally unwell the next day, as well, she sent a message to Rhys saying she would return when she was recovered.

She missed him. And not only for the lovemaking. She missed watching him walk through the game room watching everything with an experienced eye. She missed sharing supper with him and sharing the trivialities of each night together. She missed being held by him.

Days passed. Sometimes by afternoon, Celia would feel the malaise leave her, but by evening all she wished was to retire early and sleep.

She had apologised to Younie and the housekeeper more than once for not being able to hold down her food and causing them such unpleasantness.

One morning Younie brought her dry toast and tea in bed.

'I do not know why I am not recovering,' she said to her maid. 'I am never ill. Adele thinks I should call the physician, but I keep thinking tomorrow I will feel better.'

Younie put her hands on her hips and frowned. 'You

are fatigued. You have nausea. Do you have any aches or pains?'

Celia coloured. 'It might be shameful to say, but my breasts are sore. I've had aches with ague before, but never in such a part of me.'

Younie cocked her head. 'When are your courses due?'

When were her courses due? She could not remember the last time she had bled. It must have been…several weeks ago. About the time she and Rhys—

She blanched. 'Younie, you do not think?'

'That you are increasing?' Her maid lifted her brows.

Celia covered her mouth with her hand. 'It is not possible!'

In all the time her husband tried to make her conceive a child, she'd failed. Failed. She was barren. Gale had called her barren. Even his physician had called her barren.

She hugged her abdomen. Could it be? Could she have a baby inside her? Rhys's baby?

What a miracle! A blessing.

'Younie! Could it be true? Could it really be true?' Was she truly carrying Rhys's child?

'Time will tell, ma'am, but it is my guess.'

For a moment Celia felt like dancing, but only for a moment. Then the reality of her situation descended upon her.

She was a respectable baron's widow and she was pregnant with her lover's child.

'Oh, Younie,' she cried, 'then what am I to do?'

Chapter Thirteen

Celia was too restless to remain in bed. She rose and dressed. The idea of a baby had firmly taken route and her head spun with wonder and fear.

Fear, because it could very well be that she merely suffered from some sort of stomach malady and her bleeding would start any day. She could so easily suffer a crushing disappointment.

But if it were true? She hugged herself in delight.

She would move to a place where no one knew her, a place where she could present the child as legitimate and no one would question it. Mentally she calculated how much money it would cost to give her child a trouble-free life—

She caught herself making plans and stopped herself. Patience, she cautioned herself. As Younie said, time will tell.

To keep her mind busy, she came downstairs to the small parlour where she kept her desk and papers. Her mother-in-law and Adele were out, so it was a good time to go through the bills that had arrived in the last few days. She counted what she owed and tallied her funds.

Being away from the Masquerade Club had hurt her finances. How could bills mount so swiftly?

She had reworked the figures for the third time when her butler knocked on the door.

'A gentleman to see you,' he announced.

She looked up in surprise. 'To see me?' Callers came to see her mother-in-law or Adele, but never Celia. 'Who is it?'

'Mr Rhysdale, ma'am,' Tucker said.

Her face heated. 'Is he waiting in the drawing room?'

'Yes, ma'am.'

Her heart beat faster. 'I'll go there directly. Bring some tea, though, will you?'

'Immediately, ma'am.' He bowed.

She took a breath and pressed her hands to her abdomen before rising from her chair.

As she approached the open door of the drawing room, he turned and her heart leapt in her chest.

She'd never seen him in daylight.

'Celia.' He crossed the room to her and he took her into his arms.

At the same instant, she closed the door behind her. 'I have been worried over you.' He let go to examine her. 'You look pale. You are still ill. What can I do?'

He could hold her again. She'd desperately missed the comfort of his arms, the warmth of his concern.

Instead she smiled up at him. 'I am better. Truly. It is an odd illness that comes and goes, but I think I am over the worst.'

His strong forehead creased. 'What does the physician say?'

She glanced aside. 'I did not consult a physician. It did not seem so serious.'

He surprised her by wrapping his arms around her

and holding her close. The sheer glory of it made her want to weep.

A knock sounded and she pulled away. 'Tea.'

Tucker entered and set the tea tray on the table.

When he left, Celia said, 'Would you sit, Rhys? I'll pour you tea.'

He hesitated, but lowered himself onto the sofa adjacent to her chair.

A glance at the biscuits Cook had provided and the scent of the tea made Celia queasy again, but she managed to pour for him and for herself.

She quickly took a bite of a biscuit and swallowed it. 'You should not have come, Rhys.'

He frowned. 'Do not say that. I had to see how you went on. There was no way I could ask anyone.' He lifted the teacup, but set it down again without drinking. 'I chose a time when you were unlikely to have other callers.'

She opened her mouth to ask him what he would have done if she'd been abed? Or if Adele had spoken to him? Or, worse, her mother-in-law? But she bit her tongue.

She was too glad to see him. 'I am truly much better. I—I might even come to the club tonight.' She needed to play cards. She needed money. 'How are things there?'

'The same.' He shook his head. 'Not the same. You are missed.' He took her hand in his. 'I have missed you.'

She warmed to his touch.

And thought of the baby inside her.

But it likely was not a baby inside her, but merely a fanciful dream.

His gaze seemed to caress her face and his hand warmed hers.

He stood again. 'I should not stay long, I know.'

She rose, as well, and he reached out and touched her

hair. 'I needed to see you for myself and now that I have—'
He pulled her into an embrace and kissed her.

Passion rushed through her, demanding release. She
hungrily kissed him back, wanting him inside her, wanting to be joined with him and together climb the heights
of pleasure. He pressed her against him and she felt his
male member from beneath his clothes.

Most of all, she wanted to be carrying his child inside her.

He broke off and leaned his forehead against hers.
'Come tonight, but only if you are well enough.'

She nodded.

He stepped away and straightened his clothes. With a
grin and another quick kiss, he walked out of the room.
She ran to the window to watch him leave and catch the
last glimpse of him.

To her horror, she saw her mother-in-law and Adele
approaching.

The front door opened and Rhys walked out just as they
reached the door. He tipped his hat to Adele and Lady Gale
before turning in the other direction and striding away.

A moment later Celia heard her mother-in-law's strident
voice quizzing Tucker.

Celia walked to the drawing-room door. 'Leave Tucker
in peace, Lady Gale. If you have questions, ask me.'

Her mother-in-law marched directly to the drawing room. Celia retreated to the middle of the room and
awaited the assault.

Her mother-in-law slammed the door behind her. 'Was
that Westleigh's bastard son leaving our rooms?'

How detestable her mother-in-law was!

Celia straightened. 'It was Mr Rhysdale.'

'He had the gall to call upon us?' Lady Gale looked
completely affronted. 'How dare he?'

Celia glared at her. 'He did not call upon you. He called upon me.'

The older lady peered at her. Her mouth worked, but no words emerged. She jabbed her finger at Celia. 'I see what it is,' she finally managed. '*He* is the one.'

Celia lifted her chin.

Adele's voice came from the doorway. 'What do you mean, he is the one?'

Celia flashed her mother-in-law a warning look. Adele did not need to know this.

But Lady Gale swung around to her granddaughter. 'He is the one she has been bedding! Imagine it, Adele. He is not only a bastard but a gambler, as well.'

'Lady Gale!' Celia cried. 'You will not speak that way in my presence. Leave the room this instant!'

The old woman tossed her head and in her outrage swirled around as nimble as a nymph. 'That suits me perfectly. I cannot abide the sight of you.' When she reached Adele, she said, 'Come with me, Adele.'

Adele shook her head, instead entering the room. 'What is she talking about, Celia? Is it true? Are you having a—a—liaison with Ned's half-brother?'

Celia put her hand to her abdomen. 'Listen to me, Adele—'

Lady Gale re-entered the room. 'And this illness of yours. This vomiting and fatigue. I know what it is about!'

Celia raised a hand to halt her.

Her mother-in-law took no heed. 'You are pretending to be with child, are you not? What a convincing act. What do you hope to accomplish from that, I wonder?' She marched off again.

Adele stared at Celia, eyes wide, mouth agape. 'Celia! Are you—?'

Celia turned to the girl. 'I do not know why I am ill.'

'You are *increasing?*' Adele was not listening to her. She tried again. 'It is impossible—'

Adele covered her mouth with her hand. 'You lied to me! You said you were gambling. But you were—were—engaging in lewd behaviour. Or were you doing both? Ned told me his half-brother runs a gambling place.' She tore at her hair. 'Oh! Ned! What will he think of me when he finds out? He will despise me. You have ruined everything! You have ruined my whole life!'

'Adele!' Celia raised her voice. 'Stop this nonsense at once.'

Adele covered her ears. 'I will not listen to you ever again!' She ran out the door and her footsteps pounded up the stairs, accompanied by loud sobs.

Celia collapsed into a chair, clutching her stomach, trying to quiet the waves of nausea, rage and fear that swept through her.

When Ned pulled up to Adele's rooms in his curricle, the door opened and she ran out to him. She climbed into the curricle before he could do more than extend his hand to assist her.

'What is it, my darling?' he asked her.

'Oh, Ned!' Tears poured from her beautiful eyes. 'Please just drive. I wish to be away from here. Is there somewhere we might be alone? I do not wish to see another person.'

As a gentleman, he ought not be alone with her, but he could not resist indulging her every request.

'We should walk, then.' They could be more private on foot. 'I can take the horses back to the stable if you wish.'

She threaded her arm through his and leaned against his shoulder.

When something troubled her, Ned wanted only to ease

it, but he did not press her to tell him what distressed her. Better wait until they could be alone.

His horses were stabled at Brook's Mews behind Brook Street. If the stablemen were surprised to see him return so soon, and in the company of a young lady, they gave no indication.

'I will not need them the rest of the day,' he told the men.

He jumped down and reached up to help Adele by placing his hands at her tiny waist and lifting her down. It was so close to an embrace that he felt the blood rush through his veins.

From the mews they walked to the park and found a path leading to a secluded bench overlooking the Serpentine.

'No one will disturb us here, my love,' Ned told her.

She flew into his arms and sobbed against his chest.

'Tell me what is the matter?' he begged, unable to bear this helpless feeling.

'Oh, Ned!' she cried. 'It is all too wretched. I must tell you, because I would not hold back anything from you, not for the world. You must know all, even though—even though—' She shuddered. 'You will despise me and I know you will never want to marry me.'

He became very alarmed. 'Come. Sit with me and tell me what it is.'

He led her to the bench. When they sat, he kept hold of both of her hands.

She took a deep breath. 'I come from a wretched family.'

Was that all? No family member of hers could be more wretched than his father.

'Today I discovered that my stepmother—although I never call her that—she is Celia to me. More like a sister, really, than a mother—' She waved a hand in front of her mouth and was too overcome to speak.

He used a soothing voice. 'I am sure it cannot be as bad as all that.'

She gulped. 'It is worse. I discovered—I discovered today that dear Celia—although she cannot be dear to me now—not after this…' She paused and held her hand against her chest. 'Celia is having an affair with your brother.'

'My brother!' He gaped at her. 'Hugh?'

'Not Hugh,' she snapped. 'Rhysdale.'

'Rhysdale?' He could not wrap his mind around it. 'But did they not just meet at the ball?' Comprehension immediately dawned. 'Oh, my God. She is…' He could not say it.

'She is gambling, as well. She goes out to gamble at night. I think that is how she met him.' Her tone was so disdainful that he dared not tell her why he knew precisely how her stepmother knew Rhysdale.

He collected his wits. 'Adele, this is not so dreadful. Surely Lady Gale has been discreet. And she is a widow. Widows are allowed some licence.'

She gazed at him with wonder. 'Do you mean you will not despise me for this?'

He put his arm around her and held her close. 'I could never despise you. It has nothing to do with you.'

'Oh, you are too wonderful.' She sighed against him and he revelled in the feel of her in his arms.

It almost made him forget the complications Rhys and her stepmother created.

'Oh…' She suddenly sounded more despairing. 'But you have not heard the worst of it.'

It could get worse?

She pulled away. 'Celia is going to have a baby.'

* * *

Celia returned to the Masquerade Club that night, but in turmoil, not anticipation. She felt more agitated than she'd been that night of the ball.

Adele refused to speak with her and Celia had been unable to explain to the girl that she could not be increasing. It was impossible. Wasn't it?

Celia had absolutely no idea how to tell any of this to Rhys. How could she say anything until her fears were confirmed once more—that she did not and could never have a child growing inside her?

'Good to see you, madam,' Cummings greeted her as he took her wrap. It was the most he'd ever spoken to her.

'I am pleased to be back.' She hoped it was wise to have returned. Her spirits were extremely low and she was still very tired.

MacEvoy grinned when she entered the cashier room. 'There she is at last. We've missed you, Madame Fortune.'

It touched her that her absence had been noticed, even in this devil's den.

MacEvoy handed her the counters with a friendly wink. 'I'll expect more from you later.'

'I will endeavour to please you, then.' She smiled and dropped the counters in her reticule.

As she approached the door to the game room, she adjusted her mask. She was dressed as she'd been the very first night she'd come here. Only then she'd not known that her heart would leap for joy to catch sight of the man who ran the establishment and that sharing his bed had taught her more about pleasure than she'd ever dared imagine. How unfair of fate to pair him with all that was dark and painful in her life.

But, then, fate had never been kind to her.

She pressed her hand against her stomach and stepped across the threshold.

The noise in the room swirled around her. She scanned the room looking for Rhys, but all she saw were men with red faces and bulging eyes playing at the gaming tables, a few women, masked and otherwise, hanging on to them with every throw of the dice or play of a card. At the card tables players kept emotion out of their faces, but their postures were tense and she knew nerves were exploding inside them.

There was nothing pleasant in view, nothing happy or peaceful. But as much as the scene revolted her sensitive stomach, another part of her was impatient to play.

A man broke away from the hazard table and approached her.

Lord Westleigh.

'Madame Fortune!' He seized her hand and kissed it. 'You have returned! I've despaired of ever being in your company again. Come, play hazard with me.'

She was due for losing at this game; she just knew it. But there was little chance she could avoid it. Others joined him in begging her to roll the dice.

'Very well,' she said, feigning enjoyment.

Another man cried, 'Madame Fortune is back! Quick. To the hazard table.'

The crowd around the hazard table grew larger as she walked closer.

'Shall we allow Madame Fortune to roll next?' Westleigh said loudly.

'I'll give it up.' The man in possession of the dice dropped them into Westleigh's hand.

Westleigh immediately gave the dice to Celia. 'Roll and make us all rich, Madame.'

She rolled, calling out, 'Six,' but made seven. She rolled

the second time and made seven again and won. The men and women around her cheered and a thrill rushed through her.

She continued to roll and to win more times than she lost. The betting was high and the winners feverish with excitement. Celia forgot she was tired, forgot that she loathed the sight and sound of gambling, forgot that she'd been looking for Rhys.

But soon it was as if a London fog parted and she suddenly saw him, watching her through the crowd like he'd watched her that first night.

She rolled a losing number.

Amidst the groans of defeat, she lifted her hands. 'That is enough for me, gentlemen!'

Westleigh scooped up the dice. 'One more roll, Madame. Have pity on us.'

She stepped away. 'My luck is turned. It is time to stop.' And time to see Rhys.

The players closed ranks around the hazard table and play continued without her. She backed away and felt a hand on her shoulder.

'Celia.' It was Rhys.

She turned to face him.

His expression was all concern. 'Are you feeling well enough to be here?'

She wanted to say her illness was merely the effect of carrying his child inside her, but that was no more than a foolish dream, one she'd dreamed before and been disappointed. She could say nothing to him about a mere foolish dream.

A week. If another week went by and she did not have her menses, she would dare to believe in it. She would tell him then.

'I am still tired.' And queasy. 'But I think it is a little better today. I need to be here. I need to play.'

He turned impassive. 'Then I will leave you to play. You no longer require my assistance gaining partners.' He stepped away.

She placed a hand on his arm to halt him. 'May I see you later?'

His eyes darkened and she felt the air between them grow alive with desire. 'Come to my room when you are ready.'

Rhys walked away from her, but turned to watch her. She remained where they'd stood together for a moment, before strolling through the room, greeting others and stopping for brief chats. Finally she joined three others for whist and he was satisfied that she was well settled.

Xavier came up to him and turned to look in the same direction as Rhys. 'She has returned, I see.'

The two friends had achieved a sort of truce while she'd been ill, but now Rhys heard something in Xavier's voice that put him on guard.

'Her illness is improved,' Rhys said in as matter of fact a tone as he could muster.

'She won at hazard again.' Xavier's voice was mild, but Rhys knew his message. 'Quite a winning streak. Unlike any we've seen these last few days.'

Rhys faced him. 'Your meaning?'

Xavier backed away. 'No meaning. A mere observation.'

In spite of himself, Rhys's suspicions were aroused and he played a version of Xavier's discourse in his head. There was still much Rhys did not know about her. How many more secrets had she kept from him? She needed money. Maybe her need was so great she was driven to cheating.

She was skilled enough to know how. Her father had been accused of it.

He stopped himself.

Her father had been killed because of cheating. Certainly that alone would serve as a caution to her. Besides, he did know her. In an intimate way, where secrets were harder to keep.

He glanced towards the doorway and saw Ned and Hugh advancing directly on him.

He met them halfway.

'We would speak with you,' Ned demanded.

Hugh looked as if he were ten years old again and ready to throw the first punch.

Rhys nodded. 'Let us go somewhere private.'

He led them up to his drawing room on the floor above.

Once inside the room, he closed the door. 'Now what is it?'

'How could you do this?' Hugh spat. 'It is abominable even coming from the likes of you.'

Rhys's brows rose. 'Perhaps you might tell me what it is I have done.'

Ned faced him squarely. 'Lady Gale is with child and you are the father.'

It was like a blow direct to his gut.

For a second Rhys could not even breathe. But he knew better than to give away his utter shock. He kept his face still, his expression bland. They obviously held all the aces and he had nothing.

'Who told you this?' He kept any emotion from his voice.

'Miss Gale,' Ned responded. 'And her distress over the matter is sufficient reason for me to call you out.'

Rhys merely raised his eyes to him. 'Are you calling me out, Neddington?'

Ned backed off. 'No. Of course not. But this is badly done of you, Rhys.'

Hugh's hands curled into fists. 'Haven't you done enough to our family?'

Rhys turned his steely gaze on him. 'You are forgetting who you came to when the family needed rescuing.'

'See here—' Hugh shot back.

'Stop it, Hugh,' Ned snapped. He faced Rhys again. 'Do you deny this? That you have been engaging in an affair with Lady Gale, who we now know must be Madame Fortune? That you have got her with child? A respectable woman from a respectable family. Think what this will mean to her stepdaughter.'

'To her stepdaughter?' Rhys laughed. 'You malign both Lady Gale and Madame Fortune and your concern is solely for the stepdaughter?'

Ned's eyes flashed. 'Miss Gale is my sole concern. Do you deny what we say?'

Hugh broke in. 'What are you going to do about it?'

Rhys made himself look blandly from one brother to the other, while inside he was furious with their implication that he was not worthy of a respectable woman. He was furious that they would criticise Celia as if her behaviour would somehow soil her stepdaughter's virginal mind. Mostly he was wounded to the depths of his soul that Celia had not told him herself that she carried his child.

Finally he spoke. 'If any of this were true, I fail to see how it is your concern. Do not come here and shout insults at me and to ladies who are not present to defend themselves. And stop spreading gossip like a set of garrulous hags.'

'Everyone knows you are having an affair with Madame Fortune!' Hugh cried.

Rhys countered, 'They suspect. They do not know.'

Hugh sprang at Rhys.

Ned held his brother back. 'Are you denying this, Rhys?'

'I am not crediting any of it with more comment,' Rhys replied in a firm voice. 'One thing I will tell you. Do not speak with Madame Fortune about this. I will not have you throwing out accusations and speculations against patrons who have chosen to be masked and anonymous. You will keep silent on this manner or you will answer to me. And, do not forget, you need the money I provide to you.'

'It is our money,' Hugh cried. 'We invested everything we had left in this.'

'And I have paid back that investment,' Rhys responded. 'We are even now.'

'You still owe us!' Hugh leaned into Rhys's face.

Rhys pushed him away. 'If I hear one more word of this from anyone else, I'm holding you responsible and these doors will be closed to you.'

'But this is our gaming house!' Hugh cried.

Rhys swung so close his face was inches from Hugh's. 'This is my gaming house. That was the bargain. I decide who may enter and who will be banned.'

Ned pulled Hugh away. 'We've said our piece. Let us go now.'

Rhys drove them towards the door. 'Remember my warning. Keep silent on this or answer to me!'

They left the room and he slammed the door shut behind them.

Chapter Fourteen

With Ned and Hugh gone, Rhys had no need to hold in his rage. He prowled through the room, wishing he were in some seedy tavern in the East End so he could pick a fight and break some furniture, smash some glass.

Why had she not told him?

With a growl he pulled the door open and ran down the stairs, slowing only when reaching the last step. Cummings glanced up at him in surprise.

'Cummings, ask Madame Fortune to come upstairs as soon as she is able,' he ordered.

Cummings gave him a queer look, but nodded.

Rhys returned to the drawing room to pace and contemplate what in the room he might smash against the wall.

She said she was barren.

Had she lied to him about that? To what purpose? Having a child would shame her and, in his station of life, make no difference to him.

Except it did make a difference to him.

He gripped the back of a chair.

No child of his would come into the world in shame. No child of his would bear the burden of being called bastard.

It seemed a long time until he heard her footsteps on the stairs. He waited in the doorway.

She climbed the stairs wearily and a wave of worry washed over him. She was still ill.

She glanced up and saw him waiting for her. 'Rhys?'

He turned and re-entered the drawing room.

She followed, pulling off her mask. 'What is it, Rhys?'

He supposed he looked like thunder. He composed his face. 'Neddington and Hugh just called upon me.'

She gave him a wary look. 'And?'

He stepped close to her and leaned even closer. 'They said you are carrying my child.'

She blanched. 'I—'

He seized her arms for a moment, but immediately released her. 'Were you planning on informing me of this fact?'

'It—it cannot be a fact,' she countered. 'I was told by a physician that I am barren, that I would never conceive.'

He seethed. 'Then why say so to Miss Gale?'

'Adele,' she whispered in an exasperated tone. She raised her head to Rhys. 'I told her it could not be true, but she would not listen.'

He held her arms again and looked down into her eyes. 'But it is true, is it not? Tell me now.'

She glanced away. 'I can only say that—that I am late in bleeding.'

'Then it might be true,' he persisted.

She bit her lips and pain contorted her features. 'It might be,' she said in the tiniest voice.

He made an angry sound and released her again, swinging away and putting some distance between them.

Celia reeled under the force of his anger, so unexpected. So crushingly disappointing.

She blinked away sudden tears and straightened her spine. 'Do not concern yourself, Rhys. If it is true, I ask nothing of you. I have enough money to care for a child.' Or she would after a few more weeks of gambling.

He swivelled back, fire shooting from his eyes. 'Do you think I am trying to shirk responsibility? Is that the sort of man you think I am?'

She was taken aback. 'Why else be angry about my possible condition?'

He seized her wrists and pulled her close. 'I am angry you did not tell me. You might have done so this morning when I called and we were private. I am angry that you excluded me from this.'

She tried to pull away. 'How could I say a word of it when everything I know speaks against it?' Her throat grew tight. 'I cannot hope it is a child.'

He released her, his expression full of pain. 'You do not want it to be true.'

The grief of many years' duration enveloped her once again. 'I want it to be true with all my heart.'

He reached out to her again, this time tenderly touching her arm. 'Then we have no conflict, no scandal. We can marry. You and our child will want for nothing.'

'Marry?' No. Never. Marriage was misery, a prison.

But this was Rhys. She might wake every morning in his arms, see his smile when sunshine filled the room. She might walk with him to the shops, sit next to him at the opera, share every meal with him across the table from her.

A knock sounded at the door and Cummings's voice carried into the room, 'Mr Rhysdale. Come. There is trouble in the game room.'

He looked at her with regret. 'We'll continue this.'

He left with Cummings, leaving the door ajar. Sounds

of raised voices reached her ears. She tied her mask in place and followed him.

From the game room door the scene unfolded.

One man lunging after another, Xavier and another man holding him back. 'You took my money! All of it! I am ruined! It is out of all fairness!'

The other man leaned threateningly towards him. 'Are you calling me a cheat? I play a fair game!'

Rhys stood between the two. 'We'll have none of this. No fighting.' He turned to Xavier. 'Take him away.' To the other man, Rhys said, 'Calm yourself, sir. I suggest you cash out and leave. Tempers are too high at the moment.'

'I won't be accused of cheating!' the man cried. 'I demand satisfaction.'

'I will have you banned if you do not calm down.' Rhys pushed him away. 'He is upset at losing, nothing more.'

Xavier and the other man dragged their charge out of the game room. As they passed by Celia, the man continued to wail, 'I am ruined! What am I to do? I am ruined.'

Rhys meanwhile stuck with the other man, waiting for him to pick up his counters and a vowel written by the loser. He walked with the man past Celia, out the door, presumably to the cashier.

The other patrons turned back to their games and soon the sounds of wins and losses returned in its familiar cadence. Celia grew cold as she watched their faces. At the hazard table all eyes were riveted on the roll of the dice. At *vingt-et-un,* the players were spellbound by each turn of a card, at faro, the dealing box. Yet one man's life was ruined and another man was willing to risk death for some dubious code of honour.

The room held perhaps seventy players and it seemed to Celia that each of the men wore her father's face. She closed her eyes only to see him again returning home with smiles and gifts, swinging her mother around and swearing that life would be easy from then on. She blinked and he was now weeping into her mother's lap, begging for forgiveness for losing money for rent, for clothing, for food.

Lord Westleigh sidled over to her. 'Might I interest Madame in some more hazard? A little luck is in order, do you not think?'

She gaped at him. The scenario played out before her eyes a moment ago might have been the way it had occurred with her father. Did not Westleigh remember that night? Should she ask him if her father won? Was that why Westleigh accused him of cheating? Was that why her father had challenged him to a duel? Should she ask how it felt for Westleigh to shoot the pistol and see her father fall? Or how he lived with himself for merely running away? He'd hid behind some gentleman's code of silence and had never been held accountable for the crime.

'No hazard, sir,' she managed.

'Then let us have some supper.' He took her arm.

She recoiled. 'No!'

He gripped her harder. 'Come now, madam, you must know I have developed a regard for you. You would do very well to take advantage of that fact.'

'Take advantage!' The very sight of him sickened her.

'I would pay handsomely for some...private time with you. You would not regret the money or the experience.' He leered at her.

'Release me, sir,' she demanded. 'I'll not bear your insults.'

He pulled her closer. 'Do not say you prefer that bastard Rhysdale? He is nothing compared to me, I assure you. A mere hireling. You cannot prefer him to me.'

She lowered her voice, so angry at him it trembled. 'How dare you call him a hireling! And I do prefer him to you. I prefer any man to you. Do not ever approach me again. For any reason.' She wrenched out of his grasp and walked out of the game room.

He caught her in the hall and pinned her against the wall, leaning down into her masked face. 'You will regret rebuffing me, madam. I have ways of retaliating against such insults.' His mouth stretched into a malevolent grin. 'Perhaps I will unmask you. You would dislike that, wouldn't you.'

When he let go of her to reach for her mask, she pushed hard on his chest, knocking him off balance.

She hurried to get away from him. As she neared the cashier's office. Rhys had entered the hallway, escorting the winning gentleman out. He gave her an apologetic glance, but she could not meet his eyes, nor tell him what just happened to her at the hands of Westleigh. She walked into the cashier's room.

MacEvoy looked up at her. 'Cashing out, Madame?'

'Yes.' She could hardly speak.

When she made her way to the hall, Westleigh was nowhere to be seen.

Xavier emerged from Cummings's coat room.

'Is Rhys in there?' she asked.

'He is. He is calming the fellow down,' Xavier responded. 'Do you wish me to get him for you?'

She shook her head. 'But I must beg a favour from you.'

'Of course.' He inclined his head graciously.

'Walk me home.'

It took all of an hour to calm Mr Poole enough to release him to go home without the intention to kill himself on the way. It also took a loan from Rhys of one hundred pounds, money Rhys suspected he would never see again.

But he did not want the pall of suicide hanging over his

gaming house. Besides, the man had a wife and children. They should not have to pay for the man's sins.

Poole had to endure a strong lecture from Rhys regarding the duty a man owed to his children. It was a lecture that had special meaning to Rhys now and he was eager to settle matters between him and Celia.

As soon as Poole walked out of the house, Rhys ran upstairs to the drawing room, but Celia was not there. He checked the bedchamber. She was not there, either.

He returned to the hall.

Cummings stood in his usual place.

'Did you see Madame Fortune?' he asked.

Cummings shook his head.

Rhys checked the game room, the supper room and the cashier. MacEvoy told him she'd cashed out.

He returned to the hall just as Xavier opened the front door and entered.

Xavier held up a hand. 'She asked me to walk her home.'

'Did she say why?' Was she ill again?

Xavier walked over to him. 'She barely said a word. Something upset her. That was evident.'

He waited for Xavier to say more or to indicate that her leaving was somehow proof that her intentions were nefarious, but Xavier said nothing.

Rhys's impulse was to rush out and run to her rooms to demand to speak with her, but it was nearly three o'clock in the morning.

He would see her when it was day and a civil time to call. He'd not wait a moment longer to discover why, after he had proposed marriage to her, she fled from him.

Chapter Fifteen

Ned spent the morning poring over his father's accounts with his father's secretary, attempting to decide which bills to pay and which to defer. Thanks to Rhys, the task was now tedious rather than desperate.

It was a task his father ought to be performing, but, ever since Ned and Hugh had discovered the dismal state of their financial affairs and confronted their father with it, their father had washed his hands of his responsibility, as if the bearers of the bad news were responsible for the problems.

Now, though, Ned had even more to worry over. Rhys had not confirmed or denied an affair with the younger Lady Gale, nor even if Lady Gale was Madame Fortune, which Ned strongly suspected. It agonised Ned that he and Hugh had managed merely to muddle matters rather than rescue Adele from this vexing problem.

Ned tallied a list of numbers for the third time, getting yet another total, when the butler knocked on the door.

'What is it, Mason?' Ned asked.

Mason bowed. 'Your mother requests your presence in her sitting room.'

What now? Ever since Rhys called that day and made

certain his mother was informed of the crisis, she'd demanded to know every detail of every decision he and Hugh made. And every problem they encountered.

He did not wish his mother to know this new scandal Rhys had created, not when it so involved and affected Adele.

He handed the ledger to the secretary and left the library to climb the stairs to his mother's private sitting room.

To his astonishment, when he opened the door to enter, she was there, his Adele, sitting next to his mother on her chaise longue.

'Adele!' He went straight to her, clasping her hands in his and looking into her beautiful eyes.

'Do sit, Ned,' his mother said impatiently. 'Miss Gale has been telling me an extraordinary tale. We wish to know what you have done about it.'

Adele's lip trembled. 'I have told your dear mother *everything*. I simply had to talk to someone and I could think of no one but her.'

'I see,' he said non-committally. He'd wanted to handle it without his mother's intervention.

'Did you speak to Rhysdale about it?' his mother asked. 'He must marry Lady Gale, of course. I hope you told him so.'

He frowned. 'Rhysdale would not speak to us of it. He called it gossip and all but tossed us out.'

'It is not gossip!' Adele cried. 'It is my life! I know that Celia is going to have a baby. Our maid verifies that it is so...' She paused as if reconsidering her words. 'Or, rather, she admits it is *possible*. Celia has all the signs, Younie said. You can ask her yourself. She came with me.'

Ned's brow knit in confusion. 'Lady Gale is with you?'

'Not Lady Gale!' Adele rolled her eyes. 'Younie. Our ladies' maid.'

His mother waved a dismissive hand. 'Rhysdale denies it?'

Ned shrugged. 'He did not confirm or deny it.'

'Then it must be true.' His mother nodded with certainty.

That logic escaped him.

'What I cannot understand...' Adele put a finger to her flawless cheek '...is how it could be true? How can Celia be carrying a baby when she was barren all those years with my father?'

'Maybe it was your father who could not...' how to put it delicately? he wondered '...father a child.'

Her eyes grew wide. 'But...but there is me! I am proof there was nothing wrong with my father.'

'Not necessarily so,' interjected his mother.

'What do you mean?' Adele turned to her.

His mother did not answer right away. 'I told you that I knew your mother, did I not?' she finally said.

Adele nodded her head.

His mother went on. 'She confided in me.' She gave Adele a very sympathetic look. 'Your mother was unhappy in her marriage to your father.'

Adele's expression darkened. 'I know that. My father was not a nice man. I remember him shouting at her when I was a little girl.' She glanced away in thought. 'He shouted at Celia, too.'

Ned's mother patted her hand. 'He was a cruel and thoughtless husband.' She grasped Adele's hand. 'You mother sought comfort elsewhere.'

Adele looked appalled. Ned wished his mother would stop. Surely this was no comfort to the poor young woman.

His mother went on. 'One Season, here in Mayfair, she fell in love with a fine gentleman, an army officer of good family, but nothing else to offer anyone. They had several months of happiness before he was sent to the Continent to fight the French.' She continued to hold Adele's hand. 'When news came to her that he'd died fighting the French in Holland, you were already growing inside her.'

Adele's eyes widened. 'Do not tell me!'

His mother turned very sympathetic. 'I am sorry to tell you, my dear.'

Ned reached over and took Adele's other hand. How difficult this must be for her. Had she not had enough to bear?

Adele squeezed his hand and broke out into smiles. She looked from his mother to him and back to his mother again. 'Oh, this is marvellous news. I disliked my father very much. I am glad I am not his daughter. I only wish I could have known my real father—' Her voice cracked and tears fell from her eyes.

'I will tell you all I know of him, but this is enough for one day,' his mother said to her.

Adele hugged his mother and all Ned could wish was that he could feel her arms around him, as well, but that, of course, would not be proper.

Perhaps if he could contrive to see her alone?

She glanced at him and concern filled her lovely face. 'Do you object very much, Neddington? I mean, I am not really the daughter of a baron. Does this change your opinion of me?'

He seized her hand again and pressed it to his lips. 'Nothing could change my opinion of you.'

His mother clapped her hands as if summoning recalcitrant children. 'We are still left with the problem of Adele's stepmother and Rhysdale. Perhaps I should call upon Lady Gale and speak to her about this.' She turned to Adele. 'As your future mother-in-law, it might be seen as my duty.'

Celia sat in her bedchamber nibbling on toasted bread and sipping tea. The events of the night before returned to her mind, even though she wanted to banish them. Rhys's offer of marriage. The nightmare that was the gaming house. Its winners and losers.

Lord Westleigh.

Her stomach heaved and she quickly bit down on another piece of toast. The queasiness was manageable as long as she could keep some food down.

Her butler knocked on the door. 'A word with you, ma'am?' he asked.

'Come in, Tucker,' she responded. 'What is it?'

'Ma'am, I thought you should know that the new Lord Gale is at this moment in the drawing room. I am of the impression that the Dowager Lady Gale summoned him. They are in deep conversation about something.'

Celia pressed her fingers against her temple.

'What is she up to now?' she said below her breath. She looked up at Tucker. 'Is Adele with them?' Had Lady Gale not given up the scheme to marry Adele off to her cousin?

'No, ma'am,' replied Tucker. 'Miss Gale went out with Younie a while ago.'

Where would Adele have gone with Younie? That was a worry. Adele had been so upset with Celia the previous day she would neither speak to nor listen to Celia. Who knew what she was thinking today?

Celia stood. 'Thank you, Tucker. I will attend to it.'

Tucker left and Celia sat at her dressing table and hurriedly twisted her hair into a chignon. She pinched her cheeks to put some colour into her face and rushed out the door, not caring if her morning dress was presentable enough for Cousin Luther.

When she approached the drawing-room door, she slowed her pace, strolling in as if by accident rather than design. 'Why, Lady Gale. Luther. What a surprise.'

Lady Gale looked lightning bolts at her.

Luther rose and did not look any more pleased to see her. 'Good morning, Celia. We have been talking about you.'

Her gaze darted to her mother-in-law. 'I dare say you have.'

Luther pointed to a chair. 'Sit down. Now you are here, I wish to talk to you.'

She advanced to the seating area, but stopped some distance from their chairs. 'I prefer to stand.' There was nothing that would entice her to sit and be scolded as if a child.

His lips pursed. 'As you wish.'

Besides, if she stood, he also had to stand. That would make it easier for him to leave.

He shifted on his feet. 'Lady Gale informs me that you have been very indiscreet and that you are attempting to entrap the owner of a gaming hell into marrying you.'

Celia glanced at her mother-in-law. How cruel and heartless could that woman be? First to tell this tale to Adele and now Luther.

Celia put on a bold face. 'Lady Gale has been busy telling stories.'

Luther baulked. 'What? Do you say it is not true?'

She straightened. 'I do not feel compelled to say anything.'

He raised his nose at her. 'As the head of the family, I believe you owe me an explanation for this scandalous behaviour.' He shook his head in dismay. 'Imagine *trying* to marry a gamester. It is the outside of enough.'

A shaft of pain impaled her at the thought that Rhys wanted to marry her. She'd been unable to face him the previous night, but tonight, she must.

Not that Luther had any say in what she did.

'Head of the family?' She shook her head. 'You are not the head of *my* family. I owe you nothing.'

'See here, Celia!' His cheeks puffed out.

Her temper was lost. She went on. 'And if you were any *decent* head of the family, you would take responsibility for those who need your protection. Adele and her grandmother should have been allowed to stay at Gale House, at least until you bring a wife there. Or you should have given them the dower house. What's more, you should have financed Adele's come-out and seen that her future was well settled. Adele and Lady Gale should have been your guests at the town house, not forced into rented rooms.' Her arm swept across the room.

'Celia!' her mother-in-law snapped. 'I will not have you speak to Cousin Luther in that manner.'

She turned her glare onto Lady Gale. 'Do not you speak to me at all.'

Lady Gale drew back as if struck.

Luther pounded the air with his fist. 'Your husband left his property and finances in such a sorry state that I am strained to the limit. You expect me to dole out more money?'

She shot back, 'A baron takes care of those in his charge. Or he should. The title comes with responsibility, not just property.'

Luther fussed at his collar. 'I do not need to stay here and listen to these insults.' He turned to Celia's mother-in-law. 'I planned to make an offer of marriage to your granddaughter, ma'am, but you may rest assured that will never happen now. I wash my hands of the lot of you.'

'Spoken like a true gentleman,' Celia said sarcastically.

For a moment he looked exactly like her husband. He looked as if he might strike her, which Gale had done. Once.

Instead, Luther started for the door.

Celia's mother-in-law rushed after him. 'Luther! You cannot credit anything she says. I beg you to reconsider.'

He threw up his hands. 'I said I wash my hands of you.'

As soon as the two of them had left the room, Celia collapsed in a chair. Her legs trembled, her stomach heaved and she could taste vomit in her mouth. She fought to keep her food down.

She rested both hands on her abdomen. If only this were indeed a baby, then at least she would not be alone.

It would be some comfort.

Celia did not know how long she sat there, but the sounds of her mother-in-law pleading with Luther faded and she heard the front door close. Soon after, the sounds of the mantel clock ticking and an occasional carriage passing by were the only sounds she heard.

The knocker sounded and Tucker's voice reached her ears.

Another caller.

She ought to have retreated to her bedchamber when she'd had the chance, so she might have avoided anyone.

Tucker rapped at the door, still slightly ajar from Luther and Lady Gale's hasty departure. 'A gentleman to see you, ma'am.'

She turned, knowing instantly who she would see.

He stepped into the room. 'Hello, Celia.'

'Rhys.' She rose. 'Do come in.'

He walked towards her and the air changed around her. Her body came alive to him with a yearning she knew could never be satisfied. Why should this man capture her heart, of all men?

'I will skip the niceties, Celia.' His face was serious. 'Why did you leave last night? What happened?'

She turned away. 'I do not know how to explain.'

He took her arm and turned her back. 'I suggest you

try.' His eyes flickered with pain. 'Explain why you left me moments after I told you I will marry you.'

She opened her mouth in an attempt to explain what settled like a pit of fear inside her, but voices from the hall distracted her.

A moment later the door opened and Adele walked in. Behind her were Lady Westleigh and Ned.

'Celia, Tucker said you were in here—' Adele stopped cold when she caught sight of Rhys. 'Oh.'

A wave of nausea hit Celia, but she had to ignore it. She curtsied, instead.

'Lady Westleigh.' She and Rhys spoke at the same time.

'Lady Gale,' the woman responded. 'Rhys. It is just as well you are here. We ought to get this sorted out.'

Tucker stood at the door, looking apologetic.

'Some tea, if you please, Tucker,' Celia said.

From behind him she saw her mother-in-law approaching. 'I heard voices. Who is here?'

Tucker gave her a sympathetic look before turning away.

Her mother-in-law strode in.

Adele stopped her. 'Grandmama, you must be civil.'

Her grandmother gave the girl a scathing look.

Rhys nodded to her and she turned her head away, instead greeting Lady Westleigh. Ned said a stiff hello to Rhys.

'Shall we sit?' invited Lady Westleigh as if she were the hostess.

Adele and Ned sat together on the sofa. Lady Gale settled in one chair and Lady Westleigh in another.

Both Rhys and Celia remained standing.

'To what do we owe the pleasure of your visit?' Celia asked Lady Westleigh.

'Adele told me about this situation of yours,' the lady answered. 'I will help devise a plan that will minimise any scandal to the family.' She turned to Rhys. 'Rhysdale, you are crucial in how we must manage it.'

Celia felt him stiffen as her ladyship spoke.

'Adele has been busy,' he remarked in a low voice only Celia might have heard.

Lady Westleigh went on. 'Now, the only thing to do, of course, is for you to marry—'

'Do not be ridiculous,' Celia's mother-in-law piped up. 'This is all a sham. She is not increasing. It is impossible. She is unable to conceive. It is a proven fact.'

Rhys put his hand on Celia's arm, a steadying gesture that surprised her as much as her mother-in-law's unrelenting abuse.

Lady Westleigh immediately swung to the dowager. 'Why do you say that, ma'am?'

The older woman straightened. 'Because my son told me so. A physician confirmed the diagnosis.' She inclined her head towards Celia. 'She was a great disappointment to him.'

Lady Westleigh shook her head. 'I dare say the problem was not your daughter-in-law's, but your son's.'

Celia's mother-in-law huffed, 'Of course it was not my son's problem. He already sired a daughter.'

'Grandmama,' Adele broke in. 'Papa was not my real father. My mother gave birth to me after a love affair with an officer.'

Her grandmother clasped her heart. 'It isn't so—' She protested in every way manageable.

But her words did not penetrate through the blood pounding in Celia's ears. She touched her abdomen. She'd been so afraid to hope, but now hope turned to possibility and possibility to certainty. The magic and wonder of it made her want to throw herself in Rhys's arms. He'd given her this life growing inside her. There was no other man she would rather be the father of her child.

Her mother-in-law's words finally penetrated. 'My son was a virile man. Her womb was as dry as an old woman's!'

'Ma'am!' Rhys gave Celia's mother-in-law a fierce look. 'I demand you apologise to her. Do you hear me? I will not tolerate it.'

'*You* will not tolerate it?' her mother-in-law went on. 'You dare speak to me that way when you are nothing but a—'

'Bastard?' He said it for her. 'Madam, none of us choose our birth, but we do choose our behaviour. I've known women forced to live on the streets who have more grace and kindness than you.'

Lady Gale gave a disparaging laugh. 'I wager you would know countless women who live on the streets—'

'Lady Gale!' Celia cried. 'Leave this room now or I will have Younie pack your trunk and I will personally escort you out of the house.'

Adele shrieked and covered her mouth with her fist.

Her mother-in-law rose and, grumbling outrage and insults, flounced out of the room.

As soon as the door closed behind her, Lady Westleigh again spoke. 'Well, that was unpleasant. But perhaps now we can address the problem at hand.'

Rhys put up a hand. 'No, Lady Westleigh.'

Celia quickly added, 'I appreciate your concern, my lady, but I have no intention of discussing anything.'

'Lady Gale—' Ned sounded outraged '—this affects Adele and that reason alone gives me the right to speak with you about this. My mother, as well.'

Celia turned to him. 'I am not going to discuss it with you or your mother. Adele should have come to me first.'

She turned to her stepdaughter. 'I tried to speak with you yesterday, you recall.'

Adele crossed her arms over her chest. 'I did not wish to speak with you.'

'No, you preferred the ravings of your grandmother to anything I might say.' Celia gave her a penetrating look. 'And then you carried tales about me.'

'See here, Lady Gale,' Ned cried. 'She came to me and to my mother. There is nothing to object to in that.'

They were Westleighs and Celia wanted nothing to do with any of them. If it made Adele happy to join that family, so be it, but Celia was not obligated.

'Your family is not my family,' Celia said to Ned. 'Adele should have respected that.'

'You are maligning my dear Ned,' wailed Adele.

'She is not maligning Ned,' Rhys broke in. 'Stop acting like a child.'

'See here, Rhys!' Ned pressed his hands into fists and leapt from his chair.

Celia faced him. 'Ned, if you had an ounce of sense in your head, you would marry Adele now. You'd get a special licence and marry without delay. I dare say even with your financial difficulties, you have more resources to care for her than I have. You do not even have the courage to officially declare yourselves betrothed. It is wrong to leave her in such a precarious position.'

Ned fumed. 'I have good reasons! Besides, you cannot tell me when Adele and I should marry. That is for us to decide.'

Celia nodded. 'And you cannot tell me what I should do. That is for me to decide.'

Lady Westleigh stood. 'Your point is well taken, Lady Gale. We have been unforgivingly presumptive. Do forgive us.' She turned to her son. 'Ned, we should take our leave.'

He gave his mother a pleading look. 'I would like some time to speak with Adele.'

Celia turned to Rhys. 'Would you escort Lady Westleigh home?'

He gave her a questioning glance.

She spoke more quietly. 'I will see you later. We can talk then.'

Celia needed time. Time to think of her child, time to think of what was best to do.

Rhys bowed to Lady Westleigh. 'Ma'am, I would be honoured to escort you.'

Lady Westleigh nodded to Rhys. 'I accept. That is very kind of you.'

'I'll walk you both out,' Celia said.

As they stepped out of the room, Tucker approached with the tea tray.

Celia shook her head. 'We do not need tea now, Tucker. Lady Westleigh and Mr Rhysdale are just leaving.'

He nodded and carried the tray back to the hall and placed it on a nearby table. He went to retrieve Lady Westleigh's wrap and Rhys's hat and gloves.

Rhys took Celia aside. 'Come tonight, Celia. We must talk this out.'

She nodded, but did not know what she would say to him when the time came.

Chapter Sixteen

That night Rhys told Cummings to send Celia up to the drawing room as soon as she arrived and to summon him immediately.

She arrived at her usual time and Rhys left the game room to go to her.

When he entered the drawing room, she was standing in the centre of the room, waiting for him. In the candlelight her white shimmering gown made her look as if she were a vision created from his dreams.

She smiled tentatively. 'Do you think we will be disturbed this time?'

He frowned. 'Not for anything.'

He walked over to her as if under a spell, his body craving her almost as much as his soul. He did not wish to need her so much. He prided himself on not needing anyone. If one was alone, one had nothing to lose. Suddenly he risked losing this woman.

And their child.

He would never do what his father did. He would never abandon her or their child.

Rhys tried to pour all those emotions into an embrace.

She sighed and melted against him and, as their bodies entwined, the need to join with her grew to an even greater intensity.

He bent his head and placed his lips upon hers in a hunger that shocked him.

But her returning kiss felt like regret.

He broke away from the intense contact and held only her arms. 'I have missed you, Celia.'

Her lips trembled. 'I have missed you, too.'

So why had she left after he'd proposed marriage to her?

He released her and walked over to the decanter on the table. 'Brandy or port?'

She pressed her stomach. 'Neither. Just the thought of spirits makes me feel out of sorts.'

He turned back to her. 'You are still ill?'

'I am now thinking it might be because of a baby,' she said. 'My ills are expected, I am told.'

'Do you now believe you are increasing?' He poured himself some brandy.

'Yes.' She walked over to the table where his stood and fingered the wood. 'Lady Westleigh made me dare hope.'

'Hope?' He was more confused than ever.

Her eyes filled with tears. 'It is a miracle for me.'

He gulped his brandy and stared directly into her eyes. 'Then finish what we started this afternoon. Explain why things are not right between us.'

She turned away.

He drained the contents of his glass and pressed on. 'Explain why you will not simply say you will marry me and give our baby my name. Is it because of my birth?'

She turned in surprise. 'Not at all. I never even thought such a thing.'

'Then why?'

She averted her gaze again. 'I do not know how to say it.'

His insides twisted in pain, but he kept his expression blank. 'Celia. Just say it.'

She took a breath. 'I went down to the game room. And the men there—the ones you were sent to deal with—it was so much like what happened to my father and Westleigh.'

He could see that. 'You must know, though, that what happened had nothing to do with you or me.'

She held up a hand to stop him from interrupting. 'After you took the men out of the room, everyone went back to gambling as if nothing had happened. One man ruined. Another wanting a duel. And they all went back to the games. And then Westleigh came up to me and wanted to play hazard...' She stopped.

Westleigh.

What was she not telling him? What had Westleigh done?

'What did Westleigh do?' His voice deepened to a growl.

She made a nervous gesture. 'Nothing.'

He did not believe her.

She paced in front of him. 'It is merely that—that this is your world. It connects you to Westleigh, but I cannot be connected to it.'

He burned inside. 'You connected yourself to it.'

'Yes,' she admitted, 'but before I knew of him. And out of necessity. I needed—still need—the money. I loathe this—*him*—I loathe all this represents.'

'I am here out of necessity, as well.' Did she think he was given a choice? It was gamble or starve. 'But you are being less than truthful. You enjoy the play.'

'That is it,' she agreed. 'That is the seduction. The fever. It robs everyone of their senses. It is what killed my father.'

'I am not your father, Celia.' Rhys never played cards with emotion. 'Cards are nothing more than a tool to me.

A means to an end.' Survival once; now something more. 'I know when to play on and I know when to cash out.'

She shook her head. 'You cannot control luck, Rhys. No one can. All it takes is a turn of luck. I've lived this all during my childhood. I'll not subject my child to such a life.'

'And if I said I would give it all up?' He'd always intended to give it up. He had figured three years would do the trick. By then the Westleighs' fortunes would be solid and he would be wealthy enough to buy a factory or a ship or something.

She gave him a direct look. 'Do you know how many times my father promised to give it up?'

He stepped towards her, seized her arms and held her gaze. 'There is a difference between those men like your father and those like me. I am a gambler because when I had nothing, it was an honest way to get food to eat. When I won, I ate; when I lost, I didn't. I learned how to win. I learned how to survive and eventually I learned how to thrive. I will not go backwards. So do not hold up my gambling as a reason not to give your child a father.'

She averted her face. 'There is another reason.'

'And that is?'

She met his eye again. 'Westleigh. You are connected to Westleigh.'

He let go and swung away. 'He should not be considered at all!'

She would refuse to marry him because he was fathered by Westleigh? How ironic. When a boy he'd hoped his father would once call him son. Now that he accomplished it out of spite, doing so meant losing the woman he loved and a child he could call his own.

Rhys felt the pain of it as if a thousand sabres cut into his flesh. 'Westleigh keeps you from me? Am I again to be punished because of my birth?'

She reached out to him with sympathy on her face. 'Not because of your birth. Because you chose to entangle your life with his.'

He turned away, too angry at her—at himself—to trust what he would say or do next. 'Then we are done here.' He looked back with a sardonic smile. 'I must return to my gaming hell.'

She picked up her mask. 'Do you object to me playing tonight?'

That she would gamble after that speech of hers, after rejecting him for his gambling life, a life that was providing her needed funds, was a final sabre thrust.

'You are still in my employ, Celia.'

He walked out.

She'd hurt him and it agonised her. Almost as much as having to turn away from him for the sake of her child.

Rhys was a good man, a man to love. She'd never know his like again and her heart shattered at the thought that she had rejected him when she wanted him more than she could bear.

It was the gambling she did not want, *could* not want around her child. She could not bring a child into the sort of childhood she'd endured.

Gambling, its seductions and its perils, was the real villain. Now it had dealt her another blow. It had robbed her of the man she loved.

Celia tied the mask to her face and peeked in the mirror above the mantel to see if it concealed her identity well enough. The bone-weariness she felt tonight had little to do with her condition. She was exhausted from the battle she'd waged inside herself, the battle her heart had lost.

She walked down to the cashier's office and picked up her counters. She made her way to the game room, pausing in the doorway while its sounds and sights enveloped her. Lifting her chin, she walked through the room, looking around.

Looking for Rhys.

She found him conversing with a masked woman and her partner at whist. He lifted his gaze to her as she moved past him and her heart ached inside her chest.

'Madame Fortune!' a gentleman cried. 'Come! Play some hazard. I'm in need of a little luck.'

Some others joined his plea.

A man came up to her from behind and leaned into her ear. 'Do play hazard, my dear. See if your luck still holds.'

It was Lord Westleigh.

She straightened her spine and took another man's arm. 'If you insist. I will play hazard.'

Her first roll was a loss and the dice passed to another player. When it came around to her again and she reached down to scoop up the dice, Westleigh beat her to it.

He took the dice in one hand and grasped her hand in the other, dropping the dice into her palm.

'Best of luck, Madame Fortune.' He smirked.

She expected to lose again, but she won the toss.

A shout rang out from the crowd, 'Madame Fortune has found her luck!'

The next bets placed were overwhelmingly with her next roll. Westleigh bet with her, as well.

With the crowd's enthusiastic encouragement, she rolled again and again, not always winning, but more often than not. More often than seemed likely. In spite of herself, it roused her excitement and she was eager for the next roll. Even Xavier's intent scrutiny did not deter her. The counters piled up and more and more players pushed their way to place their bets.

Rhys appeared next to Xavier, watching her play. She

froze, dice in hand. She might be winning, but she was losing him a great deal of money. Bets were already placed and her next roll called. She had no choice but to roll, telling herself she'd stop after this.

She'd called seven and the dice fell into a three and a four. A cheer went up and the wagerers collected their counters.

Westleigh picked up the dice from the table and bounced them in his palm. 'They are weighted!' he said in a loud voice. 'I declare. The dice are weighted.'

She stared at him.

'Watch,' he said pointedly to Rhys and Xavier.

He placed one die on its corner and tried to make it spin. It fell immediately to the number four. He tried to spin the other die. It, too, failed and fell to a two.

Loud rumblings went up from the crowd.

'Weighted dice,' Westleigh intoned.

The voices grew more outraged.

'But, I never—' Celia tried to protest.

Rhys broke in. 'The hazard table is closed.' He walked around the table and seized Celia's arm. 'Come with me, madam.' He inclined his head to Westleigh. 'You, too, sir.' He turned to Belinda. 'Pay the winners, then you and Xavier come find us.'

'Rhys, I did not cheat,' Celia tried to tell him. He nearly dragged her through the room. 'I know nothing of fixing dice.'

But she did instantly understand her part in it. She'd chosen favourite numbers, not realising that the dice themselves were training her which numbers were more likely winners. She also knew that Westleigh had somehow planted the dice.

But why would he do such a thing? It lost money for the house and his family if he planted weighted dice.

Xavier had suspected her all along, though. He often watched her at hazard and she'd even admitted to him that she counted cards at *vingt-et-un*. Counting cards was not cheating, precisely, but it did put her in a class beyond the typical player.

As they reached the door, Ned and Hugh were walking in. 'What is this?' Hugh asked.

His father looked triumphant. 'She was caught cheating.'

Ned gaped at her. 'Cheating!'

Rhys led Celia to the hall. Westleigh and his sons followed.

Cummings became very alert when they all strode in.

Rhys said to him, 'We will be in my private drawing room. Tell Xavier and Belinda to come to us there.'

'Yes, sir,' Cummings responded.

Rhys practically dragged her to the room where he had just embraced her and kissed her and where she had spurned him.

Once inside the drawing room with the door closed, Ned blurted out, 'My lady, what more scandal are you going to bring to your family?'

His father's brows rose. 'My lady? Who is she?'

Celia did not want Westleigh, of all people, to know her identity, but, even more, she did not wish for someone other than herself to reveal it.

She pulled off her mask.

He looked at her blankly.

'Do you not recognise her?' Ned looked aghast. 'She is Lady Gale.'

Westleigh still appeared mystified.

'Miss Gale's stepmother,' Ned tried. 'You met them both at the ball.'

'He still doesn't know!' groaned Hugh.

Westleigh protested, 'I cannot be expected to recall every person ever introduced to me.'

Celia broke in. 'Perhaps he would know me better as Mr Cecil Allen's daughter.'

Westleigh's eyes flickered with comprehension.

'Yes,' she said in a low voice. 'I hoped you would remember him.'

Xavier and Belinda walked in the room.

'Sit, everyone,' Rhys said.

Westleigh shot him a withering glance, but did as he was asked. He turned to Ned and Hugh. 'She was using weighted dice at hazard. I dare say the house had some big losses.'

'If the dice were weighted, I knew nothing of it,' Celia retorted.

'I didn't know.' Belinda turned to Rhys. 'I put out new dice each night, as you ordered.'

Westleigh pointed to Xavier. 'You suspected Madame-whoever-she-is, did you not? You've watched her play.'

Xavier nodded. 'I did suspect her.'

Celia looked from him to Rhys. 'I do not cheat. It was not me.'

Rhys and Xavier both remained standing and Rhys gave nothing away in his expression.

He had every reason not to believe her. He knew she needed money, knew she was the daughter of a gamester, knew her father had been accused of cheating.

She also had hurt him.

'Who, then?' Hugh asked.

Rhys's brows rose.

Celia turned to Belinda. 'Have I always won at hazard?' she asked.

Belinda's forehead furrowed. 'Mostly.'

'But always?' Celia persisted. 'Was there not a time I did not win so much?'

The young woman seemed to be thinking hard. 'Only for a little while once.'

'What was different about that time?' she asked.

Belinda shrugged. 'I can't think of anything.'

Celia leaned forwards. 'Was Lord Westleigh with me that time?'

'When you lost?'

Celia nodded. 'When I lost.'

Belinda glanced away. When she turned back, she said, 'I can't remember him there that time.'

Rhys picked this up. 'When Westleigh was there, did he touch the dice?'

'What is this?' Westleigh sounded outraged. 'Do not accuse me. I am the one who showed you it was she who played the bad dice.'

Rhys turned to him. 'Where would she procure the dice?'

Westleigh's eyes shifted as if he was composing the answer. 'Why, from her father, of course. He was a cheat.'

Xavier looked pensive. 'Westleigh was always with her. He was always asking her to play hazard. And he always touched the dice.'

'You cannot remember all that!' Westleigh raised supplicating hands. 'Besides, what reason would I have to cheat? The profits come to me anyway. I have no motive to steal from myself.' He laughed, but his laugh rang false.

Belinda looked puzzled.

Hugh glared at his father. 'Except that the profits are under Ned's control, not yours. You have no money except what Ned gives you. You are cheating to have more money to gamble with!'

'You cannot prove that.' Westleigh pointed to Rhys.

'You just want to blame me. You sleep with her. Everyone knows that. You are behind this. So you can keep her in your bed.'

Rhys appeared to ignore him. 'It should be easy to discover proof,' Rhys said to the others. 'Whoever has the original set of dice is the culprit.'

Celia stood up and stretched her hands out to her sides. 'Search me.'

Rhys walked over to her, and, as he did so, she removed her gloves and handed them to him. There were no dice in her gloves. She had no sleeves in which to hide the dice.

Westleigh harrumphed. 'She would not put dice in her gloves. She dropped them down her dress.'

Rhys signalled to Belinda. 'Would you step out of the room and check her dress?'

When the two women walked out, Westleigh continued his barrage. 'Who is to say she did not drop the dice on the floor or conceal them in the table? You want to refute what I say, but I saw her rolling the weighted dice. I called your attention to it. Why would I do so for any other reason than an abhorrence of cheating? She is cheating our gaming house, after all.'

Rhys let him go on, but only with difficulty.

Celia would not cheat. It went against everything he knew of her, everything he'd countered when Xavier suggested she was not to be trusted. She was being set up and he knew precisely who was behind it.

He caught Xavier's eye. Xavier was perhaps the only one who could tell how near Rhys was to murderous rage. He would control it. He'd spent a lifetime perfecting control of his emotions.

He'd settle his accounts with this man once and for all.

This man had made a fatal mistake. He'd involved Celia in his dealings, and in the most hurtful way possible.

Hugh looked over at his father. 'Would you stubble it, Father? Your accusation of this woman does you no credit at all. What do you have against her?'

'She prefers the son over the father,' Xavier said.

That was it, Rhys thought. Westleigh had decided to make Madame Fortune a conquest, because Rhys had warned him off. Westleigh had moved from complete indifference towards his bastard son to resentment and rivalry.

The two women returned.

'I could not find anything,' Belinda said.

Celia did not appear steady on her feet. Rhys crossed the room to her and gave her his arm for support.

'This is too taxing for you,' he murmured.

She gave a dismissive wave of her hand. 'I am managing.'

He helped her back to her chair.

'Touching display,' Westleigh said sarcastically.

Rhys swung around to him, losing his composure momentarily.

Ned spoke first. 'This is enough, Father.'

'Stand up, Father,' Hugh ordered. 'It is time to search you.'

Westleigh's eyes bugged out in alarm. 'Me? Why me? This is an outrage. I will tolerate no such thing. You forget who I am.'

Hugh released an exasperated breath. 'We know precisely who you are. Stand up.'

'I will not!' Westleigh gripped the arms of his chair.

Hugh commenced to search his father's sleeves while the man sat in the chair and tried to wave him away. Westleigh gave up the fight as Hugh searched though the pockets in his father's coat and waistcoat and patted him to see if he could feel the dice underneath his clothing.

He moved away, his hands empty.

Celia spoke in a weary voice, 'Check around his chair.'

Ned crouched down and felt the carpet under Westleigh's chair. He looked up and shook his head. Hugh reached behind his father, who tried to prevent access. 'This is a humiliation!' Westleigh cried.

But Hugh pulled his arm out from behind his father and lifted the dice in the air for all to see.

'Oh!' exclaimed Belinda. 'The dice.'

'You are an abomination,' Ned said to his father.

'Which is worse?' Rhys asked Ned. 'What you lately accused this lady of, or your father cheating his own sons and attempting to put the blame on an innocent person?'

Ned glanced away, chastened.

Xavier inclined his head towards Westleigh. 'What will you do with him?'

'I am not certain.' Rhys knew what he would like to do with him, but that punishment belonged to the Middle Ages. 'Would you and Belinda return to the game room? You can reopen the hazard table with new dice.'

'What shall we say to the patrons?' Xavier asked.

'Say only that we do not tolerate cheating and that we have stopped it.' He was not certain what other action he wished to take.

After Xavier and Belinda left the room, Rhys turned to Ned and Hugh. 'Are you able to keep your father in your custody and return him here tomorrow?'

'You are not going to accuse me of cheating! I will be ruined,' Westleigh ranted. 'I will ruin you first. I will take this gaming hell to the devil and all of you with it. I have powerful friends.'

Rhys had no doubt that Earl Westleigh did indeed have

powerful friends, but the code of honour for gambling was sacred among the highest reaches of the *ton*. Would they tolerate even a friend who cheated his own sons at hazard and tried to place the blame on a woman?

'You have contrived to make me look guilty,' Westleigh went on, 'because of *her*. You do not want it known that you were duped by a common cheat.'

Rhys leaned into the man's face and his rage turned his voice low and treacherous. 'Do not say another word about her.'

Westleigh flinched, but quickly recovered. He waved a finger at his two legitimate sons. 'Do not believe this man! You traitorous pups. I am your father. You owe your allegiance to me!'

Hugh wheeled on him. 'You were cheating *us*, Father. You knew the profits went to us.'

'And to him!' Westleigh pointed to Rhys. 'Besides, I needed more money than you provided me.' He glared at Ned, but quickly caught himself. 'But I did not cheat. The weighted dice are not mine.'

'Rise, Father,' Hugh ordered. 'We are taking you home.'

Westleigh's two sons pulled him out of his chair and each held one of his arms.

Rhys turned to Celia. 'I will see them out.'

But he would return to her afterwards to assure himself that these stressful events had not done an injury to her health.

As he followed the three Westleighs down the stairs, he had to admit that Celia had the right of it. Gaming houses were ugly places where greed and desperation drove men to unseemly acts. Rhys might be able to control himself and his emotions around gaming and gamblers, but he could not control others. The veneer might be pretty, but a gaming house was not so different than the desperate streets he'd been thrown into at age fourteen.

When they reached the hall, Westleigh demanded, 'I want to cash out. I need to cash out.'

'Let us just give the cashier the whole lot,' Hugh said to his brother.

On their way to the cashier's office, the game-room door opened. Westleigh seized that moment to break free.

He ran into the game room and shouted, 'Rhysdale is making an unjust accusation. He says he will accuse me of cheating. But you all saw it! It was Madame Fortune!'

Rhys dashed into the room after him.

Westleigh swung around to him. 'I will not be unjustly accused! I demand satisfaction!'

'Here! Here!' some of his cronies shouted. 'Cannot have this!'

One gentleman stepped forwards and said, 'I will be your second, if you wish, Westleigh. It is an outrage. We saw her cheating with our own eyes. Now we know why she always won. How many other cheats are here, I wonder?'

The patrons started to glance at each other in sudden suspicion.

'Lord Westleigh planted the weighted dice on Madame Fortune,' Rhys shouted above the din. 'There is no false accusation here.'

Westleigh smiled a malevolent smile. 'Let us settle this with a duel.'

'A duel! A duel!' others shouted.

'What say you?' Westleigh challenged Rhys. 'We can settle this like gentlemen—'

Chapter Seventeen

Celia heard the shouting from below and feared something had gone wrong. She hurried out of the drawing room and down the stairs, tying her mask to her face as she went.

She reached the doorway of the game room in time to hear Westleigh say, 'Pistols at dawn, Rhysdale?'

'No!' Her voice pierced through the room.

She ran to Rhys's side and grasped his arm. 'No, Rhys! You mustn't do this.'

He pulled her fingers away. 'I will manage it. Trust me.'

Westleigh laughed. 'Madame Fortune, have you come to admit to cheating at hazard?'

Celia's heart pounded. She could stop this! All she had to do was admit to cheating.

She stepped forwards, but Rhys held her back.

'You, Westleigh, are still trying to blame her,' Rhys said. 'Even your sons saw proof of your lies.'

'You set me up!' Westleigh cried. 'You and—and your lover here.'

'Nonsense,' Rhys countered. 'What gaming-house proprietor conspires to lose money?'

Several men nodded their heads.

'You have not answered my challenge, sir.' Westleigh returned to that horrible question. Would Rhys accept a duel?

Because of her.

Rhys glanced around. 'Forgive me, gentlemen. You may know this better than I, but is a gentleman allowed to issue a challenge to one such as me? I am certainly his social inferior.'

'You are his natural son,' one man blurted out.

The murmurs of the crowd grew louder.

'And I am older than you,' Westleigh said. 'That more than cancels out the inferior blood of your mother.'

Celia's gaze darted to Rhys. Surely he would react to such an insult.

But if he felt the blow, as she had, he did not show it. His face was as composed as if he were strolling through the room watching the gamblers.

'What say you, gentlemen?' Westleigh asked the crowd.

'I say pistols at dawn,' one man shouted.

Others cheered.

Ned walked up to his father and seized his arm. Hugh hurried over and grabbed the other one.

'We are leaving now!' Ned said.

As they pulled him past where Celia and Rhys stood, she heard Ned say, 'Are you mad? We could have kept this quiet and now all London will know of it. A duel, Father? With your son?'

'He's naught but a bastard, Ned,' Westleigh said.

She knew Rhys heard, as well.

Xavier walked up to him. 'That was unfortunate. What will you do?'

'Meet him,' Rhys said.

She grasped his arm. 'No, Rhys! I will not let you!'

He took her chin in his fingers and lifted her face to

his. 'I must, Celia. But trust me in this. I know what I am about.'

It was akin to what her father had said to her mother—
It is something I must do.

'Please, Rhys!' she begged.

He walked her into the hall. 'Celia, you were barely able to stand on your feet a while ago. You must be exhausted. When does your coachman come?'

'Not for an hour.'

He touched her cheek. 'Go upstairs. Lie down. Rest. I need to be visible in the game room. I cannot be seen as hiding from what just occurred.'

She nodded. 'But promise me you will not fight a duel.'

'I cannot promise that.'

Celia was too tired to argue. She walked up to his bed-chamber and took off her mask and let down her hair. She kicked off her slippers, climbed onto his bed and fell asleep immediately.

She woke to his arms around her and rolled over to face him. All the candles had been extinguished and the only light came from the glow of the coals in the fireplace. He was shirtless and his face was shadowed with beard. He was warm and comfortable.

And comforting.

His eyes opened for a moment and he gathered her closer, so that her head rested against his heart, lulling her with its rhythmic beat. She wanted to stay in his arms for ever.

But she pulled away. 'What time is it? My carriage.'

He gathered her close again. 'I sent your coachman away. I told him to leave word you were staying here to-night.'

She ought to protest. Her mother-in-law and Adele would have fits of apoplexy.

But she could not care. Not when he held her, when the scent of his skin filled her nostrils, and the even sound of his breathing lulled her into an illusion that everything was as it should be. Everything was wonderful.

She fancied she could feel his baby inside her and she thrilled anew with the wonder of it. She imagined them as a family, saw herself rocking their baby to sleep while she and Rhys quietly conversed about the day.

But it would never be that way. Because she refused to listen to tales of men and women winning and losing, elated and despairing. She could not live in fear of bad luck or challenges to duels.

She did not want him to face Westleigh with pistols. Rhys could die as her father died. It was the greatest cruelty that he would not refuse for her sake, if for no other reason.

And even if he did not die, what would happen to him? An earl might escape arrest, but the proprietor of a gaming hell would certainly be hanged.

He purported to know how to play the odds, but in this case the odds were stacked solidly against him.

She clung to him tighter as tears rolled down her cheeks.

She must discover where the duel was to be held. She would stop it. Somehow, she would stop it.

She might not be able to live with Rhys and his gambling ways, but life would be unbearable if he did not live at all.

If it was wonderful to fall asleep in Rhys's arms it was glorious to waken in them. When Celia opened her eyes he was already gazing at her. They each lay drinking in the sight of the other for several long moments before he closed the space between them and kissed her.

Silently, he helped her out of her clothing and made

love to her. Quietly. Gently. So gently that she thought she would shatter under the sheer beauty of it. He stroked her body as if worshipping it, and every sensation inside her lit up like the illuminations at Vauxhall Gardens. She'd missed him so terribly that her desire burned white-hot for him.

She would have taken him fast and hard. Her body urged her to do that very thing, but his pace remained lazy and leisurely, as if they had all the time in the world.

As if this would not be their last time.

As if he were not intending to engage in a duel at the next sunrise.

When he entered her, she moaned in relief. He'd already driven her to a fevered state with his hands and lips. Now her body could take over, meet his thrusts and urge him to go faster.

But, still, he built the passion slowly and she finally surrendered to his pace, savouring every moment, every sensation.

Even her climax built slowly, like a stack of wood meant to last most of the day instead of the flash of brush she'd initially craved. Once released, it seemed as if the culmination of their lovemaking would have no end. Inside her she felt him spill his seed while she still convulsed with unbelievable pleasure.

An act like this had resulted in a new life, a baby for Celia to love. She said a prayer of thanks that her child had been created out of love. That in itself was a miracle.

He collapsed beside her, holding her as if she would disappear if he let go.

That was not too distant from the truth.

'How are you this morning, my love?' he asked.

He'd never before used such an endearment. 'I feel very

well,' she responded. 'I think you have found a cure for the morning sickness.'

He stared into her eyes. 'Then let me treat you every morning.'

He kissed her again.

Later they sat across from each other at the small table in his bedchamber. She was wrapped in a banyan he'd lent her to wear. He was in shirtsleeves and trousers.

Over a cup of hot tea, he continued what he'd begun after lovemaking. 'We could make a marriage work for us, Celia,' he insisted. 'The gaming house is temporary. No more than three years or so and I'll be done with it.'

He thought he was telling the truth, she knew, but she'd heard her father promise to quit gambling over and over. *Tomorrow I'll quit. Just one more game. A chance to recoup.* If he won he could not interrupt his winning streak. If he lost, he still needed one more game. Then it would start all over again.

But even that would be preferable to his death.

She lifted her chin. 'Give up the duel with Westleigh and I will marry you, Rhys.'

He frowned at her. 'I cannot.'

'You could! You could admit to him and the world that Madame Fortune was cheating. She could vanish, then. All who know I am Madame Fortune would have good reason not to tell anyone.' She gave him a pleading look. 'I do not mind giving up being Madame Fortune. It could work.'

He shook his head. 'I am going to stop Westleigh once and for all. He has had this coming for a very long time.'

Did he mean to kill Westleigh? She shuddered. 'I burn to have my father's death avenged, but not at the risk to your life.'

He did not waver. 'I said before, you must trust me on

this matter.' He rose. 'And do not use marriage as a bargaining chip. Either you wish to marry me or you don't. But you know marriage would be best for the child.'

'I am not so certain.' She raised her eyes to his. 'I lived that life, Rhys.'

He reached across the table and took her hands. 'You need to trust me, Celia. If I tell you I will give up the gaming house in three years, I will.'

It was not that simple, Celia thought.

He went on. 'If I say I will come out of the duel without a scratch, I will.'

Celia pulled her hands away. 'How can you promise that? You cannot.' Her voice broke. 'My father promised the same thing.'

'Trust me.'

'Tell me how you will do it,' she countered.

He shrugged. 'My plan is not yet in place, but it will be. This duel will solve everything.'

Celia wanted to believe him. She supposed her mother wanted to believe her father, too.

'No. I will not listen.' She waved his words away. 'A duel is too big a risk.'

'Everything in life involves risk, Celia.' He spoke in a low, firm voice. 'The best we can ever do is stack the odds in our favour. Trust me to do that.' His gaze was intense. 'I am not your father. I've never trusted my life to fate. I've made my own luck against all the odds. That is what I will do and can do again.'

She wanted to believe him.

One thing she knew. She'd always been a victim of fate. No more.

If he could make his own luck, so could she. She had no intention of leaving his life to fate. Somehow, she would stop this duel.

* * *

It was about noon when he sent her home in a hackney coach. She walked slowly into her set of rooms, passing Tucker in the hall.

'Good morning, ma'am,' he said in a concerned tone.

'Do not worry,' she responded to his implicit question. 'I am well.'

She walked straight to her bedchamber, but Adele appeared before she made it inside.

'Celia, I must tell you something.' Adele's voice was still cold.

'Very well,' Celia said. 'Come into my room. You can help me change my clothes.'

Adele followed her inside. 'Younie is here somewhere. I'll get her to help. I only need a minute of your time.'

Adele would not even help her with her laces?

Celia stepped into her dressing room and managed to remove her dress by herself. She put on one of her morning dresses. 'What is it you wished to tell me?' she asked, walking back out to the bedchamber.

'Ned and I are getting married. As soon as he can procure a special licence. I need you to secure my guardian's permission.'

So they were following her advice. 'I will send a letter today.'

'Good.' Adele started towards the door, but stopped before opening it. 'After my wedding, I will be moving in with Lord and Lady Westleigh until Ned and I can find rooms of our own.'

'And your grandmother?'

Adele lifted her chin. 'She does not wish to live with you or with me. We are not relations, she says. She wishes to retire to Bath. Ned will pay for her.'

They both would be free of the woman.

And Celia would be free to leave London in perhaps a matter of days.

Unless she agreed to Rhys's proposal.

Assuming he lived.

Anxiety clenched her insides. 'Will you see Ned today, Adele?'

'No,' the girl answered mournfully. 'He sent word that he has business to attend to. He will not see me tomorrow, either.' She narrowed her eyes. 'I do hope his absence is not due to some trouble you or your lover have caused.'

Adele's barb hurt.

Celia spoke quietly. 'That was not well said of you, Adele. Nothing I have done was meant to hurt you, but you deliberately wound me.'

Adele looked chastened for a moment, but she cried, 'You are going to have a baby out of wedlock!'

Celia put a hand on her abdomen. 'I am going to have a baby. What greater happiness could there be for me?'

Adele's expression remained obstinate. 'Why did you ask about Ned?'

She certainly was not going to confide in Adele. 'No reason. I merely wanted to know your schedule for the day.'

Adele opened the door. 'I am calling upon some of my friends. Younie will accompany me.' She walked out.

Celia went in search of Younie. She had decided to make a call of her own and needed Younie to help her dress again.

Younie helped Celia into a walking dress and she soon was off again, walking through Mayfair to the Westleigh town house. She knocked upon the door and was admitted by the butler.

A few minutes later she was escorted to the second floor

and announced to Lady Westleigh. Fortunately the lady was alone. Even her daughter was not present.

Lady Westleigh remained on her chaise longue when Celia was admitted into a small parlour. The lady's private sitting room, Celia suspected. It was a very feminine room, with upholstered chairs in blue brocade and gilded tables with white marble tops. Celia immediately felt comfortable. She could not imagine Lord Westleigh setting foot in such a room.

'Ma'am, thank you for receiving me.' Celia curtsied.

Lady Westleigh nodded. 'I confess I am surprised to see you.' She gestured for Celia to sit.

'May I enquire whether your sons or your husband are at home?' Celia asked.

Lady Westleigh raised her brows. 'They are not. They all went out. I confess they sounded as if in a quarrel.'

Celia could believe it. 'I am guessing you do not know of any of this, but your husband has challenged Mr Rhysdale to a duel.'

'A duel?' Lady Westleigh sat up straight. 'Whatever for?'

Celia explained the circumstances. 'I must stop this.'

'Certainly we must,' the lady agreed.

A footman served tea.

Lady Westleigh said to him, 'Tell Mason I wish to see him.'

The butler presented himself shortly. 'You asked for me, my lady?'

Lady Westleigh spoke in an officious tone. 'It has come to my attention that my husband is fighting a duel at dawn. I want you to tell me where it will be held.'

The man blanched. 'I am certain I do not know such a thing, my lady.'

Lady Westleigh did not back down. 'And I am certain

you do. One of the valets will have heard of it and I am certain it was mentioned in the servants' quarters. It is imperative you tell me.'

Chapter Eighteen

At first morning's light the next day, Rhys and Xavier stood on Hampstead Heath, fog swirling around their ankles.

'I wonder how many duels have been fought here?' Rhys mused.

'It is popular with those of us with no imagination.' Xavier, as Rhys's second, had had to attend to all the details of the duel. 'It is not too late to get out of this.'

Xavier had suggested the same thing as Celia. Blame Madame Fortune and have her disappear. But Xavier lacked the imagination to use this duel as an opportunity.

'Westleigh will pay this day. Madame Fortune did nothing wrong.' He walked the spot where they would take their positions.

'You don't truly plan to shoot him?' Xavier asked. 'He is your father, after all.'

Rhys turned as he would turn to fire. 'I intend to finish it here.'

They heard a carriage approaching.

'They are here.' Xavier shivered. 'Blast. It is as cold as winter this morning.'

Rhys turned at the sound. 'The coldest summer anyone recalls,' he remarked.

A curricle emerged through the mist and a moment later two men climbed down. It was not Westleigh who had arrived, but Ned and Hugh.

Rhys nodded to them. 'You came after all.'

Ned shivered. 'We said we would.'

Ned and Hugh had called upon Rhys the day before and discussed the duel and its likely aftermath. They had parted in agreement, which surprised Rhys.

It also surprised him that he'd come to a grudging respect for these two men with whom he shared a father. Ned might make a cake of himself over Miss Gale, but he took his responsibilities to his family and his people very seriously. Hugh, as volatile as Rhys was controlled, none the less did not suffer fools gladly. Neither of them exhibited the self-conceit of their father.

'Our father is not here yet?' Hugh asked, his tone contemptuous. 'Perhaps he will not show.'

Rhys was probably the only one who knew that their father had fought a duel at least once before. 'He will show.'

Sure enough, the sound of a carriage reached their ears. It, too, came through the mist and stopped nearby. Westleigh and his second climbed out of the carriage, the surgeon after them.

Rhys looked back to where he would stand in a few minutes. The sky was lightening by the minute.

Time to deal the cards and play the game.

Rhys and Xavier walked towards the new arrivals, followed by Ned and Hugh.

His second drew Xavier aside for the final task. Loading the pistols.

'What are you doing here?' Westleigh gave his sons scathing glances.

Hugh smiled. 'We would not miss this.'

Westleigh waved a hand at him as if he were an annoying fly. He turned to Rhys. 'Do you have anything to say to me?'

'Only that you are a fool.' Rhys spoke calmly. 'Did you not recall that I spent almost a decade in the army? I am very used to killing.'

Westleigh's brows knit.

'And I am steadier and thinner than you.' He looked Westleigh up and down. 'You'll make a bigger target.' He let Westleigh contemplate that for a moment before adding, 'And since you made the challenge, the weapons are mine. I will be firing a pistol I've fired many times before.'

Westleigh wiped his forehead with his sleeve. 'All that is to no purpose.'

'Suit yourself.' Rhys folded his arms across his chest and waited for Xavier and the other man.

Westleigh tossed the two seconds worried glances. As Rhys had suspected, Westleigh had hoped he would back out. He underestimated Rhys's resolve.

Ironically, only Celia and his brothers believed he would truly go through with it.

The two seconds approached them.

'We agreed the duel will allow for one shot each at thirty paces. No shooting into the air,' Westleigh's second said.

Xavier opened the case containing the duelling pistols. 'Choose first, Westleigh.'

Westleigh tossed Rhys one nervous glance and his hand shook as he selected a pistol. Rhys remained impassive.

'Take your positions,' Xavier said.

Rhys walked at a brisk pace to the spot he had chosen. Westleigh breathed hard to keep up. They stood back to back and Westleigh's second counted the paces. '...nine. Ten. Eleven—'

Ned and Hugh sprinted to Rhys's side and paced with him.

Westleigh's second paused, but Xavier gestured for him to continue.

'Twelve. Thirteen. Fourteen. Fifteen. Turn and fire!'

Rhys, Ned and Hugh turned quickly, as if they were one unit.

Westleigh turned, as well, but his arm faltered when he faced, not only Rhys, but his heir and his spare, as well. 'See here! This is not how it is done.'

Rhys's arm was raised and his aim steady. 'You would know precisely how it is done, would you not, Westleigh?'

Westleigh gestured with his free hand. 'Get them away.'

'Fire, Father,' Hugh said. 'We are not moving.'

'We chose to watch from here,' Ned added.

'Do not fire,' his second cried. 'What if you hit one of your sons?'

'That is the point, is it not, Westleigh?' Rhys held his aim. 'To shoot a son? You are bound to succeed, are you not? Who knows? With luck you might even hit me.'

'You are traitors,' Westleigh cried. 'Siding with him.'

'Should we side with you, Father?' Hugh asked. 'A liar and a cheat? A man who hides his guilt behind a skirt?'

'You cannot shoot your own sons,' his second cried. 'The scandal will ruin you.'

'Shoot, Westleigh,' Rhys called again. 'Or shall I fire first? I am an excellent shot.'

Westleigh's arm trembled.

'Do not do it!' his second begged.

His legs began to shake, as well.

Rhys's arm did not waver. 'You can end this another way.'

Westleigh's face contorted. As the sun lightened the sky it showed a sheen of perspiration on his brow.

Rhys was unshaken. 'Apologise. Confess that it was you who cheated, then leave the country and never return.' He wanted Westleigh far away. Out of his family. Far from Celia. He wanted her to never see the man again. 'Or fire so I can kill you.'

Westleigh fired the pistol into the air and collapsed to his knees. 'Very well. I did it. I planted the dice and blamed Madame Fortune or whoever she is.'

Rhys, Ned and Hugh strode over to him.

From the mist came a cry, 'No!'

The men turned to the sound.

A woman appeared, running towards them. 'Rhys!' she cried.

'Celia,' Rhys whispered. He stepped in her path.

She came to a halt, then vaulted into his arms. 'I thought he'd shot you.'

'No one is shot.' He held on to her. 'Celia, what are you doing here?'

'I came to stop you,' she cried.

He touched her stomach. 'You should not have exerted yourself. I told you to trust me. It is all over. All over. I have fixed it.'

Ned and Hugh pulled their father to his feet and another woman appeared.

Ned peered at her. 'Mother?'

'She would meddle,' Westleigh mumbled.

'You sorry creature,' she spat.

Rhys released Celia and faced Lord Westleigh. 'Here is what you will do. You will leave today for the Continent. You will stay there. You'll have an allowance large enough for comfort, but if you gamble it away or waste it on carousing, there will be no other money. You will leave your family alone, with Ned in charge and empowered to act on your behalf in all matters. What say you?'

'You had better agree,' Lady Westleigh demanded.

Westleigh nodded. 'Yes. I agree. I'll do as you say.'

'Your word as a gentleman?' Rhys persisted.

'I give you my word,' Westleigh said.

'Louder,' Rhys said.

'I give my word as a gentleman!' he shouted.

Ned and Hugh walked him past his second. The man made a sound of disgust and signalled to the surgeon to come with him. They left in the carriage.

Xavier walked up to Rhys and Celia. 'Lady Gale, I am not surprised to see you.' He bowed. 'I would have expected no less from you.' He turned to Rhys. 'Well done. Quite clever, actually.'

Rhys grinned. 'I suppose it violated some part of the gentleman's code, but, as we all know, I am no gentleman.'

'Rhys,' Ned called to him. 'We'll take charge of Father. Hugh and I will take him directly to our solicitor in the curricle. We'll be on our way to Dover by noon and to Calais on the morrow.'

'Take him in the carriage with me,' Lady Westleigh said. 'Rhys can take the curricle back to the stables.'

'I'll take our horses back,' Xavier said.

Before Rhys knew it, everyone had left them, except Ned's tiger. He helped Celia into the curricle and the tiger hopped on the back.

'Where do I take you, Celia?' he asked.

'To your house.' She caressed his cheek. 'I believe I can trust you at the Masquerade Club.'

He peered at her. 'Are you saying you have reconsidered?'

She nodded and put her arms around him. 'I trust you will do as you say.'

Epilogue

Rhys walked through the game room watching the play. The Masquerade Club was as popular as ever—and as profitable. It was hard to believe that so much had happened in under a year.

Change had come to the monarchy in this year, with the mad king's death and George IV inheriting the throne.

But there were even more important changes in Rhys's life. His friend Xavier was still at his side, but also were his brothers. Ironically, he was now accepted as a Westleigh, after all, but only because his father was gone, still banished to the Continent and keeping his word to leave his family in peace.

Best of all, Rhys had married Celia.

At Ned's insistence, they'd been married by special licence in the drawing room of the Westleigh town house on the same day and place as Ned and Adele's wedding, very shortly after he'd almost lost Celia because of the duel.

But he'd managed to rid them all of Westleigh, save the Westleigh estates, and convince Celia that he was a man of his word. In return he'd been given happiness greater than he ever thought possible.

He glanced towards the game-room door. To his surprise Celia stood there. She never came downstairs during the night's play, not since she'd grown so large.

A memory flashed of his first glimpse of her in her mask and deep red gown that now would never contain her full breasts and rounded abdomen.

She braced herself against the door jamb and signalled for him to come to her. He was already heading there.

He touched her arm. 'What are you doing down here?'

She smiled. 'I don't want to alarm you, but I think it is time.'

'Time for what?' he asked.

She looked him in the eye. 'Time for our baby to be born.'

He blanched. 'Indeed?'

She nodded. 'I had Xavier send for Lady Westleigh and the physician.'

'You should not have risked the stairs.' He took her by the arm. 'We must get you back upstairs.'

They'd prepared one of the rooms upstairs for the birth, with a comfortable bed, a tiny cradle and a window for fresh air.

He helped her up the stairs and stayed with her, letting her grip his hand when the contractions came, wishing he could ensure that nothing went wrong.

Lady Westleigh arrived and immediately took charge, telling even the physician what he should do.

'You must leave, Rhys,' she told him.

'Do not waste your breath arguing with me over it,' he told her. 'I am staying with her.'

'I want him to stay,' Celia managed as yet another contraction came.

He endured twelve hours of witnessing Celia in more pain than he could ever imagine, even after being in battle.

Finally Lady Westleigh, not the physician, declared that it was time for the birth. Rhys let Celia grip his hand as hard as she wished as she bore down, trying to push the baby from her body.

Finally, after yet another of her agonised cries, another sound erupted. The cry of a newborn baby.

'You have a son,' Lady Westleigh announced.

'A son,' he rasped.

Celia laughed in relief and reached out for her baby.

Later when she, the baby and the room were cleaned up and she put the baby to her breast, Rhys sat back and just gazed at his lusty-lunged son and his beautiful wife.

He made a wager. He wagered this baby would never be hungry or alone, not if Rhys could help it. He would always be loved. Rhys also wagered that Celia, too, would always be loved and that he'd give her the security she had lacked as a child.

He knew the odds of winning these wagers were extremely high.

'Is he not the most handsome baby you have ever seen?' Celia said. 'And so clever to learn how to nurse right away.'

'He is as wonderful as his mother,' Rhys replied. He leaned down and kissed the baby on top of his head. He kissed Celia, too, a kiss of thanksgiving that she and their son had come through the ordeal so well.

'I love my family,' he murmured, kissing her again.

* * * * *

A Marriage
of Notoriety

For my new daughter-in-law, Beth,
beautiful on the inside and outside,
and a wonderful addition to our family.

Prologue

London, Spring 1814

'Mr Xavier Campion,' Lady Devine's butler intoned in a baritone voice.

'Adonis is here!' gasped one of the young ladies standing near Phillipa Westleigh. The others shared furtive smiles.

Phillipa knew precisely who her friends would see when their gazes slipped towards the doorway. A young man tall and perfectly formed, with broad shoulders, a narrow waist, and muscled limbs. His hair would be as dark as the ebony keys on a pianoforte and longer than fashionable, but an excellent frame for his lean face, strong brow, sensitive mouth.

The young ladies had been tittering about him the whole evening. Would he come to the ball? Could they contrive an introduction? He'd been the main topic of conversation since they'd discovered him at the opera the night before. 'He is an Adonis!' one had proclaimed and the name stuck.

Phillipa had not attended the opera that night, but heard before all of them that he'd come to town. She, too, glanced to the doorway.

Clad in the formal red coat of the East Essex infantry,

Xavier Campion looked as magnificent as a man could look
in regimentals.

He scanned the room, his brilliant blue eyes searching
until reaching Phillipa. His lips widened into a smile and
he inclined his head before pivoting to greet Lord and Lady
Devine.

'He smiled at us!' cried one of Phillipa's friends.

No. He'd smiled at her.

Phillipa's cheeks flushed.

Did he remember her? They'd been childhood friends in
Brighton during the summers, especially the summer when
she fell and suffered her injury.

Phillipa's hand flew to her cheek, to where the jagged
scar marred her face. Not even the clever feather her mother
insisted be attached to her headpiece could hide the disfigurement.

Of course he remembered her. How many scar-faced girls
could be known to handsome Xavier Campion?

She swung away, while the others giggled and whispered
to each other. She heard their voices, but could not repeat
a word any of them spoke. All she could think was how it
might be if her appearance were different, if her right cheek
were not branded with a jagged red scar. How she wished
her complexion was as unflawed as her friends'. Then she
could merely have a pretty ribbon threaded through her hair
instead of the silly headpiece with its obvious feather. She
wished just once Xavier Campion could look upon her and
think her as beautiful as he was handsome.

Her companions suddenly went silent and a masculine
voice spoke. 'Phillipa?'

She turned.

Xavier stood before her.

'I thought that was you.' He'd noticed her scar, he meant.
'How are you? It has been years since I've seen you.'

The other young ladies stared in stunned disbelief.

'Hello, Xavier,' she managed, keeping her eyes downcast. 'But you have been at war. You have been away.' She dared glance up to his face.

His smile made her heart twist. 'It is good to be back in England.'

One of her friends cleared her throat.

Phillipa's hand fluttered to her cheek. 'Oh.' She looked from Xavier to the pretty girls around her. It was suddenly clear why he had approached her. 'Let me present you.'

When the introductions were complete the other young ladies surrounded him, asking him clever questions about the war, where he'd been and what battles he'd fought.

Phillipa stepped back. She'd served her purpose. Her introductions made it possible for him to ask any of them to dance. She imagined their minds turning, calculating. He was only the younger son of an earl, but his looks more than made up for a lack of title. And he was reputed to have a good income.

Her friends were solidly on the marriage mart. They'd all been bred to hope for the perfect betrothal by the end of their first Season. Phillipa's hopes had quickly become more modest and certainly did not include snaring the most handsome and exciting young man in the room. Not even ordinary eligible gentlemen paid her the least attention. Why should Xavier Campion?

In Brighton, when she'd been a young, foolish child, she'd been his companion. Although a few years older, he played children's games with her. He filled buckets at the water's edge with her and built castles out of the pebbles on the beach. They'd chased each other through the garden of the Pavilion and pressed their faces against its windows, peeking at the grandeur inside. Sometimes when they were at play, she'd stop and stare, awestruck at his beauty. Many a night she'd fall asleep dreaming that some day, when she was grown, Xavier would ride in like a prince on horseback and whisk her away to a romantic castle.

Well, she was grown now and the reality was that no man wanted a young lady with a scar on her face. She was eighteen years old and it was past time to put away such childhood fancies.

'Phillipa?' His voice again.

She turned.

Xavier extended his hand to her. 'May I have the honour of this dance?'

She nodded, unable to speak, unable to believe her ears.

Her friends moaned in disappointment.

Xavier clasped her hand and led her to the dance floor as the orchestra began the first strains of a tune Phillipa easily identified, as she'd identified every tune played at the balls she'd attended.

'The Nonesuch'.

How fitting. Xavier was a nonesuch, a man without equal. There were none such as he.

The dance began.

Somehow, as if part of the music, her legs and feet performed the figures. In fact, her step felt as light as air; her heart, joy-filled.

He smiled at her. He *looked* at her. Straight in her face. In her eyes.

'How have you spent your time since last we played on the beach?' he asked when the dance brought them together.

They parted and she had to wait until the dance joined them again to answer. 'I went away to school,' she told him.

School had been a mostly pleasant experience. So many of the girls had been kind and friendly, and a few had become dear friends. Others, however, had delighted in cruelty. The wounding words they'd spoken still felt etched in her memory.

He grinned. 'And you grew up.'

'That I could not prevent.' Blast! Could she not contrive something intelligent to say?

He laughed. 'I noticed.'

The dance parted them again, but his gaze did not leave her. The music connected them—the gaiety of the flute, the singing of the violin, the deep passion of the bass. She would not forget a note of it. In fact, she would wager she could play the tune on the pianoforte without a page of music in front of her.

The music was happiness, the happiness of having her childhood friend back.

She fondly recalled the boy he'd been and gladdened at the man he'd become. When his hand touched hers the music seemed to swell and that long-ago girlish fantasy sounded a strong refrain.

But eventually the musicians played the final note and Phillipa blinked as if waking from a lovely dream.

He escorted her back to where she had first been standing.

'May I get you a glass of wine?' he asked.

It was time for him to part from her, but she was thirsty from the dance. 'I would like some, but only if it is not too much trouble for you.'

His blue eyes sparkled as if amused. 'Your wish is my pleasure.'

Her insides skittered wildly as she watched him walk away. He returned quickly and handed her a glass. 'Thank you,' she murmured.

Showing no inclination to leave her side, he asked polite questions about the health of her parents and about the activities of her brothers, Ned and Hugh. He told her of encountering Hugh in Spain and she told him Hugh was also back from the war.

While they conversed, a part of her stood aside as if observing—and judging. Her responses displayed none of the wit and charm at which her friends so easily excelled, but he did not seem to mind.

She had no idea how long they chatted. It might have been ten minutes or it might have been half an hour, but it ended when his mother approached them.

'How do you do, Phillipa?' Lady Piermont asked.

'I am well, ma'am.' Phillipa exchanged pleasantries with her, but Lady Piermont seemed impatient.

She turned to her son. 'I have need of you, Xavier. There is someone who wishes a word with you.'

He tossed Phillipa an apologetic look. 'I fear I must leave you.'

He bowed.

She curtsied.

And he was gone.

No sooner had he walked away than her friend Felicia rushed up to her. 'Oh, Phillipa! How thrilling! He danced with you.'

Phillipa could only smile. The pleasure of being with him lingered like a song played over and over in her head. She feared speaking would hasten its loss.

'I want to hear about every minute of it!' Felicia cried.

But Felicia's betrothed came to collect her for the next set and she left without a glance back at her friend.

Another of Phillipa's former schoolmates approached her, one of the young ladies to whom she had introduced Xavier. 'It was kind of Mr Campion to dance with you, was it not?'

'It was indeed,' agreed Phillipa, still in perfect charity

with the world, even though this girl had never precisely been a friend.

Her schoolmate leaned closer. 'Your mother and Lady Piermont arranged it. Was that not clever of them? Now perhaps other gentlemen will dance with you, as well.'

'My mother?' Phillipa gripped the stem of the glass.

'That is what I heard.' The girl smirked. 'The two ladies were discussing it while you danced with him.'

Phillipa felt the crash of cymbals and the air was knocked out of her just like the day in Brighton when she fell.

Prevailing on family connections to manage a dance invitation was precisely the sort of thing her mother would do.

Dance with her, Xavier dear, she could almost hear her mother say. *If you dance with her, the others will wish to dance with her, too.*

'Mr Campion is an old friend,' she managed to reply to the schoolmate.

'I wish I had that kind of friend.' The girl curtsied and walked away.

Phillipa held her ground and forced herself to casually finish sipping her glass of wine. When she'd drained the glass of its contents she strolled to a table against the wall and placed the empty glass on it.

Then she went in search of her mother and found her momentarily alone.

It was difficult to maintain composure. 'Mama, I have a headache. I am going home.'

'Phillipa! No.' Her mother looked aghast. 'Not when the ball is going so well for you.'

Because of her mother's contrivance.

'I cannot stay.' Phillipa swallowed, trying desperately not to cry.

'Do not do this to yourself,' her mother scolded, through clenched teeth. 'Stay. This is a good opportunity for you.'

'I am leaving.' Phillipa turned away and threaded her way quickly through the crush of people.

Her mother caught up with her in the hall and seized her arm. 'Phillipa! You cannot go unescorted and your father and I are not about to leave when the evening is just beginning.'

'Our town house is three doors away. I dare say I may walk it alone.' Phillipa freed herself from her mother's grasp. She collected her wrap from the footman attending the hall and was soon out in the cool evening air where no one could see.

Tears burst from her eyes.

How humiliating! To be made into Xavier Campion's charity case. He'd danced with her purely out of pity. She was foolish in the extreme for thinking it could be anything else.

Phillipa set her trembling chin in resolve. She'd have no more of balls. No more of hopes to attract a suitor. She'd had enough. The truth of her situation was clear even if her mother refused to see it.

No gentleman would court a scar-faced lady.

Certainly not an Adonis.

Certainly not Xavier Campion.

Chapter One

London, August 1819

'Enough!' Phillipa slapped her hand flat on the mahogany side table.

The last time she'd felt such strength of resolve had been that night five years ago when she fled Lady Devine's ball and removed herself out from the marriage mart for good.

To think she'd again wound up dancing with Xavier Campion just weeks ago at her mother's ball. He'd once again taken pity on her.

No doubt her mother arranged those two dances as well as the first. More reason to be furious with her.

But never mind that. The matter at hand was her mother's refusal to answer Phillipa's questions, flouncing out the drawing room in a huff instead.

Phillipa had demanded her mother tell her where her brothers and father had gone. The three of them had been away for a week now. Her mother had forbidden the servants to speak of it with her and refused to say anything of it herself.

Ned and Hugh had a rather loud quarrel with their father, Phillipa knew. It occurred late at night and had been loud enough to wake her.

'It is nothing for you to worry over,' her mother insisted. She said no more.

If it were indeed nothing to worry over, then why not simply tell her?

Granted, in the past several days Phillipa had been closeted with her pianoforte, consumed by her latest composition, a sonatina. Pouring her passions into music had been Phillipa's godsend. Music gave her a challenge. It gave her life meaning.

Like getting the phrasing exactly right in the sonatina. She'd been so preoccupied she'd not given her brothers or her father a thought. Sometimes she would work so diligently on her music that she would not see them for days at a time. It had finally become clear, though, that they were not at home. That in itself was not so unusual, but her mother's refusal to explain where they had gone was very odd. Where were they? Why had her father left London when Parliament was still in session? Why had her brothers gone with him?

Her mother would only say, 'They are away on business.'

Business, indeed. A strange business.

This whole Season had been strange. First her mother and brother Ned insisted she come to town when she'd much have preferred to remain in the country. Then the surprise of her mother's ball—

And seeing Xavier again.

The purpose of that ball had been a further surprise. It was held for a person Phillipa had never known existed.

Perhaps *that person* would explain it all to her. His appearance, the ball, her brothers' and father's disappearance—all must be connected somehow.

She'd ask John Rhysdale.

No. She would *demand* Rhysdale tell her what was going on in her family and how he—her half-brother, her father's illegitimate son—fit into it.

Rhysdale's relationship to her had also been kept secret from her. Her brothers had known of him, apparently, but no one told her about him or why her mother gave the ball for him or why her parents introduced him to society as her father's son.

A member of the Westleigh family.

Her mother had given her the task of writing the invitations to the ball, so she knew precisely where Rhysdale resided. Phillipa rushed out of the drawing room, collected her hat and gloves, and was out the door in seconds, walking with a determined step towards St James's Street.

She'd met Rhysdale the night of the ball. He was very near to Ned's age, she'd guess. In his thirties. He looked like her brothers, too, dark-haired and dark-eyed. Like her, as well, she supposed, minus the jagged scar on her face.

To Rhysdale's credit, he'd only given her scar a fleeting glance and afterward looked her in the eye. He'd been gentlemanly and kind. There had been nothing to object in him, except for the circumstances of his birth.

And his choice of friends.

Why did Xavier Campion have to be his friend? Xavier, the one man Phillipa wished to avoid above all others.

Phillipa forced thoughts of Xavier Campion out of her mind and concentrated on being angry at her mother instead. How dared her mother refuse to confide in her?

Phillipa had a surfeit of her mother's over-protection. She could endure a ball with no dance partners. She could handle whatever mysterious matters led to her family's aberrant behaviour. Just because an ugly scar marred her face did not mean she was a child.

She was not weak. She refused to be weak.

Phillipa took notice of passers-by staring at her and pulled down a piece of netting on her hat. Her mother insisted she tack netting on to all her hats so she could obscure half her face and not receive stares.

She turned off St James's Street on to the street where Rhysdale lived. When she found the house, she only hesitated a moment before sounding the knocker.

Several moments passed. She reached for the knocker again, but the door opened. A large man with expressionless eyes perused her quickly. His brows rose.

'Lady Phillipa to see Mr Rhysdale,' she said.

The man stepped aside and she entered the hall. He lifted a finger, which she took to mean she should wait, and he disappeared up the staircase.

The doors to rooms off the hall were closed, and the hall itself was so nearly devoid of all decoration that it appeared impersonal. Perhaps a single gentleman preferred no decoration. How would she know?

'Phillipa.' A man's voice came from the top of the stairs.

She looked up.

But it was not Rhysdale who descended the stairs.

It was Xavier.

He quickly approached her. 'What are you doing here, Phillipa? Is something amiss?'

She forced herself not to step back. 'I—I came to speak with Rhysdale.'

'He is not here.' He glanced around. 'You are alone?'

Of course she was alone. Who would accompany her? Not her mother. Certainly her mother would never make a social call to her husband's illegitimate son. 'I will wait for him, then. It is a matter of some importance.'

He gestured to the stairs. 'Come. Let us sit in the drawing room.'

They walked up one flight of stairs and Phillipa glanced

into a room she presumed would be the drawing room. She glimpsed several tables and chairs.

'What is this?' she exclaimed.

Xavier looked dismayed. 'I will explain.' He gestured for her to continue up another flight of stairs.

He led her into a comfortably furnished parlour and extended his arm towards a sofa upholstered in deep-red fabric. 'Do be seated. I will arrange for tea.'

Before she could protest, he left the room again. Her heart beat at such rapid rate that her hands trembled as she pulled off her gloves.

This was ridiculous. She refused to be made uncomfortable by him. He meant nothing to her. He'd merely been a boy who'd once been her playmate. Defiantly she swept the netting over the brim of her hat. Let him see her face.

He stepped back in the room. 'We'll have tea in a moment.' Choosing a chair near her, he leaned close. 'I do not know when—or if—Rhys will come back.'

'Do not tell me he has disappeared as well!' What was going on?

He touched her hand in a reassuring gesture. 'He has not disappeared. I assure you.'

She pulled her hand away. 'Where is he?' she demanded.

He leaned back. 'He spends most days with Lady Gale.'

'Lady Gale?' What did Lady Gale have to do with anything?

Lady Gale was the stepmother of Adele Gale, the silly young woman to whom her brother Ned was betrothed. Both Adele and Lady Gale had been guests at her mother's ball, so Rhysdale might have met them there, but was there more to that connection?

Xavier frowned. 'You do not know about Rhysdale and Lady Gale?'

Phillipa waved a frustrated hand. 'I do not know anything! That is why I am here. My brothers and my father have disappeared and my mother will not tell me where they have gone or why. I came to ask Rhysdale where they were, but it seems I've been excluded from even more *family* matters.'

There was a knock on the door and a manservant entered, carrying the tea tray. As he placed the tray on a side table, he gave Phillipa a curious look.

Because of her scar, no doubt.

Xavier nodded to him. 'Thank you, MacEvoy.'

The servant bowed and walked out, but not before tossing her another glance.

Xavier reached for the teapot. 'How do you take your tea, Phillipa? Still with lots of sugar?'

He remembered that? She'd had a sweet tooth as a little girl. That had been a long time ago, however.

She stood. 'I do not wish to drink tea. I came here for answers. I am quite overset, Xavier. I do not know why everything is kept secret from me. Do I look as if I cannot handle adversity?' She jabbed at her scar. 'I am well practised in adversity. My mother—my whole family, it seems—apparently thinks not.' She faced him. 'Something important has happened in my family—something more than Rhysdale's appearance—and I am to be told nothing? I cannot bear it!' She pressed her hands against her temples for a moment, collecting herself. She pointed towards the door. 'What is this place, Xavier? Why does my half-brother have a room full of tables where the drawing room should be and a drawing room on a floor for bedchambers?'

Xavier stared back at Phillipa, considering how much to tell her.

He preferred this version of Phillipa to the one he'd so recently encountered at her mother's ball. That Phillipa barely looked at him, barely conversed with him, even though he'd danced twice with her. She'd acted as if he were a loathsome stranger.

Her present upset disturbed him, however. Ever since they'd been children, he'd hated seeing her distressed. It reminded him of that summer in Brighton when the pretty little girl woke from a fall to discover the long cut on her face.

He admired Phillipa for not covering her scar now, for showing no shame of it or how she appeared to others. Besides, her colour was high, appealingly so, and her agitation piqued his empathy. He understood her distress. He would greatly dislike being left out of family matters of such consequence.

But surely she'd been told of Rhys's arrangement with her brothers?

'Do you not know about this place?' He swept his arm the breadth of the room.

Her eyes flashed. 'Do you not comprehend? I know nothing.'

'This is a gambling establishment.' All of society knew of it. Why not Phillipa? 'Nominally it is a gambling *club* so as to adhere to legalities. Have you not heard of the Masquerade Club?'

'No.' Her voice still held outrage.

He explained. 'This is the Masquerade Club. Rhys is the proprietor. Patrons may attend in masks and thus conceal their identities—as long as they pay their gambling debts, that is. If they need to write vowels, they must reveal themselves.' He made a dismissive gesture. 'In any event, it is meant to be a place where both gentlemen and ladies may enjoy cards or other games. Ladies' reputations are protected, you see.'

She looked around again, her expression incredulous. 'This is a gambling house?'

'Not this floor. These are Rhys's private rooms, but he is not here very often these days.'

She pressed fingers to her forehead. 'Because he is with Lady Gale.'

He nodded. Rhys's connection to Lady Gale ought to have been roundly discussed at the Westleigh residence.

He could tell her this much. 'Sit, Phillipa. Have some tea. I will explain.'

He reached for the teapot again but she stopped him with a light touch to his hand. 'I will pour.' She lifted a cup and raised her brows in question.

'A little milk. A little sugar,' he replied.

She fixed his cup and handed it to him. 'Explain, Xavier. Please.'

'About Lady Gale and Rhys,' he began. 'Earlier this Season Lady Gale came masked to the Masquerade Club.'

She lifted her cup. 'She is a gambler? I would not have guessed.'

He lifted a shoulder. 'Out of necessity. She needed money. She attended often enough for Rhys to become acquainted with her. In learning of her financial need, he began paying her to come gamble.'

'Paying her?' Her hand stopped before the teacup reached her lips.

He gave a half-smile. 'He fancied her. He did not know her name, though. Nor did she know his connection to your family.'

She looked at him expectantly. 'And?'

'They became lovers.' He took a breath. 'And she is with child. They are to be married as soon as the licence can be arranged.' He paused. 'And other matters settled.'

'Other matters.' Her brows knitted. 'Ned's courtship of Lady Gale's stepdaughter, do you mean?'

He nodded. 'And more.'

Rhys's gambling house and his affair with Lady Gale had hardly caused her a blink of the eye. Surely she was made of stern enough stuff to hear the whole of it.

She gave him a direct look. 'What more?'

'Do you know of Ned and Hugh's arrangement with Rhys?' he asked.

She shook her head. 'I am depending upon you to tell me all of it, Xavier. All of it.'

How could he resist her request?

Ever since her injury. What age had he been? Twelve? She'd been about seven and he'd never forgotten that summer.

How it pained him to see that little girl so wounded, so unhappy.

If only he could have prevented it.

He'd felt it his duty to cheer her up. He'd learned that summer that one should act, if one could. Not hold back.

So he'd made her his responsibility and worked to cheer her up.

It was not his place to tell her about her family's affairs, but....

He set his jaw. 'This past April Ned and Hugh came to Rhys and asked him to open a gaming house. They had scraped together the funds for it, but they needed Rhys to run it.'

'They asked Rhysdale to run a gaming house for them?' She sounded incredulous.

He took a sip of tea. 'Out of desperation. Your family was in dire financial straits. Did you know of that?'

She shook her head.

He might as well tell her all. 'Your father's gambling... and carousing...brought your family to the brink of ruin. You, your mother, everyone who depended upon the Westleigh estates for their livelihood would have suffered terribly if nothing had been done.'

Her eyes widened. 'I had no idea.'

'So Ned and Hugh hit upon the idea of a gaming house. Rhys agreed to run it, although your father gave him no reason to feel any sense of loyalty to the family. Besides taking half the profits, though, Rhys asked that your father publicly acknowledge him as his natural son.'

'Hence my mother's ball.' She caught on quickly.

'Indeed.' The ball was part of Rhys's payment. 'The scheme worked perfectly. The element of masquerade has made this place successful beyond anyone's hopes. Your family is rescued.'

She looked askance. 'If all has gone so well, where are my father and brothers?'

'They went to the Continent. To Brussels.' Ought he tell her this part? He peered at her. 'Phillipa, are you close to your father?'

She laughed. 'I dare say not.' She glanced away, her face shadowed. 'Should he chance encounter me, he looks through me. Or away.'

His heart constricted.

'Your father made trouble for Rhys, I'm afraid. He detested Rhys being the family's salvation.' She did not need to know all the details. 'Suffice to say your father challenged Rhys to a duel—'

'A duel!' She looked aghast.

'It did not take place,' he assured her. 'Your brothers stood by Rhys and together they forced your father to relinquish all control of the family's money and property to Ned.' Either that or publicly shame the man. 'They offered your father a generous allowance, but only if he moved to the Continent. Your brothers travelled with him to make certain he reaches his destination and keeps his word. He is to remain there. He will not come back.'

'He is gone?' She turned pale, making her red scar more vivid. 'I had no notion of any of this.'

He feared she would faint and he rose from his chair to sit beside her on the sofa, wrapping an arm around her. 'I know this is a shock.'

He remembered how he'd held her as a little girl, when she cried about being ugly. He'd never thought her ugly. Certainly not now, although to see her face, half-beautiful, half-damaged, still made something inside him twist painfully.

She recovered quickly and moved from his grasp. 'How could I have been so unaware? How could I have not had some inkling?'

'It is not your fault, Phillipa. I am certain they meant to protect you,' he said.

'I do not need their protection!' she snapped. She looked at him as if he were the object of her anger. 'I do not need pity.'

He admired her effort to remain strong.

'I must leave.' She snatched up her gloves and stood.

He rose as well. 'I will walk you home.'

Her eyes shot daggers. 'I am fully capable of walking a few streets by myself.'

He did not know how to assist her. 'I meant only—'

She released a breath and spoke in an apologetic tone. 'Forgive me, Xavier. It is unfair of me to rail at you when you have done me the honour of exposing my family to me.' She pulled on her gloves. 'But truly there is no need to walk me home. I am no green girl in need of a chaperon.'

'If that is your wish.' He opened the door for her and walked with her down the stairs.

She stopped on the first-floor landing and pointed to a doorway with a half-closed door. 'Is this the game room?'

'It is.' He opened the door the whole way. 'You can see the card tables and the tables for faro, hazard and *rouge et noir*.'

She peeked in, but did not comment.

As they continued down the stairs, she asked, 'Why are you here in a gaming house, Xavier?'

He shrugged. 'I assist Rhys. As a friend.'

He was useful to Rhys. Because of his looks, men dismissed him and women were distracted. Consequently, he saw more than either sex imagined and, for that, Rhys paid him a share of his profits.

'Do you have the gambling habit, then?' she asked.

Like her father? 'Not a habit,' he responded, although once it had been important to prove himself at the card table. 'These days I play less and watch more.'

They reached the hall and Xavier walked her to the door. When he turned the latch and opened it for her, she pulled down the netting on her hat, covering her face.

The action made him sad for her.

He opened his mouth to repeat the offer to escort her.

She lifted a hand. 'I prefer to be alone, Xavier. Please respect that.'

He nodded.

'Good day,' she said in a formal voice and stepped away.

Xavier ducked inside and grabbed his hat. He waited until he surmised she would have reached the corner of the street, then stepped outside and followed her, keeping her in sight, just in case she should require assistance of any kind. He followed her all the way to her street and watched until she safely entered her house.

It was a familiar habit, looking out for her, one he'd practised over and over that long-ago summer in Brighton, when his duty towards her first began.

Chapter Two

Phillipa walked briskly back to her family's town house, emotions in disharmony. Her mind whirled. Rhysdale's gaming house. Her father's shameful behaviour.

Xavier.

She had not expected to see Xavier and her face burned with embarrassment that it had been he who exposed her family's troubles to her.

Her family's shame. Did there ever exist such a father as hers? What must Xavier think of him? Of them?

Of her?

She hurried through the streets.

How could she have been so insensible? Her family had been at the brink of ruin and she'd not had an inkling. She should have guessed something was awry. She should have realised how out of character it was for her father to hold a ball for anyone, least of all a natural son.

Seeing Xavier there distracted her.

No. It was unfair to place the blame on Xavier. Or even on her family.

She was to blame. She'd deliberately isolated herself, immersing herself in her music so as not to think about being in London, not to think of that first Season, that first dance with Xavier, nor of dancing with him again at the ball.

Instead she'd poured everything into her new composition. With the music, she'd tried to recreate her youthful feelings of joy and the despairing emotions of reality. She'd transitioned the tune to something bittersweet—how it had felt to dance with him once again.

Her mind had been filled with him and she'd not spared a thought for her family. In fact, she'd resented whenever her mother insisted she receive morning calls, including those of Lady Gale and her stepdaughter. It surprised her that she'd paid enough attention to learn that Ned intended to marry the artless Adele Gale. The girl reminded Phillipa of her school friends and that first Season when they'd been innocent and starry-eyed.

And hopeful.

Phillipa had paid no attention at all to her father, but, then, he paid no attention to her. She long ago learned not to care about what her father thought or did or said, but how dared he be so selfish as to gamble away the family money? She would not miss him. It was a relief to no longer endure his unpleasantness.

Phillipa entered the house and climbed the stairs to her music room. She pulled off her hat and gloves and sat at the pianoforte. Her fingers pressed the ivory keys, searching for expression of the feelings resonating inside of her. She created a discordant sound, a chaos, unpleasant to her ears. She rose again and walked to the window, staring out at the small garden behind the town house. A yellow tabby cat walked the length of the wall, sure-footed, unafraid, surveying the domain below.

Her inharmonious musical notes re-echoed in her ears. Unlike the cat, she was not sure-footed. She was afraid.

For years she'd been fooling herself, saying she was embracing life by her study of music. Playing the pianoforte, composing melodies, gave her some purpose and activity. Although she yearned to perform her music or see it published for others to perform, what hope could she have to accomplish that? No lady wanted a disfigured *pianiste* in her musicale. And no music publisher would consider an earl's daughter to be a serious composer.

There was an even more brutal truth to jar her. She was hiding behind her music. So thoroughly that she had missed the drama at play on her family's stage. All kinds of life occurred outside the walls of her music room and she'd been ignoring it all. She needed to rejoin life.

Phillipa spun away from the window. She rushed from the room, startling one of the maids passing through the hallway. What was the girl's name? When had Phillipa begun to be blind to the very people around her?

'Pardon, miss.' The girl struggled to curtsy, even though her hands were laden with bed linens.

'No pardon is necessary,' Phillipa responded. 'I surprised you.' She started to walk past, but turned. 'Forgive me, I do not know your name.'

The girl looked even more startled. 'It is Ivey, miss. Sally Ivey.'

'Ivey,' Phillipa repeated. 'I will remember it.'

The maid curtsied again and hurried on her way.

Phillipa reached the stairs, climbing them quickly, passing the floor to the maids' rooms and continuing to the attic where one small window provided a little light. She opened one of the trunks and rummaged through it, not finding for what she searched. In the third trunk, though, triumph reigned. She pulled it out. A lady's mask, one her mother had made for her to attend a masquerade at Vauxhall Gardens during her first Season. It had been specifically designed to cover her scar.

She'd never worn it.

Until now.

Because she'd decided her first step to embrace life and conquer fear was to do what Lady Gale had done. She would wait until night. She would step out into the darkness and make her way to St James's Street.

Phillipa would attend the Masquerade Club. If Lady Gale thought it acceptable to attend, so could she. She would don the mask and enter a gaming house. She would play cards and hazard and faro and see what sort of investment Ned and Hugh had made in Rhysdale.

He would be there, of course, but that was of no consequence. If she encountered Xavier, he would not know her.

No one would know her.

That night Phillipa stepped up to the door to Rhysdale's town house. No sounds of revelry reached the street and nothing could be seen of the gamblers inside, but, even so, she immediately sensed a different mood to the place than earlier in the day.

She sounded the knocker and the same taciturn manservant who'd attended the hall that morning answered the door.

'Good evening, sir.' She entered the hall and slipped off her hooded cape. This time she did not need netting to hide her face; her mask performed that task.

The manservant showed no indication of recognising her and she breathed a sign of relief. The mask must be working.

She handed him her cape. 'What do I do next? I am new to this place, you see.'

He nodded and actually spoke. 'Wait here a moment. I will take you to the cashier.'

The knocker sounded the moment he stepped away, but he returned quickly and opened the door to two gentlemen who greeted him exuberantly. 'Good evening to you, Cummings! Trust you are well.'

Cummings took their hats and gloves and inclined his head towards Phillipa. 'Follow them, ma'am.'

The gentlemen glanced her way and their brows rose with interest. How novel. Without her mask most men quickly looked away.

'Is this your first time here, ma'am?' one asked in a polite tone.

'It is.' She made herself smile.

The other gentleman offered an arm. 'Then it will be our pleasure to show you to the cashier.'

This was how she would be treated if not disfigured. With pleasure, not pity.

How new, as well, to accept the arm of a stranger when she'd been reared to acknowledge gentlemen only after a formal introduction took place. Would he think her fast for doing so? Or did it not matter? The gentleman would never know her.

She'd already defied the conventions of a well-bred lady by walking alone on the streets at night. She'd gathered her cloak and hood around her and made her way briskly, ignoring anyone she passed. Gas lamps lit most of the way and there had been plenty of other pedestrians out and about to make the trek feel safe.

Taking the arm of a stranger for a few seconds seemed tame after that.

He and the other gentleman escorted her to one of the rooms that had been hidden behind closed doors earlier that day. It was at the back of the house and, judging from the bookshelves that lined one of the walls, must have once been the library. Besides a few lonely books on the shelves, the room was as sparsely decorated as the hall. A large desk dominated the room. Behind the desk sat the man who had served her tea.

'MacEvoy,' one of her escorts said. 'We have a new lady for you. This is her first time here.'

MacEvoy looked her straight in the face. 'Good evening, ma'am. Shall I explain how the Masquerade Club operates?'

'I would be grateful.' She searched for signs that this man recognised her. There were none.

He told her the cost of membership and explained that she would purchase counters from him to use in play in the game room. She could purchase as many counters as she liked, but, if she lost more than she possessed, she must reveal her identity.

This was how patrons were protected, he explained. They would know who owed them money, and those who needed their identity protected dared not wager more than they possessed.

Phillipa had little interest in the wagering, but hoped she purchased enough counters to appear as if she did.

'We will take you to the gaming room, ma'am,' one of her escorts said.

'That would be kind of you.' She knew the way, but did not want the gentlemen to realise it.

When they entered the room, it seemed transformed, a riot of colour and sound. The rhythm of rolling dice, the hum of voices, the trill of shuffling cards melded into a strange symphony. Could such noise be recreated in music? What might be required? Horns? Drums? Castanets?

'Ma'am, do you wish to join us in cards?' One of her gentlemen escorts broke her reverie.

She shook her head. 'You have assisted me enough, sir. I thank you both. Please be about your own entertainment.'

They bowed and she turned away from them and scanned the room as she made her way to the hazard table. To her great relief, she did not see Xavier. A pretty young woman acted as croupier at the hazard table, which surprised Phillipa. She'd not imagined women employed to do such a job. She knew the rules of hazard, but thought it insipid to wager money on the roll of dice. Phillipa watched the play, interested more in the people than the gambling. Several of the croupiers were women. The women players were mostly masked, like she, but some were not. She wondered about them. Who were they and why did they not worry about their reputations? Perhaps she was in the company of actresses. Opera dancers. Women who would not hide from life.

There certainly seemed to be great numbers of counters being passed around in the room. Those who won exclaimed in delight; the losers groaned and despaired. Happy sounds juxtaposed with despairing ones. She'd never heard the like.

She glimpsed Rhysdale. He circulated through the room, watching, stopping to speak to this or that person. He came close to her and her heart raced. He looked directly at her, nodding a greeting before passing on. She smiled. He had not recognised her.

She walked over to the faro table. If hazard was an insipid game, faro was ridiculous. One wagered whether a particular card would be chosen from the deck. If you placed money on the banker's card you lost, if on the winning card you won double.

Still, she ought to gamble. To merely gape at everything would appear a bit suspicious.

She stifled a giggle. Out in society, people treated her as if she did not exist. Here she feared them noticing her.

She played at faro and became caught up in the spirit of the game. She cried with joy when she won and groaned at her losses, just like the other patrons. She was merely one of the crowd. Even her deep-green gown blended with the tableau as if she were a part of the décor of reds, greens and glinting golds. Her anonymity became like a cloak around her, protecting her so well she forgot that, besides Rhysdale, there might be someone at the club who could recognise her.

Xavier defused some escalating tempers, interrupted some reckless wagers and otherwise performed the same tasks as always at the Masquerade Club. His mind, however, continued to wander back to that morning.

Ought he have sent Phillipa to Rhys? Should it have been Rhys's choice of whether to tell her about her father, about the gaming house?

No. Rhys might have some of the same blood flowing through his veins as Phillipa, but she was a stranger to him. Xavier had known her for ever, even before her injury. He'd been close to her once. Her injury bound them together.

Or at least it bound him to her.

He'd been wrong to neglect her since the war ended. He should have sought her out before this. Made certain she was in good health and in good spirits. Perhaps that was why she was so cold to him at the ball.

Perhaps he would call upon her soon. See how she was faring after what he'd told her this afternoon.

Satisfied with that thought, Xavier circulated throughout the room, perusing the players and the croupiers, remaining alert to any potential problems. Most of the players here tonight were familiar to him as regular attendees. Even the masked ones were familiar, although there were a few whose identities he'd not yet guessed.

A new woman caught his eye. He'd not seen her arrive and did not know in whose party she might be included, but there was something about her...

She dressed expensively in a gown of dark-green silk. Its sheen caught the lamplight and transformed the rather

plain style into something elegant. Who was she and why
she was here for the first time?

Xavier watched her.

And came more disturbed.

His brows knit as he walked closer to her. He knew her,
did he not?

Xavier stood across the faro table from her, waiting for
the puzzle pieces to sort themselves. She glanced up and her
gaze held his for a brief moment. She quickly looked away.

He walked around the table and leaned towards her ear.
'May I have a moment to speak with you, miss?'

She bowed her head and allowed him to lead her out of
the room.

He brought her to a private corner of the hallway and
backed her against the wall. 'What the devil are you doing
here, Phillipa?'

She glared at him. 'How did you know it was me?'

How did he know? The set of her shoulders. The tilt of
her chin. Her smile. 'It was not that difficult.'

'Rhysdale did not recognise me.' That chin lifted.

'He does not know you as I do.' But he would not allow
her to change the subject. 'Why are you here?'

She shrugged. 'To gamble. Why else?'

'Who is with you?' Her brothers were gone. And, if they
had not been, they would have had to answer to him for
bringing their sister here.

'No one,' she said.

'No one?' She could not have come alone. 'How did you
get here?'

She gave him a defiant look. 'I walked.'

Walked? 'Alone?'

She did not waver. 'Yes, alone.'

He seized her arm. 'Have you taken leave of your senses?
You cannot walk about alone at night.'

'It is only a few streets.' She continued to stare into his eyes. 'Besides, Ned and Hugh taught me how to defend myself.' She lifted her skirt and showed him a sheathed knife attached to her calf.

As if she would have time to draw it, if a man accosted her. As if such a man could not easily grab it from her hand.

'And that makes you safe.' He spoke with sarcasm.

'There were plenty of people about and street lamps were lit along Piccadilly. It was like walking in daytime.'

He doubted that. He also doubted that she was there for the simple reason of gambling. 'Come,' he said. 'Let us talk in the supper room.'

The supper room served wine and spirits and a buffet supper. Designed in the style of Robert Adam, its décor was light and airy, the opposite of the game room with its darker colours. Chairs and tables covered with white linens were arranged for conversation. Along one wall stood a huge buffet table upon which were set out a variety of cold meats, cheeses, cakes and compotes. Patrons could help themselves to the food and sit at tables covered with white linen. Servants attended the room, providing drink.

The supper room was a needed respite from the high emotions in the game room, Xavier thought.

'Be seated. I'll get you something to eat.' He led her to a table set away from the few people seated in the room and made his way to the buffet.

To his dismay, Rhys was in the room, chatting with some gentlemen seated not too far away from the white pianoforte in the corner.

Xavier glanced back at Phillipa, whose posture had stiffened. She, too, had noticed Rhys.

Rhys excused himself and crossed the room to Xavier. 'I noticed we have a new woman patron.' He faced Xavier but his back was to Phillipa. 'What is wrong with her? She did not seem to be falling at your feet like other woman.'

Xavier's good looks did not matter one jot to Rhys. In fact, Rhys was perhaps the only person, besides Xavier's own family, of whom he could say such a thing. Rhys was no fool, though. He knew women were attracted to Xavier.

Xavier evaded the question. 'I am reasonably sure she is merely here for the gambling. Not the sort to cause trouble.'

Rhys laughed. 'I thought you'd met your match.'

Xavier shook his head.

Rhys put a hand on Xavier's arm. 'I have a favour to ask of you.'

During the war, Rhys twice saved Xavier's life. At Badajoz. At Quatre Bras. Xavier would have done the same for Rhys. 'What is it?'

Rhys glanced around. 'Take over the club for a few days, will you? The gentlemen with whom I was conversing have an investment that may interest me, but it would require a few days' travel.'

'Certainly,' Xavier agreed. 'What sort of investment?'

'Steam engines,' Rhys replied.

'Steam engines?' The machines that had caused such riots and unrest in the textile industry?

'Expanding their use. Making them smaller. Steam engines will do great things, you will see.' Rhys wanted another way to build wealth besides a gambling house. He'd never intended to make gambling his life.

Gambling and soldiering had enabled Rhys to survive after Rhys's mother died and Lord Westleigh abandoned him to the streets. Xavier, on the other hand, had grown up amidst luxury and the devotion of his parents and siblings. They made unusual friends.

Xavier nodded. 'If it looks to be a good investment, make certain I have a share.'

Rhys leaned forwards. 'If it is the sort of investment I expect, I may be asking you to take over the gaming house altogether.'

Run the gaming house? Xavier would do it. He delighted at doing the unexpected. Nearly everyone he'd ever met expected him to coast through life on his looks, but that was the last thing Xavier intended to do. He'd prove himself by skill, cunning, strength. Character. He'd already proved himself a good gambler, a brave soldier; he'd not mind proving he could run the best gaming house in London.

He glanced back at Phillipa. 'I'll take over the gaming house, if it comes to that, Rhys. But now I had better not keep this lady waiting.'

Rhys clapped him on the back and left the room.

Xavier brought two plates of food to the table where Phillipa waited.

'You must not have told him,' she said as he placed a plate before her.

'Told him?' Ah, she thought he would tell Rhys about her. 'Of course not.' He meant no one to know she'd come here. 'I am going to get you through this folly of yours without injury to your person or your reputation.'

'Reputation?' She made a disparaging sound. 'After what you told me about my father today, is not the whole family drenched in scandal? What does my reputation matter now?'

He signalled to a servant to bring some wine. 'Society has always known your father to be a gambler and a philanderer. His self-exile to the Continent will seem like an honourable act. Your family's reputation should stay intact.'

The wine arrived and Phillipa took a sip.

Her voice dipped low. 'No matter. I have no need to preserve a reputation. That is for marriageable young ladies or matrons concerned about children.'

He felt a stab of sympathy. 'You do not intend to marry?'

She glanced away. 'Do not be absurd. You know what is beneath this mask.' She turned back to him with a defiant gaze. 'So there is nothing to risk. If I am attacked on the street, what will it matter?'

'Do not pretend to be stupid, Phillipa,' he growled. 'A horror could befall you much worse than a cut on a face.' At Badajoz he'd seen what violence men could inflict on women.

She blinked. 'I know.'

He pushed the plate closer to her. 'Have a bit of cake and let us speak of other things besides horrors.'

She obliged him and he found himself fascinated by the small bite she took of the cake, of her licking a crumb off her lip. Her lips were a most appealing shade of pink.

'I am not really so much in the doldrums, you know,' she went on. 'I was merely trying to provoke you.'

He grinned. 'Poke me and I'll poke you back.'

They'd played that game as children. Much to his annoyance, as he recalled.

She pursed her lips. 'You had better not poke me. I poke back much better than I used to. I am no longer a little girl, you know.'

He could not help but let his gaze peruse her. 'I know.'

Her eyes flashed. 'Do not make a jest of me, Xavier.'

A jest? He was seeing her as a man sees a woman. 'You ought to know me better, Phillipa.'

'I do not know you at all now.' Her expression turned bleak. 'It has been a long time since we were children.'

'I have not changed.' He had changed, though. He'd once told himself he'd always look out for her, but he'd left her behind, a mere memory, as he grew to manhood and went to war.

'I have changed.' She lifted her chin again. 'I have become quite independent, you know.'

'Hence the excursion to a gaming hell.' He touched her hand, but quickly withdrew.

Her fingers folded. 'A gaming hell makes it sound so nefarious. It is rather staid, though. What a disappointment.'

He frowned. 'What did you expect?'

'Some debauchery, at least!' She laughed. 'I did not know what to expect, but my curiosity was piqued to see what my brothers thought would be the saving of our family. And of our village and its people. There are a great deal of counters being won and lost.'

'In gambling, the house always has the advantage. Rhys's success has been beyond everyone's expectations.' And Xavier vowed he'd make even more money from it.

Phillipa finished her wine. 'May I return to the tables, Xavier? I still have money left to lose.'

He didn't want to take her back to the game room. Not all the patrons of the place were gentlemen. She was too attractive—alluring, even—and she was alone. 'Rhys is in the game room.'

'Are you afraid he'll recognise me this time?' she asked.

'You should worry over it,' he countered. 'He might recognise you. Or someone else might.'

Her eyes shifted. 'No they won't. They have never looked at me long enough to recognise me in a mask.' She stood. 'I wish to return to the tables. I was getting accustomed to faro. I believe I will play some more.'

He had no choice but to stand. 'Very well, Phillipa.'

When they walked back to the doorway, she inclined her head towards the piano. 'Who plays for you?'

He shrugged. 'No one. It is left from the previous owner.' Who also ran a brothel here as well as a gaming house, but she did not need to know that. A young fellow played the piano and the girls sang and flirted with the men.

He escorted Phillipa back to the game room and left her at the faro table where he had found her.

'Campion brought you back?' One of the men gave her a flirtatious look. 'We despaired of ever seeing you again. Has the pick of the ladies, that one has.'

Xavier did not hear Phillipa's response.

He could not hover around her, though. He'd only call more attention to her. There were gossips in the crowd who would make it their business to discover who she was.

He would watch from afar, in case she needed assistance, and when she made ready to leave, it would not be alone.

He stepped in to the hall where Cummings attended the door.

No one entered or left without Cummings knowing of it. 'Do you recall the new woman who came earlier, the masked one in the dark-green gown?' Xavier asked.

Cummings nodded.

'When she is ready to leave, detain her and alert me. Do not allow her to leave until I speak with her.'

Cummings nodded again and, if he thought anything odd in this request, made no comment. But, then, Cummings rarely commented about anything.

'I thank you, Cummings.'

Xavier returned to the game room, glancing first to see that Phillipa still played at the faro table. He'd keep an eye on her as well as on the other gamblers, and he'd be ready to see that Phillipa arrived safely to her town-house door.

After Xavier left her at the faro table, Phillipa's very limited interest in gambling waned even further, but she persisted, merely to show him he could not drive her away.

One of the gentlemen who'd escorted her to the cashier and to the gaming room approached her. 'Are you enjoying yourself, ma'am?'

How unexpected it was to be called 'ma'am' as if she were a married lady.

Xavier glanced in her direction so she smiled at the gentleman. 'I am indeed. I even win sometimes.'

The gentleman laughed. 'That is the main purpose of coming here.' One brow rose. 'Or do you have another purpose in mind?'

By his very significant look, she knew he meant something of consequence. She was not sure, but it could be flirtation. How very unexpected, if so.

'The gambling attracts me, of course.' Why not simply ask him what he means? 'What else could there be?'

His eyes flitted over her person. 'I saw that Mr Campion singled you out for notice. Are you to be another of his conquests?'

Her smile stiffened. This was the second man to suggest such a thing. '*Another* of his conquests? Goodness! How many does he have?'

He slid Xavier a jealous look. 'He can have any woman he wishes.'

That did not precisely answer her question.

No matter. What difference to her how many women fell for the handsome Xavier Campion? What woman would not? She'd always known women found him irresistible.

For some odd reason, it bothered her to hear this man say so.

'Does he wish to claim you?' the man persisted.

Surely this was impertinence. Apparently impertinence was acceptable behaviour in a gaming house. And perhaps this gentleman did not think her a young lady worthy of respect.

That was why most of the women in the room wore masks, was it not? They would be scorned and their reputations ruined if their identities were known here. The masks protected them.

Ironically her mask merely assured that a gentleman would speak to her. He certainly would not have done if he had seen her face.

She turned back to the faro table. 'I do believe Mr Campion merely wished to welcome me to the house.'

The man bowed. 'I do understand.'

He understood? She wished she did. She'd intended to merely avoid his question. There was nothing to be understood.

He walked away.

She shook her head. If that man intended a flirtation, he gave up too easily.

She caught Xavier looking at her and, as she turned away from him, caught a woman glaring at her. Out of jealousy? Now this *was* a unique experience. A woman shooting daggers of jealousy at her instead of melting with pity.

All this was new. New people. New experiences. If she'd not consumed a little too much wine when with Xavier and if the hour were not so dreadfully late, her heart would be racing with excitement. She found it difficult to keep from yawning, though. Her mask itched and her feet hurt and she yearned to be between the cool linens of her bed.

She should leave.

Phillipa walked out of the room and cashed in her counters with the cashier. She'd lost money, but it hardly signified since the money simply went back to her family. She made her way to the hall to collect her cape and gloves. The same taciturn hall servant stood there.

And so did Xavier.

When the servant walked off to get her things, she faced him. 'Making sure that I leave, Xavier?'

'No.' He did not look pleased. 'I will walk you home.'

'That is not necessary, I assure you,' she responded. 'I am perfectly capable of walking by myself.'

'Regardless, I will walk you home.'

The servant brought her cloak and Xavier took it from him. He stepped towards Phillipa and placed it around her shoulders. The touch of his hands on her shoulders caused a *frisson* of sensation down her back.

She disliked being so affected by Xavier Campion. It made her think of how she'd felt dancing with him. The thrill of coming close to him, of touching him.

The servant opened the door and the cool evening air revived her.

Phillipa crossed over the threshold with Xavier right behind her. 'I do not need an escort.'

He fell in step with her. 'Nevertheless, I need to do this.'

She scoffed. 'Do not be absurd. You can have the company of any woman you like. One of the gentlemen told me so.'

His step slowed for a moment. 'Phillipa, if any danger should befall you on this walk home, I would never forgive myself for not preventing it.'

He sounded so serious.

'So dramatic, Xavier. I am not your responsibility.'

His voice turned low. 'At this moment, you are.'

It was very late. Three in the morning, at least, and she had never walked the streets of Mayfair at such an hour. Certainly not with a man at her side.

A man like Xavier.

But she must not think of him like that.

They crossed Piccadilly and as they headed towards Berkeley Square, their footsteps sounded a rhythm broken only by the echoing of a carriage or hackney coach somewhere in the distance. Other sounds—voices, music— wafted to her ears, only to fade quickly. She concentrated on the sounds, searching for a melody she might recreate on her pianoforte, a melody that would sound like the night felt. Cool, peaceful, empty.

'Are you talking to yourself, Phillipa?' Xavier asked.

She'd been lost in her music. 'Why do you ask?'

'Your lips were moving.'

She'd been playing the music to herself. How daft she must appear. 'I—I hear music in the sounds of the night. I try to remember them.'

'Music?' He could not hear the music, obviously.

'In our footsteps. The carriages.' She shrugged. 'The other sounds.'

He paused before responding. 'I see.'

Her mask irritated her face. She untied it and pulled it off, rubbing her scar before concealing her face with the hood of her cloak.

'I like music,' she explained. 'I have studied music and the pianoforte a great deal over the last few years.' Since that ball when she'd first danced with him. Of course, she'd never played 'The Nonesuch' again, though it had once been a favourite of hers. 'It is my greatest pleasure.'

'Is it?' He acted as if interested. 'I should like to hear you play.'

Such a polite thing to say. The sort of thing one says when pretending an interest that doesn't truly exist. Like choosing a dance partner as a favour to one's mother's friend.

'I play the pianoforte alone. It consumes my time.' She made it seem as if she preferred not to have an audience when she really longed to play for others, to discover if her compositions and her technique had any merit.

He stopped speaking for a half a street.

She regretted snapping at him. 'I think I spend too much

time with my music. I think that is why I did not notice that
my family was in distress.'

'You isolated yourself.' He sounded as if that would be
a sad thing.

'Too much, perhaps,' she admitted. 'That is the main
reason I decided to visit the Masquerade Club.'

'Could you not simply decide to attend balls and routs
and musicales instead?' His tone disapproved.

She was invisible in such places. No one looked at her if
they could help it. No one spoke to her if they could avoid it.

When she donned the mask this night all that changed.
'Perhaps balls and routs and musciales are not exciting
enough for me.'

His fingers closed around her arm and he stopped walking. 'Too much excitement can be dangerous. You must not
play with fire, Phillipa.'

'Fire?' She laughed. 'What do you mean?'

'I mean that men will notice you at the gaming house.
They will not expect you to be an innocent young girl.'

'Innocent girl? Young? I am three and twenty. Quite
on the shelf.' But devoid of any experience, of that he was
correct.

They walked again. 'You have had your excitement,' he
went on. 'Go back to playing your music now.'

She was eager to return to her music room, to write down
the notes she'd heard in the sounds of the street at three in
the morning, the sounds of a gaming hell, of his voice.

But she could not be done with the Masquerade Club.
She wished to see and hear more; she wished to experience more.

Too bad for him. 'I plan to return.'

'No!' he growled.

She lifted her chin. 'I fully realise you do not wish me

around you, Xavier, but it is you who have insinuated your-self into my company, not the reverse.'

'You wrong me again.' He sounded angry. 'We are old friends, Phillipa. I owe you my protection as sure as if you were one of my sisters.'

'Once, perhaps, you were under an obligation to do me a kindness.' Her chest ached in memory. 'Not any more.'

A carriage clattered by and she forced herself to listen to the horses' hooves clapping against the cobbles, the wheels turning, the springs creaking.

She made it into music inside her head so she would not have to speak more to him, nor think about the thrill of him walking beside her, a sensation distracting in the extreme.

Would her old school friends still envy her as they'd once done when she'd danced with him all those years ago? Her friends were all married now. Some very well. Some very happily. She'd lost touch with most of them, although on the rare occasion her mother convinced her to attend some society event, she often saw some of them. Her most regular correspondence was with Felicia, who moved to Ireland when she married and never returned to England. Felicia's letters were all about her children, her worries about the poor and her fears of typhus. Felicia would probably not even remember when Phillipa had danced with the most handsome man at the ball. How trivial it would seem to her if she did.

They reached Davies Street and the Westleigh town house.

'Will someone let you in?' Xavier asked, walking her directly to the door.

She pulled a key from her reticule. 'No one will even know I've been gone.'

He took the key from her hand and turned it in the lock. As he opened the door, she stepped closer to slip in.

'Farewell, Phillipa,' he murmured, handing her back the key, standing so close his breath warmed her face. His voice felt as warm around her.

'Xavier,' she whispered back, unable to thank him for doing something she didn't want, battling a familiar yearning she thought she'd defeated years ago.

She closed the door quietly and set her chin. 'I will see you when night falls again,' she said, knowing he could not hear.

Chapter Three

The next day Xavier saw Rhys off to travel north to look into this steam engine venture. That night, as other nights, Xavier walked through the gaming room, watching to see if all ran smoothly. From the beginning of the Masquerade Club he'd assisted Rhys in this task. The croupiers and the regular patrons were now used to him, but he'd needed to earn their respect.

It was not unusual for other men to underestimate him. He knew their thinking—that a man with his looks could not possibly have anything of substance to offer. Soldiers in his regiment had scoffed at his capacity to lead them until he proved himself in battle. Even the enemy on the battlefield took one look at him and dropped their guard. He could still see the surprised faces of those who felt the sharp edge of his sabre.

Xavier always believed he possessed courage, strength, cunning, but battle had tested it and proved it to him once and for all.

But he was done with war and fighting. He'd seen enough blood and suffering and death.

Xavier shook off the memories and made another circuit of the room. He paused at the hazard table, watching the men and women throw away fortunes with the roll of the dice, paying close attention to the dice, making certain they were not weighted.

Hazard, so dependent upon chance, had never interested him. To own the truth, even games of skill had lost their appeal. He'd demonstrated to the sceptics—and to himself—that he could win at cards. He possessed a tidy fortune to show for it.

Running the Masquerade Club was his latest challenge. Making it a success, in terms of popularity and profitability, was a game he intended to win. When Rhys returned, the house would be showing greater profits and more patrons than ever before.

Xavier knew he could be good at this. Hadn't he been the one to notice the irregularities at the hazard table, the ones that so involved Lady Gale and ultimately Lord Westleigh?

Good riddance to that man. Everyone was better off with him gone. Especially Lord Westleigh's family.

Especially Phillipa.

Lord Westleigh had been on the brink of ruining Phillipa's life.

She had changed from that waif-like little girl he'd vowed to protect at Brighton. He'd been nearly five years older than she, but after her injury that summer, he'd made himself her champion, doing his best to distract her from her scar and keep sadness and despair at bay. He'd repeated this charge every summer until his family no longer summered at Brighton.

He'd never forgotten her.

In 1814, when Napoleon had been banished to Elba and peace briefly reigned on the Continent, Xavier found her again and danced with her at one of the Season's balls. She'd seemed as light-hearted and gay as her many friends. And as pretty—if one ignored her scar. He'd looked forward to a second dance that night and a chance to spend more time with her, but she'd taken ill, her mother said. And he'd left for his regiment the next day.

Phillipa had changed in these last five years, though. She was remote. Guarded. As if she'd built a wall around herself, too deep and high to breach.

At least he'd seen her home safely last night. It had been foolish of her to come to the Masquerade Club alone. Still, he wished he could see her again.

Two men and a woman at the faro table parted and his wish came true.

There Phillipa stood.

She'd come back, even though he'd told her not to.

She glanced at him at that moment, straightening her spine defiantly. He acknowledged her with a nod.

He had a mind to march over, seize her arm and drag her out of this room, out of this gaming house and back to her home. Such a disruption would not be good for the house. And he certainly did not want to cause her undue attention.

He waited.

Finally she walked out of the room. He leaned over to one of the croupiers. 'I'll be right back.'

He caught up to her in the hallway. They were alone. 'Phillipa.'

She turned and held her head high.

'Are you leaving?' He would not allow her to walk home alone.

She did not answer right away. 'I am going to the supper room.'

He took her arm. 'I will come with you.'

When they entered the room, she strode directly to the buffet and made her own selections.

He asked one of the servants to bring wine to his table, selecting one far enough away that the other diners could not hear their conversation. The wine arrived before she left the buffet.

She turned and paused as if trying to decide whether to join him or not. Tossing her head, she carried her plate to his table and sat down in silence.

He leaned towards her. 'What possessed you to return here, Phillipa? I told you not to.'

She sipped her wine. 'You *told* me I'd had enough excitement, as if you could know.'

'This is not a fit place for you.' How could he convince her? 'Not all who come here are gentlemen and ladies.'

'Enough, Xavier.' She glared at him. 'I will not be treated as if I am still seven years old. My half-brother made this a place ladies could gamble and so I shall gamble here. You cannot and will not stop me.'

She was right. He could not stop her. But he did have an obligation to her. He'd always had an obligation to her. 'Do you intend to come again?'

'Of course.' She smiled smugly. 'As often as I wish.'

'Name the nights you will come and the times. I will escort you to and from the place.' He could at least see she was safe on the streets.

'No!' she snapped.

'Why?' This was more foolishness. 'It is to keep you safe.'

She held his gaze with an obstinate look. Finally she said, 'Very well, but only if you agree not to tell Rhysdale.'

He'd never had any intention to tell Rhys. 'Very well.'

Their conversation became more companionable after that. She asked about some of the patrons and he told her frankly which men were gentlemen and which were not. She asked questions about the running of the Masquerade Club, about the collection of the money, especially for the card games. She asked about profits and the potential for losses.

She had a quick mind, grasping the workings of the place as quickly as did her brother Hugh.

After half an hour, she rose to leave. As they walked towards the door and passed the pianoforte, Phillipa ran her fingers over the keyboard. 'It seems a shame that no one ever plays. This is a pretty instrument.'

'It has a nice sound, as I recall.' Under Madame Bisou, the previous owner, music and raucous singing had filled the room for part of the night.

Phillipa looked at him with a careful expression. 'I will play for you, if you will allow me to.'

He cocked his head, thinking. It would keep her out of the gaming room, at least.

He gestured to the piano bench. 'Give it a try, Phillipa. Play whatever you like.'

She smiled. 'Not tonight. Tomorrow night.'

The next night Xavier met Phillipa outside her town house at the agreed upon hour. He walked with her through Mayfair, crossing Piccadilly to St James's Street and finally to the gaming hell. She headed straight to the supper room and the pianoforte.

He stayed to listen to her. If she was dreadful, he could stop her. Amateurs were often dreadful. Enough wrong notes, enough singing off-key and people would find another house in which to gamble. That would not happen under his watch.

Her first song he'd heard before—'I Have A Silent Sorrow Here', a song of unrequited love. The strings of the pianoforte and her voice resonated with emotion. She sang the song so beautifully it convinced him she had once loved a man who did not love her.

Who the devil was that man? That man who hurt her so?

Was that what caused her to isolate herself? Had he made her bitter and unhappy?

The second song had a similar theme, although he'd never heard the tune before. Even more melancholic than the first, she sang of watching her beloved across a room and of being invisible to him.

He forgot about anything but the pain and sadness of her song, the emotion in her voice. He'd failed at his youthful vow to protect her. He'd not been there when this man wounded her. He clenched a fist. He'd like to find that fellow now.

She next played something light-hearted and he woke from his reverie. He glanced at the faces in the supper room. The people seated there abandoned their conversations. With rapt expressions, they all turned toward Phillipa.

The only way Phillipa would be a liability to the gaming house was if patrons abandoned the gaming tables to come hear her perform.

Xavier yearned to abandon his duties to stay to listen to her, but he'd already spent enough time away from the gaming room. He reluctantly left the supper room. In the gaming room the sounds were not melodic. Voices humming, dice rolling, cards shuffling. Although the sound of her voice and of the pianoforte sometimes broke through the din.

She did not stay long that evening, only a little more than two hours. As she promised to do, she sent word to him when she wished to go home. To escort her home would take little more than a half-hour. For that amount of time he could leave the club in the hands of Rhys's employees.

They stepped out into the cool night air.

Her spirits were so high, she seemed irrepressible. It reminded him of that long-ago ball.

'You enjoyed yourself tonight?' he guessed.

She almost danced down the pavement. 'I did. No one seemed disappointed in my playing.'

'You did very well.'

She did more than very well.

'Did I?' She skipped ahead of him and faced him while walking backwards. 'Do you truly think so?'

She pulled off her mask and the gas lamps illuminated her face, making it glow. Her happiness made her beautiful.

His heart swelled for her. 'I know little of music, but I enjoyed what I heard.'

She grinned and twirled around. 'That is all I wish!'

She chattered on about the songs she'd sung and played, reviewing her mistakes, assessing what went well. He liked listening to her. It reminded him of when she'd been a little girl and he'd been able to get her to happily chatter on.

In no time at all they reached her door and he put the key in the lock.

She reached up on tiptoe and kissed him on the cheek. 'Thank you so much, Xavier. You have made me very happy tonight.'

Her lips felt soft and warm.

He wrapped his arms around her and brought his lips within a hair's breadth of hers. He felt her breasts rise and fall against his chest, further tantalising him. Her eyes grew wide as her mouth opened in alarm.

Banking his impulses, he lightly touched his lips to hers.

When he released her, his breath came faster. 'I want you always to be happy, Phillipa,' he murmured. 'Same time tomorrow?'

She blinked up him, her brow puzzled. 'Same time tomorrow.'

He opened the door and she slipped inside.

It took him a moment to move away.

He'd appointed himself her protector, but perhaps his hardest task would be to protect her from himself.

For the next four nights Xavier met Phillipa at her town house and returned her home again. They walked side by side through the night with only the occasional gaslight or rush light to break through the darkness. There were few carriages in the streets and fewer still pedestrians sharing the pavement. They talked of her music and the patrons who attended the gaming house, traded stories of what transpired in the supper room and in the game room.

Xavier was careful not to touch her, at least not to touch her in the way he most desired. The old camaraderie from their childhood days might have returned, but what consumed Xavier's senses was the woman Phillipa had become. So graceful. So quick-witted. So passionate.

So unaffected by him.

How ironic that he should desire a woman who gave no sign at all of desiring him.

It was fortunate, he supposed, because this idyll could not continue indefinitely. When Rhys returned her performances would stop, and, Xavier suspected, Phillipa would have no more use for him. Still, he did not regret his decision to allow her to perform.

It brought her joy.

It even brought increased profits. People came to The Masquerade Club to hear her play and they stayed to gamble.

Could he contrive to see her when it was over? Would she receive him? Did he want to push himself on a woman who did not want him? God knew, he detested being pursued by someone he did not want.

This night she performed for two hours, as had become her custom, and sent word to Xavier that she was ready to leave. As they'd done on previous nights, they stepped out into the night air and began to share the night's events with each other. This night, though, when they crossed Piccadilly and made their way to the unlit streets of Mayfair, Xavier felt a change in the air. It was nothing more than an odd sound, an unfamiliar shadow, but the soldier in him went on alert.

When he and Phillipa reached Hay Hill, the hairs on the back of his neck rose and he could almost hear the drum beat of the *pas de charge*.

He stopped her and lowered his voice. 'Do you still carry your dagger?'

'Yes.' She caught his nerves.

'Pull it and hand it to me now.'

She did as he asked.

As soon as the knife was in his hands, three men burst from the darkness. One, stinking of drink, seized him from behind and dragged him into the Brunton Mews. Xavier twisted his way free and slashed the dagger at the man, slicing in to a tattered uniform. In his ears he heard the sounds of battle. Muskets firing. Cannons booming. Men and horses screaming.

But this was not battle.

Another man grabbed for his wrist and tried to wrest the knife from his grasp. Xavier whirled on him, kicked him in the groin and sent him sprawling.

The third man had Phillipa in his grip. Xavier strained to come to her aid, but the first man set on him again.

'We need money,' the man cried. No doubt he was a former soldier now driven to theft and violence.

'Leave us! Release her!' Xavier lunged at him, slicing the man's cheek and neck with his blade.

The man cried out and clapped his hand to his face. Blood dripped through the man's fingers and on to his uniform. Xavier turned away at the sight and saw the second man regain his feet. Xavier's thoughts were only on Phillipa.

She struggled to free herself. She gripped her captor's hair and pulled it hard, before stomping on the man's foot.

The second man went to aid the man fighting with Phillipa. Xavier launched himself forwards and seized the man's collar, pulling him away.

That man pulled a knife. 'Not so brave now, pretty boy.' He laughed. 'Give us your money.'

One more man underestimating him.

Xavier lifted his hands as if surrendering. 'I want no trouble.'

The man sneered in contempt and lowered his hands slightly, the chance Xavier anticipated. He let out a cry, so fierce and wild, the man shrank back. Xavier charged straight for him, his fist connecting to the man's chin. The man's knife dropped to the street.

Xavier slammed him against the wall of the building and put the dagger to his throat. 'Not so brave now, are you?'

'Don't cut me! Don't cut me!' the man pleaded.

Xavier snarled, 'Leave now and you leave with your lives.'

The man nodded in fear. 'We're leaving. We're leaving!' He raised his hands in the air and Xavier stepped away. The man sidled away and grabbed the arm of the man still trying to stop the bleeding of the cut to his face.

The third man now had Phillipa's reticule in his grip. She would not release it. His eyes widened when his companions ran off and Xavier advanced on him. Phillipa blocked the man's escape. He picked her up and thrust her aside.

She hit the pavement flat on her face, her forehead bouncing on to its hard surface.

She did not move.

'Phillipa!' Xavier ran to her.

* * *

Phillipa heard a man call her name.

She scented sea air and heard waves rolling on to the shore. She felt small and frightened and in pain. Her face hurt and she tasted blood.

She tried to move, but the wind had been knocked out of her. 'Phillipa!' the voice called again.

A man's hands turned her on her back. The darkness had melded into dusk and the air was briny.

'Wake up, my girl,' the voice said.

She opened her eyes and her vision filled with the face of a man. A stranger to her, but she'd seen him before, in this exact way—or so it felt.

'Phillipa, wake up.' The face changed before her eyes, turning into Xavier's face.

She gasped.

'Are you hurt?' Xavier's hands were all over her, touching her arms, her legs, her torso. 'Did he hurt you?'

This was not at the seaside?

No, it was London. She and Xavier had been walking home. This was not Brighton. She was not a little girl. This was Xavier with her.

'I'm not hurt,' she managed.

She tried to sit up. His arms embraced her and lifted her to her feet. He held her against him. 'I thought you were hurt.' He held her tighter. 'I thought I had lost you.'

She remembered men jumping out of the darkness at them. She remembered fighting to be free.

But for a moment she'd been back in Brighton. She'd seen a different man lean over her. He appeared as real as Xavier appeared now.

She trembled. She'd seen something that was not really there.

Panic rose inside her, kept at bay only because of the

strength of his arms. He comforted her. She was safe. Xavier held her.

He loosened his grip. 'I must get you home.'

Supporting her weight with one arm, he led her out of the mews, past Berkeley Square to Davies Street.

Her head throbbed as she remembered he'd had to fight off two men. 'Did they hurt you?' she asked. 'Did they get your money?' Her reticule still dangled from her arm.

His voice turned low and fierce. 'Not that miserable lot of ruffians.'

They reached her door and he embraced her again. 'I should have prevented that attack. We should not have been walking at this hour. I was wrong to agree to this.'

If he had not been with her, what would have happened to her? There had been three of them.

Her heart pounded, anticipating what would come next. He intended to forbid her to come to the Masquerade Club. He would stop her performances right when she was learning about how to make the music most entertaining. He would take it all away.

She could not bear it.

'Do not forbid me this, Xavier.' Her voice trembled and her head ached.

'It is not safe, Phillipa,' he insisted. 'You simply cannot take the risk.'

The hood of her cloak had fallen away, exposing her disfigurement. She pulled it up again and put the key in the lock, turning it.

He covered her hand with his. 'Phillipa, do not come to the gaming house. Do not try it alone.'

She opened the door and turned to him. 'May I have my dagger back?'

He hesitated, but finally handed it to her.

'Thank you, Xavier.' Impulsively she threw her arms around him. 'You saved us both.'

To her surprise, he returned her embrace with one of his own. He held her against him so tightly it seemed as if he would never release her.

'Phillipa,' he rasped in her ear, as if wanting something more of her, but she did not know what.

She only knew she felt even more shaken when he finally released her and she hurried inside the house.

Chapter Four

Phillipa tossed and turned in her bed. If she drifted into sleep, her attacker returned, jarring her awake. Worse, in her dream, the attacker bore the face of the man she'd seen in her vision.

She must call it a vision. What else could it be? She'd seen something that did not exist. Not only *seen*, she'd actually *been* in another place, a place that smelled and sounded like the seaside.

Like Brighton.

Was she going mad?

She closed her eyes and made herself imagine the image of her real attacker. And then she purposely recalled the face of the phantom man. She could remember both, but remembering was not remotely akin to what she had experienced. Seeing the phantom face, feeling as if she were in another place, those were not mere memories.

Even now, safe in her home, in her bed, she trembled in fear. It made no sense to feel afraid now; she'd not been excessively afraid during the attack. Fear had not been a part of fighting off her attacker and refusing to give him her reticule. The terror had come when she fell and that phantom face appeared.

It had seemed so very real.

If it were not enough to worry about going mad, her head also hurt like the dickens. She rose from bed and, by the dawning light from the window, peered at herself in her dressing table mirror. Her forehead bore a nasty scrape.

Phillipa walked back to her bed and pulled off a blanket. She wrapped it around herself and curled up in a chair to watch the light from the window grow brighter.

Her maid entered the room quietly and jumped when Phillipa turned towards her in the chair. 'My lady!'

'I could not sleep, Lacey.' Phillipa stretched. 'I might as well dress, I suppose.'

Her maid helped her into a morning dress and stood behind her to pin up her hair as she sat at the dressing table.

The girl glanced at her in the mirror. 'What happened to your forehead?'

'It is nothing,' Phillipa answered quickly. 'I…I bumped into the wall by accident.'

The maid looked sceptical.

Lacey was younger than Phillipa and had been hired as Phillipa's lady's maid after the Westleighs arrived in London for the Season. How nice it would be if Phillipa could confide in her about how her injury came about.

'I'll just wear a cap today,' Phillipa said as the maid pinned up her hair. 'We need not mention my injury to my mother. No need to worry her.' A cap should hide the scrape well enough. Besides, her mother never looked at her too closely these days.

The girl nodded. 'Yes, miss.'

Once dressed, Phillipa went straight to her music room. She placed her fingers on the keys of the pianoforte and tried to release the emotions inside her. The keys produced dissonant, unharmonious sounds and her fear returned, as if her world were crumbling around her and she could not stop it, the same feeling she experienced when she fell.

Her music reflected the confusion inside her. No phrase complemented any other.

She became dimly aware of a rapping at the door, but she did not stop playing. Whoever it was would eventually go away.

Suddenly her mother stood before her, shocking her as much as if her mother had been a vision herself.

'Gracious, Phillipa! At least play a tune. This noise grates upon my nerves.' Her mother pressed her fingers to her forehead.

Phillipa and her mother had barely spoken since the quarrel that sent Phillipa in search of answers about her family. And led her to Xavier. Now she could not speak of what she'd learned without revealing that she knew of the Masquerade Club.

Phillipa lifted her hands from the keys. 'As you wish, Mama.'

She softly played 'The Last Rose of Summer', reciting the words in her head—*Tis the last rose of summer, Left blooming alone; All her lovely companions Are faded and gone.*

She'd not felt alone since Xavier allowed her to perform at the Masquerade Club.

'When do Ned and Hugh return from wherever they are?' She knew her mother would not tell her, but it might make her leave the room before noticing Phillipa's bruise.

Her mother, still straight-backed and regal though in her fifty-fifth year, pursed her lips before answering, 'Please do not tease me about their whereabouts. I have no wish to have that discussion with you again.'

Phillipa continued to play *pianissimo*.

'Do you come to Lady Danderson's musical evening with

me tonight?' Her mother's tone dripped with disapproval. No doubt she expected Phillipa to refuse.

She was correct 'I think not.'

Her mother swept a dramatic arm encompassing the pianoforte and half the room. 'Why not? I thought you loved music.'

Phillipa shot her a sharp look, but averted her eyes. No sense revisiting her mother's displeasure at her retreat from society. 'It is to be an amateur performance, is it not? Lady Danderson's daughters and other young ladies and gentlemen of her choosing?'

'It is,' her mother admitted.

'But she has not chosen me.'

Her mother cleared her throat. 'That is true, but…'

Phillipa stopped playing. 'I do understand it, Mama. The performers are eligible young people. She wishes them to show off to good advantage.' Phillipa did not need to explain to her mother that she would never show off to good advantage. Her mother would be first to agree. 'There is no reason for me to be there.'

'Well, there is the music,' her mother added.

Phillipa resumed playing and the final lines of the song came to her—*Oh! Who would inhabit this bleak world alone?* 'I would not enjoy it.'

'I will attend without you, then.' Her mother turned away and then swung back. 'Perhaps I will ask Miss Gale if she will come with me. She is at least a sociable sort.'

Miss Gale was the young woman Phillipa's brother Ned wanted to marry. She was also the stepdaughter of Lady Gale, the woman carrying Rhysdale's child, the woman who also came masked to the Masquerade Club.

'Miss Gale will be glad of my company.' It was her mother's parting shot. She strode out of the room.

Phillipa's head suddenly ached, but she moved her fingers over the keys, barely pressing them this time, searching for a melody, any melody to erase this unrest within her.

Xavier waited for Phillipa that night at their appointed place, at their appointed time. This time, however, he waited with a hackney cab.

He paced the pavement, rather hoping she would not show up, yet yearning to see her, needing to know for certain that her injuries were minor. A blow to the head could be deceiving. What if she had been truly hurt, like that long-ago time in Brighton?

He'd have failed her again, that was what. And this time it would be his fault.

The jarvey leaned down from his perch atop the coach. 'How much longer, sir? My time is money.'

'I'll pay you for your time, do not fear.' Xavier paced some more.

Her town house door finally opened and a shadowy, cloaked figure emerged.

Phillipa.

She glanced towards where he stood near the coach, pausing briefly to put on her shoes before heading in his direction. She showed no sign that she knew it was he and looked as if she intended to walk past him.

'Phillipa,' he called out.

She drew back.

'It is Xavier.' He stepped in her path. 'I have a hackney coach.'

'Xavier?'

He opened the coach door.

She looked uncertain. 'You brought a hackney for me?'

'I feared you might try to walk alone.' *Or be too injured to make the attempt*, he added silently as he helped her climb into the coach.

She settled in the seat and pulled her cloak around her. 'I did not expect this.'

Xavier sat beside her in the close quarters of the coach's dark interior. He felt her warmth, inhaled the scent of jasmine that clung to her. Her face was shrouded by her mask, but he longed to see her for himself. Was she bruised? Did her injuries again show on her face?

'Have you suffered any ill-effects from last night?' he asked.

She did not answer right away. 'A scrape on my forehead and little headache is all.'

'That is all?'

There was something she was not telling him. He resisted the temptation to pull off her mask to see this scrape for himself. He also resisted the temptation to check her arms, shoulders, ribs, legs—all over her, as he had done the night before.

At the very least, he was tempted to hold her, like he'd done when she was a little girl and had been in need of his comfort.

The distance to the Masquerade Club made for a short walk and an even shorter ride. In no time the coach pulled up to the gaming house and they disembarked.

Xavier paid the driver generously. 'You'll earn that much again if you return in three hours.'

The jarvey grinned. 'In that case, I will, sir!'

Cummings opened the door, nodded to them both and took Phillipa's cloak.

'Thank you, Cummings,' Phillipa said, sounding more tense than other nights.

Xavier faced her. 'Give me your word you will wait for the hackney coach. Do not leave without me.'

'You have my word,' she assured him.

Xavier watched her climb the stairs to the supper room,

but he was not perusing her for possible injuries. He was admiring her form and grace.

He glanced away and noticed Cummings regarding him curiously. Cummings turned and disappeared with Phillipa's cloak.

Xavier shrugged. Who ever knew what Cummings thought? Xavier crossed the hall in the opposite direction and checked in with MacEvoy.

'Our numbers continue to run high.' MacEvoy handed him the ledger where he kept count of the numbers of patrons attending and the amount of profits at the end of the night.

When Rhys returned he would look through the books and ask Xavier about the spike in patrons and profits. Xavier would tell Rhys about the *pianiste* who'd briefly performed in Rhys's absence.

He simply would not tell Rhys the *pianiste* had been Phillipa.

MacEvoy added, 'A woman asked for you.'

'Indeed?' Women often asked for him.

'Don't know her. She's wearing a mask. I told her you'd be back directly.' Most of the time MacEvoy recognised patrons, even when they wore masks. He knew the *pianiste* was the woman who'd called on Xavier that first day, but he did not know her real name.

Unless he had asked Cummings. She'd announced herself to Cummings. Both Cummings and MacEvoy probably knew Phillipa's identity. Xavier would have to deal with that.

'Thank you, Mac.' He returned the ledger to MacEvoy.

Xavier's next stop was the gaming room. He wound his way around the room, stopping to chat with patrons or the croupiers. He stepped to the side and surveyed the room, looking for signs of potential trouble. A reckless loser. Or an angry one. Or, a gaming hell's worst trouble—cheaters.

A masked woman approached him. The woman who'd asked for him, he surmised.

'Hello, Xavier.' Her voice was low and lustful.

'Ma'am.' He was usually as skilled as MacEvoy in recognising patrons beneath their masks, but she was new to him.

She laughed. 'Do you not know me?'

He smiled. 'I make it a practice not to know anyone wearing a mask.'

Except Phillipa.

She touched his arm. 'You must know me!'

He had no idea.

'It has been an age. Ten years. But I have never forgotten you.' Her fingers squeezed his arm in too familiar a manner.

Ten years? A dampening feeling spread over him.

Yes. He knew her suddenly. She'd nearly ruined her marriage, her reputation and the good name of his family when last he'd encountered her.

'But I do not know you,' he said, untruthfully. 'The mask disguises you. Your identity is safe here, I assure you.'

'Xavier.' Her tone turned sharp and her fingers dug tighter. 'You would not forget me.'

Indeed he would not.

He'd been barely eighteen. She'd been two years older and unhappily married. She'd pursued an affair with him with all the force of a regimental attack.

And now she was back.

He was careful to remain no more than civil. 'I assure you, ma'am. Those who choose anonymity may be secure in it.' Illusory though it was. 'I will not know you.'

She pulled him over to a corner of the room and pulled down her mask. 'It is I. Daphne. Lady Faville. Surely you remember me.'

She had not changed. Same pale, unblemished skin. Same flaxen hair and wide-set blue eyes. A perfect beauty.

He put her mask back in place. 'Of course I remember you, my lady.' He remembered her desperate loneliness and her belief that an affair with him could alter her unhappiness.

'My lady?' She sounded as if she would cry. 'Can it not be Daphne and Xavier between us?'

'No, it cannot.' He softened his expression, but glanced around the room. 'Is Lord Faville here with you?'

Her eye sparkled. 'Did you not hear? He is dead.'

'I am sorry to hear it.' He really ought to peruse the newspapers more carefully. 'My condolences.'

She waved a hand. 'I am out of mourning. I have attended some of the Season's parties, hoping to see you. Then I learned you were here.'

She'd come looking for him. This was not good.

She smiled. 'There is no one to stop us now.'

Xavier gritted his teeth. 'Daphne, I am stopping it. You caused a great deal of trouble and pain to my family as well as nearly ruining your good name and your marriage—'

Her eyes lit up. 'You called me Daphne!'

Oh, good God.

'Enough of this.' He held up a hand. 'You are welcome here. To play the tables, or cards or refresh yourself in the supper room, but what is past is over.'

He strode away and did not look back.

In the supper room Phillipa played only pieces that were so well practised she need not look at her music. If the patrons recognised that she was not challenging herself to play her best, they showed no indication.

She knew the exact moment Xavier entered the supper

room, if not by her senses alone, by the way other women's heads turned in his direction. She glanced at him, too.

He stood near the door, arms folded across his chest, listening to the simple tune she played. His handsome face was composed—such a contrast to how he'd looked fighting their attackers.

Strong and fierce.

He did not stay long. He never stayed long, but she also sensed the moment he left.

The gentleman who'd met her that first day entered the room, looking gloom-faced. He sat near the pianoforte, drink in hand. He was one of her admirers. There were several men who always listened to her play and spoke pretty words to her.

Imagine. Several men, none of whom would give her a second glance if they first saw her scar.

The idea usually amused her, but not this night when other faces flashed through her memory. The men who attacked her. The man in the vision.

After performing for an hour and a half, Phillipa's head ached. She rose from her bench and those in the room, the gentleman included, clapped their appreciation.

She curtsied to them. 'Thank you. Do go gamble. I will play again after a brief respite.'

The patrons who left the room at that point were unlikely to return once they were deep in their cards or dice, but it did not matter. The more men and women gambled, the more improved her family's finances would be.

A gentleman she had not seen there before approached her. 'Excellent performance, ma'am.'

Was this to be another admirer? 'Thank you, sir.'

He inclined his head in response. 'I did not expect to

hear such excellent music. I confess I did not know of the fine entertainment when learning of the Masquerade Club.'

'You flatter me.' The flattery she received here always surprised her.

'Nonsense. I speak the truth,' the gentleman said.

Like most of the men who attended the club, he did not wear a mask. His face was pleasant, as was his manner. It put her at ease.

He bowed. 'Allow me to present myself. I am Mr Everard.'

'How do you do, Mr Everard,' she responded. 'You have not been to the Masquerade Club before?'

'It is my first time,' he admitted. 'I have especially enjoyed the music.'

'Not the gambling? There are several tables and games to enjoy.'

He shook his head. 'I never gamble. I am a man of business, you see, and I believe it is not a good thing to risk money on cards or dice.'

Had her father's man of business possessed the same philosophy? Had the man warned her father against gambling the family fortune away? Perhaps her father simply ignored him. Xavier might know.

'Surely you did not come here just to hear me.'

'I confess I did not.' He smiled. 'Although I might have done so had I known of your excellent music. I am here in the capacity of escort.'

'Escort?'

'I was my lady's husband's man of business until his death, but I will say no more, else risk revealing her identity.' He looked wistful. 'Suffice to say I try to serve her in whatever way she needs me.'

'How very generous of you.' Phillipa glanced towards the servant attending the supper room. 'If you will excuse me, my throat is very dry. I need to ask the servant for something to drink.'

He raised his hand. 'Tell me. I will order it for you.'

'Some sherry would be very nice.'

He crossed the room to speak to the servant.

The gentleman who assisted her the first day rose from his chair and walked over to her still carrying his drink. 'I see you have another admirer.'

'One more is always welcome.' She'd learned to banter with gentlemen.

He lifted a hand and counted on his fingers. 'Mr Campion is certainly an admirer. This new gentleman...and me, of course. How many more?'

Phillipa sat down at a nearby table. 'Do not talk nonsense. I think you are peeved for some reason. Perhaps you have lost too much at cards and now you are seeking distraction at my expense.'

He rubbed his forehead. 'How very astute. You are right, of course.' He looked genuinely contrite. 'Forgive me. I have lost a great deal of money and I am very uneasy about it.' He gestured to one of the chairs. 'May I join you for a moment?'

Such a request was commonplace to her here. 'As long as you behave properly.'

'Agreed.' He sat.

Mr Everard hurried over, carrying a wine glass. 'Please forgive me. My lady is here.'

'Thank you for the sherry, Mr Everard,' she called to the already retreating figure.

Everard hurried to the doorway where a masked lady stood.

Phillipa's eyes widened. She'd expected a stooped-over dowager, not this elegant creature in a gossamer confection of a gown that seemed to glow from the candlelight of the chandeliers. Her blonde locks shone equally as brightly as she gracefully stepped into the room, immediately greeted by Mr Everard.

The gentleman seated with Phillipa cocked his head towards the doorway. 'That is Lady Faville, the great beauty. I recognise her even with the mask.'

She glanced at him in shock. 'You should not tell me who she is!'

He shrugged. 'I know. I know. Supposed to be anonymous. But it is quite easy to guess who is under a mask.' He regarded Phillipa. 'I have not the least notion who you are, however.'

Of course he had no notion. 'You have likely never met me before.'

'Likely not.' He smiled and extended his hand. 'I am Mr Edward Anson.'

Anson? Oh, Goodness. She'd once met John Anson, the heir of Earl Wigham. One of her schoolmates had married him. This must be his younger brother.

She accepted his hand.

He released it and glanced back at Lady Faville. 'What a shame she wears a mask. Her beauty is truly extraordinary.' His tone turned reverential. 'She married Viscount Faville for his title and fortune. I believe there was some scandal attached to her shortly after she married. I don't recall what precisely, but it involved another man. All hushed up very quickly.' He took a sip of his brandy. 'The Viscount kept her on a short leash after that. She can take her pick of any man now, though. Faville had the courtesy to die on her. Left her very well off.'

Phillipa watched Mr Everard pull out a chair for Lady Faville. The woman had certainly caught Everard's affections. The poor man. A beautiful, wealthy widow of a viscount was way above the touch of a man of business.

She sipped her sherry and felt her senses heighten.

Xavier had returned.

'There is Campion checking on you,' Anson said.

Xavier stood in the doorway, perusing the room. His gaze did not seek out Phillipa, however, instead riveting on Lady Faville. He quickly backed away and disappeared into the hallway.

Anson finished his drink. 'I wonder if I discouraged him.'

'I wish you would not say such things,' Phillipa snapped. 'I dislike it very much.'

He sobered. 'My apologies once more.'

Phillipa returned to the pianoforte and began 'Bright Phoebus', a song much happier than she felt. Her audience had thinned, as she'd expected, with more comings and goings of those left.

The reputedly beautiful Lady Faville departed after a time, but Mr Everard remained. Presumably, the lady returned to gambling. Anson also left, but Phillipa hoped he'd gone home and not stayed to risk losing more. Xavier appeared briefly. Was he checking on her welfare? Her heart warmed with the idea.

After she finished she stopped in the ladies' retiring room. Lady Faville was also there.

'I wonder if you would help me,' the lady asked. 'My dress has come apart on the shoulder seam and I cannot pin it in place.'

'Certainly,' Phillipa stepped forwards to do the task.

'I pulled at a thread and all the stitching came apart. Can you imagine?' She handed Phillipa some pins. 'How my lady's maid overlooked the problem, I cannot say.'

Phillipa worked one pin through the fabric.

'You are the songstress,' Lady Faville went on.

Phillipa would have rather been recognised as the *pianiste*. 'Yes, I am.'

'You have a lovely voice,' she said. 'And you play beautifully.'

'Thank you.' Phillipa held the extra pins in her teeth.

'This wretched mask is such a bother.' The lady pulled it off. 'Don't you hate wearing a mask?'

'No. I prefer it, actually.' Phillipa placed the pins so they would be secure, but not show.

'I think I will go without a mask.' The lady paused for a moment. 'Tell me. Do you know Mr Campion well?'

The question took Phillipa completely off guard. 'I know him, certainly. I—I play the pianoforte here most nights.'

'Do you know if he has any attachments? He's been out of society of late and I have seen or heard nothing about him.'

Phillipa worked on the last pin. 'I do not know of his personal affairs.'

Lady Faville's voice turned to a wistful whisper. 'I knew him long ago.'

Phillipa lifted her hands from the dress and stepped back.

And saw Lady Faville's face.

She saw an angel. Skin so pale and smooth it appeared other-worldly. Beautiful azure eyes. Full lips the tint of summer roses.

No wonder Mr Everard was smitten and Mr Anson prosed on about the woman's beauty.

Lady Faville touched her gown's shoulder. 'Oh, you have done a marvellous job.' She glided over to the mirror and smiled. 'It is perfection! I am so grateful.'

Her smile made her even more beautiful.

Phillipa could hardly speak in the presence of such physical perfection. 'My pleasure,' she managed.

The lady looked at herself in the mirror. 'I wonder if

I need the mask.' She turned to Phillipa. 'What do you think? I am a widow. Widows are allowed certain licence, are they not?'

Phillipa lowered her gaze. 'I would not presume to advise you.'

'I believe I will forgo it!' she said brightly. She gave Phillipa another dazzling smile. 'Thank you again. I am indebted to you.'

Phillipa waited a few minutes before following the beauty out of the retiring room. She was shaken. For the second time in two days she could not explain her reaction to a face. The first one was certainly imaginary, but Lady Faville was all too real.

With a glance towards the door, she turned back to the mirror and lifted her mask.

The contrast between her image and Lady Faville's face caused sheer pain.

She put her mask back in place and shook herself as she walked to the hall. It had been years since she'd so directly compared her appearance with another woman's. Years since envy had so plagued her. She'd worked very hard to accept what could not be changed and to be grateful for what she did possess. Talent and musical skill.

Ever since the attack—and her vision—her emotions had been in disorder. She'd been in such excellent control of herself before last night.

No longer.

Cummings brought her cloak and Xavier's hat and gloves.

A moment later Xavier strode into the hall. 'Forgive me. I was detained.'

'I only just got here,' she responded.

Xavier took the cloak from Cummings and placed it

around Phillipa's shoulders. She pulled up the cloak's hood and waited while he donned his hat and gloves.

Cummings opened the door for them.

'Goodnight, Cummings,' she said.

The servant nodded.

As they stepped out into the street to await the hackney coach, Phillipa felt a shiver up her spine. The night strongly resembled the previous one, which had started out so comfortably. She'd not been comfortable since, and now the whole experience repeated itself in her mind's eye. Including the vision of the man's face.

She'd seen him before, she was certain, but the only memory she could retrieve was the one of the vision.

The coach pulled up and Xavier helped her inside. When he sat next to her, she felt his warmth, inhaled the scent of bergamot that would forever make her think of him. She removed her mask and, covering her face with her hood, thought of Lady Faville.

'With the hackney coach you no longer need to come with me,' she said into their silence. Neither of them had spoken heretofore.

It seemed as if he needed to rouse himself from his thoughts to answer her. 'I will escort you, hackney coach or no.'

Why inconvenience himself in this way? She could only suppose he felt some obligation to her family. Fancied this was his duty.

Like dancing with her.

When the coach reached Hay Hill, near where the attack took place, he put his arm around her and held her close. She blinked away tears. He might escort her out of duty now, but he was still her childhood friend, comforting her when she became sad.

And she selfishly thought only of herself. Never mind that she interrupted his duties at the gaming house. Never mind that she'd caused him to be attacked by ruffians. She wanted to perform her music.

She did want to perform her music. She wanted it so badly she would have braved the streets alone and risked another attack, just for this chance.

He held her the rest of the way to the town house and walked her to the door. They'd not spoken a word.

She wanted to wish him goodnight, to thank him for his kindness, but words would not come. She took his hand and he squeezed hers in return. With his other hand, he cupped her cheek—the scarred one—and leaned his forehead on to hers.

The moment was brief, but Phillipa's heart raced as if she'd run from the Masquerade Club to here.

She hurriedly opened her door and slipped inside.

Chapter Five

Xavier returned to the hackney coach and rode it back to its stand on Piccadilly. He paid the jarvey and walked the rest of the way back to the gaming house.

Phillipa had been very quiet this night. So had he, but taking her in his arms when they passed the scene of the attack had shaken him nearly as much as the attack itself. He wanted to hold her and never let anything hurtful happen to her again.

He hadn't wanted to leave her this night. When they reached her door, he wanted to follow her up the stairs to her bedchamber. He wanted to show her the delights that sharing a bed offered, delights that would erase the pain in her eyes, the pain that had not been there before the attack.

Instead he must return to the gaming house, which he dreaded.

Daphne would still be there, no doubt, waiting for him, like a spider waits for a fly to become ensnared by its web.

He could not deny her beauty, beauty that had almost seduced him when he'd been eighteen. She had dazzled him. Tempted him.

And ultimately got him sent away to the army. That had

been the agreement with Lord Faville—send Xavier away or Faville would drag his family's name through the mud.

Xavier's father had purchased a commission for him and the army had made him into the man he was today. Xavier would not have wished it to be any other way.

As soon as he walked into the gaming room again, he saw her there. For the rest of the night, Daphne's eyes followed him wherever he went.

To Xavier's dismay, Daphne, no longer wearing a mask, returned to the gaming house again and again. The newspapers quickly reported that the lovely widow, Lady F—, had developed a new passion for gambling at the Masquerade Club.

The gossip brought in more patrons than ever.

Daphne's man of business, a non-gambler, escorted her each time. As far as Xavier could tell Daphne had several fawning admirers, but she seemed to have no friends. Certainly no women friends. The women who attended the Masquerade Club turned away or shot daggers at her with their eyes.

He felt sorry for her, but only enough to keep him from speaking too sharply to her. Each night Daphne found some opportunity to speak with him. He was cordial, nothing more. She made no more presumptions about him.

Phillipa, too, attended the gaming house. Although she seemed more recovered from their attack, her initial exuberance about performing had disappeared.

Gone, too, was the ease between them. He missed it.

She was still determined to perform and for that he was grateful. At least he could be with her. He would see her tonight. And Daphne, too, he supposed.

But first he must appear for dinner at his parents' town house.

He'd received the invitation the previous day. He'd neglected them, he had to admit. He trusted that they wanted merely to see he was in one piece, rather than bearing some bad news for him. Bad news did not wait for a dinner invitation.

He was a bit late when he knocked on their town-house door.

'Good evening, sir.' The footman grinned widely as he took Xavier's hat and gloves.

'How are you, Buckley?' Buckley was a long-time retainer for the Campions.

'No complaints, sir. Thank you for asking.' He bowed.

Xavier gave Buckley a conspiratorial look. 'And my parents? Anything I should know?'

'They are in good health, if that is what you mean.'

Xavier touched the man's arm. 'Be sure to get word to me if that changes. They are not likely to tell me.'

'I will, sir.' He inclined his head towards the drawing room. 'I dare say they are waiting impatiently for you.'

'I had best hurry.'

Xavier opened the drawing room door and both his parents sprang to their feet, welcoming him with loving embraces.

'We had about given up on you,' his mother said, hugging him tightly.

'Not I.' His father clapped him on the shoulder. 'I told her you would come late.'

The butler appeared to announce dinner, also greeting Xavier warmly. He and his parents headed straight for the dining room.

The meal passed pleasantly, filled with news about his older brothers and his sisters and their assorted children. He was the youngest of four boys, with two older sisters and two younger ones. Every one of his brothers and sisters was married. All his brothers were occupied in what his father deemed worthy occupations. It took a great deal of the meal to fill him in on everyone, from his eldest brother to the youngest niece.

When dessert arrived their attention turned to him as he knew it eventually would.

'You cannot spend your life running a gaming house,' his father said after lamenting Xavier's lack of direction.

'I do not intend to,' Xavier assured him. 'I am merely assisting Rhys.'

'I do like Rhys very much.' His mother took another bite of custard. 'But I cannot like that he runs a gaming house. It isn't at all the thing.'

'I agree,' Xavier assured her. 'It is only temporary.'

Rhys already had bigger plans. He'd be in manufacturing, if not of steam engines, then something else. He'd make a fortune and prove himself to the father who sent him penniless into the street.

Xavier's desire to succeed was equally as strong as Rhys's. He did not want a factory, though.

At least his mother and father could be grateful for that. Owning a factory would probably be less genteel in their eyes than a gaming house.

His father took a sip of wine. 'I admit that I am glad you have given up the army. You know I never wanted that life for you. So dangerous. Kept you far away, as well.'

His father did not have to add that Xavier had been sent to the army because of Daphne and her husband's threat.

Xavier winked. 'Well, do not ask me again to read for the law or to join the church—'

His father held up a hand. 'I know better.'

Xavier wished to avoid a heated exchange with these dear people. He loved them too much.

His father brightened. 'How about farming? We can help you purchase a pretty estate—'

Xavier interrupted him. 'I have money enough to buy land. I do not need yours. Perhaps I will end up doing exactly that, but farming is suffering since the war. So much is changing. It may not be the wisest course.'

It would be the simplest one. Become a gentleman farmer, overseeing others doing the actual work.

Where was the challenge in that?

Xavier finished the custard Cook had prepared especially for him. 'Do not worry over me. I will manage something.'

He did not remain long after that. He kissed his mother, shook hands with his father and walked out of the town house feeling unsettled. It was just turning dusk and on this mild night the streets were still busy, the shops still open.

Xavier trusted that he'd know when the right opportunity came his way. It must spark his interest. It must test him in some way, make him more than he was right now.

He walked on Piccadilly past St James's. As always happened, women turned to look at him. A few streets over in Covent Garden, the women would openly proposition him. He would not walk that far.

He reached the new Burlington Arcade and stepped inside. What a grand idea Cavendish had to make this property into an arcade of shops. It was said Cavendish had built it to prevent oyster shells, bottles and other refuse from being thrown into his garden. No matter the reason, the shops employed many workers. Having employment was precious in these difficult times.

He walked past shop after shop. Lace makers, hosiers, milliners. Shoemakers, watchmakers, umbrella-makers. Even a music-seller.

On impulse Xavier entered the music-seller's shop.

'Music for pianoforte. Whatever is newest and best,' he requested of the shopkeeper.

He purchased 'Bid Me Discourse', a song written from Shakespeare's poem *Venus and Adonis*.

Bid me discourse, I will enchant thine ear,
Or, like a fairy, trip upon the green,
Or, like a nymph, with long dishevell'd hair,
Dance on the sands...

Would it please Phillipa? He hoped so.

He walked out of the shop and noticed the beadles in uniform, standing tall, watching over matters, making certain the rules were enforced. Cavendish had recruited them from his former regiment, the Tenth Hussars. A clever way to provide work for at least some of the former soldiers whose regiments were disbanded and who were left to fend for themselves.

Xavier left the arcade and headed back towards St James's and to Rhys's gaming house. He passed former soldiers on the street, wearing their old uniforms for want of other clothing. Some begged. Some were filled with too much drink.

One man leaned against a building, his eyes watchful. His face bore a still-healing cut on his cheek and neck, the cut Xavier had inflicted.

The man nodded towards Xavier. 'Spare a penny for a soldier?'

Xavier advanced on him and the man's eyes widened.

'Do you remember me?' Xavier asked in a low, deep voice.

The man lowered his gaze. 'We should not have done what we done to you and the lady. No forgiving that.' He touched the cut on his cheek. 'I got what I deserved.'

'Why did you do it, then?' Xavier demanded.

'Too much drink, sir. Our bellies were filled with gin.' The man looked ashamed.

Xavier eyed him. 'You were hungry?'

The man nodded.

'Are you hungry now?'

The man nodded again.

Xavier reached into his pocket and drew out several coins. He dropped them into the man's hand. 'Meet me right here tomorrow at noon.' He pointed to the coins now in the man's open palm. 'There will be more of that tomorrow.'

The man looked from the coins to Xavier. His eyes narrowed. 'How do I know you won't bring the Watch with you?'

Xavier held his gaze. 'You don't. But I'll tell you this. I was in the East Essex. I was in the battle, too.' He did not need to tell the man which battle. They both knew he meant Waterloo.

The man bowed his head respectfully. 'I will be here tomorrow when the clock strikes twelve.'

That night, as before, Phillipa crept down the stairway in her stocking feet and quietly let herself out the town house door. After stopping to put on her shoes, she walked quickly and confidently to the corner where she knew Xavier would be waiting with the hackney coach.

He greeted her as she walked towards him. 'How are you, Phillipa?'

He never complained about accompanying her, yet she knew she inconvenienced him in a myriad of ways.

'Very well, Xavier,' she responded as he helped her in to the coach. 'And you?'

'Tolerable.' He sat next to her.

'Just tolerable?' Perhaps she inconvenienced him once too much.

He waved a hand. 'Nothing dire. I dined with my parents tonight.'

'I hope they are in good health.' She had not seen Lord and Lady Piermont since her mother's ball.

How long ago that seemed.

'They are in perfect health. As is everyone in the family. The Campions are a hearty lot, you know.'

There were eight Campion children. When she'd known Xavier in Brighton, the oldest sons had been at Oxford. She'd hardly glimpsed them during those summers. Xavier's younger sisters were near her age, but it had been Xavier who'd singled her out for friendship.

He still acted her friend even with the trouble she caused him.

'What made dinner with your parents merely tolerable?' It was rare he talked about himself, she realised.

Even in the dim light of the carriage, she could see him smile ruefully. 'As you might imagine, my parents wish me settled. They would prefer I occupy myself in ways other than helping to run a gaming hell.'

'It is not a hell, surely!' It seemed quite tasteful to her, not dark and dangerous.

'No, it is not a hell. But it is not what they would choose for me.'

'Of course they would not choose that for you.' The aristocracy did not run gaming houses. Her brothers had got Rhys to do it for them. 'My parents would not choose for me to play the pianoforte in a gaming house either. That is, my mother would not. I doubt my father would trouble himself to give it a thought.' But she was talking about herself again. 'I do not think we should be confined to society's expectations. The question should be, are you happy doing what you are doing?'

He grinned at her. 'Phillipa Westleigh. I did not know you espoused such an enlightened philosophy.'

She turned away. 'Now you are making a joke of me.'

He put his fingers under her chin and turned her back. 'Perhaps a little, but, believe me, as vexing as you've been, wanting to walk the streets alone, I admire your determination to do what you most wish to do.'

She looked into his startlingly blue eyes. 'I have you to thank for it, Xavier. You provided me this opportunity to perform my music and my songs in front of an audience. It has been a joy for me and I thank you.'

His eyes darkened. 'Show me your gratitude.'

'Show you?' She was puzzled.

One corner of his mouth turned up. 'With a kiss.'

She felt the blood rush to her cheeks.

He averted his gaze. 'I am teasing you.'

Of course. He'd meant it as a jest. What could be more amusing than the scar-faced lady kissing the man once called Adonis by her friends?

He placed his hand over hers. 'I almost forgot.'

This gesture of affection confused her more. 'Forgot what?'

He stroked her hand with his thumb. 'I purchased a piece of music for you today. The store clerk assured me it is quite new, so you are unlikely to have it already.'

'Xavier.' Her throat tightened. 'Thank you.'

Impulsively, she touched her lips to his.

He held her and prolonged the kiss, a wondrous sensation of soft flesh somehow firm and strong against hers. She felt the kiss throughout her body, filling her with yearning.

The driver rapped against the side of the coach and they

jumped apart. Phillipa's heart pounded so hard she thought Xavier must be able to hear it.

'I guess we have arrived,' he said, his voice thick.

He climbed out to help Phillipa and pay the driver. They entered the house and, as usual, Cummings took her cloak.

Xavier touched her hand again. 'I will come to listen to you when I am able.'

She nodded, but she was still under the power of the kiss and everything else seemed unreal.

Checking to make certain her mask was in place, she made her way to the supper room where the tables were filled with patrons waiting only to hear her sing and play.

Mr Everard sat at a table close by the pianoforte. That meant the beautiful widow, Lady Faville, was here again. She'd been at the gaming house every night Phillipa had performed.

Not to listen to Phillipa, though.

Mr Everard nodded a greeting as she sat on the bench. She smiled.

In front of her sat a new music sheet with a brief note written in pen on its cover—

For your pleasure,
X

Her fingers trembled as she opened the cover and scanned the first pages.

These lyrics caught her eye:

Love is a spirit all compact of fire,
Not gross to sink, but light, and will aspire.

Phillipa took a deep breath. She must never aspire. No matter the kiss, which surely was part of his jesting with her. She'd come perilously close to aspiring after one dance, after one Season. No more.

She glanced over to the door and saw Xavier…with Lady Faville upon his arm. Xavier, tall and dark, his blue eyes fringed by dark lashes. Lady Faville, dainty and light in contrast. They were so beautiful, so perfect, she had to look away, only to notice that all eyes were on the stunning couple. Lady Faville seemed to bask in the attention. Xavier looked as if he'd not noticed. He escorted Lady Faville to Mr Everard's table.

Poor Mr Everard appeared stricken.

You also must not aspire, Mr Everard, Phillipa thought.

To her surprise, Xavier stepped away to stand at the back of the room.

Phillipa put the sheet of music he'd given her behind her other music and selected another song to play.

She sang:

Her hair is like a golden clue
Drawn from Minerva's loom.
Her lips, carnations dropping dew,
Her breath a perfume...

The room applauded when she finished. Lady Faville beamed.

Xavier bowed his head and rubbed his forehead.

Lady Faville remained in the room when Phillipa stopped playing to take her usual respite about halfway through her time there. The lady leaned towards Mr Everard and said something to him. He immediately jumped up and hurried to the buffet. To fill a plate for her, Phillipa supposed.

She straightened her music and rose, flexing her fingers.

'You play beautifully,' Lady Faville said to her. The lady smiled and patted the chair next to her. 'Please do sit with me a little. I've asked Mr Everard to fix us both some plates of food and to order you something to drink.'

Phillipa had no choice but to sit. 'That is kind of you… and Mr Everard.'

Lady Faville tossed him a fond glance. 'He is such a dear. I do not know how I would cope without him.' She turned back to Phillipa. 'I believe I told you I am a widow.'

'You did, indeed.' What possible reason could this woman have for inviting this conversation?

The lady glanced around the room again. 'This club is finely decorated, would you not say?'

Phillipa could easily agree. She especially loved this room, decorated in the Adam's style, all pastels and carved plasterwork.

Lady Faville did not give her time to say so, however. 'I suspect the décor was influenced by Mr Campion. I understand he has been at Mr Rhysdale's side throughout everything. All the rooms show such refined taste. I quite did not expect it. But seeing how involved Mr Campion is in the running of the house, I just attribute it to his influence.'

Phillipa's hackles rose. How dare she assume her half-brother would have no taste if not for Xavier?

She immediately smiled inwardly at herself. She certainly had accepted Rhysdale into the family if she felt like flying to his defence.

She tried to keep her tone neutral. 'I presume you have never met Mr Rhysdale?'

Lady Faville laughed. 'Goodness, no. How would I?' She looked down at her wine glass and twirled it absently by its stem. 'I also understand that Mr Campion escorts you to and from the gaming house.'

'Yes, he does.' Now she understood why Lady Faville had sought her out.

She supposed everyone knew that she came and left in Xavier's company. She'd been attending the Masquerade Club for so many nights, it would certainly have been noticed. But this lady would have had to deliberately seek out this information.

Lady Faville continued to fiddle with her glass. 'When you so generously helped me with my dress, you did not leave the impression that there was any…attachment between you and Mr Campion.' She glanced up and looked earnestly into Phillipa's eyes. 'Because I would not for the world come between a woman and her—her—*paramour.* If there is one thing I respect above all other things it is the *love* between a man and a woman.'

Phillipa held the woman's gaze. Inside her Lady Faville's words felt like a daggers stabbing her heart, but she did not know why she should feel so.

Except for the kiss.

She found her voice. 'Why do you ask me such a question? I do not know you and your question is of a very personal nature.'

Lady Faville coloured slightly. 'Oh, I am being presumptuous, am I not? It is merely that I do like you excessively. I wish us to be friends. And I would not in the world do injury to a friend.'

This was sincerely said, but Phillipa felt wary. Perhaps it was her own envy of the woman that made her doubt.

Lady Faville reached over and touched Phillipa's mask. 'I assume Mr Campion has seen the face beneath this mask and has fallen desperately in love with you.'

Phillipa lowered her gaze. Xavier had indeed seen beneath her mask.

Lady Faville went on. 'I think you should remove your mask and let all the gentleman admire you.'

Could the woman be mocking her? How could she know of Phillipa's disfigurement? No one here knew her except Xavier and she did not wish to believe he had talked of her to anyone.

He certainly had seen beneath her mask, though. How could he not compare her scars to this lady's perfection?

Phillipa resisted the urge to touch her marred face.

A servant brought her a glass of sherry. She lifted the glass and took a sip before answering Lady Faville. 'The mask suits my purposes.' She took another sip and met Lady Faville's eye deliberately, smiling enigmatically. 'I can tell you that Mr Campion and I are...friends.'

Let her stew on that!

A tiny line appeared between the beautiful lady's eyes.

Phillipa glanced away for a moment and noticed that Mr Everard stood with two plates of food, watching them. Lady Faville nodded to him slightly.

He immediately brought the plates to the table. He served his lady first.

She beamed at him. 'Oh, you have picked all I could like.'

His expression softened and his hand shook as he placed the second plate in front of Phillipa. 'My lady thought you would enjoy some delicacies.'

'Thank you, Mr Everard,' Phillipa said.

The poor besotted man.

Mr Everard bowed. 'I will leave you to your conversation.' He looked pointedly at Lady Faville. 'I remain at your disposal, ma'am.'

'You are a treasure, sir,' the lady said.

Mr Everard backed away.

Lady Faville smiled at Phillipa again. 'Did he not do a fine job of selecting treats for us?'

Phillipa selected a piece of cheese. 'He seems quite devoted.'

'Devoted.' Lady Faville nodded. 'That is such a lovely word to describe him.' She shook her head as if ridding herself of Mr Everard. 'But we were talking of Mr Campion, were we not?'

'You were,' agreed Phillipa.

A determined look came into Lady Faville's eyes. 'I assumed that because Xavier—I mean Mr Campion—escorted you here every night that it meant there was a relationship of a personal nature between the two of you.'

'A friendship of a personal nature,' she said enigmatically.

Just as she pretended to be worthy of the flirtation the gentlemen of the Masquerade Club sometimes engaged in with her, Phillipa could pretend she and Xavier were lovers, that she could indeed be a rival to this ethereal creature.

Phillipa knew better, though. Xavier was merely an old family friend, now forced by her to act in a protective role.

She should not step in the way of what might make him happy.

But she still could not resist creating these implications. 'I do not assume that you and Mr Everard have a relationship of a personal nature. He escorts you to and from the Masquerade Club, does he not?'

Lady Faville's eyes widened in surprise. 'Certainly he does, but—' She blinked. 'Oh, I comprehend your meaning. Your connection to Mr Campion is more in the nature of employer and worker!'

No, that was not what she wished to imply at all. Xavier was not her employer. He'd given her a gift—*For your pleasure*, he had written. He was a friend.

He'd returned her kiss.

Phillipa pretended to attend to her food and to enjoy the sweetmeats and other confections Mr Everard had brought her.

Lady Faville leaned closer. 'I must confide in someone! I am only here at the Masquerade Club because of Mr Campion. We—we were lovers once, but I was married and nothing could come of it. I needed to be certain that no

one stood between us. You are so clever and so lovely that
I feared his affections were engaged and I had for ever lost
my chance with him.'

Lovers? Lovers?

The word was a new dagger to impale her, but it should
not matter to her. It should not.

'I cannot be your confidante, my lady. It is not my
place—'

Lady Faville gripped her wrist. 'Oh, but you must. I do
not care if you are below me—'

Below her? Phillipa was an earl's daughter.

'I confide in my maid, as well.' Lady Faville smiled pa-
tronisingly. 'But you *know* Mr Campion. You will understand and you may be able to help.'

Phillipa raised her brows. 'A low person like me? A mere
pianiste?'

Her sarcastic tone was lost on the lady. 'He must talk to
you when he brings you here and takes you home. Has he
ever mentioned me?'

Phillipa had talked to him more than he'd talked to her.
Might he have confided in her about Lady Faville if she had
given him the chance?

'He has not mentioned you to me,' Phillipa answered
honestly.

Lady Faville's face fell, but she quickly recovered. 'But
you will tell me if he speaks about me? I know you will!'
She clasped Phillipa's hand. 'We are friends now.'

Phillipa pulled away. 'It is time for me to perform.'

'Of course.' The lady smiled. 'And it would be a delight
to listen to you. But I should put in an appearance in the
gaming room, should I not?'

Phillipa rose and returned to the pianoforte. She began
with a tune she'd written herself. It was about a sailor's

return from the sea and into the arms of the woman who waited faithfully.

A happiness she would never know.

The music, as always, filled her spirit and drove all else away. She abandoned herself to it, so much so that she blinked in surprise when the audience applauded. When the time drew near for the hackney coach to arrive, she announced the last song, one of farewell. It was a composition of hers with which she ended each performance. She had written the first notes of the song not long after that first Season ball when Xavier danced with her.

A few minutes later she waited for Xavier in the hall. She'd already donned her cloak with her new piece of music tucked safely in a pocket.

Xavier came from the gaming room. He strode up to Phillipa, close enough that no one else would hear him. 'I cannot ride home with you, Phillipa.'

This had never happened before. 'Is there trouble?'

He glanced up to the gaming-room door. 'There might be if I leave. Shall I send someone else with you? Or do you trust our hackney coachman? I will pay him extra to see you safe to your door.'

'I will be entirely comfortable with the coachman,' she assured him.

He took her arm. 'I'll see you to him and explain matters.'

Phillipa glanced up and saw Lady Faville watching them from the landing. Would he end his night with her? she wondered.

Outside the hack awaited and Xavier quickly explained matters to the jarvey before turning back to help Phillipa into the coach.

Phillipa took his offered arm, but did not immediately

climb into the coach. 'Remember I will not be coming to-night.'

He nodded. 'You'll be missed.'

She settled in the seat while he closed the door. Before the horses moved, she leaned out the window. 'I forgot to thank you for the music. I should have it ready to perform when next I come.'

He smiled. 'I will look forward to hearing it.'

When the coach pulled away, Phillipa sat in darkness, alone, uneasy, but not fearful. She missed Xavier. Their brief rides alone in the dark hackney coach were precious, she realised. And unique. Even without her mask, her face was obscured.

She was not so far removed from that silly girl she'd been in her first Season, when she'd momentarily believed in impossible dreams. Even now she clung to the slimmest straws, spending mere minutes with him, performing and knowing he could hear her play, hear her sing.

How long could she keep this up?

When Rhysdale came back it would be over. He would ask questions about the *pianiste* Xavier allowed to play and Xavier would tell his friend who it was behind the mask.

She would return to her music room and her reclusive existence, and some day she feared she would read in the *Morning Post* that Xavier Campion had married Lady Faville.

Perhaps that day she would compose a mournful funeral dirge.

Chapter Six

Xavier kept his appointment with the former soldier who'd attacked him and Phillipa. As he walked to the appointed spot, the soldier already waited. The man looked watchful and wary.

And much too thin.

He shifted nervously from foot to foot as he watched Xavier approach. 'I am here, sir. As you wanted.'

Xavier extended his hand to shake. 'Good day to you. I am pleased you came.'

The man haltingly accepted Xavier's hand. 'You said there would be more money. What must I do for it?'

'Perhaps nothing,' Xavier responded. He was unsure himself why he asked for the meeting. He had no plan. Xavier clapped the man on the shoulder. 'I am famished. Let us make our way to Bellamy's Kitchen. Would you fancy a pork pie?'

The man was the very picture of hunger, but he had pride. 'I might, if you are buying.'

'I'm buying.' Xavier extended his hand again. 'I am Mr Campion, lately a captain in the East Essex.'

'Jeffers.' The man was more willing to shake hands this time. 'Tom Jeffers, sergeant. From the 42nd.'

'You lost many men in the battle.' Almost three hundred if Xavier's memory served him.

'It was a bad business.' Jeffers's voice turned thick. He rallied. 'But we had Boney running in the end, eh?'

'That we did,' Xavier agreed.

The battlefield of Waterloo gave them common ground. Those who fought there were a select group. Only they could know what a day of death and honour it had been.

They chatted more about the battle until reaching Bellamy's, a place frequented by members of the House of Commons. Xavier found a table where Jeffers's battered uniform would not stand out against more elegantly dressed men.

They ordered pork pies and ale and talked more about the war. Jeffers finished his pie very quickly and Xavier ordered him another.

'What did you do before the war?' Xavier asked.

'I'd just finished an apprenticeship as a cabinetmaker. Should have looked for work instead of listening to those tales of adventure the recruiter told us.'

'A cabinetmaker?'

'That's the right of it.' Jeffers took a big gulp of ale. 'Was pretty good at it, too, if I don't say so myself.'

'Have you looked for work here?' Surely such a skill would be valuable.

'No one's hiring. I'm too old, they say, and not enough experience.' He stared into his ale. 'If they'd give me a chance, I'd show them.'

The tavern maid came up to the table and leaned provocatively over Xavier while pouring more ale. 'Anything else you have a fancy for?' she asked.

'Bread and cheese,' Xavier said without expression.

After she walked away Jeffers's gaze followed her. 'I'd say she had a fancy for you.'

Xavier shrugged.

'I'll wager that happens a lot to a pretty fellow such as yourself,' Jeffers said.

Xavier hated being called pretty. 'Often enough.'

'Lucky bloke,' muttered Jeffers.

Other men always considered him lucky. After all, men such as Jeffers endured much worse. He knew that. But his looks did affect his life, much like Phillipa's scar affected hers. It was all a matter of degree.

'I have an idea,' An idea that formed itself as Xavier spoke. 'Could you run a shop? Make furniture?' Now here was a new challenge.

Jeffers's jaw dropped. 'What is your meaning?'

'Exactly as I said.' Xavier took a sip of ale. 'If you think you can open a shop, I'll finance you.'

Jeffers turned pale. 'I do not understand you. By the right of it, you should hand me over to the magistrate. I attacked you and your lady. I should be in Newgate for it.'

'You should. But I have a whim.' If Cavendish could create an arcade of shops, perhaps Xavier could open one shop…and make some employment for his fellow soldiers who, like he, came back from war with nothing to do. 'Do you know other men with your skill? You could take on others.'

'Others? I dare say I can find others,' Jeffers rasped.

'Excellent.' Xavier dug into his pocket and took out a purse. 'I'll pay until the shop is profitable, then you pay me a portion.' Not unlike how Rhys arranged the gaming house.

They talked on, about what steps to take. First find a shop to let, then purchase wood and tools. The proposition became more expensive as they spoke, but Xavier did not care. The more he thought of this plan, the more certain he became.

Was it a risk? Certainly. But it was also a new way to test himself. Could he turn men like Jeffers away from a life of crime and create a successful business at the same time? He was determined to do it.

Xavier parted company with Jeffers. As the man walked away, he stood taller, prouder. Xavier smiled.

He almost laughed aloud. The last thing he ever expected to become was a shopkeeper. That was worse in the eyes of the *ton* than running a gaming hell. Cavendish might have pulled it off under the guise of a whim, but he was the brother of a duke.

Phillipa's words came back to him. *I do not think we should be confined to society's expectations.*

He was certainly taking it to heart.

What she would think of his impulsive offer? He'd made it to one of their attackers, after all. Would she understand why he'd done it? She'd become more subdued since the attack. Although she did not speak of it, he suspected she was not entirely recovered.

He would not mention this to her. At least not right away.

Xavier missed Phillipa that night. He found himself listening for strains of the pianoforte to rise above the din in the gaming room. When he entered the supper room, his gaze immediately turned to where the pianoforte sat. He expected to see her there, masked and mysterious, charming the patrons with her music and her voice.

Unfortunately, Lady Faville was present and he was convinced she'd not given up her pursuit of him. She was clever enough not to plague him too much, though. Still, she found some opportunity to talk to him each night, some moment when he could not avoid her.

Like the night before when she'd appeared in the hallway the exact moment he made his way to the supper room.

Others were in earshot when she asked him to escort her there, so he could not refuse.

She divided her time between the supper room and the gaming room, never wagering much, but always attracting a great deal of attention from the men, each very willing to partner her, to assist her, to teach her how to play.

She basked in the attention, the admiration, as if she could not exist separate from it, as if she were nothing but how she appeared to others, as if her beauty was all she was worth.

That she was a beauty was indisputable. When he'd been eighteen she'd been a young man's dream, so lovely it hurt to look at her. He'd been smitten.

Until he realised it was his looks that held the most appeal to her. And finer elements of character, like being faithful to her husband, paled in comparison to what a beautiful couple she and Xavier would make.

He'd not bedded her at eighteen. Of that he was grateful, and grateful, too, for a husband wise enough to send temptation away from his obsessed young wife.

Xavier left the gaming room to check on the supper room, and a moment later she appeared by his side, looking as if she merely wished to pick some delicacies from the array of food available.

'Where is your songstress, Xavier? Have you let her go?' Daphne's tone, always sweet, grated on his nerves.

He frowned. He did not wish her to plague Phillipa. 'She does not play every night.'

'It is not the same without her, is it?' She sighed and tossed a glance towards the pianoforte. 'I confess, I miss her immensely. We've become great friends, you know.'

He would not wager on that.

She kept him there chatting for a time longer before he could escape without appearing to the others to deliberately cut her. Someone might remember the trouble she caused him all those years ago. He did not want those rumours resurfacing.

He went next to check on MacEvoy in the cashier's room. Cummings remained always a shout away from MacEvoy, should he need him. For that matter, either of the former soldiers was well able to take care of any nonsense, but if any trouble brewed, Xavier wanted to be aware of it.

When he stepped into the hall a familiar gentleman handed Cummings his hat and gloves.

'General Henson?' Henson had been at Waterloo. Xavier met him in Brussels before the battle and, before that, at Salamanca, another ghastly but triumphant battle. Xavier always had the sense he'd met Henson somewhere before that, but he could never place where.

The general swung around. 'Campion, is it not?'

'Yes, indeed, sir.' He nearly stood at attention, but instead extended his hand. 'A pleasure to see you here.'

Henson shook his hand. 'Good to see you, Campion. Just returned to town and heard of this place. Honest games, they say.' The man seemed in an uncommonly good mood. 'I heard Rhysdale runs it.'

'Indeed he does, sir,' Xavier answered.

Henson clapped him on the arm. 'Friend of yours, I recall. Brave fighter. Done very well for himself. Who would have guessed his fortunes would have turned in this direction?'

Rhys had not been a typical officer like Xavier, a younger son whose choices might include the clergy, the law, or the army. Rhys made his way in life through gambling. Perhaps Henson did not know that Rhys purchased his commissions with his gambling winnings. Rhys's skill and bravery on the battlefield earned him his promotions.

'Rhysdale always does well,' Xavier told him. 'He is out

of town at present and I am running the place for him. I will show you to the cashier.' He led the way.

They entered the cashier's room and MacEvoy immediately stood.

Xavier gestured to him. 'General, MacEvoy here was also in the East Essex. Cummings, too, whom you met in the hall.'

Henson shook MacEvoy's hand. 'Good to see soldiers like you, MacEvoy.'

'Sir!' MacEvoy responded.

MacEvoy went on to explain how matters worked at the gaming house, how those who came in masks—ladies, mostly—could only receive credit or write vowels if they revealed their identities.

'Having the ladies here is quite refreshing, I must say.' Henson purchased his counters.

Henson was not married, as Xavier recalled. Perhaps he was in town to find a well-dowered wife, like many an officer without a regiment.

'Certainly it has contributed to Rhys's success,' Xavier responded. 'I'll show you to the gaming room, if you like.'

The general shook MacEvoy's hand again before they left him.

As they walked to the gaming room, Xavier said, 'I lately encountered one of your infantrymen. Tom Jeffers. Do you remember him? He was a sergeant.'

'Ah, yes!' The general nodded. 'Jeffers. A fine sergeant. He was one of the men who carried Moore from the battlefield.'

General Sir John Moore died from wounds at the Battle of Corunna and was much mourned by his men. Sir Arthur Wellesley had had big shoes to fill when he took Moore's place as the Commander of the British army in the Peninsula—no one knew then that Wellesley's victories would result in him becoming the Duke of Wellington.

'A good man,' Henson went on. 'Hope he is doing well.'

'Matters are improving for him,' Xavier said.

They chatted a bit about the great numbers of former soldiers who were out of work and suffering, before reaching the gaming room.

It did not surprise Xavier to see Daphne hovering near the doorway.

She smiled. 'Have you brought someone new for us, Xavier?'

Xavier gritted his teeth. She'd been lying in wait for him. 'Lady Faville, may I present to you General Henson.

Henson bowed. 'Charmed, my lady.'

She lifted her hand for him to clasp. 'I am delighted, General.'

Xavier stepped back and out of the room, but not before seeing a disappointed look in Daphne's eye.

Phillipa had not slept well, even though she'd not gone to the Masquerade Club the night before. The visions of the mysterious man's face had abated, but now her mind filled with the memory of Lady Faville on Xavier's arm.

It should not matter. *Could* not matter. She must be content with being able to perform her music for others. That was the gift Xavier had given her and all she could expect from him.

Besides the piece of music he'd purchased for her.

And the kiss.... She'd practised Xavier's music all the previous day and had already committed it to memory.

Tired of tossing and turning, she rose and summoned her maid to help her dress. She might as well eat breakfast and she fancied a walk outside in the sunshine, a visit to the shops, perhaps.

She entered the dining room and saw her mother seated at the table, sipping a cup of chocolate and looking through the mail.

Her mother looked up at her entrance. 'Goodness! You are up early. How are you this morning, my darling girl?'

Her mother was in uncommon good spirits. Perhaps her father's absence was the cause. It was certainly reason to celebrate.

'I woke early,' Phillipa responded. 'It is early for you, too, is it not?'

Her mother smiled. 'It is, but I feel quite well, none the less.'

Phillipa chose her food from the sideboard and sat adjacent to her mother.

A footman appeared. 'Chocolate, m'lady?'

'That would be excellent, Higgley.'

He poured her the last of it from the chocolate pot. 'Shall I bring you more, Lady Westleigh?' he asked.

'Do, Higgley,' her mother responded as she picked up an envelope to read the address.

When he left the room, Phillipa asked, 'Have there been any letters from Father or Ned or Hugh?'

Her mother's smile faded. 'I had a letter a few days ago. They arrived at their destination and all is well.'

'And will you tell me now where they are?' Would her mother say they had arrived safely in Brussels?

Her mother waved a dismissive hand. 'On the Continent.'

This was more information than her mother had given before. '*Where* on the Continent?' she pushed.

Her mother put her cup down hard on the table. 'Do not plague me with this! It is men's business and you need know nothing of it. There is absolutely no cause to worry.' She fussed with the collar of her morning dress. 'I—I do not know the half of it myself. They tell me nothing, you know.'

She knew more than the half of it, Phillipa thought. It was useless to pursue, however.

Her mother went on. 'I thought I would call upon Lady Gale and Miss Gale this morning. Will you come?'

Lady Gale was the woman carrying Rhysdale's child and the woman who had come masked to the Masquerade Club. Miss Gale was betrothed to Ned. She had not given them much thought when meeting them before, but now that she knew of their interesting connection she could admit to being curious about them.

'I believe I will. I have a need to be out of doors. The walk will do me good.'

Her mother beamed. 'I am glad of your company.'

Phillipa and her mother stepped out after noon to make their call to the Gale house. The day was warm and sunny enough to carry parasols. It had not been the family habit to spend the summer in London. Indeed, it was unusual for any of the aristocracy to be in London in summer, but Parliament remained in session and, though the company had thinned, there were still plenty of social engagements to interest her mother.

And now Phillipa knew that their stay in London could also be attributed to the family's financial woes.

Her mother opened her parasol. 'I do wish you would wear one of the hats I had made for you. They are so flattering.'

Phillipa wore a hat, just not one contrived to cover her scar. 'Mother, I like this hat. The others make my face itch.'

It had been so long since Phillipa had ventured out in daylight that she looked upon everything with fresh eyes. The lovely green of the trees and grass, the creams and reds of the houses, were vibrant compared to the various shades of grey she and Xavier had walked past.

They crossed Mount Street and passed Berkley Square and Gunter's Tea Shop where several people gathered outside to cool themselves with pistachio or elderflower ices. Her mother nodded a greeting to people she knew, who never quite looked Phillipa in the face. At least at the gaming house people looked at her. Because her mask concealed her.

They turned on to Curzon Street and strolled to Half Moon Street where Lady Gale and her stepdaughter lived. Phillipa sounded the knocker and tried to remember when she'd last made calls with her mother. She'd not come to this house before.

The butler opened the door to them and announced them to Lady Gale and Miss Gale. Both women stood at their entrance.

Lady Gale stepped forwards. 'How good of you both to come.' She turned to her butler. 'Tucker, we will have some tea, I think.'

'Very good, ma'am.' He bowed and left.

Miss Gale rushed over to them, her hands extended. 'Lady Westleigh, I am so happy to see you!' She clasped her future mother-in-law's hands and turned to Phillipa. 'What a treat to see you, as well, Phillipa!' The girl could not quite look at Phillipa for more than a moment.

'We thought it past time to see how you both are faring,' Phillipa's mother said.

They sat, Phillipa's mother and Miss Gale together on a sofa. Phillipa took a chair near Lady Gale.

'Have you any news from our dear Ned?' Miss Gale asked.

Her mother answered, 'He wrote only to say they had arrived and all was progressing well.'

Phillipa assumed her mother's vague reply was for her benefit. Why should all this be a secret from her?

'Have you any letters from Ned?' Phillipa asked Miss Gale. 'Did he write you from where he is?'

'Brussels?' the girl chirped.

Miss Gale was so easily led.

Phillipa could feel her mother stiffen. 'Yes, Brussels.'

'He did write me a very sweet letter about how he hoped to be home very soon.' Miss Gale sighed.

Phillipa persisted. 'How much more does he need to accomplish in Brussels?'

Miss Gale jumped into the snare. 'He said he and Hugh would leave the moment your father is settled in suitable lodgings.'

'I see.' Phillipa stole a glance towards her mother, who sat with pursed lips.

But not for long. 'Did you enjoy the musicale we attended?' her mother asked Miss Gale.

'I did,' the girl responded brightly, her blonde curls bobbing as she inclined her head towards her stepmother. 'Celia does not attend the social functions in her state and Grandmama is not available.'

'Oh?' Phillipa feigned surprise and turned to Lady Gale 'Are you and Miss Gale's grandmother not well?'

Lady Gale put a hand on her abdomen. 'I am very well. Celia's grandmother has recently moved to Bath where she has many friends and should be very happy.'

Phillipa's mother frowned.

Just one more secret to bring out in the open. 'Were you ill, though?'

Miss Gale, of course, answered. 'She was ill at first, but the doctor said all women are at the beginning. All is fine now. In fact, I have asked Celia and Rhysdale to say their vows when Ned and I do. We'll have a double wedding! Will that not be wonderful?'

'It will indeed.' Phillipa smiled at her mother. 'Do you not agree, Mama?'

'Yes. Yes,' her mother responded in a testy tone, but simpered towards Miss Gale. 'You must attend more functions with me, my girl. My daughter refuses all invitations.'

Miss Gale glanced at Phillipa and her expression turned sympathetic. 'I do understand.'

The tea arrived and the conversation turned to the other invitations her mother had received and which should be accepted. Miss Gale wisely ceded all decisions to Phillipa's mother.

Obviously her mother approved Ned's choice of a wife. Miss Gale was pretty, malleable and hungry for approval.

Phillipa stared into her tea cup and thought of all the secrets kept among them. Her father's transgressions, his whereabouts, Lady's Gale's interesting condition. The best-kept secret might be hers, though. None of them knew she ventured out at night and played the pianoforte at a gaming house.

Lady Gale leaned towards her. 'You play the pianoforte, do you not?'

For a moment Phillipa wondered if Lady Gale somehow knew her secret, but more probably her mother had mentioned it to Miss Gale that Phillipa closeted herself with her music all day. Miss Gale likely told all to her stepmother.

'I do play,' she admitted.

If it were not for secrets, she could ask Lady Gale about her experience at the gaming house, if people treated her differently when she'd worn a mask.

Chapter Seven

That night Xavier stood by the wall in the supper room while Phillipa played 'Bid Me Discourse', the music he'd purchased for her.

If he were able, he'd stay the whole time she performed. She played and sang with skill, but also with passion. He not only heard the music, he felt its emotion though her.

'Bid Me Discourse' showed Aphrodite's enchantment by Adonis. She saw only Adonis's physical beauty. Daphne shared Aphrodite's misconception.

Appearances could obscure the truth of a person. He'd realised as much since he'd been a young boy. His face and his physique were the least important things about him. He had strength, courage and prowess. He had determination. When he'd finally joined the East Essex regiment, he'd had the chance to prove his true self. Phillipa's true self—her beauty, her sensibility, her complexity—was revealed through the performance of her music.

He'd seen flashes of this true self in her childhood. The intensity with which she examined a flower. The unanswerable questions she asked that showed an understanding far beyond her years—and his, at the time. The empathy she showed to those less fortunate than she.

'It is better to have a scar than to be poor and hungry, is it not?' she said to him once when they'd given coins to a mother begging for her two unfortunate children.

It was indeed.

They were an odd pair in those childhood days, both trying to overcome the handicap of their faces.

Neither had done too badly, he thought as he watched her fingers move confidently on the keyboard.

Still, he wished that he could have prevented the marring of her face back then and saved her the struggle to acceptance.

Phillipa finished the song.

...By law of nature thou art bound to breed,
That thine may live when thou thyself art dead.
And so, in spite of death, thou dost survive,
In that thy likeness still is left alive.

Xavier would not mind seeing a little girl such as she had been, one who could grow up without the pain of disfigurement. But, as for himself, he would not wish his face on any son.

He clapped appreciatively after the last chord was played. She looked directly at him and smiled.

'Wasn't that lovely?' a woman's voice piped up. Daphne, grabbing the attention to herself.

Cummings appeared at the doorway and gestured to him. Xavier crossed the room to him and followed him into the hallway.

'MacEvoy says come talk to him,' the man said.

Xavier hurried down the stairs to the cashier's room. 'What is it?'

'Those fellows in masks you worried about the other

night are back,' MacEvoy said. 'I'm thinking they are up to no good.'

'You were right to tell me,' Xavier responded. 'I believe I'll spend some time in the gaming room.'

MacEvoy grinned. 'My hackles tell me that is a grand idea.'

Xavier sauntered into the gaming room and immediately saw the two men that worried MacEvoy. They'd found two partners for whist and were making a grand show of being deep in the cards, but something about their manner rang false. Xavier alerted a couple of the croupiers to the men and tried to keep a close eye on them without seeming obvious.

General Henson strolled up to him. 'Your house seems busy tonight.'

'It is,' responded Xavier.

The general remained next to him, as if wanting more conversation.

Xavier decided to confide in him. 'See those two fellows there?' He gestured to the men.

The general turned in that direction. 'I do.'

Xavier's voice deepened. 'I believe they are trouble.'

'You do not say?' The general nodded. 'I will watch them.'

It did not take much time for Xavier to see the sleight of hand. 'We have a pair of Captain Sharps, sir.'

He made his way to the table and grasped the arm of the man dealing the cards. 'One moment, gentlemen.'

He pulled a card from the man's sleeve.

The man and his partner bounded to their feet. The man Xavier grasped knocked over the table. A shout rose from the gamblers. Women shrieked. The man tried to shove Xavier away, but Xavier did not let go.

The second man tried to make it to the door, but the general blocked his way and one of the croupiers seized him.

Xavier and the card sharp careened against another table, scattering the players, cards and counters. Fists flew.

Phillipa heard shouts and screams coming from the gaming room. She'd seen Cummings summon Xavier. Something was wrong. She jumped from her bench and ran from the room.

When she reached the door to the gaming room, a dishevelled Xavier dragged a man, nose bleeding, from the room. Others held a second man.

The second man made an attempt to get away and, in the struggle, careened into Phillipa. She lost her balance and, as she fell, felt the aura of her vision.

No! It was gone. She'd been certain it was gone. It must not return. She did not wish the loss of her mind in this public place.

But strong arms steadied her, preventing her fall. She breathed a sigh of relief and lifted her gaze to thank the man.

She froze.

An older gentleman held her, but his face was that of the man in the vision.

'Nothing to fear,' the man said. 'I've got you.'

She blinked, but his face did not change. He was real. This was the man in her vision, but this time he was real.

'Who—who are you?' she managed.

He released her and bowed. 'Allow me to present myself. I am General Henson and you must not be alarmed by this commotion. Campion spotted some men cheating at cards and he made short work of them.'

She barely heard. Cheaters? 'Why are you here?'

He looked puzzled for a moment, but immediately assumed a kindly expression. 'I came for a little gambling, is all.'

The grey hair was wrong. It had been black in her vision.

But the face was the same. *The same.* A few more lines, perhaps, but the same face.

'Have you come to gamble?' he asked conversationally. 'I would be pleased to escort you into the gaming room. It should be straightened up by now. I assure you, all the excitement is over.'

'No, I—I wanted to speak to—to—Mr Campion.' Her voice sounded shrill.

If he thought that odd, he made no indication. 'I suspect he will be busy for a time. Is there somewhere you would like to wait? I will be honoured to convey your request to him. Whom shall I say asks for him?'

She almost spoke her name, but caught herself. 'Say his *pianiste.*'

He smiled. 'So you are the *pianiste* I have heard so much about? I came last night for the first time, having heard the Masquerade Club had both gambling and fine music. You were not here.'

She could not absorb the compliment.

Lady Faville appeared. 'What was the commotion?' she asked Phillipa, but then noticed the general. 'Oh, General Henson. How nice to see you again. When our Miss Songstress ran out, I wanted to follow, but dear Mr Everard convinced me to stay. You do recall Mr Everard, do you not, General? You met last night.'

'I do indeed,' he answered.

Mr Everard stood behind Lady Faville, but addressed Phillipa. 'You should not have dashed out, miss. You might have encountered danger.'

'She had a brush with it,' Henson said. 'Nothing of consequence, but it has upset her, I think.'

Lady Faville's eyes widened. 'What happened?'

General Henson explained about the men caught cheating and, while Lady Faville listened and asked questions, Phillipa backed away and returned to the supper room. It was abuzz. There had been a fight, they said. Xavier had overpowered the culprit. A big fellow, they said. Imagine. A man who looked like Campion overpowering a man like that.

Phillipa had seen him fight. Xavier had taken on three men the night they were attacked.

And once again the man in her vision appeared to her.

This time he was real.

She asked the servant to bring her a brandy. Mere sherry would not do to calm her nerves this night. She retreated to a table far in the corner and, after the servant set the glass in front of her, she picked it up and took one sip, then another. Her hand shook.

She closed her eyes and tried to make sense of it all.

The man was real…

'Phillipa?'

She opened her eyes and Xavier stood before her.

It had taken Xavier some effort to find Phillipa tucked away at this corner table. Reaching her had been even more difficult. The patrons delayed him, asking questions about what transpired in the gaming room.

She looked grateful to see him.

He sat. 'Were you injured?'

She shook her head.

'What possessed you to come to the gaming room, Phillipa?' He put her hand in his. 'It could have been dangerous.'

She averted her gaze. 'I feared for you.'

He squeezed her hand. 'Foolish girl. I have plenty of men to come to my aid, if necessary. Think of Cummings. What man could be a match for him?'

'I was not thinking. I heard the sounds—' Her brow furrowed and she looked at him with an uncertain expression.

'May we talk alone? I know it is presumptuous, but could we talk in Rhys's drawing room, perhaps?'

He immediately stood. 'Of course.'

Only a few people slowed him down with questions and comments as he led her through the room and out into the hallway. When they started up stairway to the drawing room, he glanced back and saw Daphne staring at him from the supper-room doorway.

Xavier leading a woman up to Rhys's private rooms? What conclusion would Daphne make? He did not care. His worry was for Phillipa. She seemed unsteady under his touch.

They entered the drawing room and he brought her directly to the sofa. 'You are shaking, Phillipa. Are you certain you are not injured?'

'It is not that. Really.' She pulled off her mask and rubbed her scar. 'I could not stand the mask another minute.'

There was more to it than the mask.

He walked over to a cabinet and brought out a bottle of brandy, pouring one glass and handing it to her before pouring another for himself.

He sat next to her on the sofa. 'Tell me what happened.'

She took another sip of brandy and reached out, almost touching his face, but withdrawing her hand. 'First, tell me if you are hurt. There was a fight, they said, and I saw the other man's bloody face.'

His skin yearned for her touch, but he spoke as if nothing had affected him. 'That fellow had the worst of it. He should not have tangled with me.' He took her hand, relishing the warmth of it. 'It is all over now. They will not be back.'

She nodded and slipped her hand away. He took a gulp of brandy. His desire for her surged, but this was not the time.

Eventually she spoke. 'There was a gentleman—he

kept me from falling. General Henson. Do you know who I mean?'

He nodded. 'I know the general.'

She turned away. 'I am fearful you will think me mad.'

'Mad?' He could never do so.

'I saw the general before.' She took another sip and swallowed. 'That night we were accosted by the three men. One man knocked me down and—and—suddenly I was someplace else. Someplace that smelled like the sea. When… when you helped me up, your face was a different face. It was that face of that man. The general.'

His face was another face?

'It was a vision.' Her voice cracked. 'I had the vision again. Several times. Falling. Smelling the sea. Seeing the face. It was always as though I was in a different place, but only for an instant.' She pressed her finger to her forehead. 'I do not understand it.' She waved a hand. 'In any event, the visions stopped and I thought them gone, but when I lost my balance it almost returned. This time, I saw the general. The real one, I mean.' She took a breath. 'I am certain it was the general's face in my vision, but now he looks older.'

Xavier's brows knitted.

She put her hand to her scarred cheek and turned away. 'You do think me mad.'

'No. No. I am trying to make sense of it.' He pulled her hand from her face. 'Are you certain it was a vision? Perhaps it was a memory.'

Because the pieces fit.

'If it was a memory, I would have remembered it!' Her voice rose. She glanced away again as if in thought. 'It was *familiar*, though. As if I ought to have remembered it.'

'Maybe it was a memory about your fall.' She'd smelled the sea. That could have been Brighton.

'My fall?' She looked confused.

He touched her scar. 'Listen to me. I know of soldiers who have memories of battles so vivid they think they are there again. This could be a memory. What do you remember of that event? When you fell at Brighton?'

She put her palm where his fingers touched. 'I was running up stone stairs and I fell. Or I must have fallen. My mother said I fell. I remember running up stone steps and falling. That is it.'

She did not remember it all, but Xavier did.

It had been dusk in Brighton and he'd been out poking around at the base of the sea wall. Sometimes people dropped things from the top of the wall, while they were gazing out to sea. He'd found coins, a watch, all sorts of treasure.

He heard the sounds of a quarrel. A man and woman, mere shadows at that time of day. He saw the man hurry away and the woman rush after him. And, then, there was the little girl—Phillipa.

He should have stopped her. The steps were too steep, too slippery to run up at that pace. Instead, he just watched. And saw it all.

The woman was Phillipa's mother. Lady Westleigh.

The man. Could it have been General Henson?

'Do you remember a man being there when you fell?'

'No one was there,' she insisted. 'My mother found me and picked me up and carried me home.'

'Do you remember that?'

She shook her head. 'Do you think the general was there?'

Xavier had never seen the man's face, but he'd worn a coat that might have been an officer's coat.

'My mother would have told me if a man was there.' She touched her scar again.

Would it help if he told her? He wanted to.

He could not tell her, though, not when he'd sworn a promise not to.

He'd given his word.

Phillipa pressed her fingers against her temple. 'I do not know what to think.'

Could her vision be a memory? It could not be the hallucination she feared, because General Henson was real. One could not conjure up a person and then discover he was real.

It must be a memory.

Xavier handed her the glass of brandy. 'Drink the rest. It will calm you.'

She took it and did as he told her.

The clock on the mantel struck the hour.

She picked up her mask. 'I should return to the supper room. People will think it odd that I am not performing.'

He stilled her hand. 'You are under no obligation to perform. You may stay here and rest until it is time for the hack to arrive.'

She had another hour. 'No, I'll play. The music will help.'

She put her mask in place.

'I'll tie the ribbons for you.' His voice turned low and soft.

What a marvellous voice he possessed. It could soothe. It could menace. It could make heat rush through her.

His fingers did the job of securing her mask gently but competently and his warm hand slid to the bare skin of her neck. 'There.' He rose from the couch and extended his hand to help her up.

This time his hand felt strong and secure. 'I'm certain everyone will wonder where you are,' Phillipa said, to cover up the silly emotions he aroused in her.

Emotions that nearly betrayed her long ago when she'd fancied herself in love with him.

He left her at the doorway of the supper room.

She entered the room and all heads turned to her. 'I am back,' she said to them in a cheerful voice. 'Do you wish me to play?'

Several voices called out their assent and she sat down on the bench to the pianoforte and quickly looked through her music for something she could manage in her shaken state.

Something joyful, she thought, to raise everyone's spirits.

Lady Faville approached her. 'Are you feeling better, Miss Songstress?'

The appellation surprised her. 'Yes. I am quite recovered.'

The lady's full pink lips turned up in an angelic smile. 'Was it not kind of Mr Campion—Xavier—to allow you some time to refresh yourself.' Her smile faltered a bit. 'I assume that was why he took you out of here. He is nothing if not the kindest of men.'

Phillipa supposed everyone knew she'd gone with Xavier to the private rooms, but surely they would think nothing of it. They thought her in the employ of the Masquerade Club, so it should not feel odd for the manager to speak to her alone.

But it rankled that Lady Faville commented upon it. 'Yes. I was shaken up by all the excitement, and—and almost falling.'

'Did you almost fall?' Lady Faville asked with a mere touch of scepticism.

'I did,' Phillipa assured her. 'And the general caught me.'

'How exciting!' cried the lady. She turned solicitous again. 'As long as you did not hurt yourself. I would have been desolate if my new friend were injured in any way.'

New friend. Even if it was merely Phillipa's envy that

prevented it, she could not ever consider this creature a friend.

'Thank you,' she said tightly and turned to her music.

Chapter Eight

The next morning Phillipa resolved to ask her mother about her accident all those years ago. If it had been possible that there was a man present, surely her mother could tell her.

Phillipa had slept late, exhausted by the night before. She missed her mother at breakfast and could only hope she had not yet gone out.

She checked her mother's bedchamber first, but she was not there. She started down the stairs and spied Mason below.

'Mason, where is Mother, do you know?' she called down.

The butler looked up. 'In the drawing room, m'lady, but—'

'Thank you!' She was near the drawing room. She knocked quickly and opened the door. 'Mama—' she began, but stopped short.

Quickly rising from the sofa was a gentleman.

General Henson.

Her mother spoke as she, too, rose. 'Phillipa! How good it is you have come. I want you to meet this dear old friend of mine.'

Dear old friend?

She stepped forwards and tried to look calm. What was he, of all persons, doing in her mother's drawing room?

Her mother took Phillipa's hand and pulled her closer. 'Phillipa, may I present my dear friend, General Henson.' Her mother gave the general a fond look. 'Alistair, my daughter.'

'This is Phillipa?' The general smiled as he had smiled the night before. In the better light of day, the lines of his face were more apparent. 'I cannot believe you are grown up.'

Phillipa's heart pounded painfully. 'Did you know me when I was a child, General?' she asked, remembering in time to extend her hand.

He clasped it in a fatherly way. 'I saw you when you were little more than a tot, my dear.'

He, of course, noticed her scar, but did not seem surprised about it. He must have known about it, but she had been much older than a tot when the accident happened. She'd been seven years old.

'I do not remember you,' she said. Although, apparently, she did.

He exchanged a glance with her mother. 'No reason why you should.'

'The general invited me for a drive in the country,' her mother broke in. 'Does that not sound delightful?'

The man looked apologetic. 'I would include you in the invitation, but, alas, my curricle is a small one.'

'Do not concern yourself,' Phillipa replied. 'I have much to do today.'

'My daughter spends her days playing the pianoforte.' Her mother's tone was disapproving, of course.

'Does she?' The general smiled in delight. 'What a worthwhile occupation.'

'How do you know my mother?' Phillipa asked. 'I do not recall her mentioning you.'

'We met in B—' He stopped himself. 'We met long ago through—through other connections. For most of the time until now I have been off fighting wars.'

'Well, enough of that,' her mother said with false cheer. 'We ought to leave, Alistair, if we are to return in time for me to dress for the opera.'

'As you wish.' He gave her mother a warm glance, but turned back to Phillipa. 'Will you do me the honour of allowing me to escort you to the opera as well as your mother? Your mother has graciously invited me to join her in her box.'

'Thank you, but I rarely go out.' Perhaps she should go. Find out more about this general. And her mother.

Her mother took the general's arm and led him to the door. She turned her head back to Phillipa. 'If you do not wish to come, Phillipa, be so good as to send a note to Miss Gale, inviting her to come with us. Do it quickly so she will have time to send a reply.'

'Yes, Mama.'

She watched them leave, her mother happier than she'd seen her in years.

Phillipa might have spent her time in near seclusion, but she was not so green a girl not to guess that her mother's relationship with General Henson was not merely friendship.

Had he been there, the day she was injured? If so, why had her mother not said so?

After her mother and the general left the house, Phillipa paced in the music room. She could not play a note, let alone compose one, although she forced herself to write to Miss Gale.

She wanted to talk to Xavier. He was the only person

with whom she could discuss this latest of events, finding the man in her vision seated with her mother in the drawing room.

Time passed much too slowly, though. She might indeed go mad if she had to wait until the middle of the night.

Why wait? She could call upon him. She'd done so once before, although she'd thought she would be calling upon Rhysdale. Calling upon one's relation, even one born on the wrong side of the blanket, would not cause too many questions, but calling upon a single gentleman could not be proper.

She did not care. She was not an *ingénue*. At twenty-three, in her situation, she was solidly on the shelf. Who would care what she did?

And her mother was not at home to question where she went or why.

She summoned her maid to help her don a walking dress and, before leaving her bedchamber, had the girl find a straw hat with so much netting her mother would have been pleased to see her in it. When she stepped out into the fine day, her face was well shaded from anyone recognising her as well as from the sun.

She walked as quickly as she could without attracting notice. As she neared the spot where she and Xavier were attacked, she slowed her pace. Anxiety fluttered inside her. She'd not walked this route since that night. Once there, the events returned to her mind, but without the darkness, the area held no lingering menace. She paused, wondering if the vision would recur.

It did not.

When she tried to recall the face in the vision, she saw only the man who'd been seated with her mother, who'd caught her when she almost fell.

She reached the door to the Masquerade Club, its innocent appearance striking her anew. She sounded the knocker and Cummings opened the door.

She almost greeted him by name. 'Lady Phillipa to see Mr Campion, please.'

'Not here,' the footman said.

'Oh dear.' She'd not considered this.

He stared at her for a moment. 'At the Stephen's Hotel, mayhap,' he finally said. It was an impressive string of words for the close-mouthed man. 'Doesn't come 'til later.'

The Stephen's Hotel was not far and it was still early enough to walk back by Bond Street. She could stop by the hotel and ask for him. It was a brazen idea, but very unlikely that anyone would know about it.

'Thank you,' she said.

Cummings nodded and closed the door.

Only after she set off for Bond Street did she realise how odd it was for Cummings to give Xavier's direction. Had Cummings recognised her? As more than the woman who had called upon Rhys that day?

She shook her head. She could not worry about that at the moment.

She hesitated once more as she approached the door of the Stephen's Hotel. Surely it was not what a lady would do, to enter this establishment that catered to army officers. She took a deep breath and opened the door, stepping in to a sparsely decorated hall. There was a desk behind which a clerk stood.

The man looked up and his brows rose.

She approached him. 'I would like to see Mr Campion, if I may.'

He looked askance. 'He would wish to know who calls.'

She had not thought that far in advance. 'Tell him his *pianiste* calls.'

'Very good, ma'am.' The man gestured to an open door on his right. 'Would you care to wait in the drawing room?'

Phillipa thanked him and hoped no one else would be in the room. Luckily she was alone amidst the assortment of chairs and couches arranged for conversation. The curtains were drawn and, although the room had more the air of a gentleman's library, fresh flowers on the mantel and on the tables made it somewhat cheerful.

The idea of coming here seemed suddenly foolish. How much could it have mattered to simply wait to talk to him that night?

A man's voice sounded in the hall and Phillipa hurried to the doorway, expecting to see Xavier.

It was not Xavier.

It was General Henson, obviously sneaking a giggling woman through the hall.

Phillipa's mother.

Xavier quickly put on his coat and ran a hand through his hair as he descended the stairs, trying not to appear too eager for the clerk's sake.

She'd come alone, the clerk said. What could have possessed her to do so? He could only think that something bad had happened.

The clerk was again behind his desk by the time Xavier crossed the hall to the drawing room. When he walked through the doorway he saw her.

She simply stood, gazing blankly towards the door.

He hurried to her. 'Phillipa, what is it? Has something happened?'

God help that it not have happened to Rhys. Or Lady

Gale, Rhys's lover. Or any member of her family. He could think of no other reason she would come to him here.

She did not answer.

Unless something had happened to her.

He lifted the netting away from her face. 'Phillipa! Talk to me.'

She blinked. 'Oh, do forgive me.' She was pale as chalk. 'I am quite speechless.'

He gripped her shoulders. 'What happened?'

She shook her head as if not believing her eyes. 'I just saw General Henson. In the hall. The real General Henson. Not a vision.'

He softened his touch and his tone, but did not cease holding her. 'The hotel caters to army officers.'

'I know.' Her voice was breathless. 'There is more. My mother was with him. They obviously came from his rooms.'

That must have been a shock.

His fingers slipped down her arm and grasped her hand. 'Come. Sit.' He led her to a sofa. 'You could not have known that before you came here.'

She smiled wanly. 'I did not, but it was why I came, none the less.'

She told him of encountering General Henson with her mother in her mother's drawing room. Of her mother professing to know him many years ago. Of the general saying he'd seen her when she was a tiny girl.

'But, this is the thing.' She touched her scar. 'He showed no surprise at seeing my scar. People are always surprised the first time they see my scar. So he must have known about it. He must have seen me—and Mama—after it happened.'

Henson must have been the man on the beach that night. Nothing else made sense.

'I think they were lovers,' she said firmly. '*Are* lovers, still. They obviously have become reunited.'

'General Henson has not been in town long, I think.' He realised he still held her hand. He released it. 'Does it upset you to discover your mother has a lover?'

'Goodness, no.' She laughed. 'If any woman deserves a lover, it is she. My father certainly gave her more trouble than care or devotion.' Her eyes narrowed. 'Were you thinking I should have a fit of the vapours? I assure you I have acquired some knowledge of the world.' She gestured to her face. 'When nobody looks at you, much can be observed.'

He felt a stab of pain for her.

'It surprised me to see them, that's all.' She glanced away as if witnessing them again. 'My mother was as giddy and silly as a girl in her first Season—' She cut herself off and turned back to him. 'I am the one who feels silly, coming to you like this.'

He met her gaze. 'I confess, I feared something much more serious brought you here.'

From the window, the sun's rays dusted her chocolate-brown eyes with flecks of gold. Her lips were moist and tempting. Her skin, too, was luminous and so smooth he itched to touch it—

He stopped himself. Why was it he'd only found one instance to kiss her? Every other time the desire overcame him, she was too overcome with emotion.

He contented himself to savour her beauty. What a pity people did not look at her. Or if they did, they saw only her scar.

Her eyes darkened and she lowered her lashes. 'It was foolish of me. I simply needed someone to tell about General Henson and my mother. There was no one else but you.' Her lashes fluttered. 'It should have waited until tonight.'

He almost touched her again. 'I do not mind it, Phillipa.'

She fussed with the netting on her hat and covered half her face. 'It is the sort of thing one runs to one's lady friends about, I suppose, but I've lost touch with most of my school friends and the others live far away.'

'You have hidden yourself away,' he said.

Her chin rose. 'I have been busy with my music. It has been my passion.'

He did indulge himself and touched his finger to her chin, but it was as he used to do when they were children and he wanted to tease her about the faintest cleft in her chin. 'You've achieved impressive results.'

Her eyes widened and she leaned back. 'Why, thank you, Xavier. I have longed to hear words of approval for my music.'

He was puzzled. 'You hear such words every night you play, do you not?'

She released a breath. 'They do not know who I am.'

'Should it make a difference?' He noticed a stray curl escaped from her bonnet.

'The daughter of an earl is not supposed to perform music. At least not in a gaming house. At a musicale, perhaps, but there everyone who plays is deemed marvellous.' She lowered her voice. 'I do not think you would lie.'

'I would never lie to you.' Withhold information, perhaps, but never lie.

'This is all of no consequence.' She waved a hand. 'The vision must be a memory, as you have said. General Henson must have been there when I fell. My mother would not tell me such a thing, if he had been her lover. What do you think?'

'It seems plausible,' was all he could say.

'I would so much rather have a memory than see things that were never there.' She leaned against him like she used to do when they were playmates. 'This seems so much like it used to be in Brighton. You were always my friend and confidant.'

He put his arm around her and enjoyed the moment of comfortable closeness with her.

'I must go.' She sat up straight again. 'I presume too much, taking up your time like this with my nonsense.'

She rose from the sofa.

He stood as well. 'Wait a moment. I'll get my hat and walk you home.'

'No,' she said quickly. 'I came on my own. I can leave on my own.' She shook her head. 'Besides I do not want my mother to see you. She might be home by now. I do not wish to endure her questions.'

He nodded.

She started for the door but turned back to him. 'Thank you for being so kind, Xavier. I truly did need a friend to talk to about this.'

'I am your friend, Phillipa,' he responded. 'I have always been.'

She smiled, but did not meet his eye. 'Good day.'

He did not want her to leave. 'I will see you tonight.'

'Yes. Tonight.'

She turned back to the door, but suddenly ran back to him, throwing her arms around him in a big hug. She would have pulled away just as quickly, but he held her there, against him, and inhaled the jasmine scent of her, relished the warmth of her.

He released her and she hurried away. He stepped to the window to watch her walk briskly away. She stopped suddenly and pulled the rest of the netting back over her face.

And he again felt a stab of pain for her.

Without hat or gloves, he stepped to the door to follow her home and make certain she arrived safely.

* * *

That night she sang songs about forbidden love.

Still thinking about her mother, Xavier surmised. He felt even closer to her than before, even closer than as children, the sort of closeness a man wants with a woman he craves.

He stood at the back of the room, his usual place, watching her as her long, elegant fingers moved over the pianoforte keys and her voice rang out with emotion. He wished she could remove her mask so he could see the emotion on her face as she played.

Her music was full of life because she'd put her whole life into it. It made him sad for her, but also appreciative of her considerable achievement.

He could listen to her for hours, but ought to spare only a few minutes more before attending to the gaming room.

Daphne sidled up to him. 'I did not know you had such an…appreciation of music, Xavier.'

She ruined the moment for him. 'You do not know me, Daphne.'

She was undaunted. 'We have become bosom bows, your Miss Songstress and me. Did you know that?'

'I believe you have said as much before.' But he doubted it. He inclined his head towards Phillipa. 'Does she know it?'

Her lips pursed for a moment, but she turned them up in a smile. 'You will make me laugh, Xavier, and then I will interrupt the music.'

He straightened. 'I cannot remain here and talk to you. I must return to the gaming room.'

He walked away from her without a second glance.

Later when he came to collect Phillipa for the ride home in the hackney, Daphne stood with her, chattering away. It was difficult to see Phillipa's reaction under her mask.

When they were in the coach, he perused her. 'Have you befriended Lady Faville?'

She did not answer immediately. 'She befriended me.'

He shook his head. 'Why?'

She stiffened. 'Is it so difficult to believe someone would befriend me?'

'Not in the least,' he assured her. 'But someone like her—'

Phillipa drew away from him. 'Because she is so lovely?'

'You know I do not mean that.' This was merely causing tension between them. 'I was surprised, that's all. She is not the sort to make friends.'

He dropped the subject and so did she, but they rode in uncomfortable silence the rest of the short journey. He felt like kicking himself. He ought to have let her talk of her mother and General Henson.

The hackney pulled up a few doors down from the Westleigh town house and Xavier helped Phillipa from the carriage. Just as they both stood on the pavement, the Westleigh town house door opened and a man emerged.

Xavier and Phillipa stood in the shadows away from the hackney coach's lamp.

General Henson walked past them.

Chapter Nine

The next day Phillipa rose early to catch her mother at breakfast.

By rights Phillipa ought to confront her mother about her affair with the general, but she didn't have the heart. Her mother deserved some happiness, after all.

But Phillipa's memory of General Henson and its apparent attachment to her injury were another matter. So when she descended the stairs and entered the dining room it was with a determined step.

Her mother was already seated there.

'You are up early,' they said in unison.

'I could not sleep,' they answered together.

Her mother laughed, a sound Phillipa had so rarely heard in recent years.

She turned to the buffet and picked out a piece of bread and jam.

Her mother spoke. 'I rose early so I could go to the shops.' Her tone was defensive. She was lying. 'I plan to shop all day, so I am certain you would not wish to keep me company.'

A wave of tenderness for her mother washed over Phillipa. 'I do not, but who do you take with you? Your maid? Higgley?'

Her mother lifted her nose. 'If you must know, General Henson will accompany me.'

'Again today?'

Her mother crossed her arms over her chest. 'Yes. Again today. I have not seen him in very many years—'

Phillipa held up a hand. 'I meant no criticism, Mama.'

'Oh.' Her mother relaxed again.

'There is something I wish to ask you, though.'

Her mother tensed again. 'Not more about your father and brothers, if you please. I am done talking about that with you.'

Phillipa chewed and swallowed a piece of bread. 'Not that,' she assured her. 'I wanted to ask you what you remember about the time I fell. When my face was cut.'

Her mother glanced away. 'Whatever for?'

'Curiosity.' She took a breath. 'Tell me about it again.'

Her mother rose and fussed at the buffet. 'Must I? It was a terrible event and I dislike remembering it.'

'Please, Mama. Just tell me again.'

'There is nothing to say.' She sat again. 'You went outside without permission and I found you on the beach. You'd fallen. That is all.'

'What was I doing out there?' Phillipa had never thought to ask this before.

Her mother threw up her hands. 'I do not know. You went out. You confessed not to remember. It was a terrible shock to find you all—all bleeding and insensible.'

Why had her mother gone out to find her? She'd never thought of it before, but her mother sent servants for tasks like that.

Her heart pounded. 'Was anyone else there, on the beach when you found me?'

'No.' Her mother's eyes darted away. 'Enough of that, now. The whole terrible event is best forgotten. I will not say another word about it.'

Phillipa persisted. 'Is there anything you can tell me now that you withheld from me as a child? I do wish to know.'

Her mother busied herself with her food. 'Nothing. Unless you wish to hear a hideous description of the skin hanging off your face.'

'Spare me that, Mama.' Her mother was being deliberately cruel.

'You would do better to forget about the past. You need to rejoin society.' Her mother straightened in her chair.

This was an old, familiar lecture.

'You are an earl's daughter,' her mother went on. 'For that reason alone, you are a desirable catch for any respectable gentleman, no matter what your age and your—' She stopped. 'No respectable gentleman would be unkind to you, because of—' Again she closed her mouth.

The word her mother refused to speak was *scar*.

'There is a ball tonight,' her mother said. 'You should attend.'

Phillipa glanced down at her plate. 'No, Mama.'

'Very well.' Her mother stood. 'I will take Miss Gale with me.' She flounced out of the room.

Phillipa rested her head in her hands. Such an attack by her mother had only one end. To force Phillipa's retreat.

There was something her mother did not wish to speak of and that something had to do with her accident. These secrets were killing her.

General Henson must have been there. Her memory told her so. Why could her mother not simply admit it and explain what really happened?

* * *

Over the next two days there was no opportunity for Phillipa to confront her mother again. Her mother spent every spare minute with General Henson. Phillipa surmised he spent at least part of the night in her mother's bed even though she and Xavier never saw him leave again. She held her breath entering the house in the wee morning hours for fear of bumping into him on the stairway.

Phillipa encountered another worry. Her maid had discovered that she was sneaking out at night. Luckily the girl was loyal. And ambitious. Phillipa paid her well for her silence.

Since General Henson was with her mother, he did not show up at the Masquerade Club. However, Lady Faville was always there.

Soon, though, it would all end. Each night that passed brought her closer to the time when Rhysdale would return. That would be the end of her performing.

The end of her time with Xavier.

It broke her heart.

This night as Phillipa took her seat at the pianoforte, she forced herself to be happy for the moment and not think of the future.

Lady Faville and the steadfast Mr Everard sat at their usual table. She supposed she would have to endure another *comfortable coze*, as Lady Faville called it, where Lady Faville would prose on about her devotion to Xavier and her determination to marry him.

Whenever Lady Faville stood next to Xavier, Phillipa was struck anew at how perfect they looked together, that contrast of light and dark. Mr Everard saw it too, she noticed. She could see it in his eyes when he looked at the beautiful pair.

Lady Faville gave her a little wave and Phillipa started

playing. She chose the happiest piece she could think of. Not one of her compositions, which all tended to more wrenching emotions, but 'La De Belombre', an old composition for harpsichord she liked because it challenged her fingering.

Xavier listened through the whole song before leaving. Phillipa always knew when he was there.

After he left, she played in waves, happy music drifting to songs of love lost or lovers' deaths, then back to something joyous or frivolous.

At the end, there was gratifying applause. She stepped away from the pianoforte and chose her refreshment, taking it to the table in the corner that gave her some privacy.

Until Lady Faville approached her, that is. 'You did very well this night, Miss Songstress.'

This lady's approval held no importance. 'Thank you.'

Lady Faville sat without being invited to. 'Does Xavier not look handsome tonight? More handsome than usual, do you not think?'

To Phillipa he looked wonderful every night. 'He is a very well-looking man.'

Lady Faville laughed. 'You are always so careful not to say too much.'

That was perceptive of her, more perceptive than Phillipa would have given her credit. 'I must be discreet.'

With this lady, Phillipa played the employee. It was what Lady Faville and most of the patrons wished to think of her. An employee would be careful what she said about an employer or his designated manager.

Lady Faville leaned across the table. 'Has he said anything about me? Did you talk to him about me?' She was forever wanting Phillipa to convince Xavier of her regard and she hoped Xavier would tell Phillipa of his admiration.

In truth, Xavier talked so very little about himself that

she truly did not know from his lips how he felt about the lady. Most of the gentleman preened and strutted around Lady Faville, but Phillipa did not ever see Xavier doing so. A man as handsome as he had no need to do so.

'I cannot presume to talk to him about you,' Phillipa told her for what seemed the hundredth time. 'And our conversations are not such that he would mention any patron.'

Lady Faville gave her a sceptical smile. 'You know I do not credit that. You do not tell me all.' She released an exaggerated sigh. 'I do not know what kind of friend you are, to hold back what is so important to me.'

She was no friend at all, Phillipa thought. 'I am holding back nothing.'

Except, perhaps, that she wished Lady Faville to leave her alone. It was painful to Phillipa to be the lady's confidante, to hear of her intent to marry Xavier, to know the wealthy young widow would be a prize any man would covet.

Lady Faville put a hand on Phillipa's arm. 'I know you will say nothing to me, but I do count on you to be my very dear friend.'

Sometimes Lady Faville was so charming that Phillipa could almost like her, but it was difficult to like someone who had everything you lacked.

She'd almost finished her final set when Xavier returned. His presence disturbed her in a pleasurable way, making her both self-conscious and bold in her piano playing.

When she was done, he walked her down the stairs. 'The piece before your last one, was that one of your compositions?'

It had been the bagatelle she'd laboured over for so many hours and days. 'Yes, it was.'

He shrugged. 'It reminded me of the gaming room somehow.'

She stopped. 'Do not say it. That is precisely the sound I was attempting to recreate.'

He grinned. 'You accomplished it.'

She felt like skipping the rest of the way.

When they sat in the hackney coach and she pulled off her mask, she asked him about his night, if there were any problems in the gaming room.

'One fellow lost too much,' he told her. 'I feared for him; he was so despondent.'

He'd told her stories of men who'd lost fortunes and killed themselves. Her father lost a fortune and merely tried to cheat his way out of it.

'What did you do?' she asked.

He turned to her, his features muted in the dark coach. 'I gave him a loan.'

'Will Rhysdale approve of that?' she asked.

'I have seen him do the same from time to time,' he responded. 'But I did not use his money.'

She knew what he would say. 'You used your own money.'

He shrugged. 'I did.'

Her breast swelled with pride for him. What a fine thing to do.

How was she ever going to give up knowing him, talking to him every day?

She promised herself that she would savour every moment at the gaming house and with him. She would hold every moment in her heart and never let go of them.

The hackney coach pulled up to its usual place on her street, but before Xavier opened the door, he took her hand. 'I enjoyed your performance tonight, Phillipa.'

Before she could speak, he pulled her into his arms and

kissed her. It was a short kiss, but one that took her breath and left her weak.

He opened the door and Xavier jumped down to help her out. 'Goodnight, Phillipa. Sleep well.'

She kept hold of his hand. 'Goodnight, Xavier. I will see you tomorrow night.'

He pressed her hand tighter before letting go. She turned to walk the short distance to her town house, but had gone no more than two steps when two men jumped from the shadows.

Xavier grabbed her arm and pulled her behind him.

'Phillipa, do not hide from us,' a familiar voice said. Her brother Ned.

'Who is this with you?' Hugh, her other brother, demanded.

The jarvey called down, 'Need assistance, sir?'

Xavier walked over to him and paid his fare and his tip. 'You may go, Johnson, I'll be walking back tonight.'

'After I'm done with you, you won't be able to walk,' Hugh said.

'You'll do nothing of the sort!' Phillipa cried.

The coach pulled away.

Xavier held her arm again, but spoke to Hugh. 'Hugh, it is Xavier. I can explain this.'

'Xavier!' Hugh was taken aback. 'What the devil? You are the man carrying on with my sister?'

'It is not what you think,' Phillipa broke in.

Xavier still kept hold of her. 'May I suggest we not discuss this in the street?'

'Come. All of you,' Ned ordered.

Xavier held Phillipa's hand as they followed him to the town house.

Her brothers were back from Brussels. The ending she dreaded had come without warning.

This had been her last night to perform her music.

Her last night with Xavier.

What a blasted mess, Xavier thought as he followed Ned into the town house. They walked directly to the drawing room where Lady Westleigh was seated.

Where was General Henson? Hiding in a closet somewhere? In Lady Westleigh's dressing room, perhaps?

'We found her, Mama,' Ned said.

'And the man.' Hugh, with a disgusted expression on his face, gestured in Xavier's direction. 'Xavier Campion.'

The countess's brows rose when she saw him. 'Xavier Campion!'

He bowed. 'Lady Westleigh.'

'I cannot believe this of you.' She shook her head in dismay. 'Your mother is my friend.'

'Mama,' Phillipa cried. 'You must allow me to explain.'

'Explain?' Ned faced her. 'We come home in the dead of night and discover you are not in your bed. Your maid, after much coercion, finally confesses that you leave the house every night after everyone retires. You return three hours later.'

Three and a half hours, to be more precise, Xavier thought.

'And it is Campion you were sneaking out to see.' Hugh glared at him. 'Taking liberties with my sister.'

'Liberties!' Phillipa cried. 'He took no liberties.'

Except that he'd just kissed her, but he could not regret that.

'Listen to her explanation,' Xavier demanded.

'Very well.' Lady Westleigh leaned back in her chair.

Phillipa spoke. 'I have been attending our gaming house. The Masquerade Club.' She held up her mask that had been gripped in her hand all this time. 'I play the pianoforte there and I sing.'

'You sing?' Hugh shot back. 'Like a common—' He did not finish.

'The gaming house?' Ned cried. 'You were not supposed to know about the gaming house.'

'I was not supposed to know many things of great import to our family, apparently.' Her chin rose.

Hugh swung towards Xavier. 'Rhys told her, didn't he? What business was it of his? Just because he joined the family did not give him the right.'

Xavier shot him a quelling look. 'I told Phillipa. Not Rhys. Rhys knows nothing of this. He is not even in town.'

Lady Westleigh tossed him a very worried look. 'Precisely what did you tell her—?'

'About Father,' Phillipa cut in. 'About our debt and how Rhys helped our family, only to have Father cheat him and challenge him to a duel. About how Ned and Hugh took Father to Brussels where he agreed to stay.'

'Good God, what didn't you tell her?' Hugh said.

There was more he didn't tell her. Couldn't tell her.

'See, Mama, I have not fallen apart.' Phillipa raised her arms. 'I learned all this and I still stand before you, the same as always. I have attended a gaming house and performed music there and I remain in one piece. I am unfazed by your secrets. I did not need to be protected from them. I do not need protection from anything.'

She was strong, Xavier did admit, but not without need of protection. What might have happened to her if she'd been alone when they were attacked?

'You obviously needed protection from Campion here.' Hugh leaned into his face. 'What the devil is wrong with you, Campion? You can have any woman you want. Why trifle with my sister? Were you bored with the pretty ones?'

Xavier seized Hugh by the front of his coat. 'Do not in-sult her. Do you heed me?'

He pushed Hugh away and Hugh lowered his head. 'I didn't mean it that way. Not how it sounded.'

Phillipa swung towards Hugh. 'Xavier has been a per-fect gentleman towards me. He escorted me to and from the gaming house, because he knew I would walk there alone if he did not.'

Ned glared at her. 'Phillipa, you cannot spend time alone with any man in the middle of the night. If this becomes known, your reputation will be ruined.'

'That is a laugh, Ned.' She pointed to her face. 'What do I need a reputation for?'

Ned turned haughty. 'Well, I, for one, will not have the lady to whom I am betrothed besmirched by your loose morals.'

'Stubble it, Ned.' Xavier wanted to strike him. 'Your sis-ter has not displayed loose morals—'

'Listen to me,' Phillipa broke in again. 'I wanted an ad-venture and I have had one. Xavier made certain I was safe while doing so. It is ended. It is over. No one else knows. Leave it. There is nothing to be done.'

Ned seemed to consider this.

Even Hugh settled down somewhat. 'He did not seduce you?'

'He did not,' she answered.

Xavier reined in his temper. Matters were calming down. Ned and Hugh were beginning to see reason.

Ned blew out a breath. 'I suppose…if no one knows…'

'Let it be as Phillipa desires,' Xavier said.

His attention shifted to Lady Westleigh, who'd developed a very calculating look in her eye.

'I must return to the Club,' Xavier said. 'I am usually gone only a few minutes.'

He slid a regretful look at Phillipa.

She nodded her approval. 'Leave, Xavier,' she said. 'It is over. There is no harm if no one knows, and who would tell?'

Not Cummings or MacEvoy, Xavier would see to that.

He bowed to Phillipa and to Lady Westleigh. 'I bid you goodnight, then.'

Lady Westleigh rose. 'Not so hasty, young man.'

He stopped and turned.

She looked like a player holding the winning cards. 'It is of no consequence that you did not steal my daughter's virtue. Or that no one will know you carted her off in the middle of the night. You still behaved very dishonourably. You have compromised Phillipa and you know what honour dictates you do.'

Yes. He understood very clearly.

Lady Westleigh intended to manipulate him into marrying Phillipa.

'No!' Phillipa cried. 'No, you cannot do this, Mama. It is not fair.'

She had never foreseen this, never even dreamed it could happen.

She turned to Xavier. 'Do not listen to her.' She swung back to her mother. 'This is wrong, Mama. You must not require this of him.'

'Must I not?' Her mother actually looked smug.

'Mother,' Ned began. 'Perhaps this is not the thing to do.'

Her mother's eyes flashed. 'Of course it is the thing to do. Mr Campion knows what honour requires of him, do you not, Mr Campion? He must marry her.'

Phillipa could not bear it. To ruin his life like this? It was all her fault. 'Xavier, do not heed her. My family will say nothing. No one will know. No reputation will be ruined. There was no harm done.'

He turned to her mother and brothers. 'Allow me to speak with Phillipa alone.'

'No.' Her mother straightened her spine. 'Call upon us tomorrow. We will discuss the particulars.'

Her mother acted as if the decision had been made.

He glanced at Phillipa, who nodded her assent.

'I'll call tomorrow.' He bowed.

Phillipa watched him walk away through the doorway until she could see him no more.

She whirled back to her mother, angrier than she had ever been in her life. 'How could you do this to him?'

Even Ned spoke up. 'Mother, maybe it would be better to hush this up.'

'Xavier doesn't want to marry her,' Hugh added.

Her mother stood. 'Go to bed, all of you. We will discuss this in the morning.' She started to the door.

Hugh rubbed his hands. 'I'm not going to bed. I'm going to the Masquerade Club. Someone should check on things if Rhys is not there.'

Ned looked wary. 'I had better go with you. The last thing we need is you getting into a dust-up with Xavier. Then there will be talk.'

'Leave him alone,' Phillipa said to their departing backs. 'He deserves none of this.'

Her mother patted Phillipa's arm as she also passed. 'Do not concern yourself over Xavier, dear. Think of this as good fortune.'

Good fortune? It was disaster. Cruelty. Pain.

She was left alone in the room, but it took several minutes until she could make herself walk to her bedchamber.

As soon as she opened the door, her maid cried, 'Oh, m'lady, I did not mean to tell them. I tried not to, but your mother was so insistent. And then she tricked me and made me say what I promised I would not say.' She reached into her pocket and took out a purse. 'Here is the money you paid me to be quiet.'

'Keep it, Lacey,' Phillipa said in a weary voice. 'I do not hold you to blame.'

'Oh, thank you, m'lady.' The girl bobbed. 'I am ever so grateful.'

'Just help me out of this dress and into bed.' Phillipa rubbed her face.

A few minutes later she was between her bed linens and her maid had gone. Her head and her heart ached.

One thing was certain. She would not allow Xavier to be coerced into marrying her. No matter how much her mother connived.

Chapter Ten

Xavier was glad for the walk to the Masquerade Club. He needed the physical exertion and cool night air.

Those cursed Westleighs. He was angry with the lot of them.

Except for Phillipa. How could they treat her so shabbily? Had they given any care to what she did before this? Perhaps if they had shown some interest in her, some support of her music, she would not have had to venture out on her own and put herself in peril.

Xavier knew he'd done what he must. She would have braved the streets alone had he not escorted her. He certainly did not regret allowing her the chance to perform. Not when it brought her such joy.

Honour might dictate that he marry her, but honour be damned. It must be what Phillipa wanted, not what suited the rest of them.

He'd speak to her alone. She alone must decide. By God, he'd marry her if that was what she wished, but only if it was her wish. Not her mother's. Not her brothers'.

Not even his.

Xavier knew what he wanted. He wanted to whisk Phillipa away from them. All of them. He wanted to find a myriad of ways to give her the joy she'd found performing her music. Because it was not only she who had found joy in this interlude. He had, as well.

But she must want it. She must choose.

He reached the town house and sounded the knocker. Cummings opened the door to him. Xavier left him his hat and gloves and went straight to MacEvoy, who informed him that nothing eventful had come to his attention.

He left MacEvoy and went next to the gaming room.

As soon as he walked in the room, Daphne was beside him.

'Did you get our lovely Miss Songstress back to Covent Garden?' she asked in her dulcet-toned voice.

He faced her directly. 'Daphne, I have no patience for your nonsense tonight. Tell Mr Everard to take you home.'

For an instant she looked as if he'd slapped her and he was sorry he'd taken out his ill temper on her.

'That was unkindly said,' he spoke more softly. 'I apologise for that, but you should spend your time elsewhere.'

A determined gleam appeared in her eyes. 'I know what I want, Xavier.'

'No, Daphne. Your happiness is not with me.'

Ned and Hugh walked in and Xavier left Daphne without another word.

'What now, gentlemen?' He braced for more insults to their sister.

Ned's expression was conciliatory. 'We simply came to see how the place is faring.'

'I have not managed to burn the place down yet,' Xavier answered. 'Do you want to see the books?'

'It seems a good place to start,' Ned replied agreeably.

They had started back for the door when Hugh leaned over to Xavier. 'Who is that beautiful creature?'

Xavier did not need to look to know of whom Hugh was speaking. 'Lady Faville. She's taken a fancy to gambling.'

'Lady Faville,' Hugh repeated quietly. 'I've never seen her before.'

Xavier took them to MacEvoy, where they glanced through the ledgers. Did they notice the rise in profits while their sister was here? Afterwards, they retired to the supper room.

When they walked past the pianoforte, Xavier glanced at Phillipa's music.

Should he send her music home with Ned and Hugh? In truth, it was too precious to trust them with it. They did not even seem to notice the pianoforte that had been so important to their sister.

He led them to a table and ordered brandy.

'All looks well here,' Ned remarked.

'Rhys did not tell us he would be away. You cannot blame us for worrying,' Hugh added. 'Our family fortune is at stake.'

'I do not blame you for seeing to your investment.' Xavier blamed them for their treatment of their sister.

The brandy was served.

Ned took a sip and nodded approvingly. 'Sorry about this business with our sister.'

Hugh peered at him with narrowed eyes. 'You had better be telling the truth. If I discover you trifled with her—'

Xavier gave the younger Westleigh a severe look. 'You'll do what, Hugh? Make me marry her? Bloody my face? I would relish the opportunity for you to try.'

'Do not tempt me,' Hugh countered.

Xavier went on as if Hugh had not spoken. 'Or will you merely insult your sister several more times? I ought to call you out for the things you said about her.'

Hugh looked genuinely surprised. 'What did I say?'

'That she was not one of the pretty ones. That her singing was common.'

'Xavier is correct,' Ned said. 'That was not well done of you.'

Xavier turned to him. 'And you accused her of loose morals. Tell me why she deserves such talk from her brothers?'

Ned looked chastened; Hugh, about to lose his temper again.

Until Daphne walked in and sat with Mr Everard. Hugh's gaze riveted on her, as well as the gazes of several other men in the room.

'When does Rhys come back?' Ned asked, changing the subject.

Xavier tasted his brandy. 'I do not know. Soon, I expect.'

Hugh dragged his attention back. 'Ned merely wishes to know when he will be able to get married.' He laughed. 'I have a capital idea. The three of you can be married together. Three at once.'

'No.' Phillipa would despise such a thing, even if she did agree to marry him. 'And nothing is decided.'

Ned leaned forwards. 'I think Phillipa had the right of it. There is no reason for you to marry her. If no one knows about her—her activities here—we can all go on as before.'

Xavier took another drink. 'It must be as Phillipa wishes.'

The next morning at breakfast, without her brothers present, Phillipa tried to reason with her mother.

'Please, Mama. Surely you see the sense in this. If we say and do nothing, all will go on as before. If I marry Xavier, then there will be talk.' She shuddered at the thought. 'A man of his appearance marrying a disfigured woman like me? No one would talk of anything else.'

'That sort of gossip is of no consequence.' Her mother was almost cheerful this morning.

Phillipa's voice rose. 'It would be wrong to force Xavier to marry me.'

Her mother made a gesture for her to speak more quietly. She inclined her head towards the servants' door.

'Do not be ridiculous, Mama.' Phillipa leaned back in her chair. 'The servants know. Or will do so soon.'

'Only when I am ready for them to know,' her mother said.

Phillipa lowered her voice. 'Why would you insist upon my marrying Xavier when I do not wish to?'

Her mother continued to eat her food, talking between bites. 'Because it secures your future, Phillipa dear. You have been hiding in your music room. That is no way to achieve a proposal of marriage. This is a godsend.'

'Mama!'

Her mother's expression turned stern. 'You have been apprised of the state of our family's finances, Phillipa. Much as I have tried to shield you from this distress, you may as well know that you have no dowry. Any money meant for you is gone.'

She had not known that part of it. Had even her dowry been squandered by her father?

Her mother went on. 'I have very little money left, as well. There is nothing to leave you when I am gone. You are a burden to this family now, and if you do not marry you will for ever be a burden.'

A burden. What cruel words.

'But if you marry Campion—' her mother smiled '—you will have a household of your own. Pin money of your own.'

'I am to marry for money?' Phillipa scoffed.

Her mother waved away her words as if they were an annoying fly. 'There are worse reasons to marry. And you know you are marrying a good man. We have known his family since before you were born. No one ever gossips about them—' She glanced away. 'Well, there was the one time, but that problem was quickly dispatched—'

What on earth did she mean?

Her mother smiled again. 'The Campions have a respectable fortune, and it is said that Xavier has his own money. From an uncle or aunt or somebody.'

'So I *am* to marry for money,' Phillipa muttered.

Her mother pursed her lips. 'My dear daughter, he is the perfect husband. He is rich. He comes from a decent family and he has been brought up to be an honourable man. He will treat you well.' She pinned her with her gaze. 'Need I go on?'

'But he is also a friend.' Phillipa felt as if her insides were in shreds. 'A friend you would have me treat quite shabbily. He has been kind to me, but he cannot regard me as a wife.'

Xavier was the sort of man who would offer, though. For honour's sake. He should not be punished so for what had been her instigation.

'Do not turn romantic on me, Phillipa,' her mother scolded. 'It will be a good marriage for you. You will see.'

'But what about him?' Phillipa cried. 'What about Xavier? You cannot saddle such a man with me. A—a man of his looks and his character. He does not deserve it.'

Her mother smiled. 'Then he should not have been running around with you in the middle of the night.'

It was no use to argue with her.

'I will not do it, Mama,' she whispered. 'I will not marry him.'

Her mother glared at her. 'You will marry him or I will make certain you regret it.'

It mattered not what revenge her mother intended. 'I will not marry him.'

She loved him too much.

* * *

Xavier presented himself at the Westleigh town house at the appointed time. The solemn-faced butler announced him to the family.

When he entered the drawing room, his eyes immediately found Phillipa. Her features were pinched and her posture taut, as if wanting to flee.

Lady Westleigh had enthroned herself in an armchair. Ned and Hugh stood at her side, like pages.

Xavier bowed to Lady Westleigh, but quickly straightened. 'I will see Phillipa alone.'

Lady Westleigh met his eye. 'I think not.'

He'd not yield the power to her. He gave her a look his soldiers once knew—he'd brook no argument. 'I will see Phillipa alone.'

He'd wrestled with the matter overnight, getting no sleep at all.

In honesty, he wanted to marry Phillipa—if for no other reason than to keep her away from this family. But also to find a way to give her joy.

In that, his motives were unchanged from their days in Brighton.

Except he also wanted her as a man wants a woman.

Lady Westleigh huffed. 'There is nothing for you to discuss together, because you will marry her.'

Phillipa leaned towards him. 'Do not heed her, Xavier.'

'Phillipa,' her mother warned.

Xavier's hands curled into fists.

'Now, Mother.' Ned's tone was quelling. 'Let them talk together—'

'Be quiet, Ned,' Lady Westleigh snapped.

A knock at the door silenced them all. The butler appeared again. 'General Henson, my lady.'

'Alistair!' The lady brightened. 'Do show him in.'

General Henson stepped into the room, but stopped as if he'd not expected to see them all gathered there. 'My dear lady. Forgive me. I interrupt you.' He noticed Xavier with even more surprise and nodded. 'Campion. Good to see you.'

'General.' Xavier said. Who else would show up? Lord Westleigh?

The general bowed to Phillipa. 'Lady Phillipa.'

She merely nodded.

Ned and Hugh exchanged puzzled glances.

Lady Westleigh simpered. 'Alistair, you have walked in on a—a family meeting, but do come forwards. I would be delighted to introduce you to my sons.'

The introductions were made as if this were the most ordinary of social occasions. The general acknowledged an acquaintance with Hugh from when both were in the Peninsula and the two of them spoke of mutual acquaintances.

Ned glanced at his mother, brows raised.

She gave him a patient smile. 'Ned, dear, General Henson and I are very old friends. We happened to meet again in town and he has been good enough to act as my escort on occasion.'

And as her lover, Xavier thought, but Ned and Hugh would work that out soon enough. Their mother's intimate manner towards Henson spoke volumes.

'I am very happy to be reacquainted with you all. My gracious, you were mere boys when last I saw you.' The general gazed from one to the other. 'But I will interrupt you no further. I take my leave.' He walked up to Lady Westleigh and clasped her hands. 'I shall return, my dear.'

He left and the room fell silent.

Hugh finally spoke. 'Mother! What the devil?'

Lady Westleigh lifted her head regally. 'I do not approve

of such language, Hugh. My friendship with the general is my affair. Not yours.'

Hugh laughed scornfully. 'Affair. Interesting choice of words, Mother.'

'What of my friendship with Xavier?' Phillipa broke in. 'Is that not *my* affair, Mama?'

The lady responded with sarcasm. 'Affair. Interesting choice of words, Phillipa.'

Phillipa's face turned red.

'Enough!' Xavier shouted. He turned to Phillipa. 'Where can we talk?'

'Here, if they will leave,' she responded.

Lady Westleigh hesitated a moment before she stood. 'Oh, very well. Ned. Hugh.' She spoke to them as if they were in leading strings. 'Come with me.'

Phillipa's mother and brothers closed the drawing-room door behind them and she was alone with Xavier.

He looked even more handsome in the light of day, as tall as her brothers, but perfectly formed and in a coat that fit him like a second skin. He'd stood tall when facing her mother, and now, gazing at her, he seemed perfectly in control.

'Do you wish to sit?' He gestured to the sofa.

She shook her head.

He waited, giving her time to speak first.

She took a breath. 'This is all nonsense, Xavier. My mother does not believe you truly compromised me. She sees this as a grand opportunity for me to snare a husband and secure my future.'

'I surmised that.' He looked directly into her face.

She wished he would glance away. 'We must stand up to her. If we do, this will all pass and things will be as they were.'

His intense blue eyes bored into her. 'Is that what you want? For things to be as they were for you?'

She lowered her gaze, fearing he would see all the way to the grief she felt at losing the Masquerade Club and the nightly time they shared. 'I always knew it was a temporary adventure.'

He lifted her chin with his finger and she was forced to look at him again.

'What if we did marry, Phillipa?' He spoke *sotto voce*. 'What if things do not have to return to what they were? I am willing if you are.'

How dare he use a voice so deep and soothing, like the rumble of the lowest pianoforte keys? How dare he say he was *willing* to marry? Such words were daggers disguised as jewels.

She turned her head from his touch. 'Do not toy with me, Xavier.'

'I am not toying with you. I want this, if you do.'

Now he was merely being honourable.

She touched her scar and moved near the window where she knew it would show in stark relief.

'No!' She lifted her hand. 'You cannot want it.'

Adonis with a scar-faced wife? How he would be pitied. How soon before he would pity himself?

His face was no less impossibly handsome even as he frowned. 'What if I told you I did want to marry you?'

She touched her scar. 'I would not believe you.'

'Why do you not believe me?' he asked.

'Why?' It hurt more that he pretended to want her. 'Because everything I've done has forced you into involving yourself with me. Whether it was dancing with me or escorting me or letting me perform. None of it has been by your choice—'

'Dancing?' He looked puzzled.

Of course, he would not remember the dance. It loomed large only in her memory.

She felt tears sting her eyes. She blinked them away. 'I will not marry you, Xavier. I refuse.' She gathered all her courage and met his eye. 'I do not want to marry you. That is the end of it. There is no more to be said.'

She could not stay a moment longer without bursting into tears. She forced herself to stand straight and to stride with a purposeful gait towards the door.

'Phillipa?' She heard his voice behind her, but she opened the door.

Her mother and brothers waited in the hallway outside the room. She walked past them.

'Where are you going?' her mother cried. 'We are not finished.'

'I am finished.' She did not stop.

Hugh dashed after her and seized her arm, a look of concern on his face. 'What happened in there, Phillipa?'

She shrugged out of his grasp. 'Xavier made an offer of marriage and I refused him. That is all.'

She reached the staircase and started to climb.

Her mother came after her, calling to her from the foot of the stairs. 'Come back here, Phillipa! If you leave it this way you will regret it. I will make you rue the day you threw away such an opportunity. You will have nothing without it! Do you hear me? Nothing!'

Phillipa did not answer her mother. She did not slow her pace. She did not turn back to see if Xavier also watched her walk away.

She merely climbed the stairs and retreated to her music room even though she was empty of music.

Xavier watched her walk past her family and climb the stairs. He watched until she disappeared on the upper floor.

He felt as if he'd been run through with a sabre.

He'd been prepared for her refusal; he'd not been prepared for the pain of it.

Although he ought to have known.

He'd been attracted to her, especially from the moment he'd witnessed her perform. She'd no longer been the little girl to whom he felt a responsibility; she'd turned into a woman who captivated him.

And his interest had never been returned.

Would people not laugh to know that he, to whom it was reputed that women flocked, could not get the one woman he wanted?

She thought him a friend and nothing more.

Hugh strode over to him. 'What the devil did you say to her?'

Xavier would not allow that hothead to see his wound. 'I offered marriage and she refused. She made her desires very clear. It is time to drop this.'

Ned spoke up. 'I agree. The best thing to do is forget this happened.'

Hugh scoffed. 'She's daft.'

'She is foolish and ungrateful.' Lady Westleigh pursed her lips before turning to Xavier. 'It is my turn to speak with you alone, sir.'

'Don't rail at him, Mother,' Ned said. 'He's done the right thing.'

His mother glared at him.

Ned seemed not to heed her. 'I beg your leave. I am off to call upon Miss Gale, who does not even know I have returned. I tell you we are done with this. Time to move on to other matters.' He extended his hand Xavier. 'This was a bad business, but we will put it behind us and act as before.'

'Certainly.' Xavier shook his hand. He'd never look at Ned in the same way, however.

'Go, if you must,' his mother snapped at Ned. 'Xavier, come in here.'

Xavier returned with her to the drawing room. She sat in her chair and gestured for him to sit, as well.

'I'll stand, ma'am.' His parents taught him well how to remain respectful, but he'd stand his ground all the same.

'I will make Phillipa change her mind,' she told him. 'And I'll hold you to your proposal of marriage.'

'Leave Phillipa be, ma'am.' He spoke firmly. 'She knows her own mind. Her wishes need to be respected.'

Lady Westleigh huffed. 'She knows nothing. She is determined to hide herself away with nothing but a pianoforte. What sort of life is that for her?'

He held her gaze. 'Give your daughter credit to know her own mind.'

She crossed her arms and raised her head defiantly. 'I will do what is best for my daughter.'

He opened his mouth, ready to threaten to spread talk about her affair with the general, but what good would that do?

He lowered his voice. 'Let go of this now.' He bowed. 'Good day to you, Lady Westleigh.'

He turned to walk away, but she called him back. 'There is another matter I wish to discuss with you.'

He looked over his shoulder. 'That is?'

'You told my daughter a great deal of family business. It was not your place to do so.' Her tone was scolding.

He faced her again. 'I do not apologise for it. She deserved to know.' This whole family sold Phillipa short.

'It was not your place,' she repeated, emphasising her words. 'However…' she paused, still giving him a haughty look '…tell me what else you told her.'

'What else?' He did not know what she meant.

She leaned forwards and her expression turned to worry.

'Did you break your word to me? You gave me your word all those years ago in Brighton. Did you break it?'

'Did I tell her the truth about her accident, do you mean?' He held something over this woman's head that was much bigger than an illicit affair, but he could not use it. 'I did not break my word.'

Lady Westleigh leaned back in her chair and suddenly looked very old. 'That is good. That is as it should be.'

'Was it General Henson on the beach that day?' Xavier asked.

She sat up straight. 'Why? Why do you ask me that?'

'Because I thought I remembered him as the man who was there,' he lied. It was Phillipa who remembered him.

'Do not say a word of this to her. Do you hear me?' She avoided his question, but her manner gave him the answer. 'You are honour-bound to keep your word.'

'I will keep my word,' he assured her. 'But you should tell her of that night. She needs to know it.'

'I'll be the judge of what she needs to know.' She waved him away. 'Leave now. I will get a message to you if Phillipa comes to her senses.'

He did not argue further, merely bowed again and left.

Chapter Eleven

Xavier walked back to the Masquerade Club, quiet at this time of day. Cummings and MacEvoy were nowhere to be seen and only the sweet scent of baking, wafting up from kitchen, revealed anyone was in the house.

He walked through the rooms still disordered from the previous night's gamblers. By the time the doors opened that night, every room would be cleaned and made ready for play. He straightened chairs here and there in the gaming room and made his way to the supper room.

All the plates, cutlery, and glasses had been cleared away the night before. Some of the tables were bare of their cloths, making the usually elegant room appear bereft.

Mimicking how he felt inside.

He felt the loss of Phillipa.

No longer would this room fill with melody. No longer would he hear Phillipa sing or the applause of others who recognised her worth. He glanced at the pianoforte. Her music still rested there, as if waiting for her to bring it to life.

He walked over to the instrument and gathered the sheets of music. Perhaps in time he could return them to her. In the meantime, he'd keep them safe.

* * *

August drifted to September and Xavier pressed on, helping with the Masquerade Club and checking Jeffers's progress on the cabinetry shop.

Jeffers exceeded Xavier's expectations. The soldier quickly found a storefront, a place with a workshop behind it and room for men to build furniture. Jeffers located the shop in Cheapside. It was a good location to sell furniture priced for the merchant class, rather than aiming for the elite of the *ton*. Jeffers procured the wood and in no time simple tables and chairs, and chests were on display in the front of the shop. Three other former soldiers who were skilled carpenters were hired. They'd all been maimed in the war. One man lost a leg, another an eye. The third reminded him of Phillipa, although the scars on his face came from burns suffered at Hougoumont. Jeffers was scarred, as well, but from Xavier's knife the night of the attack. He, too, was a reminder.

This venture seemed so ensured of success that Xavier was on the lookout for more challenges. There were all sorts of goods that might be manufactured and sold. They'd already found men to start a candle shop and Jeffers was keeping an eye out for other soldiers who might be able to do skilled work.

These ventures functioned much like Rhys's gaming house. The men ran the shops and he, like the Westleighs, provided the investment.

It was still not enough for Xavier.

He was restless.

Rhys had returned a fortnight after Phillipa's last night at the Masquerade Club and Xavier told him about her having performed her music there. Once Ned knew, Rhys was bound to find out. He told everything, except about the attack, and Phillipa's visions of General Henson. He told about Ned and Hugh discovering them. About his offer of marriage and her refusal.

'But you did not trifle with her.' Rhys did not accuse, merely stated a fact.

'You know I would not.' That was also a fact.

Rhys had leaned back in his chair, still regarding him. 'Phillipa took a risk, coming here night after night. At least no harm came of it.'

Except to Xavier. And Phillipa.

'I am not so certain,' he'd admitted to Rhys. 'Check on her for me, if you can, would you?'

Rhys had contact with the family, especially with Ned and Hugh, who kept an eye on the gaming house. He called upon Lady Westleigh with Lady Gale and Miss Gale to discuss the wedding. He'd never seen Phillipa, but when he enquired, Lady Westleigh always assured him she was in good health.

Ned and Hugh said the same thing.

Xavier never felt easy, though. He needed to see for himself.

He would get the chance at Rhys's wedding, the double wedding with Ned and Miss Gale.

The day of the wedding came quickly, about three weeks after Rhys returned. Both Rhys and Ned procured special licences so that they could marry in the privacy of the Westleigh town house. Because of the scandal Lord Westleigh had created—and Lady Gale's obvious condition—Lady Westleigh declared that the weddings should be as private and unobtrusive as possible. There would be no guests, only family.

Xavier was an exception. Rhys asked Xavier to stand up with him. Another exception was General Henson, who, according to Ned and Hugh, had become a fixture in the

Westleigh home, constantly to be found at Lady Westleigh's side.

Xavier knew Phillipa would be present at the wedding. He was eager to see her, to see for himself if she was in good health. If she was content. He also hoped to restore some of the *bonhomie* between them, to be friends again.

He missed her. He missed her more than he'd ever missed his family when he'd been off to war. He'd not expected this intensity.

Without her he had lost the music in his life.

The morning of the wedding Xavier and Rhys walked the distance to the Westleigh town house. At Lady Gale's request Rhys had spent the night before at the Masquerade Club.

'I spent so much time away from her, I could not see this one more night away,' Rhys said.

'But it was what she wanted, was it not?' Xavier responded.

'That is so.' Rhys smiled. 'Which is enough to explain why we are walking across Mayfair this morning.'

'Will this steam-engine venture take you away from her in the future?' Xavier asked.

'Undoubtedly.' Rhys sounded regretful. 'I am convinced it will secure our futures, however.'

Xavier was happy for Rhys. Soon he'd have a wife and a child and a business with a future. Quite a feat for a bastard son left alone on the streets to fend for himself.

And Xavier, whose upbringing had provided him everything he could want and a loving family to boot, had lost what he wanted most.

Phillipa.

Xavier turned off that train of thought. 'I confess I am surprised you agreed to this double wedding. Do you feel so much a part of that family?' Lord Westleigh had been Rhys's father, but Rhys had never been accepted by the family, not until they needed his help to deliver them from financial ruin.

'I no longer resent and despise them,' Rhys admitted. 'Lord Westleigh, perhaps, but not the others.' They crossed Charles Street. 'The wedding decision was Celia's. Her step-daughter wanted it and Celia was most anxious to please the girl. There'd been such a breach between them since— since the news of the baby.'

'Miss Gale seems incredibly young, do you not think?' Lady Gale's stepdaughter could not be more than nineteen.

Rhys gaped at him. 'And you are so old? You're not yet thirty.'

Xavier felt old, however.

They reached the Westleigh town house and were admitted to the drawing room where they'd once waited together for the Westleighs' ball to begin, where he'd danced with Phillipa. It also was the room where Phillipa had refused to marry him.

The furniture in the room had been placed against the wall so that a space was opened for the wedding ceremony. In a corner a trio of musicians were setting up. A nearby table held wine and glasses and vases of flowers stood on almost every other surface.

The butler poured them sherry, a drink not nearly strong enough for Xavier.

'How are you faring?' he asked Rhys after the butler left.

Rhys finished his sherry. 'Eager to have it done. It has been a very long time since I have belonged to anyone.'

It reminded Xavier he ought to call upon his parents.

They would be shocked at what he was up to. Virtually becoming a shopkeeper. On good days his mind whirled with possibilities to employ other craftsmen. His goal was to employ as many former soldiers as he could. The fewer such men he could see on the street, the better.

How was Phillipa spending her time? Was she composing music?

He turned his thoughts away from her and from music he would never hear.

He examined the room. The last time he'd stood in this room he hadn't noticed if Lady Westleigh had replaced the portrait of her husband that dominated this room with one of her own. But her portrait was certainly on display now. Unless he missed his guess, it was by Gainsborough. The artist had painted her against a wild landscape and a cloud-filled sky when she'd been young and beautiful.

He could see Phillipa in the image.

At that moment the door opened and Phillipa entered, wearing a lovely day dress of green-and-white stripes that shimmered in the light and accentuated her slim figure. In fact, she looked thinner than when he last saw her. Her hair was a cascade of curls that appeared to be held in place with a feather headpiece. One feather of the headpiece brushed her cheek and obscured her scar.

It did not hide the fact that she looked pale.

She hesitated when she saw the two of them, but recovered and briskly approached Rhys with a smile. 'Once again I am the first in my family to greet you. You make a handsome bridegroom, Rhysdale.'

Rhys took her extended hands and kissed her cheek. 'I am a happy one. It is good to see you, Phillipa.'

She turned to Xavier, but did not quite look at him directly. 'Xavier. How nice of you to come.'

He bowed. 'Phillipa.'

She looked ill! He wanted to ask why, but knew women better than to make such a remark on a day when one's appearance was important.

Footsteps sounded outside the door. 'Higgley, find her! If she has left, I shall be very vexed.' Lady Westleigh entered, but turned back to the door. 'Never mind, Higgley. She is here.' She quickly surveyed Phillipa and gave a little approving nod.

Xavier felt Phillipa stiffen in response.

But Lady Westleigh did not see. Instead she put on a smile and swept over to Rhys. 'Rhysdale, how good it is to see you. You look in excellent health. This is a very special day, is it not?'

Rhys bowed. 'I am pleased you think it special on my behalf, my lady.'

She inclined her head towards Xavier. 'Xavier,' she said, adding a significant look in her daughter's direction. What was that about?

He bowed. 'My lady.'

The butler appeared at the door. 'General Henson,' he announced.

Lady Westleigh's expression brightened. 'Alistair!'

She stepped forwards to greet him. He took her hand and clasped it in a fond gesture. 'My dear lady, what an honour it is to be invited to such a happy event.'

'Nonsense, Alistair.' She covered his hand with hers. 'You know how I value your friendship. You must be at my side.'

Xavier glanced at Rhys, who returned a comprehending look. He'd told Rhys about the general and Lady Westleigh.

A visibly nervous Ned entered with the clergyman and introductions followed. The servants filed in and Lady Westleigh sent the butler out to tell Hugh and the brides that all was ready. The clergyman stood at the far side of the room, holding his Book of Common Prayer. The musicians started to play, a Haydn piece, one Phillipa played often on the pianoforte.

He glanced at her, but could not see her expression.

'Stand by Reverend Peck, gentlemen.' Lady Westleigh waved a finger at Rhys and Xavier. 'The two of you on one side. Ned, you stand on the other. Quickly now, before they come in.'

The butler opened the door and the two brides walked in, escorted by Hugh.

Xavier watched Rhys's face as Lady Gale—soon to be Mrs Rhysdale—approached. Rhys adored her so strongly, Xavier felt it in the air. If he reached up, he fancied he could touch it. He was happy for his friend and envious. There was no doubt in his mind that these two people each knew—and loved—the essence of the other.

The ceremony began.

'Dearly Beloved. We are gathered together here in the sight of God, and in the face of this congregation...'

Vows for Miss Gale and Ned went first, then Rhys and Lady Gale.

Rhys looked into his beloved's eyes. 'I, John, take thee, Celia, to my wedded wife, to have and to hold from this day forward, for better for worse, for richer for poorer, in sickness and in health, to love and to cherish, until death us do part...'

Xavier glanced over at Phillipa, whose gaze was averted, as if she were deep into her own thoughts. Was she thinking that this could have been her wedding?

He was.

Very quickly the minister came to the end, 'I now pronounce that they be Man and Wife together, in the Name of the Father, and of the Son, and of the Holy Ghost...'

With those words it was done. Rhys and Celia's lives had changed. So had Ned's and his wife.

All that was left were a few sonorous prayers and then

the congratulations. Champagne was served and the musicians started playing again.

Xavier walked up to Rhys and his new wife. 'You make my friend very happy, Madame Fortune.' He used the name the patrons gave her when she had gambled at the Masquerade Club.

She laughed at that. 'I think you should call me Celia after all we've been through.' She threaded her arm through her husband's. 'Or Mrs Rhysdale.'

Rhys put a hand on Xavier's shoulder. 'Call her Celia. She is too beautiful to be Mrs Rhysdale.'

General Henson's loud voice filled the room. 'This is a fine day. A fine day!'

Rhys leaned towards Xavier. 'He is acting as if he is the man of the house.'

Xavier nodded. 'Lady Westleigh looks ten years younger when she looks at him.'

'Well, I am certainly not going to judge either one of them,' Celia said, touching her abdomen. 'We all must seize our happiness when we can.'

Xavier was willing to seize it, if he ever saw a chance for it.

At least he'd tried once.

Hugh came up to them, champagne glass in hand and a frown on his face. 'I feel like planting him a facer.' He inclined his head towards the general. 'He's quite taken over our mother.'

He moved on to speak to the butler before any of them could respond.

The servants left the room and Hugh returned to the wine table.

Xavier noticed Phillipa standing alone, listening to the music being played quietly in the corner.

He walked over to her. 'Do they play well?' he asked.

She looked surprised to see him. 'Well enough.' She turned back to the musicians.

'The ceremony went well.' He could not think of anything better to say.

'Yes, it did.' Her voice held little expression.

He listened to the music with her until the violinist, flautist and violoncellist finished their piece and turned to a new page of music.

She walked away just as the musicians began to play 'I Serve a Worthy Lady'.

The butler announced the wedding breakfast.

Lady Westleigh sat at the head of the table. The general, of course, was at her side. Xavier was seated between Ned's wife and Phillipa, which he thought was a cruel touch on Lady Westleigh's part.

There was no speaking to the new Lady Neddington, who was too enthralled with her new husband, and Phillipa showed no signs of wishing to converse with him.

He noticed she made a show of eating, pushing her food around the plate without actually consuming it. No wonder she was getting thin.

He very much wished they could regain at least a piece of their friendship. Perhaps be cordial to each other. He searched his mind for something to say to her that would serve that purpose.

He remembered the sheets of music she'd left at the Masquerade Club. 'I have your music, Phillipa,' he told her. 'Forgive me for not returning it to you. I will have it brought to you tomorrow, if you desire it.' Perhaps he would deliver it himself.

'There is no need.' She stared at her plate.

'No need?' He did not understand.

'I do not play music any more,' she said.

Not play music? 'Why not, Phillipa? What about your pianoforte?'

'I no longer have a pianoforte.' She faced him directly and her eyes seemed like walls, closing her off from him. 'Mama had the pianoforte removed.'

'Removed?' He could not believe his ears.

She resumed toying with her food. 'Mama has this notion that, if she makes my life miserable, I will somehow bend to her will.'

'She took away your pianoforte.' This was cruelty in the extreme. 'Because you refused my proposal?'

Her voice trembled. 'She said she is done indulging me.'

Xavier lost his appetite as well.

Phillipa speared the piece of lobster with her fork and brought it to her mouth, not for wanting it, but to have a reason not to say more to Xavier. She'd not meant to tell him about her pianoforte, about her music.

It had been difficult to see him, especially during the ceremony, listening to words that might have been spoken between them.

If her mother had got her way.

Her mother was still furious at her for refusing Xavier. Taking away the pianoforte had been done in a fit of temper, but her mother would not back down from that decision. To be deprived of music was like being starved of sustenance. Hearing the trio play had been more gratifying than witnessing the marriages of her brothers. She devoured every note.

Now the musicians had packed up their instruments and departed, and again she was empty inside.

No one spoke to her about music. The servants certainly would not mention it. Her brothers seemed to have forgotten about it. Initially they had argued with their mother on her behalf, insisting she return the pianoforte to Phillipa, but her mother sold it. Phillipa would never get it back. After a few days, Ned and Hugh became involved in other matters and that was the end of her music.

Captain Henson stood with glass raised. 'I propose a toast. To the happiness of these two fortunate couples.'

Phillipa's mother joined in. 'To their happiness!'

Phillipa dutifully drank, but anger bubbled up inside her. Logic told her that her mother deserved a man who truly cared for her, but at the same time Phillipa resented that her mother possessed what never could be hers—a man who loved her.

Phillipa always felt the vision pushing forwards when the general spoke. Or when he came to dinner. Or arrived to take her mother to some social event.

Xavier spoke to her. 'I cannot decide if he is encroaching or merely greatly attached to your mother.'

She longed to talk about it with him. He was the only one who knew everything.

Her throat tightened. She pretended to keep eating.

She'd not been wrong to refuse him, she told herself again. A man so perfect could only be unhappy with an imperfect wife.

When the breakfast was over, Phillipa slipped away while the couples were busy saying their goodbyes. She was certain no one would notice. She returned to her bedchamber and tried to play in her head the music she'd heard that day.

And erase the image of Xavier Campion from her mind.

Chapter Twelve

Two days later the house was so quiet Phillipa thought she would go mad. If she'd had her pianoforte she would have loved such a day. She would have filled the air with music.

Her mother now spent all her spare time with General Henson. Ned and Adele were on their honeymoon trip, and Hugh had gone to the country, to Westleigh House, to oversee the harvest. Phillipa had begged her mother to allow her to go with him—there was a pianoforte there—but her mother refused and Hugh would not counter their mother's wishes.

Phillipa was alone with no way to fill the days.

Out of desperation she turned to needlework. And to winding her music box over and over.

Higgley knocked upon her door. 'A gentleman to see you, Lady Phillipa.'

Her spirits drooped lower. 'Who is it?'

'Mr Campion.'

She knew even before he spoke the name. What other gentleman would call upon her? 'I will see him in the drawing room.'

She looked at herself in the mirror. She wore an old dress

and an old cap and looked her very worst. She changed nothing.

Instead she wound the music box once more and closed her eyes as it played. Unfortunately the tune it played was 'Plaisir D'amour'.

The pleasures of love lasts only a moment.
The pain of love lasts a lifetime.

She closed the box and left the room.

The door to the drawing room was open and she paused for a moment.

He stood at the window. Even in profile, he could take her breath away. His coat and pantaloons were superbly cut, fitting him well, as did all his clothing. His dark hair was slightly longer than fashionable and untamed.

She stepped in to the room. 'Xavier?'

He turned to her and did not speak for a moment. 'Good day, Phillipa.' He seemed to scrutinise her. 'Are you in good health?'

That was a way of saying she looked so dreadful she must be at death's door.

She waved a hand and crossed the room to a chair. 'I am well enough. Why are you here?'

She might as well force him to the point.

He sat in a chair near her. Too close for her comfort. Surely now he could see the dark circles under her eyes and the lines etching her forehead.

And her scar.

'It is about your music.'

Of course. He'd said he would bring her music.

'You should not be without your music.' He leaned towards her. 'It is plain to see that you are not doing well without it. I propose to give it back to you.'

'*Propose* to give it back? Have you not brought it with you? You said you would.' Although what could she do with it besides hide it from her mother?

'I do not mean your sheet music,' he said.

Then what did he mean? 'Do not say you have purchased a pianoforte. My mother will be rid of it.'

'Your mother will have no say. The music will be all yours.'

'Stop talking in riddles, Xavier.' She pinched the bridge of her nose. Must she get a headache, too?

'Marry me, Phillipa.' His voice dropped. 'Reconsider and marry me. Do so and you may work on your music to your heart's content.'

His words were stabs of pain. 'We have been through this before.'

He held up a hand. 'No. Not this. When you refused me before you could not think your mother would take away your music. Marriage to me will restore it and more. I promise I will buy you the finest pianoforte to be found in all London.'

She could not believe her ears. 'I should marry for a pianoforte?'

He smiled. 'Why not? Other women marry for a title or wealth, why not marry for a pianoforte?' He turned serious again. 'You can perform at the Masquerade Club, if you wish, and I promise to help you sell your music. I already showed one piece to a music seller. He agreed it was good. He gave me a list of music publishers here.'

Her head whirled. He'd done all that for her?

He went on. 'You ought not to be deprived of what you most love. Your music.'

'But that is not your doing.' She knew where the blame rested. 'It is mine. And my mother's.'

'But I have the power to fix it.' He touched her hand. 'We

can put it in the settlement papers, if you wish. That you will always have any musical instrument you desire. That I will endeavor to sell your music. That the money goes to you.'

She swept a hand around the room. 'The weddings that took place here? Those couples had a regard for each other. We do not.'

His eyes pierced hers. 'You do not have a regard for me?'

She glanced away.

'I assure you…' his eyes bored into hers '…I have a regard for you, Phillipa.'

'Do not jest with me.' She pointed to her scar. 'Look at me.'

He pulled her hand away from her face. 'Your scar has never mattered to me. Listen to me. In your family you will always be dependent—'

This was no argument. She cut him off. 'You will make me dependent upon you.'

'No. Because I can give you independence. Money of your own.' He paused as if thinking of something for the first time. 'If you prefer, I can simply support you, but I fear that will cause both our families some distress and it will limit you in society.'

She almost laughed. Think of the gossip. The handsome Xavier Campion taking disfigured Phillipa Westleigh under his protection.

But the ridicule would be the same if he married her.

What was she thinking? 'I cannot do this to you, Xavier. Or to myself. You cannot want me for a wife.'

His gaze did not waver. 'I do want you for a wife.'

'Why?' It made no sense. A man like him wanting to marry her.

'You are being treated shabbily,' he said. 'I can fix it.'

She turned away.

'Think of it, Phillipa,' he pressed. 'You may play your

music to your heart's delight. You will run your own household, decide on your own invitations. Your own activities. You will not be dependent upon your mother or brothers.'

She would only be answerable to him.

'Trust me.' It was as if he read her mind.

She stared into a future with her mother. She would be a spinster. As her mother aged she would be called upon to be her companion. When her mother was gone, she'd be shifted from one brother's home to the other.

If she married, though, she could live her own life. Was that not what her mother had always done? Her parents had paid little heed to each other's activities. Would marriage with Xavier be like that?

Could she endure it?

There must be something of self-interest in this proposition. 'What advantage would marrying me provide you?'

He glanced into her eyes. 'Would you believe me if I told you I would marry you because I love you?'

The words pierced her heart. 'Of course not.'

'I thought as much.' He smiled, but the sadness did not leave his eyes. 'Marry me anyway and leave this place.'

It was as if he'd offered freedom from a dungeon. The question was, could she resist, when she knew it was guilt or obligation or honour or whatever that led him to make this offer?

She could not.

He offered her music and that was the one offer she could not resist.

'Very well, Xavier.' She would marry him.

He seized her hand. 'Good, Phillipa. Good.'

'But there is one thing.'

His brows rose. 'That is?'

'We must marry quietly. Only you and me.' She refused to be put on display, not even in front of family.

He raised her hand to his lips. 'It will be as you say.'

* * *

Xavier released a pent up breath. She'd said yes.

Music was the key.

She could not live without music.

He appearance this morning was even more alarming than the day of the wedding. She wore her hair pulled back into a simple cap that hid all her curls. Her lips were thin and her eyes pained, and she was so pale, the discolouration of her scar became even more prominent. He wanted to see her flushed with pleasure again. He wanted to see her joy at making music.

He pulled a paper from his coat pocket. 'I took the liberty of procuring a special licence. We can marry anywhere, any time. We want only witnesses and a clergyman.' He smiled. 'We could do it today, if you wish.'

'Today?' She looked alarmed.

'Tell me when.' He wanted to assure her the independence he'd promised her. She must decide.

Her chin rose in determination. 'Tomorrow, if you can manage it.'

He reached across the distance between them and touched her cheek. 'I am determined it should be exactly as you wish. I will send word if I am unable to make the arrangements.'

Her eyes searched his as if trying to determine whether she should believe him.

'Do not worry,' he told her. 'Leave it to me. I will call upon you at eleven o'clock.' He stood. 'I should take my leave. I have much to accomplish.'

She rose as well and walked with him to the drawing-room door.

He reached for the latch, but her hand stilled his. 'Are you certain of this, Xavier?'

He lifted her chin and leaned down to place his lips on hers. 'I am certain, Phillipa.'

The butler, who was attending the hall, handed Xavier his hat and gloves and walked to the door to open it for him.

Xavier turned to the man as he reached for the door-knob. 'If you have any affection towards Lady Phillipa, sir, perhaps you could refrain from mentioning my visit to Lady Westleigh.'

The butler's expression did not change, but he said, 'If her ladyship does not ask if Lady Phillipa received any callers, I see no reason I should mention it.'

Xavier smiled. 'Thank you. That is all I ask.'

He walked out to the street and turned towards Bond Street. There was much to be accomplished and only one day to accomplish it all.

Which he was determined to do.

Phillipa's heart pounded as she watched Xavier leave the house and hurry down the street. Could it really be true? Would she be able to leave this prison her mother had created for her and be free?

She walked out of the room and made her way to the stairs, feeling as if she were sleepwalking.

Mason stood in the hall. 'Is there anything you require, m'lady?'

She wanted to tell him not to tell her mother about Xavier's visit, but was he an ally or would he report to her mother?

No, she must pretend Xavier's visit was nothing of significance, nothing worthy of mentioning.

'If you would find Lacey and ask her to attend me, I would be grateful.' She had to risk asking for Lacey's help. Even more, she needed to tell someone what had happened. And what was going to happen.

'Very good, m'lady.' He bowed and she started up the stairs. 'One moment, m'lady,' he called to her.

She turned to him.

He looked up at her. 'Lady Westleigh never enquires if you have had callers.'

How odd for him to say. 'I rarely do have callers.'

'Precisely.' His voice did not change from its typically formal tone. 'Which is why Lady Westleigh never asks.' He paused. 'And I, therefore, have no reason to answer her.'

She suddenly understood. 'Thank you, Mason.'

He bowed.

On impulse she rushed down the stairs again and gave him a hug. 'Wish me happy,' she whispered in his ear. 'I am going to be married. Say nothing to my mother or anyone else.'

He broke into a smile, but just as quickly composed his features. 'If Lady Westleigh asks me if you are to be married, I shall be compelled to answer.'

She laughed. 'If she asks, do tell her!'

She ran up the stairs to her room. It looked remarkably unchanged. Her needlework lay on the chair by the window. Her music box sat on the table. Her brush and comb remained on the dressing table. She glanced in the mirror.

Even she did not look changed, even though everything she expected in her life would now be different. She turned a full circle, scanning every corner.

'I'll not see this room after tomorrow,' she said aloud. 'Of that I am immensely glad.'

A knock sounded at the door and Lacey entered the room. 'You wished to see me, m'lady? Is there something I may do for you?'

Lacey felt sorry for her, Phillipa knew, and also very guilt-ridden for telling her family about sneaking out at night.

Phillipa was about to give her a second chance. 'I have something to tell you, but you must promise to tell no one.'

Lacey wrung her hands. 'Oh, m'lady! I will swear on everything holy. I will say nothing. Not even if they torture me or threaten to sack me.'

'You won't be sacked, but you may be promoted.' Phillipa made the girl face her. 'Do you know that Mr Campion called today?'

Lacey nodded. 'One of the maids saw him walk to the door. She and I took a peek at him when he left. He is a sight to see, as you know.'

Even the maids were not immune to his good looks. 'Will you tell the maid to say nothing to anyone about seeing him?'

'Yes, m'lady. If you wish it.'

Phillipa hugged herself. 'You see, I have agreed to marry him.'

Lacey squealed. 'You do not say! Marry him? A man like him? Who would have thought?'

Even Lacey could not believe a perfect man like Xavier would marry an imperfect woman like herself.

'But you must tell no one.' Phillipa repeated. 'No one.'

'Yes, m'lady.' The girl giggled. 'No one. I promise. Not even the maids.'

'Especially not the maids.' She told Lacey of the plans for the next day. 'We must pack a portmanteau for me. I will write my mother a letter, which you may tell her about if she asks for me, but not before noon. I'll send word where to deliver the bag. I have not the faintest idea where it will be. We must sneak a portmanteau into this room without anyone knowing. Can you do it?'

'I can, m'lady.' She returned a calculating look. 'But what did you mean by a promotion?'

'If you wish it, you may come live with me. I'll need a

lady's maid. Because you will be maid to the lady of the house, you must receive more pay for what you do.'

The girl's eyes widened. 'I would live with you and Mr Campion?'

'When we are settled.' Phillipa did not know where they would live. She did not care as long as it was not here.

And as long as it had a pianoforte.

Chapter Thirteen

Xavier searched out the jarvey who had driven them to and from the gaming house. He hired him for the day so that he would be directly at hand. None of the distances they would travel were too far to walk, but he would not have her walk this day.

At precisely eleven o'clock in the morning the hack pulled up to the Westleigh town house. Xavier had no more alighted than the door opened and Phillipa emerged.

Against the pale-grey brick she was a bloom of colour. Her dress was pale pink with a matching coat fastened only at her bosom so that its skirts billowed behind her as she walked towards him. Her face was hidden under her bonnet and her customary netting.

He strode towards her and took her hand in his. 'Look who drives us.'

She lifted the netting up to see the driver. 'It is you!'

He pulled his forelock. 'It is, indeed, miss. I am yours for the day. And what a day it is, eh?'

'I am happy to see you.' She sounded happy.

Xavier's heart swelled. 'Phillipa, you look lovely.'

She cringed at his words.

He bit his tongue. He did not wish anything to spoil her day.

'Come. Let us set off. Johnson knows all the stops.' He helped her into the coach as he had done so many times before.

'Where are we bound?' she asked.

He took her hand again. It trembled under his. 'Allow me to surprise you.'

The coach stopped on Piccadilly in front of a red-brick church.

Xavier said, 'This is our first stop.'

He helped her out. 'St James's,' he said.

'We are to be married in a church?' Her voice was breathless.

'We are indeed.' He'd made the right choice. 'We'll enter on the south side.'

They walked up to an elaborate Ionic doorway and went inside.

As soon as they entered, the church's organ exploded into Handel's music.

Phillipa gasped. *'The Arrival of the Queen of Sheba!'*

The organist had informed Xavier that the organ dated back to the late 1600s. The man suggested playing Handel, but Xavier had not known what pieces he'd select. As it was, the first piece was rather appropriate.

Phillipa laughed, but the sound was almost a sob. 'Oh, Xavier!'

She threw her arms around his neck and he held her close against him, surprised that the music pleased her that much. She wept on his shoulder and he could feel her whole body shaking. Curse her mother for depriving her of this—this food for her soul.

The feel of her in his arms affected him more than he'd ever have expected. He did not want to release her.

But she did pull away and they walked slowly towards

the altar, the music wrapping itself around them like a warm cloak against harsh weather. In the centre of the church, she paused, her eyes closed and he waited, letting her have the moment to herself.

The first piece ended and the second began, much softer than the first.

'Water Music.' She smiled and she took his arm as they walked down the aisle, past the Corinthian columns, beneath the vaulted ceiling with its rich plasterwork, to the altar where the clergyman waited, prayer book in hand.

Phillipa let the music sink into her, filling all the empty spaces inside her. She had not expected this. She thought he'd bring her to the Masquerade Club and they would be married in the drawing room there. She'd start weeping again if she dwelled on how wonderful this was of Xavier.

Nothing could have been better.

As they neared the altar the clergyman stepped forwards to greet them. He was a young man, younger than Phillipa herself, she'd guess. Newly ordained, perhaps, and so very obliging to perform this ceremony on such short notice.

Standing nearby were MacEvoy and Belinda, one of the Masquerade Club's croupiers. MacEvoy winked at her and Belinda smiled. They knew her, she realised. Xavier must have told them.

'Are we ready?' the clergyman asked, glancing from one to the other.

'One moment.' Xavier took the netting on her hat and lifted it away from her face. 'I must see you,' he murmured.

Her impulse was to cover her face, not to hide her scar, but to preserve her identity, although that was silly, because soon the world would know that Adonis-like Xavier Campion had married the scarred Phillipa Westleigh.

Xavier indicated he was ready. Was she? Her heart

pounded. It was not too late to change her mind. Save the handsome Adonis for a Venus worthy of him.

The music swelled.

No. She would not change her mind, selfish as it was. She needed music too much.

'Dearly Beloved, we are gathered here in the sight of God...' The words the clergyman spoke were the same they'd heard only a few days before, when Ned and Rhys married, both for love.

Not for a pianoforte.

She faced Xavier as he repeated his vows. 'I, Xavier, take thee, Phillipa, to my wedded wife...'

The sun shone through the stained-glass windows, casting his face in a riot of colour. His blue eyes were as clear and bright as the glass and they gazed upon her with abundant good will.

It was her turn to make the vows that would alter her existence. And his.

She made her voice strong. 'I, Phillipa, take thee, Xavier, to my wedded husband....'

When she finished her vows, the clergyman asked for the ring. Phillipa expected a thin gold band. Xavier, instead, placed a large ring festooned with diamonds upon the prayer book.

The clergyman handed the ring back to Xavier. He spoke. 'With this ring I thee wed, with my body I thee worship, and with all my worldly goods I thee endow....'

He placed the ring on her finger. It sparkled in the light, like a musical composition with many notes. She stared at it. Why had he chosen this ring? This very special ring?

The clergyman recited the prayers with more meaning than had been evident in the other weddings. The words sound more personal, created just for them.

'...Those that God has joined together let no man put

asunder…' And finally to the end. 'I pronounce that they be Man and Wife together.'

The music grew louder, more joyous. The allegro from the *Music for the Royal Fireworks*, composed over half a century ago, but still as beautiful and happy as one could wish.

Xavier captured her hands and squeezed them. 'We have done it, Phillipa.'

She pulled him down to whisper in his ear. 'Thank you, Xavier.'

MacEvoy and Belinda hurried up to them with congratulations. They all went back to the church office to sign the papers. In no time at all Xavier and Phillipa were back in the coach, headed to the next destination.

It was back to her mother's town house. Phillipa's spirits sank. Was he going to leave her there?

'I thought you might want to collect some of your things,' he said. 'We'll have to have it all sent to us eventually, but I did not have time to find us a place to live.'

'You have done much more than was necessary.' She swallowed, relieved. 'I have a portmanteau packed, but I do not want to go inside. I do not want to speak to anyone or to have them see me. Especially my mother.'

He moved to climb out of the coach. 'I am counting on your mother being out.' He jumped down and turned to her. 'I will go in. How do I ask for it?'

'Have Mason send for my maid. She will hand over the bag.'

He strode to the door, walking with a masculine power that seemed unique to him. He sounded the knocker and, as she had hoped, Mason opened the door.

The butler glanced to the coach and met her gaze. She smiled at him. His expression softened and he nodded. A

very few minutes later Xavier reappeared with the portmanteau. As he carried it to the carriage, Lacey appeared
at the window, waving.

Phillipa waved back.

Xavier climbed back in. 'Here it is.'

'My mother—?' Phillipa started to ask.

'Not at home.'

She leaned back against the leather upholstery. 'Good.
I wrote her a letter. My maid will see that it is put into her
hands.'

The hackney coach started off.

'Where to next?' she asked.

He grinned. 'Another surprise.'

The coach took them back to Piccadilly and stopped in
front of the Pulteney Hotel, so fashionable that the Tsar
of Russia himself once chose to stay there rather than at a
royal palace.

'We are staying here?' she asked.

'We are.' He opened the door. 'One night, at least.'

They said good day to the hackney driver and entered
the hotel, its hall as grand as the hotel's reputation. Soon
they were escorted up to their set of rooms.

The servant opened the door and Phillipa entered first.

She gasped.

Prominently displayed in the room was a pianoforte, the
prettiest she had ever seen. Its mahogany rectangular case
was adorned with chevron-string inlay and hand-painted
with pink roses above the keyboard.

She crossed the room to it, running her fingers down
the keys.

'It is yours,' Xavier said.

She swung around to him. 'Truly?'

'Unless you want another.' His voice turned deep. 'I

asked for the best one in the shop, but if there is another you would like—'

'There could never be one more beautiful.' She played a few keys. Its sound was wonderful, as well. 'You have been too good.'

Her throat twisted and she thought she would dissolve into a puddle of tears if she said more.

'Feel free to play.' He gestured for her to sit. 'Your music is there.'

'My music?' He'd thought of everything.

'And a book of country dances. Something frivolous I bought on impulse.' He pulled up a chair nearby. 'Play. Whatever you like.'

A maid appeared and Xavier handed her Phillipa's portmanteau. While the girl unpacked her clothing, Phillipa pulled off her gloves and sat at the pianoforte's bench. From memory, she played a few bars of *The Arrival of the Queen of Sheba*. 'Did you pick the music for the church?'

He shook his head. 'I left it to the organist. I know very little of music.'

'It doesn't matter.' The pianoforte had a lovely sound. 'You thought of music.'

She began to play the minuet from Haydn's *Surprise Symphony*, which she knew by heart. She was happy and this was happy music.

When she finished, he said, 'You make me feel like dancing.'

She started playing another piece. 'If I could play and dance at the same time, I would. I do not think I have ever been so happy.'

Xavier dismissed the maid and settled in a chair to enjoy hearing Phillipa play. He watched her face as her fingers flew over the keys. All the nights she played at the Masquerade Club, he had longed to see her face, to watch her expression as the music poured out of her.

He was not disappointed.

Her pallor disappeared and her face was flushed with pleasure. Her eyes shone with joy. She looked beautiful.

When he'd called upon her yesterday, she'd looked as if she were shrinking into herself. She'd looked as if she were dying. The music filled her, like nourishment. Ironically the music was also a feast for anyone lucky enough to be her audience. He felt content, just for listening to her.

He was satisfied with himself. It had been a new challenge for him to arrange a wedding with music and a set of rooms with a pianoforte in less than a day, but he'd done it.

He poured himself a congratulatory glass of brandy from a sideboard and sat back to simply take in the music.

He had the strong sense again that he was listening, not to music, but to her emotions. The emotions swirling inside her flowed into her fingers and emerged as music.

Even in the joyous pieces she chose to play there was an undertone of melancholy, as if she could not imagine being happy for very long, but that was another challenge he intended to meet.

This marriage would be a good one for her. And for him. He cared nothing for what others might say of it. He was determined to succeed as a good husband, one who made certain nothing hurt Phillipa again.

She looked up from the music and smiled at him.

Today was an excellent start.

Chapter Fourteen

Phillipa played all the music in her head, all her sheets of music Xavier brought to the hotel for her. He interrupted her once to tell her he must go out briefly, but she lost track of time and did not know how long he'd been gone. When he returned he sat in one of the brocade-upholstered chairs, his long legs stretched out in front of him. She resumed playing, soaking in the music like a flower parched from lack of rain.

She lost herself in the music again until she felt the touch of his hand on her shoulder. 'Our meal has arrived. You need to eat something.'

He'd ordered a lovely meal, dismissing the servant, saying he would serve the meal himself. Turtle soup. Salmon. Roast beef with side dishes of courgette and potatoes. Peach tart waiting for dessert.

The scent of it roused Phillipa's appetite. 'I am suddenly famished.'

'I can imagine,' he responded. 'It has been hours since breakfast.'

She pressed her stomach. 'I did not eat very much breakfast.'

In fact, she'd not thought of food all day. She'd hardly

thought of him either, or of being married, so lost was she in the music. It shamed her to realise it.

He uncovered the tureen of soup and served her. 'Have you enjoyed the pianoforte?'

She felt tears sting her eyes. 'I cannot tell you how wonderful it has been. I have missed the music so very much.'

His expression warmed. 'I am glad it made you happy.'

When had anyone been concerned with her happiness? Her father certainly never gave her a thought. Her brothers thought of her as much as brothers think of sisters. Her mother's attention had not been concerned with her happiness, but with a determination that she mix well in society. The only person she could recall who'd ever purposefully wanted to cheer her had been Xavier. When they'd been children, she'd worshipped him for it.

He poured her a fine claret.

She could not talk of the pianoforte or his kindness or she would weep in a manner he could not possibly understand.

'I wonder if my mother has yet discovered my absence,' she said instead.

Had her mother read the letter? Was she gloating in triumph or angry that her daughter had acted without her?

'I suspect your mother will approve,' Xavier said, piercing a morsel of salmon with his fork.

'She will approve of the marriage,' Phillipa responded. 'She will probably take full credit for it.'

He turned their conversation to her music. What she preferred to play. What she liked to write. It made it quite comfortable to converse with him.

When it was time for the last course, that lovely peach tart, Phillipa stood. 'You must allow me to serve.' She cut him a piece and placed it on his plate.

'Where did you go when you went out?' she asked him

as she cut her own piece. 'If—if I may ask, that is.' Did she have the right to ask where he went, what he did?

'Of course you may ask.' He took a bite of the tart. 'I went to the *Morning Post*. An announcement of our marriage will be printed in two days' time.'

She froze, her fork in midair. 'Everyone will know.'

'The sooner the better, do you not think?' He looked concerned. 'Everyone must learn of it eventually.'

'I suppose.' She expected the notice would generate a great deal of gossip. *The Adonis married the scarred spinster. Can you imagine it? What was he thinking?*

He reached over and clasped her hand. 'I am happy to announce it, Phillipa. Let the whole world know.'

He was merely being kind again. Surely he would find the talk uncomfortable.

She slipped her hand away and cut him another piece of tart.

She changed the subject. 'Will you be at the Masquerade Club tonight?'

A quizzical look came over his face. 'Not tonight, Phillipa. MacEvoy will watch things there. I am not needed.'

She thought he would go about his routine. This wedding was not like Ned's and Rhys's. It was more like a favour he'd done her.

Tea arrived and the servants removed the dinner dishes.

Phillipa's eyes kept wandering to the pianoforte. It was much more comfortable to play her music than to think about him.

Her husband.

He placed his cup in its saucer. 'Teach me to play something.'

'You?'

'Certainly!' He took her hand and led her back to the pianoforte's bench. 'My sisters once insisted I learn to play.

My lessons did not last long. I was much more interested in swordsmanship and shooting.'

'As a soldier ought to be,' she said.

He joined her on the bench and together they picked out the notes to some of the country dances he'd purchased for her. Fairly soon they managed a pretty terrible rendition of 'Miss Louisa Johnstone's Fancy' and 'The Fairie's Revels'.

Laughing too hard to finish, she covered her mouth with her hand.

He touched her ring. 'Does the ring please you?'

She held it up and watched the diamonds capture the light from the candles. 'It is the most beautiful ring I could ever imagine,' she answered truthfully, ashamed she'd not told him so before this.

A smile flashed across his face. 'I am glad.'

He stared at her, his eyes darkening. 'Have I made you happy today, Phillipa?'

Her heart beat faster. 'Yes.' Her voice trembled. 'Very happy.'

He leaned closer to her. And closer.

Very suddenly Phillipa forgot about music and piano-fortes and rings. Nothing existed but Xavier, so very handsome and so very close. She felt his breath on her face, as soft as a butterfly's wing. His lips came nearer. They touched hers gently and she felt every part of her flare with sensation.

The kiss lasted only a moment, but when he moved away it felt like abandonment. He smiled again, but she was bereft. She needed that intimate connection with him. She needed to not be so alone any more.

He closed the distance between them again, wrapping his arms around her and again seeking her lips. This kiss demanded more of her. She pressed her lips against his and savoured the warm fullness of his mouth. His tongue touched hers, tasting of peaches and claret, a sensation that surprised her, especially because it made other parts of her ache in response.

She melted into his embrace, her hands flat against his back, feeling his muscled body even through his coat.

He broke away again. 'Shall I send for a maid to help you prepare for bed?'

Had she displeased him?

Something must have shown in her face because his brows knit. 'It is our wedding night, Phillipa. Do you not wish to share my bed?'

She blinked. 'I thought you were sending me away.'

He pulled her into an embrace. 'Phillipa, you are my wife. I would not send you away on our wedding night.'

Was he being kind again? She averted her face, hiding her scar from his view. 'I—I never thought you would wish to bed me.'

His expression hardened. 'We are married, are we not?'

'But—but I thought you merely were marrying me out of pity.'

'Pity?' His eyes narrowed in pain.

Her heart sank. The last thing she wished was to upset him. 'I will share your bed if you wish it, Xavier.'

'I wish it. I wish for a marriage in every sense of the word.' His eyes pierced hers. 'In fact, I will not send for a ladies' maid. I will perform that function myself.'

He would undress her? Her eyes widened.

He cupped her chin. 'I will show you what a husband will do.'

Felicia, her best friend, had hinted at the pleasures of being married and Phillipa knew what occurred between a man and a woman in bed. Who could not know who grew up on a farm? Or attended school where older girls were only too willing to tell. She had just given up hope of experiencing it for herself.

He took her hand and led her to the bedchamber, a room so beautifully appointed she could understand why the Tsar of Russia chose this hotel over St James's Palace.

By the coals glowing in the fireplace she could see the maid had turned down the bed and laid out her nightdress. She watched the fire as he stood behind her and undid the laces of her gown, his fingers creating sensations so unexpected. So pleasant.

Her dress slid to the thick carpet beneath their feet. She stepped out of it and slipped off her shoes. He ran his hands down her bare arms, his palms warming her. His touch felt comforting. And thrilling. His lips touched her neck and sensation flashed through her. She'd never guessed that a man's kiss—Xavier's kiss—could be felt all over her body.

He untied her corset and loosened its laces so that it, too, joined her gown on the floor. All that covered her now was her thin muslin shift. He pulled the pins from her hair and combed through her curls with his fingers. To have him touch her hair was glorious. Who could imagine it to feel so different from a maid's ministrations?

Was this arousal? This feeling inside her? It surprised her and made her want more from him. He slipped his hands around her and cupped her breasts, stroking her until she thought she would go mad for yearning. He swept her into his arms and carried her to the bed. While she lay upon the feather bed, he rolled down her stockings, another sensation so intense she could not bear it. Nor bear for him to stop.

But he stepped away from the bed and removed his clothes, peeling off first his coat, then his waistcoat, then his shirt. His skin glowed from the firelight and she could not look away when he removed his pantaloons and stood before her like a Greek statue.

Adonis.

He climbed on to the bed. Closer, she could see scars on his abdomen.

She touched them. 'Xavier?'

He covered her hand with his. 'A few battle wounds.'

'You must have been gravely hurt!' He'd been stabbed. Sliced.

He took her hand away and kissed it. 'Your half-brother carried me off the battlefield.'

Rhys had saved him? She thanked God for her new brother.

Xavier took her face in his hands and kissed her again, a long, lingering kiss that made her forget about battlefields.

He lifted her shift and broke off the kiss long enough to pull it over her head. She lay naked next to him, a feeling so decadent she marvelled that it felt so right. Tentatively, she touched him again, this time feeling the contours of his muscles beneath her fingers.

He kissed her again and ran his hands down her naked body and back to her breasts. He traced around her nipple with his fingers and the glorious sensations returned. Who knew a man's fingers could create such sensations?

He lay her on her back. 'I will be gentle with you, I promise.'

Gentle? She was not certain she wished him to be gentle. She wanted all of this experience, not *pianissimo* but *forte*.

He touched her. Down there. And his fingers created new sensations, as *forte* as she could imagine, so intense she thought she could not bear it another moment. At the same time, she did not want him to stop.

She moaned with pleasure and need.

'It will bring you pleasure, Phillipa,' he reassured her.

He had already brought pleasure.

His fingers were clever, bringing her body to new heights

of experience. Her muscles reacted on their own, rising up to give him more access, to keep him from ever stopping.

But he did stop and her body throbbed in disappointment. His body covered hers and she felt his male member touch her, press against her and then, as she trembled beneath him, slip inside her.

A quick stab of pain seized her and her muscles stiffened in response.

He froze, still inside her. 'Did I hurt you?'

She shook her head. 'No.' But she felt the dampness of her maidenhood flow from her.

A moment later, the pain receded and her need grew.

He moved inside her, slowly, rhythmically.

She must remember this rhythm, she thought. She must try to recreate it. In her mind she heard what it might sound like on the pianoforte. Low notes with a unique timbre and vibrato.

The tempo increased and the music he created inside her grew louder, more intense. Her need grew as well, so strongly that it frightened her.

Suddenly a sound from deep within his chest escaped him and he plunged into her and held her in place. She felt his seed spill inside her.

A child, she thought. They might create a child from this act.

The thought fled just as quickly. He pressed inside her once more and something exploded inside her. A crescendo of sensation. She cried out for the pleasure of it.

He collapsed on top of her and she felt his weight for the first time. His skin was hot, damp, and his muscled body firm. He slid to her side and she took a breath. A strange languor came over her, as if her body had turned to melted candle wax.

'Did I hurt you?' he asked again.

She shook her head. She wanted to tell him how marvellous it felt, but words would not come. The music of it resounded in her mind, but even that faded and suddenly the idea that she was naked beside him made her shy. It had happened so fast, this lovemaking, this marriage, she'd not had time to think.

She'd certainly had no time to realise he'd want the physical side of marriage with her.

He rose on one elbow and stared down at her. 'Are you certain you are unharmed? I ought to have been more gentle. I am sorry for it.'

She found the bed sheet and covered her body with it. 'I am unharmed.'

He smiled and brushed her hair away from her face. 'The first time can be painful for a woman sometimes,' he explained. 'It will get better, I promise.'

It could be better than this? That defied logic.

He lay at her side, but continued to play with her hair, threading it through his fingers. He gazed at her face. 'You are beautiful, Phillipa.'

She tensed and turned her head away, hiding her scarred cheek. She was not beautiful. This she knew. He could not possibly think so.

Her body turned numb and she turned away from him.

He cupped her cheek and made her look back at him. 'You must believe me. You are beautiful.'

She could not. He was merely being kind. He had been kind to marry her.

She thought of Lady Faville and all the other beautiful women he might have married and she was sorry he'd felt obligated to marry her. It could not have been more than pity for the shabby way her mother had treated her that led him to choose her over such worthy women.

'Phillipa?' He looked concerned.

She owed it to him to pretend everything was perfect, even though she knew it was not. He'd tried so hard to please her. He'd made such a sacrifice.

She reached over and kissed him, not a very good kiss, more like one given to an elderly uncle, but the best she could muster.

'Thank you for a perfect day.' She made herself smile. She made herself snuggle against him and pretend to fall asleep.

Although it took a very long time for sleep to come.

Chapter Fifteen

Xavier woke to sun streaming through the windows. And to an empty bed, an empty bedchamber. He rose and wrapped his banyan around him and walked into the sitting room. She was seated there, dressed in her nightdress, gazing out the window.

'Phillipa?'

She turned at the sound of his voice and smiled. 'Good morning.'

There was a reserve in her voice he could not like. He wanted her to feel comfortable with him, but perhaps the night before had upset her. He had not been gentle enough. His own need for her had surged too strong, too urgent. He had been able to bring her pleasure, of that he was certain, but they had a long way to go.

In any event, he must tread carefully with her and not expect too much of her. Theirs was not a typical marriage. It would take time for her to realise that he wanted them to get on well together, to forge a life together.

'Have you been up long?' he asked.

'Not too long,' she replied, which could have meant hours or minutes.

'And you have been sitting here the whole time?'

'Not all the time,' she said. 'I used the water closet. How marvellous for a hotel to have such a thing! I read about them, of course.'

He did not want to talk about the water closet. 'Did you sleep well?'

'Yes,' she replied.

This was still like talking with a stranger. Much too polite.

He sat in a chair across from her, but she seemed distant. 'Shall I order breakfast?'

She glanced down. 'May I be dressed first?

'Of course.' He paused, uncertain how to anticipate what would make her most at ease. 'Shall I send for a maid?'

Her smile seemed stiff. 'Now? That would be fine.'

He sent for a maid and a valet and, after they were both dressed, he'd ordered breakfast. When they were eating it, she asked, 'What happens today?'

He wanted to please her. 'We need to find a place to live, but that is not likely to be accomplished today. Would you like to stay here? Or we can stay at the Masquerade Club. Rhys no longer uses his rooms there. And he is away.' With his wife.

Having agreed to watch the Masquerade Club in Rhys's absence, Xavier could not take Phillipa on a bride trip of her own. Perhaps later she would fancy a trip to Paris or Italy. Or Vienna. Wherever great music might be found.

'I cannot see staying here if you will be needed at the gaming house,' she responded. 'It must be very expensive to stay here. You do not need to spend so much money on me.'

He wanted to spend money on her, but something in her tone told him to simply do as she said.

* * *

Later that morning Cummings opened the door to the gaming house and they entered. MacEvoy happened to be in the hall as well.

'I am glad you are both here.' Xavier said.

'Come closer.' MacEvoy gestured. 'Let us have a look at you.'

Phillipa stepped forwards and, with only brief hesitation, lifted the netting away from her face.

Xavier gestured to Cummings. 'Let me present you to my wife.'

Cummings bowed. 'Mrs Campion. Welcome back.' The corner of his mouth twitched.

'Welcome back? You remember me?' Phillipa asked.

'The *pianiste*,' Cummings said. Phillipa extended her hand. 'It is good to be back.'

Cummings rubbed his hand on his coat before accepting hers.

'Hope you slept well last night,' MacEvoy said with a wink.

'Yes.' Phillipa blushed. 'We slept well.'

Xavier said, 'We will be staying here until we find a house.'

Cummings took something from his pocket. 'This arrived. Delivered from Stephen's Hotel.'

'Thank you, Cummings.' It was from his parents. 'A pianoforte will arriving here today. You may have it put in the drawing room.'

He'd already closed his rooms at Stephen's Hotel and had his trunk delivered here. Perhaps today they could arrange for Phillipa's things, as well.

When they reached Rhys's private rooms, Phillipa asked, 'Is the letter from my mother?'

He shook his head. 'From my mother.'

He showed her the bedchamber and placed their bags there. 'Would you like to unpack?'

'In a moment.' She removed her hat and gloves and unbuttoned her coat.

He stepped over and embraced her from behind. 'Everything will turn out well, Phillipa. Do not fear.'

She stepped out of his embrace and he helped her remove her coat. 'I am trying to get used to it.' She looked around the room, turning away from the bed. 'Should you not open your letter?'

'I should.' He broke the seal and unfolded the paper. 'They are in town.' He glanced up at her. 'Would you be willing to call upon them with me?'

She turned away. 'Perhaps you had better see them yourself and tell them. You must tell them before they read it in the newspaper.'

'I agree, but come with me.' He wanted her to be used to them together. The more people who saw her as Mrs Xavier Campion, the better.

She faced away from him. 'This will not be happy news for them.'

He laughed. 'Do you jest? They will be over the moon about it! They have wanted to see me settled since the end of the war.'

'But to me?' Her voice was almost inaudible.

He made her look at him. 'Our families have always been friends. Why would they not want to see me married to you?' She tried to turn away, but he would not let her. 'I insist. You must come. We should call on them right away.'

She took a deep breath and released it. 'Very well. Help me with my coat again. Let us go now, before I lose courage.'

It was as Xavier predicted. His parents were surprised. Shocked. And Phillipa supposed they were also mystified as to why he had chosen her, of all women, but they had always been kind people.

Like their son.

Lord and Lady Piermont welcomed her with open arms, broke out a bottle of sherry to toast to their future and insisted that Xavier and Phillipa come to dinner. Worse, Lady Piermont also sent an immediate invitation to Phillipa's mother to also come to dinner and she sent her kitchen staff into a flurry of activity to produce a dinner worthy of celebrating a marriage.

Xavier and his father set off to look for lodgings for the newly married couple and Lady Piermont enlisted Phillipa's help in writing letters to all Xavier's siblings, informing them of the marriage. Fortunately none of Xavier's siblings was in town. Lord and Lady Piermont were only there on their way to the country house for the harvest and hunting season.

'You and Xavier must come to the country with us,' his mother said.

Her natural good cheer could not help but lift Phillipa's spirits. 'He must attend to the gaming house in my brothers' absence. He promised Rhys.' At her new mother-in-law's disappointed look, Phillipa added, 'Perhaps when Rhys returns.'

That made Lady Piermont smile.

Phillipa took the opportunity to write letters of her own, to her brothers, to Felicia, and even to her father, who was not likely to care much. They had not finished their task when a footman brought Lady Piermont her mother's response.

Phillipa was confident that her mother would refuse the invitation. She never went anywhere on short notice. She kept writing as her mother-in-law opened the note.

'Oh, excellent!' the lady cried. 'Your mother accepted.'

'She accepted?' She did not wish to face her mother.

'Yes, indeed,' Lady Piermont went on. 'She is going to bring a friend. General Henson. I do remember him from Brighton several years ago.'

Of course her mother would bring General Henson.

'Isn't that lovely?' Lady Piermont exclaimed.

Phillipa stifled a groan. 'She will expect me to dress. I should get a note to my maid to send over a dinner dress.'

Lady Piermont rose to her feet. 'Nonsense. You are similar in size to me. I will wager I have a dress that will fit you.'

She led Phillipa up the stairs to her bedchamber. Phillipa longed to ask the woman if she and her husband shared a bed, if their marriage had been a love match, or had they made it one after the ceremony?

Lord Piermont was a handsome, silver-haired man with kind blue eyes as brilliant as his son's, but it was clear that most of Xavier's looks came from his mother. In her early sixties at least, her dark brown hair was only threaded with grey. Her lips were full like Xavier's and her face was oval, like his. Like her son's, her nose was straight and perfectly formed. She moved with grace, as did he, although in a masculine way.

She was tall, like Phillipa, and slender. Though her waist was thicker—she'd had eight children, after all—Phillipa thought a dress of hers might, indeed, fit her.

Lady Piermont summoned her maid and instructed her what gowns to bring. One was a lilac silk with embroidered flowers in matching thread on the bodice and puffed sleeves so unusually made they reminded Phillipa of lace, but it was just the fabric.

Lady Piermont smiled. 'I see by your eyes you like this one. Let us have you try it on.'

The maid helped her into the dress and both she and Lady Piermont pulled and tucked the fabric.

'It needs only a *leetle* bit of sewing.' The maid spoke in a French accent.

Phillipa gazed in a full-length mirror and thought it looked lovely—if you looked at the dress, that is, not at her. 'I do like it.'

'I have a *leetle* something to make you look *très belle, madame.*' The maid touched her scar. 'We paint this and it disappears. *Voila!*'

Phillipa covered the scar with her hand. Her mother had always suggested she paint her face to make her scar less visible, but she always resisted. If people wished to meet her, then they would have to take her precisely as she was.

But no one at this dinner had seen her any other way than scarred.

Or masked.

Late in the afternoon Xavier came to collect Phillipa so they could walk back to the gaming house and dress for dinner, only to find Phillipa had made other arrangements. Or his mother had done.

'We shall surprise you,' his mother said, sending him off.

He returned and found the surprise. Phillipa's mother... and General Henson. Surely this would not please Phillipa.

'Lady Westleigh.' Xavier bowed. 'General.'

They were alone in the drawing room, which was fortunate. He did not mind speaking frankly.

Lady Westleigh greeted him warmly. 'Xavier, my boy! I am in raptures that you succeeded in convincing Phillipa to do the right thing. It was wrong of her to decline in the first place.'

Xavier glared at her. 'No. You were in the wrong to deprive her of her pianoforte. Wrong and cruel.'

'See here, Campion!' the general piped up.

Lady Westleigh motioned for him to keep quiet. 'It is all

right, Alistair. Xavier and I may speak with frankness.' She turned back to Xavier. 'If you are blessed with children, you may then choose to criticise me. You will learn that sometimes a parent must be cruel for a child's own good.'

'She is a grown woman who knows her own mind,' he countered. 'You made it impossible for her to do as she wished.'

'I made her see what was best for her. To see what her life would be like if she remained a spinster, subject to the whims of her relations.' She spoke with conviction. 'She made the right choice. Although she made a terrible mistake to keep the wedding secret. It ought to have taken place amongst family and special guests. She ought to have had a wedding breakfast.'

'I am grateful she could choose for herself how to be married,' he countered. 'She did not want to pretend a celebration she did not feel.'

Lady Westleigh rolled her eyes in exasperation. 'She has been running from attention since—since you-know-when. How could she expect to get married if she hid herself away?' Her eyes narrowed. 'I did what needed to be done and now all is as it should be.'

Except that Phillipa had not wished to marry him and he would need to work hard to convince her not to regret it.

His father entered the room. Xavier presented the general to him.

'We've met.' His father shook the general's hand. 'In Brighton. Years ago, I am certain of it.'

'That is so, my lord,' the general responded. 'I'd not expected you to recall it. So long ago.'

The two men talked of mutual acquaintances until Xavier's mother came and more greetings took place. They were all talking at once when Phillipa walked in.

Xavier was first to notice her.

She wore a flowing gown in a light purple colour that make her skin look luminous. It seemed to flow around her, like a dress a fairy might dance in. Her hair, too, looked fanciful, curls floating around her face, moving when she moved.

Her gaze went directly to him. He crossed the room to her, leaned down to her ear and whispered, 'You look lovely, Phillipa.'

Her hand flew to her cheek and she lowered her eyes.

'There she is,' his father boomed. 'Our new daughter! And does she not look a treat!'

His mother came up to Xavier's side and took his arm. 'I told you we had a surprise for you.'

He blew out a breath. 'I thought the surprise was her mother.'

She laughed. 'I suppose that was a surprise as well, wasn't it?'

A footman poured glasses of claret and handed one to each of them. 'A toast to our new member of the family.' His father lifted his glass. 'May she and our son be happy and fruitful!'

Xavier tapped his glass against Phillipa's. 'Happy and fruitful,' he repeated in a low voice.

After the toast, Phillipa's mother walked up to her. 'Phillipa, dear.' She touched Phillipa's cheek. 'You have applied cosmetics. Well done.'

'Very well done,' added the general. 'You can hardly see the scar.'

Phillipa's face turned red.

Xavier stared at her again. He'd not noticed what was immediately obvious to her mother.

The dinner went well enough. Lady Westleigh enquired about all the details of the wedding, which Xavier was obliged to tell.

Except he said nothing about the music played during their nuptials, nor did he tell them about her new pianoforte.

Lady Westleigh asked to see Phillipa's ring and Phillipa, her expression frozen on her face, extended her hand.

'Oh my!' her mother exclaimed. 'That is quite a ring.'

Xavier felt a quiet triumph.

When Phillipa put her hand back at her side, Xavier clasped it. She squeezed his fingers in return, a small gesture, but enough to cheer him.

After dinner they were forced to accept a ride in Lady Westleigh's carriage.

'I do think you should not be living atop a gaming house, Phillipa,' her mother said. 'It will cause talk.'

'No one will know unless you tell them,' Phillipa countered.

Xavier admired her. For the whole evening, Phillipa had more than held her own with her mother. The only time Xavier had seen her mother rattle her had been with the comment about her scar.

The ride was a short one, thank God. And they were soon back at the Masquerade Club. Phillipa covered her face with the netting on her hat when they entered.

The place was already abuzz with activity. There was not much to do in London at this time of year, so those remaining there used the Masquerade Club as their entertainment.

Xavier and Phillipa hurried inside and climbed the stairs to the private rooms. Once inside the bedchamber, Xavier helped Phillipa off with her coat.

'Tomorrow I must send for my maid,' she said.

He grinned at her. 'I take it my services are unsatisfactory?'

She coloured. 'I hate to trouble you.'

Could he not even jest with her? 'It is my pleasure to

help you. I can help you out of your dress before I go downstairs, if you wish it.'

She frowned. 'I thought I would go to the supper room
and play.' She faltered. 'With your permission, that is.'

He put his hands on her shoulders and made her look at
him. 'You do not need my permission. Play, if that is what
you want to do. We have missed you in the supper room.'

She lifted her chin. 'But I do not want anyone to know
who I am. Who I am to you. I want to wear a mask, the
same as before.'

'I'll let Cummings, MacEvoy, Belinda and anyone they
might have told to keep mum about who you are.' He stroked
her neck with his thumbs. 'Who you are to me.'

Suddenly he wished for nothing else but to share her bed
and try again to please her with lovemaking.

When a masked Phillipa entered the supper room carrying her music, she expected nothing more than to sit at
the pianoforte and play.

The room was unchanged from when she'd last been
there, even though her life had gone topsy-turvy. Some of
her regulars sat at their regular tables, Mr Anson and Mr
Everard among them.

Anson rose when she entered the room. 'Miss Songstress! You are back!'

Others also rose and soon she was encircled by a throng
of gentlemen, all asking questions of where she'd been. Had
she been ill? Had she been in Brighton? On the Continent?
Was she back to stay?

She laughed, more gratified by her reception than she
wanted to admit. 'I am well. I was not ill. I was away, but
I am back.'

She asked them about their lives in the past weeks. She
was a bit sad to see Mr Everard here still. It meant that Lady

Faville was also still here and that Everard was still pining for a woman who did not see he existed.

Phillipa knew all too well what it was like to be invisible.

As the wife of Xavier Campion, she would no more be overlooked. She would merely be talked about.

'What would you like me to play?' she asked her admirers.

They all wanted her to sing, which she did not mind, but it was her skill on the pianoforte that was the more important to her.

She sat and played and, as before, knew the instant Xavier appeared in the doorway. With him was the ever-present Lady Faville. They still made the perfect couple. How much more suited to each other were they than Phillipa was to Xavier. Xavier, though, walked away from Lady Faville and stood alone to watch Phillipa play. He did not stay long, but he had never stayed long when his duties lay primarily in the gaming room.

During her break Lady Faville approached her. 'Miss Songstress! I have missed you so! It has not been at all the same here without you.' She laughed charmingly. 'You can see I am still here, still making a cake of myself over dear Xavier. He is more comfortable with me now, I think, so I am progressing, I suppose.' She took a breath. 'But you must tell me all about where you have been. I do hope it has been for a romance!'

The beauty did not give Phillipa much of a chance to respond. 'I have been away, that is all. Now I am back.'

Lady Faville laughed again. 'Oh, so secretive. Yes. It must have been for romance. I hope soon to have a romance of my own to keep secret!'

What would Lady Faville think if she knew the object of her desires had married? She would find out, perhaps that very morning if she read the *Morning Post*. Phillipa could almost feel sorry for her.

'Well, I suppose I ought to return to the gaming room. Xavier will be wondering where I am, no doubt.' Lady Faville gave Phillipa her most beaming smile. 'Please do say I will see you again tomorrow?'

'I think so,' Phillipa managed before the lady turned and swept out of the room, all masculine eyes following her every move.

By the time the last card players finished their game, dawn's light was appearing in the sky. Daphne and three gentlemen who were obviously vying for her favour finally stacked the cards and scooped up their counters. The croupiers running the tables had already left and the only other person in the room was a very weary Mr Everard seated at a table near the door.

And Xavier.

She laughed her musical laugh and glanced his way. He stood, arms crossed over his chest, impatient to go upstairs.

And join his wife in bed.

Maybe this would be the last he'd see of Daphne. He could hope anyway. He'd done nothing to encourage her, but still she attended the Masquerade Club several nights a week with the poor, faithful Mr Everard in tow. Xavier had made it clear her interest in him would never be returned, but still she persisted. Flirting with other men in hopes that he would become jealous. Always at his side at some point in the night lest he forget her.

The other men left the room while she handed her counters to Everard. 'Will you turn these in for me? And have Cummings fetch my cloak?'

Of course Everard would.

And, of course, Daphne would linger, giving herself an opportunity to speak to him.

She came too close. 'I won tonight, is that not marvellous?'

She more often lost. 'Very good, Daphne. You are the last to leave. Please do not dally. I am eager to go to bed.'

Her voice turned low and breathy. 'Why, Xavier, is that an invitation?'

His face grew hot. 'You know it is not. You waste your time here, Daphne. I have made that clear from the beginning. You've compromised your reputation for nothing, coming to this gaming house.'

'What we once had together cannot be changed.' She touched the lapel of his coat.

He pushed her hand away. 'It was nothing then and it is nothing now. It never will be.'

He walked out of the room, but waited on the other side of the doorway to close the door after she finally walked out.

She approached him again, putting her arms around his neck. 'Change your mind, Xavier. Come home with me.'

Mr Everard was waiting with her cloak. His features twisted in agony.

Xavier seized Daphne's wrists and peeled her off, not gently. 'Stop this, Daphne!'

She looked for a moment as if she would cry, but she collected herself and, instead, smiled brightly. 'Eventually you will stop being angry at me. I will be waiting right here.'

With any luck, in a few hours she would read the *Morning Post*. Seeing the marriage announcement would convince her.

Daphne allowed Everard to place her cloak on her shoulders and escort her to the door. Cummings opened it and they left.

'Are they the last to go?' he asked Cummings.

The man nodded.

'Thank God.' He crossed the hall to the stairs. 'Do you and MacEvoy need me any further?'

'No.' Cummings gestured to the stairs. 'Go to your wife.'

Xavier grinned and clapped him on the back. 'With pleasure!'

He climbed the stairs with renewed energy and quietly opened the door to the bedchamber.

She would be in bed. Asleep, of course, and he would try not to disturb her, but he greatly wanted the comfort of her lovely body sleeping next to him. Once inside the room, his senses heightened as he caught sight of her, exactly where he expected, curled up on her side, her hair in a loose plait that he longed to take apart and wind through his fingers.

He washed his face and hands and brushed his teeth, trying to be as quiet as possible. It was a novel experience to be thinking of another's sleep instead of his own. He quite liked it. He quickly shed his clothing and laid it on a chair. Eager for her warmth, he climbed into bed, moving close to her. To his delight, she nestled against him and even though her nightdress prevented him from the glorious contact with her skin, he was content. He put his arm around her and, too tired for words, fell instantly to sleep.

A voice roused him from slumber. 'No, Mama. Wait for me, Mama. Wait for me.'

Phillipa was talking in her sleep. She sounded exactly as he remembered her sounding on that fateful day in Brighton.

She thrashed about. 'Mama! Mama!'

Should he wake her?

She cried out again, 'No!' and sat straight up in bed, blinking.

The dream had jolted her awake.

He sat up, too. 'You were having a dream.'

She peered at him as if puzzled to see him there. 'You slept with me?'

'Yes.' He wanted to touch her, but hesitated. 'We are married, remember.'

She could not meet his gaze. 'I just thought—' She waved a hand. 'Never mind what I thought.'

He could not resist. He reached over and swept some loose curls from her face. 'What was the dream?'

She lifted her hands to her head. 'It was as though I was there again.' She stared into his eyes. 'Xavier.' Her voice was little more than a whisper. 'I—I remembered something.'

Chapter Sixteen

Xavier moved behind her and held her against him.

'Tell me what you remembered,' he murmured.

Her muscles tensed as she began to speak. 'I remembered following my mother all the way to the beach. It was getting dark and I was scared, too scared to go back alone. She was on the beach, arguing with a man.' She turned her head towards him. 'It was General Henson, I am sure of it.' She turned back. 'They were so angry. I pulled on my mother's skirts, but she did not heed me.' She paused. 'She ran after the man and then I woke up.'

His muscles tensed. 'Can you remember anything now.'

She grew still, as if trying to bring the memory back.

She shook her head. 'Nothing.'

She moved out of his arms and scooted around to face him. Her gaze flickered over his bare chest and, to her credit, she did not turn missish.

She looked directly at him. 'I thought you would sleep in a different room.'

He was puzzled. 'Why?'

She lowered her gaze. 'This is not a love match.'

That was a sabre thrust. 'Maybe not, but I do want a real marriage. Children. All of it. Not separate beds and married in name only.' He lifted her chin to look at him. 'We will do well together as man and wife. Tell me you are willing to try.'

She covered her cheeks with her hands.

He pulled them away. 'I want you to be happy.'

She averted her gaze. 'You have done nothing to make me unhappy.'

He moved until she was forced to look at him again. 'Does my sleeping with you make you unhappy?'

'No.' She recovered more of her courage and looked at him again. 'I merely did not expect you would want such—such intimacy with me.'

He released her hands and stroked her hair. 'You must shake off this idea that I would not want you as a husband wants a wife, because, I assure you, I do.'

He leaned forwards and touched his lips to hers, but she was not so warm and willing as she'd been for that first kiss. Still, he'd accept the challenge of winning her over. He knelt in front of her, placing her between his knees so he could hold her close. He kissed her again, this time lingering on her lips. His body flared into response, all too visibly.

She trembled beneath his kiss and strained against his embrace.

He released her and backed slowly away. 'We have a lifetime to sort this out.'

She gazed at him with wide eyes, as if she had not expected either the kiss or his retreat.

Perhaps, later on, he could ask her what had made her withdraw from him. She had passion—their first lovemaking surely revealed that. It was not unlike what came out in her music. All he needed was to make her want to express that passion with him.

He rose from the bed and opened his trunk for clean

linen. 'What would you like to do today?' He glanced back at her and caught her staring at him.

Yes. They would sort out the lovemaking. He was confident of it.

She quickly averted her gaze and rose from the bed herself. 'I would say play music, but since you rescued me from my mother's prison, I have quite refilled the well. Performing at the gaming house tonight will be sufficient for me.' She poured some clean water into the basin and washed her face.

'There is some place I would like to take you.' He turned away purposely so she could remove her nightdress without him watching. There would be time for watching eventually.

'I will be at your disposal, then,' she said.

'First thing,' he said, pulling on his pantaloons, 'we send for your maid and your trunk. I had hoped it would be here by today.'

'I expect my mother delayed it.' He heard her moving behind him. 'So that we would have to call upon her in order for it to be sent.'

'Then we must call upon her first thing.' He donned his shirt and dared a glance.

She was in her shift and corset, but was struggling with its laces. He strode over to her.

She allowed him to tighten them. 'I suppose we have no choice.'

He tied a bow. 'Shall I call upon her alone with a coach and Cummings? We could take your trunk by force, if necessary.'

She laughed. 'Surely you do not mean it.'

She stepped into her dress and put her arms through its sleeves.

'I do mean it.' The gown had buttons down the back. 'I'll call upon your mother, fetch your maid and your trunk and you may amuse yourself here. Play the pianoforte.' He glanced around. There was clothing and such scattered everywhere. 'Or pick up this room.'

She swung around. There were mere inches between them. 'I would scrub the chamberpots rather than call upon my mother today.'

Hardly words to provoke passion.

Undaunted, he leaned down, closer, his eyes fixed on her lovely pink lips. 'Play music,' he murmured. 'Leave the pots to the maids. In fact, leave this room to the maids. Play music.'

He forced himself to move away lest he seize her in his arms and take the kiss he so very much desired. The ease between them had returned and he had no wish to risk losing it again.

Their comfort with each other lasted through breakfast and Xavier saw Phillipa comfortably seated at her new pianoforte, now in the drawing room, before setting out to call upon Lady Westleigh.

He walked to Davies Street, telling Cummings to meet him there in a short time with a hackney coach.

The September day was chilly and damp and he quickened his pace to keep warm. When he reached the Westleigh town house, he sounded the knocker.

The butler answered the door, his quizzical look something more than expected.

'Mr Campion to see Lady Westleigh,' he told the man.

'Right away, sir,' the butler responded. 'You may wait in the drawing room.'

He gestured for Xavier to follow him, but instead Xavier said, 'I can find my way.'

The man nodded and started to climb the stairs. He

stopped and turned back to Xavier. 'Begging your pardon, Mr Campion, but how fares your wife?'

Xavier grinned. 'She is very well. I will tell her you asked about her. Last I saw her she was playing her new pianoforte.'

The corners of the butler's mouth turned up for a fleeting moment. 'How very good, sir.'

Moments later Lady Westleigh swept into the drawing room. General Henson was right behind her. 'What is it, Xavier? Is something wrong?'

'Good day, my lady. General.' He bowed. 'Nothing is wrong. I am here to pick up Phillipa's trunk and to bring her maid to her.'

'Where is Phillipa?' Lady Westleigh asked. 'I wanted to speak with her.'

'To beg her forgiveness?' he asked.

Her eyes flashed. 'No. To tell her you should live here. Or with your parents. Until we find you rooms of your own.'

'Lady Westleigh.' His voice was firm. 'Stop managing. Release the trunk and the maid and let us go about our lives.'

'Watch your tongue, sir!' the general broke in.

Lady Westleigh motioned for him to be quiet. 'You cannot leave Phillipa to her own devices, Xavier,' she told him. 'She will simply closet herself away. You must make her mix in society. Limit her music—'

'Never.' His voice deepened and he leaned closer to her. 'I will never limit anything she wishes to do. Certainly not her music.' He stepped back. 'Now, if you please, summon her maid. My coach will be here very soon.'

She walked to the door and stepped out of the room to speak to the butler. 'Find Lacey and bring her to me,' Xavier heard her say.

The general took that moment to talk to him. 'Campion, I will not have this insolence towards Lady Westleigh. She does not deserve it. The welfare of her daughter has been her greatest concern, I promise you.'

Xavier straightened. 'Removing Phillipa's pianoforte was a terrible cruelty. It will take time for either one of us to forgive her that.'

'She meant it to be instructive.'

It had almost taken the life out of Phillipa.

Xavier met the man's gaze. 'Keep Lady Westleigh entertained, General. Keep her busy. Do not let her interfere. No more involving herself in what Phillipa does or does not do.'

Lady Westleigh re-entered the room. 'I will always involve myself with my children.'

'Not with Phillipa,' Xavier said. 'Not unless asked.' He made certain she knew he was speaking in all seriousness. 'No more interference or I will break my vow to you and tell what I've sworn never to tell.'

About Phillipa's accident.

Lady Westleigh blanched. 'You would not dare!'

He did not back down. 'I suggest you do not test my resolve.'

A few minutes later the maid appeared, her gaze sliding towards Xavier. 'Yes, m'lady?'

'Apparently my daughter wishes you to be her lady's maid, but I must tell you that it means living above a gaming house which is not at all respectable. You do not have to go if you do not wish it. You may stay here.'

The woman was attempting to manage the maid's life as well as her daughter's. And his.

'I do not mind living atop a gaming house,' the maid said.

Lady Westleigh took a breath. 'Very well. Pack my daughter's things, and yours, as quickly as you can. Mr Campion will take you there right now.'

'All is packed, m'lady,' the maid said. 'Since yesterday.'

The hackney coach arrived and Cummings and a footman carried Phillipa's and the maid's trunks out to the coach. The maid said quick goodbyes to the other servants and, in no time, they were on their way.

In the coach the maid looked tiny seated with the two men.

'It is Lacey, is it not?' Xavier asked her.

'Mary Lacey, sir,' the girl replied.

He introduced her to Cummings, who nodded.

'Lady Phillipa will be very glad to see you,' he told the girl.

'Yes, sir.' She blushed.

Phillipa heard the carriage pull up in front of the gaming house. She left the pianoforte and walked to the window. Xavier returned. With Lacey.

She hurried down the stairs and opened the door for them.

'M'lady!' Lacey cried, skipping to her.

'I am so very glad you decided to come.' Phillipa clasped her hand. 'Come in. I will show you around.'

'I cannot believe I'll be living in a gaming house!' the girl cried.

'It is just temporary, but I'm sure you will find it very comfortable.'

She introduced Lacey to MacEvoy, who bowed and looked very pleased to meet her. Xavier introduced both Phillipa and Lacey to the kitchen servants and the maid-of-all-work. They left Lacy to the disorder in the bedchamber and went out again.

'I almost forgot.' Phillipa pulled a note from her pocket. 'This came from your father.'

He stopped to read it. 'He says there is a small town house very near here that we might be able to let. Shall we go see it?'

'I am willing,' she said. 'But where else were you going to take me?'

He placed the note in a pocket. 'Let me surprise you.'

The leasing agent was not far and, after a surprised glance at Phillipa's scar, declared himself delighted to show the Earl of Piermont's son the town house.

'Tenants are few and far between this time of year,' the man said as he led them to a second-rate town house on Dover Street, directly across Piccadilly from St James's Street.

'The walk would be only a little more than a street,' Xavier remarked.

The agent unlocked the door. 'I am certain the interior will please you.'

The hall was unremarkable, but there was a comfortable study and a dining room behind it. The first floor had a nicely decorated drawing room, with plenty of space for a pianoforte, and a bedchamber behind.

One bedchamber with dressing rooms on each side.

There was another bedroom on the second floor and a maids' room with three beds. They descended the stairs again and examined the kitchen area and more servants' rooms.

She could be living here with Xavier, Phillipa thought. She would be in charge of the house, the meals, the servants.

'We can assist you in finding excellent servants, as well,' the agent said. 'There are several good people from whom to choose.' He smiled. 'Do you wish to take the house?'

Xavier looked to Phillipa.

She was to make the decision? 'It—it seems satisfactory.'

Xavier turned to the man. 'We will take it.'

They returned to the agent's office, signed the papers and received the keys.

'Shall I send some servants for you to interview, ma'am?' the agent asked.

This was all too sudden.

Xavier answered for her. 'Let us contact you about that tomorrow.'

By the time they walked out of the agent's office Phillipa's head was spinning. She walked numbly at Xavier's side, not even heeding where they were headed.

Xavier finally spoke. 'Please tell me you wanted that house, Phillipa.'

She slowed her pace. 'I assure you, it is all I could want.' She took a breath. 'I am simply dumbfounded. Two days ago I was completely under my mother's thumb. Now I am a married woman with a house to manage.'

He threaded her arm through his. 'I share your amazement. These are good changes, Phillipa. You must believe me.'

She wanted to assuage his concerns, but could not. 'I am too shaken by the changes to declare them good or bad.'

He pulled her closer. 'They will be good.'

They walked towards Piccadilly.

'Where do we go now?' she asked.

'To the hack stand,' he replied. 'To Cheapside.'

'Cheapside?' What could be there?

They walked to Piccadilly and Bolton Street, where the hackney cabs waited for passengers. They were immediately hailed by a familiar voice. 'Mr Campion! Over here.'

It was their hackney coach driver. He stood with his horses while they drank from buckets of water. The waterman waited nearby.

When the jarvey saw Phillipa, he pulled on his forelock. 'G'day to you, ma'am. Will you be wanting a ride today?'

Xavier opened the door of the coach. 'Take us to King Street in Cheapside.'

The waterman picked up the buckets and the driver climbed up to his seat. Xavier helped Phillipa into the carriage. She'd no sooner settled in their seat than the horses set off.

'Why do we go to Cheapside?' she asked. 'Are we to do some shopping?'

'You will see,' he answered cryptically.

The coach wended its way through streets filled with wagons, horses and other carriages, until it pulled up to a shop with a newly painted sign, Jeffers Cabinetry.

Why bring her here? He could not have known they would lease a house. Besides, that house already had all the furniture one could wish.

Phillipa and Xavier alighted and Xavier paid the jarvey.

'I can wait for you at the stand, if you like.' The jarvey gestured to a place down the street where several hacks waited.

'Good of you,' Xavier said. He rejoined Phillipa.

'We are visiting a furniture shop?' A furniture shop was his surprise?

'We are indeed.' He reached for the door handle, but paused. 'Phillipa, I must tell you. This shop is run by one of the men who attacked us.'

She shrank back. 'No! Then why bring me here? Are you going to see to the man's arrest?'

'Not at all.' He turned the handle and held the door for her to enter.

The shop displayed a variety of wooden cabinets, tables and chairs, all of simple, unembellished but pleasing design. She could hardly heed them, however, wary at encountering a man who had attacked them in the street and attempted to rob them.

A shop clerk—not the man she feared—greeted them. 'May I be of assistance, sir?'

Xavier answered, 'I am here to see Jeffers. Tell him Mr Campion wishes to see him.'

The clerk's eyes widened. 'Mr Campion!' He snapped to attention. 'I will find him right away, sir.'

The clerk's reaction seemed very odd.

It took no time at all for this Jeffers to emerge from a doorway covered by a thick curtain. It was the man Xavier cut with her knife. It must be the man, because a scar remained, still red from recent healing. But rather than gaunt and menacing, this man wore a pleasant, welcoming expression. His pleasure at seeing Xavier was genuine.

'So good of you to come.' He shook Xavier's hand.

'I brought someone with me.' Xavier stepped aside so Jeffers could see Phillipa.

The man blanched. Even through the netting on her bonnet, he recognised her.

'Ma'am. Ma'am,' he entreated. 'I beg you to forgive me. It was a foolish act to accost you. I am heartily ashamed of my part in it.'

She stiffened, the anger from that night resurfacing. 'Why did you do it, then?'

Xavier interrupted. 'Phillipa, first allow me to present Mr Jeffers to you. Mr Jeffers, this is Lady Phillipa, my wife.'

The man bowed respectfully.

Xavier gestured to the doorway behind the clerk's counter. 'Let us go in the back. I would like my wife to see it.'

In the back, three men worked on building furniture. One put the finishing touches on a cabinet. Another worked on a chair. The third, a table.

Jeffers led them to a corner where a set of completed chairs and table stood, far enough away from the workers that they would not be overheard. 'Let me pour us some tea.'

Phillipa did not want to share tea with this man!

But Xavier held a chair for her and she had no choice but to sit. Jeffers took a water kettle from the fireplace and poured water into a teapot.

After he poured the tea into cups, he sat as well. 'I will answer your question now, m'lady. There was no good excuse for attacking you. It was wrong of me.'

'He was starving,' Xavier explained.

Jeffers lowered his head. 'That I was, ma'am, but, even so, I should not have done what I did. Not to you, not to anybody.'

'No, you should not,' she said curtly, not so willing to forgive him as Xavier had apparently done.

Jeffers nodded. 'I agree, ma'am. I do not deserve this opportunity Mr Campion has given me. I do not know what would have become of me if he had not found me that day.'

'Opportunity?' She did not understand.

'Mr Campion provided the money for this shop. We are just getting started, but we will make a success of it.' He gestured to the men at work. 'It has been manna from heaven to these men and to me. We had no work, but now—' He glanced around the room again. 'Look at us.'

Xavier tried to gauge Phillipa's reaction. Would she disdain him for running a shop? For helping Jeffers? Her face was too shrouded by her hat's netting for him to tell.

'They are all former soldiers,' he explained to her. 'Let go from their regiments and reduced to begging on the streets. Or worse.' Like Jeffers, turning to crime. 'I had money to invest. I thought why not make good use of it?' He might as well tell her all. 'I also have a candle maker.'

'And I've a line on an ironmonger, if you fancy an ironmonger's shop,' Jeffers said.

Xavier glanced to him. 'Excellent idea.'

She gaped at them both.

He faced her again and continued. 'I had the idea from the Burlington Arcade. I was tired of seeing so many soldiers begging on the street. Why not put them to work.'

'You did this to give men work?' Her voice sounded stunned.

'Never you fear, my lady,' Jeffers broke in. 'We will be paying Mr Campion back and then some. He will have a share of our profits, from now to for ever.'

He was a shopkeeper. Better for her to know it now.

It would have been better still if he had told her before marrying her, but he'd wanted nothing to keep her from saying yes.

He waited for her to speak now.

She turned to Mr Jeffers. 'Did you make all the furniture in the front in this short space of time?'

Jeffers looked proud. 'We did our best. Cannot make money without goods to sell.'

'It is a remarkable feat,' she said.

Jeffers beamed. 'It is furniture for ordinary folk. That is who we expect to buy our cabinets.'

She stood. 'I spied a cabinet in the shop that interested me.'

She'd given no indication.

Jeffers popped out of his seat and led her back to the front of the shop. She pointed to a small commode, lacking the usual elaborate decoration.

'I quite like this piece,' she said. 'What is its price?'

'My lady.' Jeffers was near fawning. 'It is yours. We shall deliver it to you today.' He turned to Xavier. 'We found a soldier with a horse and cart to make our deliveries.'

'Deliver it to my residence.' He gave Jeffers the direction to the gaming house.

* * *

After the arrangements were made, they were back on the street, walking towards the coach stand.

Once back in the hack, Xavier could wait no longer. 'You needed to learn about the shops. About Jeffers.' He paused. 'It is not the sort of business a gentleman engages in, but soldiers needed jobs and I could create them. I'm not stopping with one or two. I'm determined to have several shops and to have them all succeed. They will make money, never fear.'

She turned to him and lifted her netting. 'I do not know anyone who would do what you did.'

'It begs for society's censure. I realise that.' He could point out that her family had invested in a gaming house. Were shops any worse? 'But no one knows, except you. And my solicitor. But not my parents. Not even Rhys.'

'Why did you tell me?' she asked.

'I could not withhold from you that I was in business with a man who had tried to rob us. Or that I'd turned shopkeeper.'

Her gaze turned even more intent. 'It is good you told me. I detest it when I am *protected* from the truth, as you well know. I would be unhappy indeed if you kept secrets from me like my family did.'

Except he was keeping one secret—what he knew about her accident, and was honour-bound not to tell.

Chapter Seventeen

They fell silent in the carriage. Phillipa pulled down her netting, but only so she could look at her husband without him knowing.

What sort of man would do what he'd done? Members of the *ton* looked down their noses at any man who ran a shop. *He smells of trade*, they would say.

But Xavier invested in shops for only one reason—to give unemployed soldiers decent jobs. He'd even saved Jeffers from a life of crime or a hangman's noose.

'Xavier.' Her voice came out low and husky.

He turned to her.

'I am glad you brought me to Cheapside.'

His features relaxed for a moment then tensed again. 'The shops will be successful, you will see.'

'I have no doubt,' she responded. 'Jeffers and the other men will work hard for you.'

He took her hand and brought it to his lips.

'There is just one thing,' she went on.

'What is it?' he asked.

She smiled. 'I believe my mother will have apoplexy if she discovers this!'

He laughed. 'My parents as well.'

She shook her head. 'You are wrong there. You could not displease your parents no matter what you did.'

The netting on her hat did not protect her from the intensity of his gaze. She felt as if he was searching to see if she really approved of his shops.

She did approve. In fact, her chest swelled with pride for him.

'Phillipa,' he whispered, lifting the netting away from her face and kissing her lips, a long, lingering, tongue-to-tongue kiss that made her body ache, a sweet ache that begged for more from him.

Before their first night together she would not have known what the yearning inside her meant. Now she knew she wanted him inside her, creating that sweet music with her.

He pulled her on to his lap and she felt his arousal. Did he want her?

He was under no obligation to make love to her at this moment.

She kissed him back to show him she intended to please him the way a wife should—in bed, or in the cab of a hackney.

The excitement inside her surged and she plunged her fingers into his hair.

He groaned and cupped her breast, his hand driving her need to greater heights. She felt giddy and light-headed and lost to awareness of anything but him.

'I have an idea.' He broke away from her and opened the window to the jarvey. 'Take us to Dover Street.'

The coach turned right off of Piccadilly on to Dover Street and stopped.

'Here, sir?' the jarvey called through the window.

'Here will do,' Xavier replied.

He opened the door and helped Phillipa out.

'What is your idea?' Phillipa asked.

He raised a finger for her to wait and paid the jarvey.

'Thank you, Mr Campion,' the man responded enthusiastically.

He turned back to Phillipa and pulled something from his pocket.

The key to the house he'd leased.

She still did not understand. 'We are visiting the house again?'

He smiled. 'We are indeed.'

He unlocked the door and they entered the house. As soon as he closed the door behind them and locked it again, he scooped her up in his arms.

'What are you doing?' she cried.

He gave her a quick kiss. 'Carrying you to our bed.'

Xavier's spirits soared as he carried her up the stairs to the bedchamber.

To the bed.

He turned the covers down and lay her on the bed linens, but she immediately sat up, untying the ribbons of her hat and pulling it off her head. She put her arms around him and kissed him with an energy that merely aroused him more.

When he had time to take a breath, he asked, 'How do you feel about making love to me in the daylight, in the afternoon? There is no one here to know. No one but you and me.'

She lowered her lashes. 'I am willing to try.'

He grinned. 'You never disappoint me, Phillipa.'

She glanced up at him as if surprised.

He was determined to convince her that he desired her. At the moment his desire was so strong he wanted to ravish her. He kissed her lips, her nose, her once-wounded cheek. 'May I love you, Phillipa?'

She nodded and returned his kisses, gently touching her lips to his mouth, his nose, his cheek, so innocently passionate it made even his heart ache for her.

He peeled off his coat and reached around her to untie her laces. As she wriggled out of her dress, he removed his waistcoat and untied his neckcloth. She spun around on the bed so that he could reach the strings of her corset. He untied the undergarment, loosened its laces and pulled it over her head. He threw off his shirt and undid the buttons of his pantaloons. Just in her shift, she watched him, her face flushed.

It was bold of her to watch him so brazenly. He felt a surge of pride in her because of it. He enjoyed her heated gaze as he stripped himself of his pantaloons and drawers and stood before her naked. And aroused.

Her eyes did not leave him as she lifted her shift and revealed herself to him. The afternoon light from the window made her skin glow. Her breasts were high and firm and her nipples a dark rose against skin, so smooth it begged for touching. She was lean, but not delicate, her waist narrow, but not tiny, her hips just full enough. He let his gaze wander over her, savouring her like one might savour a fine wine. His eyes lowered to the dark patch of hair between her legs.

He climbed up on the bed and took her in his arms, lifting her on top of him, luxuriating in the feel of those breasts, that skin.

His body urged him to lift her on to his erection and take her quickly, but he forced himself to a slower pace. He did not want to cheat her of her climax. She'd learned of that pleasure in their first lovemaking and he would not deprive her of it now. His pleasure alone was not enough. This time he was determined to show her what pleasure they could create together. He rolled her to his side and stroked her arms, her neck, and let his hand slip down to her breasts.

His palm scraped her nipple and she moaned with pleasure.

This was what he'd longed for between them all those nights when they'd been alone. He'd never truly compromised her, but it was not for want of desiring to. Now she was his wife. He could look forward to night after night like this. Making love. Sharing passion.

He slowly rubbed the tip of her nipple with palm of his hand until she trembled against him. Was there any sensation to compare? This intimate touch. This skin against bare skin.

His hand moved down her body until he fingered her most feminine place. Her legs parted for him and he circled his fingers, feeling her grow wet for him.

As before he slipped his fingers inside her, immediately relishing the sensation of warmth that greeted him. She writhed beneath him, covering his hand with hers as if she feared he would move his away.

No chance of that. He stroked her most sensitive spot, feeling her sensation build, greater and greater. He would show her. He could give her pleasure this way first and still bring her to climax with him inside her. He stroked with his fingers until her glorious spasm erupted.

'Xavier!' Her voice was half-question, half-demand.

He could wait no longer. He needed to be inside her.

'There is more, Phillipa,' he rasped.

'Show me,' she cried.

He rose above her, his erection rock-hard and demanding release, but he banked the urge, instead forcing himself to ease into her slowly. Her body was still unused to this and he wanted to spare her any pain or soreness.

Her hands flattened against his rear, pressing him against her, and her hips rose to meet him.

This was what it meant to be joined with her in marriage. Nothing would put them asunder, he would see to that. Nothing would stop them from making this a marriage even stronger than his parents'. He and Phillipa were meant for each other and had been since they were mere children.

A moment later those thoughts fled, all thought fled. His body moved faster, urgently plunging into her.

She kept pace with him, making it a physical kind of music with him that turned louder, stronger, and stronger still.

He felt her climax, a convulsion around him that drove him over the edge. His seed burst from him, long and gratifying.

He collapsed on top of her and moved to her side before his weight crushed her. He held her against him, never wanting to release her.

'Xavier,' she murmured.

'This is what it will be like for us,' he whispered to her before closing the distance between his lips and hers.

A little later they played the music again. Low and slow, but building to a frenzy of pleasure. He could have gone on to a third performance, but this was enough for one afternoon's interlude.

They had the rest of their married lives to complete the act.

Phillipa lay sated in his arms, her lids and limbs heavy, but her happiness danced upon the ceiling. Was it possible that this was what married life would be like? Could their nights be like this? Their afternoons?

He had desired her in this way. They'd created pleasure together. It was a good place to start making a real marriage.

He grinned at her. 'We have had quite a day, Mrs Campion.'

She sighed. 'Quite a few days.'

Her female parts still throbbed with pleasure. She wondered if they'd created a baby this afternoon. How wonderful that would be! She'd never dreamed she'd have babies of her own, but, because of Xavier, she could dream of it now.

She pressed her hand against her abdomen.

With Xavier anything seemed possible.

They sat propped up against the pillows. 'This is an adequate bedchamber, do you not think?'

A thrill rushed through her. This was *her* bedchamber. They would share their nights together here. 'I think it is a lovely room.'

'We should move in here as soon as possible,' he said.

They talked about hiring servants, how many they would need, agreeing on as few as possible to start.

'I'll contact the agent tomorrow,' he said. 'We can set up the interviews for the next day and perhaps be in this house in three days' time.'

She laughed. 'Will my head never stop spinning?'

He hugged her. 'First thing we move in is your pianoforte.'

Events might still resemble a whirlwind, but one thing was certain. She felt easy with him again. She could say whatever she wished to him and he would always be open with her.

'I have no need of living extravagantly,' she said, confident he would understand. 'In fact, I prefer to live quietly.'

He frowned. 'Do not hide yourself away entirely, Phillipa.'

She dreaded the thought of attending a ball or musicale with him. She could almost hear the talk. *He is so handsome, why did he marry her?*

He hugged her. 'And we must do something for your music. We must see about publishing some of your songs.'

'Do you think they are good enough?' She knew he would tell her the truth.

'To me they seem as good as the other songs you perform,' he replied. 'Some are better.'

She felt a rush of pride and delight.

Perhaps he had been correct. Even though he'd been honour-bound to marry her, perhaps they could be happy together. She loved him and perhaps in his way he loved her, too.

She snuggled against his bare chest and marvelled at the feel of the rough hairs peppering his skin and of the hard muscles beneath.

She had always loved him.

The marred and imperfect Phillipa Westleigh was in love with Xavier Campion, the perfect man.

Chapter Eighteen

It was near the dinner hour when they returned to the Masquerade Club. To Xavier it seemed as if they'd been gone for weeks.

So much had changed between them.

Cummings and MacEvoy did not mark their absence as anything extraordinary, though. Even Phillipa's lady's maid had kept herself busy organising the bedchamber and sorting out their clothes. She'd already put to use the commode that had been delivered from Jeffers's shop.

Perhaps their absence had only been remarkable to the two of them.

Xavier felt altered. Not only was he becalmed as only sexual satiety could accomplish, but he felt hopeful and content. He'd made Phillipa happy today.

He wanted to make her happy every day.

By the time he and Phillipa had changed out of their clothes into their evening attire, dinner was ready and was shared in the comfortable camaraderie they'd engaged in since making love. After dinner they sat in the drawing room. He sipped some brandy and listened to her play her pianoforte, the one that would soon be moved to their own house.

It astonished him how comfortable the time was spent in this manner, as if they had always shared a life together.

When the time came, he left her to attend to the gaming house. Patrons had begun to trickle in, even as the croupiers were still setting up. Because the announcement of his marriage to Phillipa had appeared in the *Morning Post* that morning, he made certain the rest of the gaming-house staff knew of it.

As Phillipa had requested, he did not tell them his wife was the masked lady who played the pianoforte and sang in the supper room. It was a fortunate thing they were soon to be in their own lodgings, because the staff would soon figure out that secret.

He made his rounds, talking with each of the croupiers and receiving their good wishes. He liked that Rhys paid them well and treated them better.

He did not mind running the gaming house now in Rhys's absence. Not now that Phillipa was back. When Rhys returned, though, Xavier wanted to pull back. He'd relish spending his nights with his wife and he wanted to take her to the opera and to concerts. He even wanted to dance with her again at a ball.

'Campion!' Anson, one of the patrons, approached him. 'You devil. I read your announcement in the paper.'

Xavier braced himself. Many of the patrons would have read the *Morning Post*.

'Bit of an epidemic here, is it not?' Anson went on. 'First Rhysdale, now you.'

'We are both lucky men,' Xavier responded.

Anson laughed. 'Except Rhysdale's off on a bride trip and you are stuck here.'

Xavier smiled. 'There is that.'

Anson leaned towards him conspiratorially. 'I wonder how Lady Faville will take this news.'

It was too much to expect that others had not noticed Daphne's single-minded obsession with him.

'I must say,' the man continued, 'I always thought she would be the one to get you in the parson's mousetrap. I am certain she always thought so, too.'

'I always made it clear to her that would never happen.' That sounded harsh, but it was the truth.

Another patron came up to them. 'Campion! Leg-shackled, are you? The Earl of Westleigh's daughter? What a coincidence, eh? The man who cheated his own son here.'

'We have known each other for many years,' Xavier explained.

The man gestured to his own face. 'Isn't she the disfigured one? Scarred on the face? Can't imagine a man like you with her.'

Xavier's eyes flashed. 'Why not?'

The man stuttered, 'D-d-don't know why. Just didn't.' He made a hasty exit.

Anson spoke. 'Damned idiot.'

'Indeed.' Xavier had nearly put his fist in the man's face.

'Expect you will hear that sort of thing more than once tonight.' Anson sounded genuinely sympathetic. He poked Xavier with his elbow. 'Take care. Here is Lady Faville.'

Daphne paused in the doorway only long enough to find Xavier in the room. She marched on him like a column of Napoleon's soldiers.

'Xavier, I would speak with you alone, please.' She sounded near tears.

'I am working, Daphne.' He did not wish to speak with her at all.

'I said alone, *please*.' She glared at Anson.

Anson, thank God, showed no inclination to move away.

Xavier also did not budge. 'Say what you have to say here.'

She sent another scathing look towards Anson before riveting her gaze on Xavier. 'Tell me that foolish wedding announcement in the *Morning Post* was a hoax.'

'I placed it myself,' he told her. 'I am married to Lady Phillipa Westleigh.'

'It cannot be!' Her voice rose. 'She is an ugly old thing! A recluse.'

Xavier glared down at her. 'Daphne, you are speaking of my wife.'

She waved her hand as if to shoo away his words. 'You cannot mean to defend her! Did she trap you? Did you need money? You should have told me. I have money! I have lots of money!'

'I need money,' Lord Anson said.

She tossed Anson another withering glance and turned back to Xavier. 'I cannot bear this. I cannot. You led me to believe—'

He held up a hand. 'I led you to believe nothing. I have been honest with you from the first night you appeared here. You simply chose not to listen to me.'

'You were not serious,' she countered. 'We were in love.'

'We were not in love, Daphne!' he snapped.

She went on as if he had not spoken. 'You should have told me you were about to be married! I would have helped you.'

'You are speaking nonsense now.'

She fell against his chest. 'I am desolate.'

He seized her wrists. 'Enough, Daphne. Stop making a fool of yourself. Calm yourself or I'll be forced to have Cummings remove you.'

She immediately stilled. He released her and walked away.

After Xavier left, Phillipa sat at the pianoforte and tried to recreate the rhythm of their lovemaking. She played the lower keys, starting slow, then increasing the tempo. It wasn't quite right, but it replayed it in her head, as well as her time with Xavier replayed in her head.

When she looked up at the clock on the mantel it was almost her usual time to appear in the supper room. She hurried to get ready, tying the ribbons of her mask last thing. Before she descended the stairs, she watched from the second floor to be certain no one would see her coming from the private rooms. The hallway below her was empty so she hurried down the stairs, stopping a moment to compose herself before entering the supper room.

Upon seeing her, several of the gentlemen stood. 'Miss Songstress, you are here again!'

Several of them walked over to her, greeting her warmly and making requests of specific musical pieces she had played before.

Two of the pieces were her own works, which made her smile.

'Please sit, gentlemen,' she said. 'Give me time to prepare.'

'Did you read in the *Morning Post* that Campion is married?' one of the gentlemen asked.

'I knew of it,' she said quietly.

She sat on the bench and put her music in order, but bits of conversation from the tables reached her ears—*Campion married…Lord Westleigh's girl…scarred.*

Lady Faville flounced up to her. 'Miss Songstress, I am in such need of a friend!' She sounded greatly distressed. 'Do you know what has happened?'

'What?' Phillipa just wanted to play her music and wait for Xavier.

'He is married!' Lady Faville's voice cracked. 'Xavier is married. What am I to do?'

'I do not know.' At least the woman did not know it was Miss Songstress who had married him.

'He is married to Lady Phillipa Westleigh and I am certain he is made unhappy over it.'

Phillipa tensed. 'Why are you certain he is unhappy?'

The lady blinked. 'Of course, you would not know. Lady Phillipa is a monster.'

Phillipa felt her face flush. 'A monster?'

Lady Faville nodded vigorously, her artful blond curls bobbing prettily. 'I should say she looks a monster. She has a horrible scar that distorts her face.'

Phillipa's hand rose. She stopped herself before touching her face. 'Have you seen her?' She did not recall ever having met Lady Faville before the Masquerade Club.

'Once. I saw her in a shop. I asked who was the deformed creature looking through the music sheets.' Lady Faville lowered herself to the bench right next to Phillipa. 'How could he have chosen to marry her? He must have been forced.'

Had he been forced? Forced by honour. By her mother? Had he preferred Lady Faville? The optimism Phillipa felt moments ago crashed to the floor and shattered.

She turned back to her music. 'My lady, I am sorry for your disappointment, but I must play the music now.'

Lady Faville squeezed her hand affectionately. 'I will leave you, then, but I know you will find out the reason he married, will you not? I am depending upon you.'

The lady rose and walked off before Phillipa could refuse.

Phillipa's hands shook as she placed her fingers on the keys. Instead of the rousing tune she'd planned to play to open her performance, she began to play Beethoven's *Moonlight Sonata*. Though she'd intended it to calm her nerves, the underlying emotion in the piece merely unsettled her more.

She transitioned to a gavotte by Hook.

Lady Faville eventually left the supper room. She'd taken Mr Everard with her, so Phillipa could only think the lady had left the gaming house as well. That was some relief.

She'd left her words behind her.

It seemed the supper room remained abuzz with news of Xavier's marriage. She overheard it over and over. He could have had any woman. Why marry her, scarred as she was? Such a marriage was destined to be notorious, they said. It would be forever talked about.

She played through her usual time for a break, because she needed the music to ease her spirit and also because she had no wish to hear more about the marriage of handsome, eligible Xavier Campion to the scarred spinster daughter of a dissolute earl.

By the end, her music calmed her and the applause gratified her and she'd reassured herself that her marriage would not be forever talked about. It might remain notorious, but people would tire of it and go on to gossip about other things. At least, wearing a mask, she'd not been required to endure the inevitable stares. People who'd forever tried not to look at her would now wish to examine her to see why Xavier could possibly pick her for a wife.

She curtsied to the patrons and stacked her music to take upstairs with her. As she walked through the supper room, several gentlemen stopped her to compliment her on her play. In those first days of performing in the supper room she'd enjoyed such attention. This night she merely wished to make her escape and return to the bedchamber above. Lacey would assist her in dressing for bed and afterwards Phillipa would wait for Xavier.

She finally reached the hallway, but needed to wait for it to clear.

When she finally thought she might make it to the upper floor unseen, she heard hurried footsteps on the stairs below. Lady Faville appeared, rushing up to her.

The lady was all smiles. 'There you are! I knew I would find you still here.' She laughed. 'Xavier is still here and he escorts you home, does he not?'

'Not always,' Phillipa said stiffly.

If Lady Faville noticed that Xavier did not leave the gaming house, she might have a clue that Phillipa had not left either.

'I have to leave,' Lady Faville said. 'I wanted to find you. I wanted to tell you that I arranged for Xavier to meet me tomorrow! Is that not grand?' She danced with excitement. 'I must give up the notion of marriage, of course, but marriages are not love, are they? Love can never be extinguished.' She made a dramatic transition from giddiness to tragic solemnity. 'If the only way we can be together is as lovers, then so be it.' She hugged Phillipa. 'Goodnight, then, my dear Miss Songstress. Tomorrow night I will tell you all about my tryst with Xavier!'

Lady Faville released Phillipa so quickly she pushed against her and Phillipa, standing right at the top of the stairs, almost lost her balance. She grabbed for the railing to keep from falling. Lady Faville did not even notice. In a flurry of skirts, she hurried down the stairs and out of sight.

Shaken again, Phillipa's vision grew dark and she smelled the briny scent of the sea. The scene changed and she was no longer at the top of the gaming-house stairs. She was running up the stone stairs of the sea wall.

Until someone turned and pushed her and her hand found nothing to grip.

Chapter Nineteen

When the gaming room thinned to only a few patrons, Xavier asked Cummings and MacEvoy to take care of things and to tend to the closing up.

'Eager to get to bed, then,' grinned MacEvoy.

'Very eager,' admitted Xavier.

In his good humour, he did not even care that MacEvoy's comment was a bit too familiar. He wanted to bound up the stairs, but took them at a sedate pace, which probably did not fool the clerk.

He opened the bedchamber door quietly. There was still a lamp burning, but Phillipa was in bed and did not move, even with the sound of the door closing.

He paused to look at her, sleeping on her side, curled up like a girl. She lay on the scarred side of her face and it gave him an idea of how she might have appeared had she never been injured.

She was beautiful to him, even with her scar, and she looked so innocent and peaceful, he did not have the heart to wake her.

He hurried to ready himself for bed, trying to be as quiet as he could be. Like the night before, he must content himself with sleeping next to her and waking in the morning with her at his side.

He extinguished the lamp and climbed into bed. In the dim light from the fireplace, he watched her sleep and remembered how it felt to make love to her.

He brushed a curl from her face and her eyes opened.

'You are here.' Her voice was husky from sleep.

He pulled her into his arms and kissed her. Sleep made her pliable in his arms, but also gave her an expression of melancholy. He knew what that felt like, too tired to smile. He promised not to tax her, he would be content to merely hold her, but he wanted the warmth of her skin against his.

She stirred in his arms, urging him on top of her.

She wanted him? He was delighted to indulge her.

She opened to him and he eased inside her, joining himself to her again. He moved slowly, unhurried now, relishing the feel of being inside her. He felt the moment she became aroused by him, how it changed her, woke her to move with him.

This sense of melancholy lingered, although it made making love to her even more poignant. Whatever its cause, even mere sleepiness, he wished to free her of it with his body. Perhaps through his lovemaking he could erase all the pain inside her. From her scars. From her abominable family. From everyone and everything that had ever hurt her.

He was willing to try. More than willing to try.

He'd had his share of bedding women. Not as many as some might suspect, but he'd had some very erotic moments with some of them, starting with the days of his youth. Those women had taken what they wanted from him.

Phillipa was the first woman he'd wanted to give everything to. He wanted to convince her she was worthy of the love he felt toward her.

The sensation intensified and their pace quickened. This

time, he did not lead her, but rather took his cues from her, responding to her every move.

With my body I thee worship. Was that not part of his wedding vow?

That was what he aspired to in this moment. He worshipped her with his body and hoped, in the end, she would feel adored.

But with the next thrust, her next rising against him, arousal took over and pushed him past the time of stopping or slowing. He rushed past the time of thinking. His need took over. It drove him into her, again and again, faster and faster, until the tortuous peak was reached and he convulsed inside her.

When he pressed against her in that final release of his seed, she cried out and he felt her reach her peak a moment after his.

As they both crashed down from that heaven, he held her tightly. He never wanted to let her go.

He loved her. He'd loved her when she was a child, but then it was as a brother loves a sister, a friend loves a friend, but from that evening before he'd been called back to war when he'd danced with her at a ball, he'd loved her as a man loves a woman.

Some day he would tell her this. Some day when she would believe him.

She mumbled something he could not understand.

'What did you say?' He wanted to add *my love*, but feared she would not yet believe even that endearment.

She answered him, only a little more clearly. 'Lady Faville.'

Daphne? Why the devil would she ask about Daphne? 'What about her?'

'Will see you tomorrow.'

He made a disparaging sound. 'Undoubtedly.' Would he

ever convince Daphne to give up her fixation on him? She was a poison he and Phillipa did not need.

'Forget about Lady Faville,' he told her.

'Can't forget.' She sounded as if she were drifting to sleep. She mumbled something else. He caught one word only when she repeated it.

'Pushed,' she said. 'Pushed.'

When Phillipa woke the next morning, Xavier was leaning down to give her a kiss. He was fully dressed.

'I have to help MacEvoy,' he told her. 'Some problem with the figures. We need to work it out with the bank. Do not fear, I'll stop by the agent's on my way back and arrange for the servant interviews.'

'You are going to the bank?' Her mind was not yet clear. 'Only the bank?'

'One or two other errands, as well,' he said cryptically. 'I'll be back in a couple of hours, if all goes well. If not, it might be later.'

He kissed her a second time and was gone.

She lay back down in the bed. She remembered that he made love to her. It had been like a dream, all soft edges like sad music played pianissimo. She remembered asking him about Lady Faville. Had he answered her? She could not remember.

Was meeting Lady Faville one of Xavier's errands?

Phillipa suddenly could not tolerate another moment in bed, a bed still filled with the scent of him. She rose and summoned Lacey to help her dress.

While Lacey chatted with her, Phillipa's mind whirled. Was he meeting Lady Faville?

He was honest with her, even when no one else would be, but would he tell her if he were arranging a romantic tryst? What man would?

No. She could not believe it of him. She could not believe he would make love to her at night and plan to see another woman in the day. That was the sort of thing her father would do to her mother. Xavier was honest and honourable, not at all like her father.

As Lacey finished arranging her hair, her doubts still nagged at her, but something else waited inside her like unplayed notes.

When she was finished dressing and walked out of the room to the top of the stairs, she remembered. She gripped the railing.

She remembered being pushed. She remembered being pushed away by Lady Faville. She remembered being pushed away on a sea wall in Brighton.

She hurried down the stairs. Could she still catch Xavier? She had to tell him. She remembered. After all this time, she remembered what had happened at Brighton.

Cummings was attending the hall.

'Is Xavier still here?' she asked.

'No,' Cummings answered. 'Went out.'

'How long ago?' Maybe she could catch up to him.

'Quarter-hour.'

That was too long of a head start. 'Did he say where he was going?'

'Bank.'

That was consistent. She could try to catch up to him at the bank—

No, that was ridiculous. She did not have to chase him all over London. She could just as easily tell him when he returned.

She glanced at the stairway and the memory again flashed through her mind.

In fact, there was something she could do first, before telling him.

'Cummings, I must go out, too. If Mr Campion returns before I do, tell him I am calling on my mother. I will not be long.'

Phillipa walked alone to her mother's house, remembering the nights that she and Xavier had walked the same route in darkness. So much had happened since then.

She passed Brunton Mews, where they'd been attacked. This time she smiled, thinking how Xavier had made something good out of the horrible experience, the experience that also jarred loose Phillipa's memories. And now she knew more of what had happened.

Today, she hoped, she could put it all to rest.

She reached the familiar door on Davies Street and sounded the knocker.

Mason answered. 'My lady!' His unguarded pleasure at seeing her quickly changed to concern. 'Is anything amiss?'

She stepped inside. 'Nothing at all,' she told him, pounding those niggling doubts. 'I wish to see my mother. Is she at home?'

'She is in her sitting room,' he told her. 'With the general.'

'Of course.' She smiled. 'No need to announce me. I'll just go on up.'

She climbed the stairs and rapped on her mother's sitting room door.

'Come in.' Her mother's voice.

She entered. 'Hello, Mama.'

Her mother's face brightened and she rose. 'Phillipa!' Her eyes narrowed in suspicion. 'What are you doing here?'

'I wished to speak with you.'

The general had been seated near her mother. He stood.

'Good day, General,' she said. 'I am glad to see you here.'

Both he and her mother looked surprised at her words.

He glanced from her to her mother. 'Shall I leave you alone, my dear?'

'No, stay,' Phillipa said to him.

He was part of the memory.

Her mother sat again. 'I will not hear you complain of your marriage. What is done is done.'

'It is not about my marriage.' She sat.

'What is it then? A social call?' Her mother's tone turned sarcastic.

'No.' She took off her hat. 'I want to talk with you about this.' She touched her scar.

Her mother dipped her head and looked concerned. 'What do you mean?'

'I mean about how it happened.'

'You know how it happened.' Her mother spoke by rote. 'You went to the beach alone and you fell from the steps of the sea wall.'

'That is what you told me all these years, Mama. But it is not what happened.'

Her mother and the general exchanged worried glances.

Phillipa went on. 'I followed *you* to the seaside that evening, Mama.' She turned to General Henson. 'You were there, too. You were quarrelling with each other. The general strode away and, Mama, you ran after him.' She paused. 'I ran after you.'

Her mother gripped one hand with the other.

Phillipa trembled. 'I ran up the steps, trying to catch you, but you turned and shoved me.'

A gasp escaped her mother's lips. 'I will throttle him,' she muttered.

'You pushed me away, Mama,' Phillipa repeated. 'And I lost my balance and fell down the stairs. How could you keep such a thing secret from me?' Her mother opened her mouth to speak, but Phillipa stopped her. 'And do not dare tell me it was for my own protection.'

'Of course it was to protect you,' her mother snapped.

'She did not mean for you to be hurt,' the general added. 'It was an accident.'

'You were little and you did not remember,' her mother cried. 'Why would I tell you such a thing?'

'You could have told me when I got older,' Phillipa countered. 'You could have told me when I asked a few weeks ago. I wanted the truth, Mama.'

'It was more complicated than that,' her mother insisted.

'Were you afraid the story would become gossip? Were you afraid your friends would know you pushed your daughter down the steps?' Phillipa went on. 'Perhaps you were not protecting me, but protecting yourself.'

'She was protecting me,' the general broke in. 'She did not want her husband to find out she was with me.'

Phillipa's mother stood and waved her hands in front of her as if to make them both stop. 'It was neither of those things! You were such a beautiful child and I had disfigured you for life! Did you think I would want you to know it? To hate me for ever? I was your mother. Goodness knows you had no father to speak of. You needed me. I could not have you thinking I could hurt you like that.'

Phillipa was struck at the intensity of her mother's emotions.

The general shot to his feet and put his arm around her. He coaxed her mother back to sitting.

She dabbed at her eyes with a handkerchief. 'It was best you went on thinking you fell, that it was just something that happened to you. I tried very hard not to let you think it would mar your chances in life, but you just had to look in your mirror to know it.' She shuddered. 'You were never going to find your rightful place in life. All because of what I'd done. You would never forgive me.'

Phillipa lowered her voice. 'Mama, I could always forgive what was an accident. What I cannot forgive is how you have kept the truth from me. About this. About our financial problems. About what my father did. About the gaming house. And Rhysdale! I had a brother. You all knew I had a brother and you did not tell me.'

Her mother pursed her lips. 'You had enough burdens. You did not have to know of all the other horrible things.'

'She did it to make life easier for you,' the general said.

'I did not need to have life made easier for me,' Phillipa insisted. 'I have always been strong. As strong as my brothers. I did not need to be treated differently.'

'But you were different,' her mother said. 'You were damaged. And it was my fault! I made it up to you as best I could.'

'My face was damaged, Mama, not me.' Phillipa stood. 'And if making it up to me meant keeping secrets from me and manipulating my life, it has to stop. Do you hear me?'

Her mother glared defiantly.

Phillipa took a breath. It was too much to expect a simple apology from her mother, a simple acknowledgement that her mother had wronged her. It must be enough that the truth was out. Finally.

She picked up her hat and curtsied to her mother. 'That is all I came to say. I will take my leave.'

The general walked ahead of her to reach the door first.

When he opened it and Phillipa put one foot on the threshold, her mother's critical tone returned. 'Tell that husband of yours I wish to see him. I will have words with him.'

Phillipa turned. 'You wish to talk to Xavier? About what?'

Her mother blinked rapidly. 'About this.'

'What about this?' There was more her mother was not telling her.

Her mother gave her a haughty look. 'I wish to tell your husband he is a dishonourable wretch. He had the gall to reveal what he promised to keep secret.'

'Keep secret?' She was confused. 'What did he promise to keep secret?'

'Bad business,' added the general. 'Not at all the thing to break a solemn vow.'

'What solemn vow?' Her voice rose.

'Come now.' Her mother huffed. 'Did he not tell you that he swore he would never tell what he saw that day? I suppose he didn't include that piece of it.' She jabbed the air with her finger. 'Why he renewed that promise just yesterday! That goes to show how much he can be trusted. What does he do? Say one thing, then hurry up to do the other?'

'What he saw?' she repeated, still unable to believe the words. 'He saw what happened?'

'Sneaking around in the dark,' muttered the general. 'Spying on people. Had no business doing that either.'

Xavier had been there that day?

'Well, do not believe a word he says. That is my advice to you.' Her mother picked up her needlework, apparently considering the conversation closed. She glanced to the general. 'It is a rare man you can trust.'

Phillipa strode back to her mother. 'If ever you tell me the truth, I beg you do so now. Was Xavier there that day? Did he see my accident?'

Her mother looked annoyed. 'Do not act the fool, Phillipa. You know he was there. How else could you know what happened? You were blessed with no memory of it. God knows why he was not at home. A boy his age should have been, instead of spying on people in the dark. He was old enough to know about vowing to keep something secret, though.'

Phillipa trembled inside, but she forced herself to speak. 'He did not break his vow to you,' she said, because that was the truth. 'I remembered what happened.'

Phillipa walked out of the room without another word. If her mother or the general said more to her, she could not even hear it. She numbly made her way to the stairs and paused, holding on to the railing for support.

Xavier had been there the day of her accident. He had seen what happened to her and, with all her struggles and fears about the memories bombarding her, he had said nothing to her. Because of some promise he made as a boy? Surely that did not count over what she had suffered? She'd thought herself insane because of the visions.

Mason was not in the hall. Or if he was, she did not see him. She let herself out, her mother's words ringing in her ears. *Do not believe a word he says.*

Chapter Twenty

Xavier hurried the last few steps to the gaming house. MacEvoy had gone on ahead while he stopped at the agent's office to arrange for the servant interviews. From there he'd made a quick trip to Cheapside to check on the candle shop. The candle maker told him a space had come available that would work for the ironmonger, so Xavier told the man to arrange for him to meet the landlord and ironmonger at the space. Perhaps that shop would be started soon as well.

Three shops. It was a good beginning, but there was always more he could do.

Xavier was finally free the rest of the day, such as it was. He was eager to get home to his wife and tell her what he'd accomplished.

Perhaps they might visit their new house again for an hour or two of lovemaking? He grinned and raised his face to the September sun before knocking on the town house door.

Cummings opened it for him.

'Thank you, Cummings,' he said in good spirits. 'How do you fare today?'

Cummings merely shrugged, but he also pointed to the hall table. 'A note came.'

Xavier picked it up and unfolded it.

The signature jumped out at him—*Yours, always, Daphne*.

He certainly had no interest in whatever she had written. He folded the note and climbed the stairs to the drawing room where he assumed he'd find Phillipa.

She was not there.

He looked in the bedchamber. The curtains were drawn and no lamps were lit. Where was she? He was about to leave the room when he spied Phillipa deep in the recesses of a wingback chair.

'Phillipa.' He dropped the note on a nearby table and walked over to her. Leaning down to kiss her on her forehead, he allowed his lips to linger a moment. 'Why are you sitting in the dark?'

'I was waiting for you.' Her voice was low and without tone.

'I hope not long.' He stepped over to the windows. 'Do you mind if I open the curtains?'

'No,' was all she said.

He tied back the curtains and the room flooded with light. He turned back to her.

She looked pale, so pale her scar shone more prominently.

'Are you unwell?' He crouched to her level and took her hands in his.

Her hands were cold.

She pulled them away and met his eyes. 'I called upon my mother today.'

He braced himself to hear of another cruelty her mother had inflicted upon her.

Her gaze drifted away and back. 'I remembered something. I remembered what happened in Brighton. How I fell. My mother pushed me down the steps.'

Yes. He could see it all again. Little Phillipa running

after her mother who wanted only to catch up to the general. Xavier knew he should stop her from running up the slippery steps, but he stayed where he was while her small legs worked hard to climb after her mother. Phillipa grabbed at her mother's skirts. Her mother whirled around and pushed her away.

He felt the horror again of seeing little Phillipa fall down the stone steps and land hard on the rocky beach below. He was the first to reach her. He saw the blood pooling under her cheek.

Phillipa spoke and he jolted back to the present. 'You were there, Xavier. My mother said you were there. She accused you of telling me what happened.'

He nodded. 'I was there.' He had no need to hide it now.

She leaned forwards. 'Why did you not tell me?' Her voice shook with anger. 'Why did you not tell me when you knew the memories were returning?'

His excuse seemed weak. 'I had sworn not to.'

'You were a boy. Why was a boy's promise more important than me? I thought I was going insane. Remember?' She choked. 'You knew how it shook me. The memories. The not knowing.'

'I wanted to tell you.' But honour was honour. A promise was a promise, no matter what age it was made. 'I gave my word not to.'

'I despise being *protected* from the truth,' she said hotly. 'You, more than anyone else, knew that.'

He stood. 'I told you as much as I could, Phillipa.'

'I thought about this,' she went on. 'You've kept other secrets. Like about meeting Jeffers and helping him.'

'I told you,' he protested.

'Not when it happened. Only after we married.' She rose from the chair.

'Did it make a difference to you?' His temper was flaring. He was honest with her. When he could be. Not when he'd given his word. 'Yesterday you did not mind me owning shops.'

'I do not mind it,' she shot back. 'I mind that you did not tell me when you first encountered him again.'

'I thought it would upset you,' he admitted.

'You wished to protect me.' She crossed her arms over her chest.

'No,' he answered. 'Yes. Yes. I wished to protect you from thinking of that night. At least until I knew what use he would make of the opportunity.'

'What else are you keeping from me?' she challenged.

'Nothing.' At least he could think of nothing. Only the events of the morning, which he'd not had a chance to mention. And some things that happened in war about which no soldier spoke.

'Nothing?' She lifted her chin. 'What about Lady Faville?'

'Lady Faville?' He forced an even tone. 'She is not important enough to speak of. If you wish to know my connection to her in the past, I will tell you, but I assure you, it is of no consequence to me now.'

'Are you not going to call upon her today?' Her voice wobbled.

He spoke through gritted teeth. 'She is the last person I would call upon.'

'You planned a meeting with her today. She told me.'

Leave it to Daphne to cause trouble. 'I planned nothing with her.'

Phillipa looked more wounded than angry. 'Do not tell me she means nothing to you. I've seen her with you so often here at the gaming house. She is always on your arm—'

'Not by my choice.'

She took in a shuddering breath. 'She believes you were

trapped into marriage with me. She believes you still love her as you once loved her.'

He looked her directly in the eye. 'I never loved her.'

She turned away.

He seized her and made her look at him again. 'Phillipa, I care nothing for her.'

She glanced to the note on the table. 'I was in the hall when the messenger arrived. I took that note from him. I read it and gave it to Cummings to give to you.'

He felt the blood drain from his face. 'Good God, what did it say, Phillipa? I did not read it.'

'She says she will see you today as planned.'

He released her and ran a hand through his hair. 'This is madness. Why would you believe her and not me?'

She avoided looking at him. 'Because what she says makes sense. It makes sense that you would fall in love with her. You must admit that you would have never married me if it had not been for my mother's manipulations.'

'I will not admit that, Phillipa.' She'd refused to be convinced.

She pointed to the mirror. 'Look at yourself. You are so handsome, and she is so beautiful...' She lifted her hand to her face and covered her scar. 'I am not.'

His stomach suddenly felt as if filled with lead shot.

He turned away from her and walked to the window to compose himself. He heard her sink back into the chair.

He remained at the window as he spoke. 'You are like her. Like Daphne. Appearances are all that matter to you. I am not like that.' He turned to her. 'Your scar has never meant a thing to me. I do not think of it when I think of you. How it has hurt you matters to me. How it has affected the treatment you receive from your mother and other people matters to me. I do want to protect you from unhappiness; I admit that and I do not apologise for it. If I give my word to keep a secret, I will keep that secret. I admit that, as well. I keep my word. And I try to do what is right.' His chest ached as he spoke. 'If you cannot see that about me and can only look at my face, I do not know how to go on.'

She glanced up at him and quickly turned away.

He left the room.

Phillipa remained in her the chair, his last words stinging in her ears. When she heard him open the door she swivelled around and watched him leave her.

Anxiety clutched at her throat.

She rose from the chair and paced the room.

What was she to believe?

So much evidence on one side. Only his word on the other.

She lowered herself on to her chair at the dressing table and peered into the mirror. Her reflection was so well lit by the light from the window, she could see every tiny line on her face, every eyelash, every inch of her scar.

Had he been correct?

For all her self-moaning and protestations about how people only saw her scar, was that all she saw of herself, as well?

She touched her scar and leaned closer to the mirror to examine it.

She'd prided herself on accepting her scar and the limitations it placed on her life. Had she really done so? Or was it the first thing she thought of when she thought of herself? It certainly was the first thing she thought of when anyone looked at her.

Did she not think of her scar no matter what she experienced?

So what if the most handsome man in the ballroom had been coerced into dancing with her? Was that only about her scar? Other young ladies in their first Season were set up with dance partners. She was the one who attributed it to her scar. And, even if that dance had been only about her scar, she was the one who used it as an excuse to leave. How might that ball have been different for her if she'd stayed and merely enjoyed herself?

She rose from the dressing table and walked over to a table near the window where she'd left some music. She picked up one sheet and played the notes in her head.

Surely her music was unrelated to her scar.

She threw the sheet down again and sank her head in her hands.

Her music had everything to do with her scar. It was her distraction from it. Her way to hide.

Her excuse to hide.

The truth was she defined where she could go, what she could do, who she could speak to, by the presence of her scar.

By her appearance, just as Xavier had accused.

He'd said the same of Lady Faville.

If Phillipa's scar was always foremost in her mind, perhaps Lady Faville's beauty was all she thought of herself? It was all anyone ever noticed about her. All Phillipa noticed about her.

Phillipa was suddenly sad for the woman. In her way Lady Faville had tried very hard to make her a friend. What if Phillipa had embraced that friendship? Perhaps she could have done the lady some good. Steered her away from Xavier and towards someone who could love her.

Assuming Xavier did not love her.

Phillipa walked to the bed and leaned against the bedpost, holding on to it as if it were the mast of a boat being tossed by stormy waves. She glanced at the bed, in contrast to her emotions so tidy, showing no signs of their lovemaking.

She stared at it, not a wrinkle on its cover. Its appearance certainly deceived.

She closed her eyes and remembered the tangled bed linens, the feel of his hands upon her skin, the firmness of his muscled body, the thrill of him entering her and making them one.

Could men lie during lovemaking? Could Xavier have pretended such tenderness towards her? Could he falsify the glow in his eyes as he gazed at her naked body? Would he have held her all night if all he'd wanted was a release?

She pushed herself away from the bed and returned to the mirror.

Could she convince herself that he had made love to her because of her scar? That he saw only her scar when he gazed upon her?

She could not.

She gasped, covering her hand with her mouth.

Do not believe a word he says, her mother said, but her mother was wrong about him.

Phillipa was wrong about him.

She loved that he'd refused to allow her to walk the streets of Mayfair alone at night, even though she protested. She loved that he arranged for her to continue at the gaming house after the attack, because he knew it meant a great deal to her. She loved his loyalty to Rhys—Xavier had managed the Masquerade Club nearly as long as Rhys. She loved Xavier's forgiveness of Jeffers, his kindness in helping him and other soldiers. She loved that he cared about her happiness.

She even loved his sense of honour, although it truly hurt that he'd not told her of Brighton.

And, yes, she did love his smile, his blue eyes, his glorious body, but they appeared pretty far down her list.

'I must tell him,' she cried aloud. 'I must tell him before it is too late! Even if he never forgives me, I must tell him he is wrong.'

She loved him for far more than his appearance.

She hurried out the door, determined to find him.

Chapter Twenty-One

Xavier needed a walk out of doors. To clear his head. Quiet his emotions. Help him forget what just happened.

Help him decide what to do.

What could he do? He was married to her.

He loved her.

Which was why it was so cursed painful that he'd misjudged her.

No matter that their wedding day had been a delight. No matter that they'd made love in the afternoon. No matter that he'd done everything he could think of to see to her happiness. Her regard for him was as shallow as any woman's.

He descended the stairs and reached the hall where Cummings was in attendance.

'Did she find you?' Cummings asked.

'Who?' One of the servants? A croupier? He had no wish to deal with anyone. Just let him be alone for awhile.

'That Lady Faville.' Cummings spoke with disapproval, using more expression than was his habit.

'Lady Faville?' What the devil was *she* doing here? First the note, now the visit.

'Said she knew where to find you.' Cummings shrugged. 'Went upstairs.'

Not to the private floor. He would have seen her. Good God. He needed to find her before she encountered Phillipa.

He took the stairs two at a time and checked the gaming room first, but it was empty. The supper room was next.

He opened the door and immediately saw that a lamp was burning on one of the tables. She was there, standing decoratively near the room's fireplace.

'Xavier!' she cried. 'I knew you would come!'

She ran to him and flung herself into his arms, smashing her lips against his.

He twisted around trying to extricate himself.

And saw Phillipa standing in the doorway.

'Xavier.' Her voice was barely audible.

He peeled Daphne off him. 'Wait, Phillipa. This is not as it seems.'

'It is as it appears to be,' cried Daphne in a triumphant voice. 'We were kissing.'

'Be quiet, Daphne,' Xavier snapped.

She seized his arm again. 'Is this your *wife*, Xavier?' She spoke the word *wife* as if it tasted rancid. 'Will you present her to me?'

'No.' He pried her hand from his sleeve. 'Leave.'

'Of course she must leave,' Daphne said, twisting his meaning. 'But it would be polite to formally introduce us first.'

'We have already met.' Phillipa stepped into the room and Xavier could not read her expression.

'We have not met.' Daphne gestured towards Phillipa's scar. 'I assure you I would have remembered.'

That was cruel. Xavier started to step in.

But Phillipa spoke first and, to his surprise, her tone was kind. 'I assure you we have met.' She covered her face with her hands as if they were a mask. 'You called me your friend.'

Daphne's eyes widened. 'Miss Songstress? But—but you pretended to be someone else.'

'I did not pretend to be someone else. I told you all along that I wished to protect my identity.' She smiled sympathetically. 'I am afraid that included not letting you know my connection to Xavier.'

'It was uncivil of you.' Daphne turned to him. 'Xavier, would you ask her to leave? I must see you alone.'

'She is my wife.' Xavier liked saying it. 'I will not ask her to leave.'

'You think you are being kind to her, Xavier,' Daphne insisted. 'But she should know the truth about how we feel about each other, about how you felt forced to marry her.' She swallowed as if experiencing intense emotion. 'About how we *love* each other.'

Phillipa looked past Daphne, directly into his eyes. 'Xavier?' Her voice was low and surprisingly calm. 'If you want her, I will not stand in your way.'

He returned her gaze. 'Phillipa, she's talking nonsense.'

'Do not say so!' Daphne's voice rose an octave. 'You love me, Xavier. You have loved me for years. Since our first meeting.'

Was the woman mad? 'Daphne.' He tried to speak gently to her, as Phillipa had done. 'There are many men who come here who, I suspect, are in love with you. But not me.'

She looked confused. 'You want me—'

'I do not want you, Daphne. Please believe me.' He turned to Phillipa and feared she would not believe him either. 'Phillipa, I love you. Forgive me. I spoke to you in anger before.'

Phillipa held his gaze. 'There is nothing to forgive. You were correct. At least in part.'

His muscles relaxed. 'I want you, Phillipa. Only you.'

* * *

Phillipa stared at him, the words *I want you* echoing in her ears. She did not need to hear anything else.

He went on, though. 'I did not ask Daphne to come here. I have nothing to hide regarding her. You must believe me in this.' He turned back to Lady Faville. 'Leave us now, Daphne. Please.'

Lady Faville's lip trembled. Phillipa now felt nothing but pity for her.

'You cannot prefer her over me,' Lady Faville cried. 'She is grotesque! And you and I will look perfect together.'

Her words still wounded.

Xavier's eyes flashed. 'I will not have my wife insulted. This ends now, Daphne. Do not come back. I will find someone to escort you home, if you wish, but you must go.'

Lady Faville looked afflicted.

Xavier softened his tone. 'It would be best if you do not come back, as well.'

Lady Faville dug in her heels. 'I will not leave. Not until I have spoken to you alone.'

'Then we will leave.' Xavier put his hand on Phillipa's back and leaned close to her ear. 'We need to end this with her.'

She nodded, more eager to be alone with him than Lady Faville could possibly be.

They walked towards the door.

'No!' Lady Faville stamped her foot. It sounded as if she pushed over a piece of furniture. 'I will not let you leave me!'

Glass shattered behind them. They whirled around to the sight of flames.

She'd thrown the lighted lamp. Its oil and fire scattered. A curtain caught fire. Xavier ran to it and pulled it down.

Lady Faville screamed and backed away in a panic. The

hem of her skirt was on fire and she was shaking it, making it worse.

'Stop her!' Xavier cried, attempting frantically to smother the flaming curtain.

Phillipa grabbed her and struggled with her, knocking her to the floor and beating out the flames. Lady Faville screamed throughout. When Phillipa released her, she scrambled to her feet and ran out the door.

'Get help!' Xavier cried.

The fire had spread to another curtain. And another. Phillipa ran to one of them and pulled it down. He battled with the other.

'Get out!' Xavier cried. 'Don't stay here.'

'No!' There was too much fire for one person to fight.

'Phillipa, go!' he cried again.

'No!' She grabbed a tablecloth and tried to beat out the small flames with it. The cloth itself caught fire and she slapped out the flame with her hands. The smoke stung her eyes and burned her throat. She was very aware that her own skirts could go up in flames, but the idea of leaving Xavier alone with the fire, risking him being engulfed in flames, was too terrible to endure.

'Phillipa, run,' his voice rasped. 'Grab your music and run. We might lose the house.'

Her music? What good was her music if she lost him?

There was a bucket of sand by the fireplace. She carried it to the fire and scooped handfuls of it on to one flame after another.

The carpet caught fire.

'Help me!' Xavier cried. He pushed the furniture away.

She ran to him and together they rolled up the carpet, smothering the flames inside it.

A voice came from the doorway. 'What? Fire!' It was Cummings, who immediately jumped in to help.

'Leave now, Phillipa,' Xavier ordered. 'Get more help.'

This time she obeyed. She ran down the stairs, shouting for MacEvoy, who appeared from the servants' floor below.

'I smell smoke,' he said.

She seized the front of his coat and pulled him to the stairs. 'The supper room. Fire.'

He ran upstairs and she went down to the kitchen, startling the cook and kitchen maids. 'There is a fire in the supper room.'

'A fire!' One of the girls screamed.

'Can you go get help?' She glanced around. 'Where is Lacey?'

Lacey entered the kitchen. 'I am here, my lady.'

Cook put down the pot she'd held. 'We must leave the house.' She turned to the maids. 'You both run ahead and find some men to help.'

Lacey wrapped her arm around Phillipa and led her outside.

When they reached the street, Phillipa began to cough.

The maids found more help and they watched more men run inside.

'Where is Mr Campion?' Lacey asked, keeping her arm around Phillipa.

Phillipa looked up to the windows on the first floor, picturing him with flames around him.

'He's in the fire,' she answered.

An hour later they sat at a table in the kitchen while Cook slathered their hands with a salve she promised would heal their burns in no time. Xavier's burns were much worse than Phillipa's and Cook wound them in bandages.

He winced when Cook touched a sore area.

Phillipa felt the pain in her own stomach. 'Your poor hands.'

He shrugged. 'Better a few burns than losing the house to fire. How could I face Rhys and your brothers if I let the place burn? Or, worse, what if the fire spread to other houses?'

'It was not worth risking your life.' She saw him again surrounded by flames, relived her fear.

He smiled. 'Actually, it was worth the risk. As long as this is all it cost.' He glanced to his hands.

Cook tied the last bandage. 'There you go, sir. All set. Keep the bandages clean and dry and I'll change them to-morrow.'

'Thank you, Cook. I feel better already.' He stood. 'But we should leave you to your work now.'

Xavier closed the Masquerade Club. The supper room was the only room damaged and that damage was primarily to the carpet and curtains, but the gaming room smelled strongly of smoke, and also the private rooms and the maids' rooms to a lesser extent. Every window in the house was open and dishes of charcoal and vinegar were placed everywhere. Still, it would take days to restore it to normal.

Phillipa and Xavier climbed the stairs to the supper room where the maids, Cummings and MacEvoy were scrubbing the floor, ceiling and walls. The carpet, the curtains and all the linen were gone. Phillipa glanced at the pianoforte, which, thankfully, seemed undamaged.

'How are you all faring?' Xavier asked them.

'Making good progress,' replied MacEvoy in a good humour. He turned to the others. 'Are we not?'

Cummings grunted, but the maids voiced their agreement.

The poor maids, Phillipa thought. This was an arduous task, but she was pleased to see the lovely paint and plasterwork emerging again.

They continued up to the private rooms and immediately

felt the chill from the open windows. In the bedchamber, Lacey wore a shawl and laid out clothes on every possible surface so they could benefit from the fresh air.

She curtsied when she saw them. 'How are your hands?'

Phillipa raised hers. 'Stinging a little, but Cook's salve has done wonders.'

'And you, sir?' the girl asked Xavier.

He showed her his bandaged ones. 'Cook says they will heal quickly if I do what she says.'

'Then you must do as she says,' Phillipa told him.

They changed into clean clothes. When done, Xavier turned to Phillipa. 'We do not need to stay here. We have a house to go to. Cook can pack us a dinner and Lacey can pack a change of clothes—'

A few minutes later they were ready to leave with a picnic basket and a portmanteau. As they opened the door, Mr Everard stood on the outside, ready to sound the knocker.

'Oh!' He startled, then bowed. 'Mr Campion. My lady. I wonder if I might have a word with you.'

'You have seen Daphne?' Xavier asked, standing aside to allow him entry. 'Was she injured in any way?'

'Nothing to signify,' Everard responded. 'But, as you can imagine, she is rather distraught.'

'She ought to be. The whole street could have burned,' Xavier said.

'She is, perhaps, not yet thinking of anyone but herself.' Mr Everard looked apologetic. 'I came to inspect the damages, however, and to inform you that she will pay full restitution.'

Xavier nodded. 'Arrange it with MacEvoy. He is in the supper room. Please include generous restitution to him, Cummings and all our servants. They bear the brunt of the cleaning up.'

Mr Everard inclined his head towards Xavier's hands. 'You are injured.'

Xavier shrugged. 'I will heal.'

'Well.' Everard cleared his throat. 'I will not keep you. I cannot tell you how sorry I am for—for all this.'

Xavier acknowledged his apology and Mr Everard started up the stairs.

'Everard!' Xavier stopped him.

Everard paused on the stairway.

Xavier said, 'Make certain she does not come here again. Or approach me in any way. Or Lady Phillipa.'

'I will, sir.' Everard continued up the stairs.

'One more thing,' Xavier called to him.

He paused again.

'She should go away.'

Everard's brows rose.

Xavier spoke firmly. 'I am serious. She should go to the Continent.'

Everard nodded. 'I will make the suggestion.'

Xavier and Phillipa continued out the door.

She stopped him, 'Why did you say Lady Faville should go to the Continent?'

'For the same reason your brothers sent your father away.' He took her hand, but winced in pain. 'Daphne has opened herself to scandal. But everyone will forget if she is away.'

She threaded her arm through his. 'I suppose the scandal will reach us, as well. People are already talking about us.'

He gave her an understanding hug. 'It will be worse for her, though. She will be alone.'

They reached Piccadilly and finally Dover Street and stood in front of the door to what would be home. He put down the portmanteau and tried to reach in his pocket for the key. His bandages made it difficult.

'I will get it for you.' Phillipa set down the basket of food.

Her fingers stung, but she reached in his coat pocket, an act that seemed very wife-like. It made her smile. With the key in hand, she unlocked the door.

Her hand was on the latch when she turned back to Xavier. She threw her arms around him and hugged him, never wanting to let him go. She'd almost lost him. To the fire. To her own folly.

'We are home, Xavier,' she cried.

It had been just as she'd dreamed as a child. Xavier had indeed whisked her away—in a hackney coach, not on horseback, and to a town house on Dover Street, not a castle—though he was and would always be her prince.

She imagined a crescendo of music, louder and faster, from the lower keys to the higher.

He returned her embrace. 'When I am with you, I am home.'

It was the perfect final note.

Epilogue

London, May, 1820

Phillipa would not say there was a crush of people in the drawing room, but there were enough that she had to crane her neck for a glimpse of her husband. He stood at the opposite end of the room, speaking to her half-brother, Rhys, father of John Rhysdale the junior, the reason for this celebration. They were probably talking business. Of Rhys's steam engines and Xavier's shops. He owned five now and she could not be more proud of it.

Watching Xavier was a thousand times more pleasurable than listening to the chatter of her sister-in-law, who'd parked herself at Phillipa's side and made no signs of ever moving away.

Or of going silent.

'It was a lovely christening, was it not?' Adele said for the thousandth time. 'Did we not make fine godparents? I am so glad you held the baby, because I am certain I was so nervous I would have dropped him....'

Xavier had indeed made a fine godfather, so handsome in his new coat, as much of an Adonis now as he had been in his regimentals all those years ago at Lady Devine's ball. He'd assured Phillipa that she looked her finest, but the old insecurities poked at her throughout the ceremony. She'd taken to using a bit of cosmetics to minimise her scar, but she'd wager a night's take at the Masquerade Club that someone in the church had commented on how unbelievable it was for Xavier Campion to marry Phillipa Westleigh— the Adonis and the scarred spinster.

Such comments had never entirely stopped.

Adele sighed. 'I do hope dear Ned and I conceive soon. It seems unfair that Celia has had the first baby in the family, although one cannot quite credit this baby as a Westleigh, seeing as they'd had to marry and my baby will be heir to the family title...'

Empty-headed Adele had no idea how insulting she could be.

Phillipa pressed her hand to her abdomen. Her sister-in-law would likely soon learn of another baby in the family, but for now it was a delicious secret, hers and Xavier's.

She glanced over at Celia, Rhys's wife, holding little John, so tiny in her arms. How would it feel to hold Xavier's baby? To know that a living creature could result from their act of love?

A woman's laughter broke into Adele's monologue. It was Phillipa's mother, arm in arm with General Henson, conversing with the clergyman who had performed the christening. Her mother was happy now and for that Phillipa was glad.

Xavier caught her eye, smiled, and started across the room to her. Phillipa's cheeks flushed, just as they had all those years ago when he'd crossed a ballroom floor to dance with her.

He winked and turned towards Adele. 'Forgive me, Lady Neddington, I must steal my wife from you.'

Adele opened her mouth to respond, but Xavier already had taken Phillipa's arm and led her away.

'You have rescued me once again,' Phillipa said. 'Where are you taking me?'

'Not far.'

It was a thrill to have his hand firmly on her arm, to be close enough to inhale the scent of him, now so familiar to her. Ladies' heads still turned as he passed and she supposed one or more of them would repeat the familiar refrain—*how could a man like that marry her?*

He loves me, ladies, she pretended to reply. *That is why.*

Two rooms had been opened into one long one to accommodate the guests. He led her to the far end where a violinist and cellist were setting up their instruments next to the pianoforte.

'Musicians!' Phillipa cried. 'I did not know Celia and Rhys hired musicians.'

'I thought this might interest you.' Xavier smiled.

'Surely they are not to have dancing as well?' That would be odd at a christening.

'Unfortunately, no dancing,' he replied.

'Unfortunately?'

He put his arm around her. 'I enjoy dancing with you.'

Their opportunities to dance together had been rare. Only one ball in the autumn and none yet this spring.

'Now that mourning for King George III has been lifted, we may dance again.' She lifted a shoulder. 'If we receive any invitations, that is.'

'We will receive invitations.' He squeezed her tighter. 'Do you remember dancing with me at Lady Devine's ball? It was right before I was to return to the regiment in Holland.'

'I remember.' That ball, that dance, had changed everything for her.

The musicians began tuning their instruments, the discordant sounds a fitting accompaniment to memories of that night.

Xavier went on. 'I do not think I ever enjoyed a dance more than that one we shared.'

She gaped at him. 'You enjoyed it?'

He looked surprised. 'Of course I enjoyed it! I'd been away so long, and home on leave so briefly, everyone seemed like strangers to me. Some of the young ladies, I certainly had never met. Then I saw you, my dear friend. I was so happy to see you, dancing with you was…' He paused. 'It was very special.'

She made him look directly into her face. 'No. My mother made you ask me to dance.'

His brow furrowed. 'Your mother? I do not recall seeing your mother until afterwards when she told me you'd gone home ill. I could not call upon you to enquire about your health, because I had to leave for Holland the next day.'

'My mother did not set it up for you to ask me to dance?' She couldn't believe it.

'Indeed not.'

Her knees suddenly felt so weak she might have sunk to the floor if he had not been holding her. All this time she'd thought—

How her life might have altered had she known at the time that he'd chosen her.

He inclined his head towards the *pianiste* and two other musicians. 'They are ready to start playing.'

Phillipa's head was already swimming. It took several bars of music for her to notice the familiar tune. 'They are playing my sonata!'

He grinned. 'As I requested.'

Before Christmas he'd sold several of her music pieces to a publisher. She'd seen them for sale at a music shop, but never performed. In fact, she'd never heard this arrangement anywhere but in her own head.

She glanced around the room, but Rhys's guests seemed to take the music in stride. 'I feel like shouting aloud that they are playing my sonata.'

'Shall I?' He made as if he would do so.

'No.' She pulled him back. 'Just listen.'

The pianoforte dominated, then the violin, then the cello. The composition had been inspired by the sounds of the gaming room at the Masquerade Club and Xavier had once remarked upon the version she'd written just for the pianoforte. It seemed fitting that this sonata should be played at this celebration of Rhys's and Celia's child. The Masquerade Club had played such an important role in their romance.

As it had in Xavier and Phillipa's romance.

She leaned her head against Xavier's shoulder as the music filled her ears and happiness filled her heart.

'You make beautiful music, my dear wife,' Xavier murmured to her.

* * * * *

MILLS & BOON®

The Regency Collection – Part 1

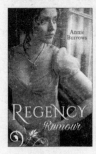